That Kennedy Girl

By the same author

CARNIVAL OF ANGELS

CLODIA

DON JUAN IN LOURDES

THE SATYR

THE DECLINE AND FALL OF AMERICA

TO BE A KING

BLOWOUT

OUTBREAK

THE EMPRESS

SECRET PLACES

A PASSION FOR POWER

SONS AND BROTHERS

STONE OF DESTINY

THAT KENNEDY GIRL

Robert DeMaria

The Vineyard Press
Port Jefferson, NY

Copyright by Robert DeMaria, 1999
first edition
Vineyard Press
106 Vineyard Place
Port Jefferson, NY 11777
Library of Congress Catalog
Card Number: 99-096639
ISBN: 0-9673334-2-3

COVER PHOTO BY PERMISSION OF
THE JOHN F. KENNEDY LIBRARY
Joseph Kennedy, Jr, Kathleen Kennedy
and John F. Kennedy, en route to Parliament
to hear Britain's declaration of war against
Germany. London, September 3, 1939.

*This is a biographical novel, a true story
told in narrative form, which requires imaginative
speculatioin about some of the dialogue
and incidental scenes.*

That Kennedy Girl

1716039205

PART ONE

THE FORBIDDEN MARRIAGE

CHAPTER ONE

Kathleen Kennedy had a secret. She had carried it around for over a month, and now it was confession time. She flew from Washington D.C. to Palm Beach to spend a few days with her parents. When she found the right moment and sufficient courage she would tell them.

She rehearsed her lines as she unpacked her bag and then again later as she sat by the pool in the warm Florida sun. The lazy palm trees and the sinfully blue sky made her uneasy. It was March, 1943, and the rest of the world was at war.

She was twenty-three years old, but in the houses of her parents she always felt like a child and was still called "Kick," a mispronunciation by very young siblings that became a permanent nickname. There were two family houses, one in Hyannis Port and one in Palm Beach. The house on Cape Cod seemed more like home, and was rich with childhood memories of good times and endless summers of sailing and swimming and first-run movies in the basement theater installed by father Joseph P. Kennedy, lord of the manor, former Ambassador to the Court of St. James, and now one of the most unpopular men in the Western World because he had opposed the war against Germany.

There had been other houses, more like the year-round houses of ordinary people. The Kennedys, of course, were not ordinary. It seemed to Kathleen that she knew this from birth, and that she was reminded of this fact every single day of her life, either by her parents or by the echo of their voices, an echo that said that the Kennedys were born to win. Yes, there had been other houses, and they had been filled with children and nannies and barking dogs. There had been the large house

1

in Brookline, Massachusetts, which they moved into the year that Kathleen was born. And there had been the even larger house in Bronxville, New York, which they acquired in 1929, when Kathleen was nine years old. And for a glorious year and a half there had been the immense embassy mansion in London just before the war.

In a half-dream she catalogued these houses, and her whole life passed before her as though she were drowning in slow-motion. There was something strange in all this, she thought, something strange in her own small life and in the larger pageant of the Kennedy clan, which had been refined by her parents into a gleaming legend of rags-to-riches success in the promised land of America. John White had felt it too. They both had worked for the Washington *Times-Herald* . He thought they were a weird family, though he himself was eccentric enough to be made fun of. But brilliant, of course. And in love with her, naturally. She liked him because he made her laugh, but she hated him because he wanted to do to her the thing that the priests had forbidden. He thought her religion was absurd, and she thought it was cruel of him to try to turn her into an atheist. He was, however, right about her parents.They did not seem to have a normal relationship. They led separate lives, even stayed at separate hotels when they occasionally happened to be in the same city. Her father was "the man in charge," and her mother was the ice-queen of domestic trivia. What they called *love* seemed to mean *control* . The whole atmosphere of the clan, said John, was charged with incestuous energy. They were attractive particles in constant motion. She had to admit that she loved her brother Jack, but not in "that way." She had discussed this more than once with Inga Arvad, another member of the *Times-Herald* staff, a beautiful, sophisticated woman, slightly older than Jack, with whom she had had a serious love affair.

The Spanish-style house was unusually quiet. The roof-tiles baked in the sun. The arches were monastic. Somewhere her mother was sleeping. And somewhere else her father was brooding over his political exile, having made an enemy of the most powerful man in the world, the president he once served, Franklin D. Roosevelt.

Being absolutely alone was a rare experience for Kathleen. She kept expecting a noisy herd of Kennedys to come galloping out of the house, all of them talking at once. But nothing happened. Where were they all? Jack and Joe were in the Navy, Jack already overseas, having shipped out of San Francisco on the 6th of March. Eunice was away at Stanford University, Pat was at Rosemont College, Bobby, Teddy, and Jean were at boarding schools. And Rosemary -- poor Rosemary, now twenty-four years old, was in a place called Craig House, near Beacon, New York, a discreet institution for the severely "impaired." She was not to be visited, nor was she to be discussed. It was her father who had decided two years ago that the operation was a reasonable gamble. It was a lobotomy, an experimental procedure that put an end to her outbursts of rage and her unacceptable sexual behavior, but also put an end to Rosemary herself. What remained of her was hardly worth keeping alive.

It was this dark happening that troubled Kathleen and forced Eunice to flee to the West Coast. The more she thought about her parents the more clearly she could see how thoroughly their lives depended upon censorship and secrets. There were certain things that could not be talked about. Rosemary's operation was one. The relationship between Rose and Joe was another. Joe's adulterous affairs made a visible hump in the rug under which all such matters were swept by Rose. Her own mother, Josie Hannon, had been involved in a tragedy that she would never forget. She had failed

3

to look after her younger sister, who, along with a friend, fell through the ice and drowned. In the closet of "Honey Fitz," Rose's father, the skeletons were living in severely crowded conditions, though there would always be room for Toodles, the cigarette girl who once lost him an election.

Secrecy was more the rule than the exception in Kathleen's family, and now she had a secret of her own, but no way to keep it. She carried it home to her parents as though it were an unwanted child. But it was nothing of that sort, just an independent decision that she had arrived at without the advice of her parents or their approval. In a normal family, independence might be considered a virtue. In this family it might very well be looked upon as an act of rebellion, even a dagger in the heart. She really had no way of knowing how her parents would react. What she had come to announce to them was her decision to volunteer for overseas work with the Red Cross, in the hope that she might be able to return to England, where she had made so many wonderful friends before the war. They called her "that Kennedy girl, the American Ambassador's daughter." One of those wonderful friends was a young man who wanted to marry her. He was William Cavendish, the Marquess of Hartington and the son of the Duke of Devonshire.

When they were in London in 1938, newspapers on both sides of the Atlantic reported rumors of a possible marriage, but those rumors were instantly denied by both families. When her parents confronted her on the subject, Kathleen played the ingenue. "I have no idea what it's all about," she said, "but isn't it nice to be talked about in the newspapers?" Her mother lectured her on the facts of her Catholic life. Such a marriage would be completely out of the question. "Of course," said Kathleen, knowing that after her next confession she would be forgiven for the small lie.

4

She withdrew from the hot sun into the shade of one of the arches. Her skin was light, almost pale at times, but it combined well with her auburn hair and her deepset eyes to give her an air of amusement and mystery. She did not like the blazing heat of Florida. She preferred the unpredictable weather of New England, or even the predictable cloudiness of England itself. She tried once again to concentrate on the current issue of *Time* , but it was no use. The headlines and the maps of the war ran together in her mind -- Guadalcanal, Stalingrad, the Kasserine Pass. She closed her eyes and heard a song left over from a night out in Washington: "Taking a Chance on Love." She had reached the point where she was willing to gamble, if not with Billy, then perhaps with one of her other English admirers-- Tony Rosslyn, William Douglas-Home, or Hugh Fraser. But he had to be English. That much she had decided. All of her close English friends were getting married and she was feeling thoroughly left out. They wrote to tell her that Billy was about to become engaged to Sally Norton, but also reminded her that Billy still loved her. She desperately wanted to be there to play her part in the courtship games. It was not a question of love; it was a question of marriage. She once said to her friend Charlotte McDonnell that she imagined love as that thing that made you forget yourself completely. Well, she had never had that, but she had had deep affection. Wouldn't that do? Charlotte shrugged her shoulders and laughed.

In the summer of 1940 Charlotte's sister Anne was getting married to Henry Ford II, who had converted to Catholicism to make the marriage possible. Kathleen was one of the bridesmaids. She wondered at the time if it was possible for a girl to marry a man that famous and still feel the usual things for him. She asked Charlotte if she thought that the importance of a man could actually excite love in a woman. "Maybe," said Charlotte. "In any

5

case, if the man you fall in love with happens to be rich, it certainly is a useful coincidence." Good old Charlotte. They all thought that she would eventually marry Jack after he had sown his wild oats, but when Jack went off to war she became engaged to Richard Harris of Southampton. No one blamed her for not waiting.

Kathleen put the magazine aside and rehearsed her confession one more time. The hard part would be explaining her preference for London and assuring her parents that it was patriotism that motivated her and not Billy Hartington. Her father was in a foul mood, and her mother was trying to protect him from anything that might upset him. It was all very unpredictable.

She closed her eyes and tried to imagine her brother Jack "somewhere in the Pacific," but all she could conjure up was an exotic jungle and snarling Jap soldiers, borrowed from a recent movie she had seen. She missed him terribly, especially now that he was out of the country. Before he left she could reach him in a hurry if she needed him. And she needed him now, before this discussion with her parents. She knew, however, how he felt about her going overseas while the war was still on. Shortly after he broke up with Inga Arvad last spring he told her that he didn't think it was a good idea, nor did he think it was a good idea to marry an Englishman, in case that was what she had in mind. She went ahead with her application to the State Department for credentials as a journalist, but she was turned down, and that was that. She never knew whether or not her father had anything to do with the State Department's decision.

When she opened her eyes again she was struck once more by the emptiness of the place and the eerie silence. There had been times in the past when important people came regularly to the house -- politicians, businessmen, and Hollywood types. Joe Kennedy was sometimes mentioned as a presidential possibility. In those days Kathleen was convinced that her father knew, literally, everyone. In her young eyes he was tall and handsome, a man who could accomplish almost anything by picking up the phone and calling a friend. Now he seemed to prefer his reclusiveness, like a wounded animal gone to ground.

Suddenly, she saw him, beyond the Spanish arches, beyond the pool, walking slowly across a stretch of lawn, his eyes cast down, as though he were searching for something. He paused, took off his glasses, wiped them and put them back on. Then he walked back the way he came. She had the impression that he was talking to himself, though she could not actually hear him. He even made an occasional gesture, as if to an invisible companion.

She let him go without calling out to him, but her vision blurred for a moment with a threat of tears. She was his favorite, and he often told her so. He was much more demonstrative with the children than his wife was. He was an extrovert who flaunted everything -- his women, his wealth, his convictions and his feelings. She remembered the time that Gloria Swanson arrived in Hyannis Port in a red Rolls Royce to visit her producer and lover Joe Kennedy. She was actually greeted and entertained by Rose and introduced to the children.

Kathleen understood the accusations that had been made against her father over the years, but she still loved him. It was not a choice but a fact, like the fact of her faith in God. And that love influenced her idea of what a man should be. He was a model, too, for her brothers, who seemed to be following in the old man's footsteps. They were all Harvard graduates, all competitive, all good Catholics and fond of vulgar language. They thought of themselves as born leaders, and were, in any case, too arrogant to be followers. Whatever they touched they had to control, and that included women.

Kathleen thought of them as "tough guys" and she loved them for being that way.

The opportunity for a confrontation with her parents did not present itself until the next day. It happened accidentally. Her father had taken her to his study to show her some old photos, and a few minutes later her mother walked in and said, "Ah, there you are, dear. I've been meaning to have a little talk with you."

"And I've been meaning to have a little talk with both of you," said Kathleen, her heart breaking into a sudden gallop.

Joe looked up from a photo taken "in the good old days," a photo of all eleven members of the family walking forward arm-in-arm on the embassy lawn, as if into a bright future, every one of them smiling and revealing the perfect teeth that only braces could produce. "What's wrong?" he said, as though he were permanently prepared for bad news.

"Nothing's wrong. I just wanted you to know that I might be doing some work for the Red Cross."

"Oh, that would be lovely, dear," said Rose with an approving smile.

"Actually," said Kathleen, "I was thinking of applying for a full-time position."

Joe squinted his eyes with suspicion. "What sort of position?"

"Well, I was reading about these Red Cross clubs for servicemen overseas and --"

He raised his voice. "Overseas?"

"Yes. They seem to be very successful, real morale builders, more like hostels than clubs. They provide all the basic needs for men on leave."

"There are only two things that soldiers on leave are interested in --"

Rose stopped him before he could go on and smiled again at her daughter.

"Now tell us, Kick, darling, what exactly do you have in mind?"

"The Red Cross is expanding these clubs and clubmobiles overseas, and they've started a big campaign to enlist qualified women. Look, I'll show you --."

From her leather purse she took a folded page from a newspaper. She opened it and held it up for them. It was the picture of an attractive young woman in a blue-gray Red Cross uniform. With a wholesome smile, she was distributing doughnuts and cigarettes to American soldiers. "What a gal!" said the caption. And then in smaller print: "She brings a touch of home to our brave men overseas."

"It's a great uniform," said Kathleen. "And the job comes with the technical rank of second lieutenant. It really would be a terrific way to contribute to the war effort. Much better than writing movie and book reviews for the *Times-Herald*. "

"I don't know," said her father. He stood up and paced back and forth in front of a wall of books and photographs. He looked agitated. Suddenly, he spun around and shouted, "Why don't you leave that stuff to the showgirls!"

"I'm not trying to join the U.S.O. I'm trying to join the Red Cross. It's not a glamorous job, Daddy. It's hard work. The coffee urns hold five hundred cups of coffee. They feed these guys. They set up ping-pong tables and card tables. They book them in for overnights and help them with everything from sewing on buttons to writing V-letters home to mama."

"Listen, kid," he said, "I don't blame you for wanting to do your bit. Now that we're in this damn war, we all want to make a contribution. I opposed the war at first. I didn't believe in it. I'm not a coward. I just didn't want my children to become hostages. But it's all happening. Who knows what will become of Joe and Jack? And now you want to put on a uniform and go overseas. I suppose you want to go to England, back to your wonderful friends. Well, I have news for you, Kick. The heavy bombing may be over, but the Germans have something deadly up their sleeve. I shouldn't be telling you this. It's probably classified information, but there are secret weapons. There's a robot plane and a rocket bomb. I'm not making this up, kid! I still have very good connections. There will be bombs falling on London again this summer, and there will be no way to stop them."

"I'm willing to take the chance," said Kathleen. "At least I'll be there to help."

"But what about us? Are we supposed to send you all off to war and turn gray sitting home worrying about you? I'll gamble away my money, but I won't gamble away the lives of my children. Don't you understand what I have been trying to tell everybody for the past five years? I think this war could have been avoided. But it doesn't matter now what I think -- now that we're in it. I love my country. I had to go crawling to that cripple in the White House. I had to beg him for a job. I wanted to make a contribution to the war effort. I know shipbuilding, I know heavy industry, I know banking. I offered him my services free. A dollar-a-year-man. But he turned me down.Then he tried to stick me in a boatyard in the boondocks. It was an insult. I'm fifty-five years old, in my profesional prime, and he's keeping me on the sidelines. That's his revenge. I expressed my opinion and he locked me out. I'm the one who should be going overseas, not you. Why don't you stay here with us and do what your mother does? She does her bit. She's very active. Tell her, Rose. Tell her what you do. You're always in a church or a hospital or a meeting. Tell her what you're doing for our boys."

"I know what she's doing," said Kathleen. "I think it's great. But I have other plans. I didn't think you would object. In fact, I thought you would

10

help me. I happen to know that you know Harvey Gibson, the Red Cross Commissioner for Europe. I bet that if I asked for London on my application, you could help me get it. Everybody wants London. It's a real plum."

Joe calmed down and shifted from foot to foot with his hands in his pockets. "Of course, I could -- if I wanted to," he said. "I just don't know if I want to. What do you think Rose?"

"Well, I'm less concerned about the risks of war than you are, but I'm against her going to London right now. I'm afraid that she may become too personally involved with her English friends, and that could lead to another embarrassment of the kind we had with the young Marquess of Hartington. Of course, if she was already married to an American in uniform it would be different --"

"Mother, I'm not planning to get married," said Kathleen.

"Well, perhaps you should give it some thought," said Rose. "And when you do, please remember what the Church has to say on the subject."

"Mother, I know what the Church has to say. You don't have to remind me. All I'm talking about right now is the Red Cross. Gosh, I got all excited about it. I was hoping you'd be pleased, but I guess I was wrong." She looked down at her hands and tried to sound as though she might actually cry.

Her parents withdrew to one side to confer in a loud whisper. Joe announced their verdict with considerable irritation in his voice: "Your mother says you can take the damn job, if you promise not to marry a Protestant."

She gave her father a big smile. "You know, you really look handsome when you're angry, Daddy," she said.

"Oh, go on, both of you," he said, waving them out. And then his face mellowed into a smile. "You're going to look great in that uniform, Kick."

11

She gave him a wink and followed her mother out.

CHAPTER TWO

"Stay with your unit. Do not leave your unit," said the P.A. voice. "Move forward when your line moves. Give your name at the check point loud and clear. As you board you will be given a cabin assignment and mess card. Repeat. You will be given two cards: cabin assignment and mess card. If your name is not on the manifest you will not be allowed to board." The troopship was the *Queen Mary* , camouflaged and renovated for wartime service.

"Look," said Tatty. "There goes Big Red One. U.S. Army First Infantry Division." Tatty Spaatz was an army brat. Her father was the Allied air commander in North Africa. It was John White who had urged Kathleen to look her up. "You think you've got a lot of gear. Look what those poor guys are carrying. An A-bag, full field equipment, helmet, gas mask, webbed belt, amunition pouches, two water canteens and weapons. Sixty or seventy pounds, plus woolen uniforms." They could hear the men shouting out their names as they moved past the bald-headed sergeant at the check point: "Randall John, Snyder Carl, Maggio Joseph."

Through the muggy air Kathleen imagined she could see the *Queen Mary* in her more glamorous days before the war, passengers lining the railing and waving to well-wishers on the docks, reporters elbowing each other to interview celebrities, flashbulbs and confetti, mink coats and poodles. She and her mother had sailed to Europe ·once on this ship. Was it in 1938, the year that her father was appointed Ambassador to England? She remembered how the photographers took her picture when she left New York and when she arrived in England. They asked her if it was true that she and Peter Grace would soon be engaged. She loved the attention and instinctively knew how to deny things with playful ambiguity. Before long, she was described in *Queen Magazine* as the most important American debutante of the season. It all seemed a long time ago. Another world! Another era!

"It's going to take a while," said Tatty. "I hear there will be about fifteen thousand troops aboard. Let's see, there are three hundred of us, counting the U.S.O. girls. Can you figure that out?"

"What do you mean?"

"You know. How many men for each woman?"

"Whatever it is, you can have my share. I'm not interested."

"How about the officers?"

"Let me know when one of them wins the Victoria Cross. I'll invite him to the club."

"Don't be such a snob, Kick. They're going to win the war for us."

"Well, I wish they'd get on with it. I'm already suffering from battle fatigue. And don't call me a snob. I like talking to people, especially men. I'm sure that most of them are nice guys and all that, but --"

"But what? Not rich? Not members of the club?"

"I'm sorry. I was brought up to keep my distance from ordinary men, working-class types. They're always trying to touch you. They seem to think that women are just waiting around to be grabbed by them."

"Some of them are," said Tatty.

"It takes all kinds," said Kathleen. "Personally, I prefer gentlemen."

"Women always do, until they fall in love," said Tatty. "Then it doesn't matter what the guy is like or how much money he's got."

"You know what the old Irish priests had to say about love?"

"What?"

14

She answered with a little recitation: " 'A subtle, odious poison, designed to set young souls in the way of eternal perdition.' I learned that from my grandmother. It's not easy being an Irish Catholic."

"You sound like John White," said Tatty.

'So do you. He was always trying to re-educate his girlfriends."

"You didn't seem to mind his company."

"He was an atheist rat, but he made me laugh," said Kathleen.

"Some of us thought you were going to marry him."

"Not a chance. We were just good friends, that's all."

"I know what you mean," said Tatty. "He was a lovable mess, wasn't he? He sure doesn't belong in the Marine Corps. Imagine winding up in the brig for taking pictures of some British destroyers."

"For a brilliant guy he's awfully dumb sometimes," said Kathleen.

"Maybe he and Inga Arvad are members of the same spy ring."

They laughed and Kathleen wrestled a cigarette from her uniform. Their line inched forward and then stopped again. "I feel like a cow in a stockyard," she said.

"At least when we get there we'll have decent jobs. Think of the poor nurses."

"I could never be a nurse. Personal sacrifice is not my strong suit. What sort of accommodations do you suppose they've given us for this trip?"

"Oh, you'll have a cabin, of course."

"Oh, good!"

"And about seven roommates."

"Oh, God! "

The *Queen* slipped away into the gathering darkness, with all the discretion and excitement of a woman going off to meet her lover, a dangerous

15

liaison. In her peasant clothes she would elude the enemy, and once on the high seas she would be uncatchable. She had once crossed the Atlantic in the record time of three days and twenty hours.

In spite of the fact that Kathleen had been one of nine Kennedy children, she was not used to the suffocating closeness of large numbers of people. She had been protected from the harsh realities of life, and had never personally felt the need to play the missionary among the poor. She thought of charitable organizations as sponsors of magnificent fund-raising balls. Her mother was always on the committee, smiling, talking in platitudes, rushing off to New York or Paris to buy a dress expensive enough to feed an orphanage full of children for half a year. It wasn't that Kathleen lacked compassion; it was just that she never gave the subject much thought.

Kathleen watched the blacked-out skyline of New York fade into the dusk. The heavy air seemed foul with the stench of humanity, and for a moment she was convinced that she was making a terrible mistake, and that all she would find in London was a circle of young aristocrats, who remembered her merely as "that Kennedy girl," that eighteen-year-old debutante who was briefly acceptable because she was the Ambassador's daughter.

Later, she lay on her bunk, fully clothed, and tried to shut out the excited voices of the other women, most of whom had never been anywhere worth mentioning. She saw no point in trying to impress them with all the wonderful things she had done and the places she had seen. In any case, if she told them that she knew the Pope and the King and Queen of England, they'd only laugh.

She slipped into the dark waters of sleep, lulled by the hum of the engines. The voices of the women became the voices of the girls at the Noroton Convent of the Sacred Heart where she had gone to school. It was very warm. She had had a fever.

16

Mother Theresa sat beside her on the bed, whispering, praying. She could feel the coolness of her robes. "Hail Mary, full of grace..."

And then she was aboard the ship again. "Are you all right, honey?" said a hefty blonde in a heavy whisper. Her shirt was unbuttoned, revealing the whiteness of her slip. "Got the queasies? A little sea-sick maybe?"

Kathleen gave her a weak smile of gratitude. "Yeah," she said. "I've never been inside a can of sardines before."

"Get some sleep," said the buxom nurse. "You"ll feel better in the morning."

When she had convinced the other women that she was asleep, she heard one of them say, "Poor little rich girl. She needs her nanny."

In her imagination she defended herself. "What's wrong with being rich? Isn't that what you all want? Isn't that what every woman dreams of?" And to escape the dreariness of the moment she slipped into a semi-dream of her Wonderful Year (actually a year and a half from the spring of 1938 to the beginning of the war in the fall of 1939.) She saw it as a book or a film: "My Wonderful Year in London." It was a magic time. In the four years that had passed since she was forced to leave, nothing in her life could match the excitement, the joy, the feeling she'd had of being at the center of things. The English thought she was marvelous. The men adored her. Her father was the American Ambassador. Her mother was an elegant beauty with all the social graces. They lived in a mansion. The Embassy residence at 14 Prince's Gate was a six-story structure with a magnificent ballroom and two beautiful reception rooms, one of which was copied from the Palace at Versailles. There were twenty-seven bedrooms, and among their guests were people who shaped the destiny of the world. Her coming-out party was one of the major events of the London season. Eighty very special young people were invited to dinner at the Embassy. They were the cream of English society, the future rulers of the Empire. In the evening they were joined by three hundred additional guests, all dressed to the hilt and dazzling in the Great Ballroom, where they danced to the music of the Ambrose band, who were enlisted from the Mayfair Hotel. What a night! What a glorious night! She was whirled around the dance floor by the likes of the Prince of Prussia and the Duke of Kent. Every man in that vast room seemed determined to dance with her. She felt courted, admired, loved.

And then, day after day for the long season there were endless dinner parties and balls, and the late-night, early-dawn windups with close friends at the clubs, the Four Hundred, the Cafe de Paris. They found her informality delightful. They were amused by her witty American way of saying things. One admirer told her that wherever she arrived she seemed to light up the place, as though she had a special glow, a special fire. She was pleased because she actually felt that way, as if all the social activity fueled her passions. And she loved the attention that she and her family received in the press. The debutantes of the Season were considered celebrities, and all the major events were covered in delicious detail, from the opening of the summer exhibit at the Royal Academy of Arts to the Royal Garden Party at Buckingham Palace. Every stitch of clothing was described and every significant person was mentioned, along with the latest gossip about pairings and potential marriages. And she was the star of the season, "that Kennedy girl." The public seemed obsessed with the whole clan, as if they didn't quite know what to make of this American equivalent of royalty. They were fascinated, amused, and sometimes outraged. Her father was sometimes very undiplomatic, too often substituting his own views for the official policies of his country. At the time she was too caught up in the glitter of the

18

Season to pay much attention to politics. Her mission in life was to have fun, and perhaps to find a rich, handsome, and aristocratic husband. Her brother Jack teased her about her romantic attraction to the British. "You're just a gum-chewing Irish kid from Boston in search of an English Prince Charming." And he showed his irreverence by arriving at the Ritz one day with a beautiful girl that he introduced as "Honeychild Wilder, the Cotton Queen of Louisiana." He was at Harvard then, and having a smashing summer in Europe.

"You American men are such immature slobs," she said to him afterward. "Englishmen your age are a lot more sophisticated. And they know how to treat their women. "

"Yeah, and how do they treat you?"

"They treat me with respect. I can get into a taxi with them without getting groped."

" 'A man's grope should exceed his grasp, or what's heaven for?' Who said that?"

"I don't know. You're the bookworm."

"It's a joke. It was John Milton."

"What did he know?"

"Anyhow, maybe they don't find you attractive enough -- in that way, I mean. On the other hand, maybe they're all a bunch of faggots."

She threw a cushion at him. He caught it and ran towards her, as though they were playing touch football again on the lawn of the house in Hyannis Port. She dove for his ankles and toppled him. They sat on the rug and laughed. "You're still my favorite kid sister," he said, "even if you aren't the most beautiful."

"Get lost!" she said.

When he was gone she found the nearest mirror and looked at herself. Maybe he was right, she thought. She was small, like her mother. She had small hands and feet and a delicate frame with square shoulders. Eunice and Pat were taller , and

Rosemary was too voluptuous for her own good. She looked a little closer. If only her nose were a little smaller and her neck a little longer. One of the English debs, Sally Norton, had a marvelous neck. But she preferred her own eyes, which were gray-blue, and her hair, which was golden brown with a hint of red and naturally curly. There were, however, shadows under her eyes at times, that made her look more serious than she ever imagined she could really be. She caught her own eye in the mirror and winked. She did a poor imitation of her father: "You got to know what they want, kid, and you got to make them feel as though they've had it when you haven't given them a thing. That's personality, baby! That's the secret!"

Men! she thought . Were they all like her father, after all, even the English under all that gentleness and gentility? Even Billy Hartington? She willed him to her bedside in the bowels of this troopship, but he did not appear, and the dark night of sleep descended on her reverie, her Wonderful Year.

The next morning when her cabin mates, made ravenous by the sea air, galloped off to breakfast, Kathleen settled for a cup of coffee on the small stretch of deck near the women's quarters. She met Tatty there by arrangement, and, since they were in different cabins, they compared notes.

"They put me in with some U.S.O. girls," said Tatty. "Listening to them last night was a whole education. I have a feeling that they do a lot more than sing to these guys. I hope they don't expect us to --"

"Forget it, Tatty. It's doughnuts and coffee and 'Goodnight Irene,' as far as I'm concerned. I didn't join this outfit to get mauled by a bunch of carpenters in uniform."

"Of course not," said Tatty, with a hint of military stiffness. "But why exactly *did* you join up?"

"To help out. To do my bit. You know, the obvious reason."

"According to the rumor mill, the obvious reason in your case seems to be a tall Englishman with a long pedigree. Does the name Billy Hartington by any chance ring your bell?"

Kathleen smiled. "Vaguely," she said. "I suppose your rumor mill is named John White. Asking him to keep a secret is like putting Dracula in charge of the blood-bank."

"John said you two were practically engaged before the war."

"That was just typical deb gossip in London. There was a lot of match-making going on in the press. We made no commitment. After I left he went out with other girls. In fact, he was even engaged for a while to another deb named Sally Norton."

"I bet you weren't too wild about that idea."

"I like Sally. She's a good friend of mine, but his parents didn't think she was right for Billy. They're a bit snobbish, just because they happen to be the Duke and Duchess of Devonshire."

"How did they feel about you?"

"Oh, we got along fine, except for the fact that I was Irish and Catholic and American. If I had been willing to give up my religion, I think they might have forgiven me the other two sins."

"So it's all over then?"

"Yeah, I'd say so, somewhere between definitely and probably. The chances of our ever getting married are not very good. And one doesn't exactly elope from a family like his -- or mine for that matter."

"I suppose your family wouldn't approve of a conversion."

"They certainly would not. My mother might even disown me. And it might be personally

21

impossible for me, after all those years of Catholic training. It really gets into your bones."

"Gee, that's tough, Kick." She pulled her sweater around her as though she felt a chill.

Kathleen shrugged. "It's water under the bridge. He went off to war with the Cold Stream Guard and managed to survive the Dunkirk fiasco. And I'm sure he'll survive the Sally Norton fiasco and go on to new and greater conquests in love and war. *C'est la vie!* "

" How romantic! 'It's still the same old story, a fight for love and glory...' But you haven't given up on him. I can tell."

"Maybe! Anyhow, I've had other offers."

"But Billy's the one, isn't he? You *do* love him, don't you?"

"I suppose so, but I don't think I'm very good at love. I'm too much like my brother Jack. I don't think either one of us is capable of anything as intense as all that. He jumps in and out of bed with women, and I'm a social butterfly. As soon as I see that net coming I panic."

"You mean you've never --"

Kathleen blushed. "Of course not!"

"But why?"

"Because it's a mortal sin."

"And what about your brother Jack?"

"He'll have to worry about his own damn salvation. Besides, things are different for men."

"They sure are, especially in the military."

"But don't get me wrong," said Kathleen, "I love my father and my brothers, especially Jack. When we were in Washington together we had a wonderful time. Then he got reassigned and Joe was finishing up his flight training, and just about everyone we knew was either going off to war or getting married. Last summer the first of our friends was killed in action. Suddenly the war was real. And there I was writing reviews of plays and movies at the *Times-Herald* . I felt completely out of it, just a pen-pal for a lot of brave guys who might lose their lives. When I saw the Red Cross recruitment ad I jumped at the chance. And here I am, lugging forty pounds of useless equipment across the ocean on a boat that's probably being stalked by submarines at this very moment, and in lousy weather to boot."

Tatty stood up. "Speaking of which, I could use another cup of coffee. Are you ready for the perils of the passageways?"

"You mean there's no room service in this floating flop-house?"

"I'm afraid not, honey, and we're lucky it's still floating."

They went off laughing and bracing themselves to run the gauntlet of men in uniform. They stepped over corpses and crap games and were serenaded by whistlers and a guy with a harmonica who was playing 'Bye, Bye Blackbird.'

CHAPTER THREE

In the soft morning sunlight the garden was a self-contained world of iris and ivy. Teardrops of dew lingered on the budding roses and birds were busy in the hemlocks. The garden belonged to the London house of Sissy and David Ormsby-Gore. Kathleen looked up from her letter-writing to watch a pair of bold sparrows scavenge in the plate where her toast had been. She had arrived the day before. The troopship had put into Greenock, Scotland, and her group had come down to London by train. At that point she abandoned them for more private and comfortable quarters. She also abandoned her uniform in favor of a sweater and skirt that made her look more like an American college girl than a wartime volunteer in England. Sissy was delighted when she called, especially since David was away at a base in Hatfield for his flight training.

For a moment Kathleen seemed hypnotized by the birds, the garden, the gentle breeze in her auburn hair. She couldn't quite believe that she was back in London again. Even Sissy found it hard to believe. "No one ever imagined that you'd make it back before the end of the war," she had said, "and a few of your old friends were willing to bet that you would never come back."

"Well, here I am," she had said, and now in the garden she wondered who had dared to imagine that she would never come back? Was it Billy?

She had grown so accustomed to the motion of the ship and the train that being on solid ground made her mildly dizzy. Two birds argued over a breadcrumb, scuffled briefly in the air, and then landed harmoniously on the edge of the small stone fountain. Kathleen lit a cigarette and looked at the letter that she was writing. "Dear John F. Brother," it began. "I'd be having a wonderful time if you were here. It may be too soon to tell, but I think I feel more at home in England than I do in America. Would you be terribly annoyed if I married an Englishman? I'm not serious. If I were, I'd probably lie about it anyway. I've arrived top-secret, so nobody knows I'm here yet. It remains to be seen if anyone really cares. The war has changed a lot of things. Sissy has promised to take me on a tour of some of our old haunts that are no more. .."

She looked up at the sound of radio music. It meant that Sissy was up and about. She recognized the voice of Vera Lynn, who was singing, "Wish Me Luck As You Wave Me Goodbye." America seemed a million miles away. At first she could not give a name to what she felt, but it was something like the sensation of lightness that one has after putting down a great burden. Or was it like the excitement that a prisoner must feel when he notices that his warden has left the key in the door and gone out to lunch?

Her speculations were interrupted by the appearance of Sissy in a summer dress. "Good morning Mrs. Ormsby-Goresby," said Kathleen. "Don't you look nice! We must be the only two women in London who are not dressed for war."

"Hardly! There are women in London who would kill for a pair of silk stockings and wouldn't be caught dead without makeup." She put her tea and newspaper on the table. Kathleen caught a glimpse of the headlines: RAF HAMMERS MUELHEIM. ALLIES POISED TO INVADE SICILY.

"I don't suppose there's much of a season with all this austerity," said Kathleen.

"Oddly enough, there is," said Sissy, " but it's all very strange. There's death in the air and it makes people reckless. You know -- that end of the world feeling. They're drinking too much, driving too fast, and getting married too soon. I suppose you've kept up with all the gossip."

"I heard about Janie and Peter Lindsay, of course. And about Billy's brother Andrew. How did the old Duke and Dukess of Dev feel about his marrying Debo? I mean, those Mitfords have gotten absolutely notorious. I suppose Diana is still in prison."

"Marrying Sir Oswald was not the smartest thing she ever did, though, I must say that if we hadn't actually gotten into a war with Germany, there would have been considerably less fuss made about his political views. He was certainly not the only member of the aristocracy who was fed up with democracy. You'd be surprised how many of our friends admired Mosley -- some of them quite close to home. As for Debo and Andrew, I suppose the family felt that it was an acceptable marriage, if not the match they had dreamed of. But they liked Debo. Everyone did. You and she were great friends, as I remember.'

"Debo and I were like classmates," said Kathleen. "You know, the Season of '38. I'm glad that she married Andrew, but jealous in a way, because the Duke and Duchess find *her* more acceptable than *me*."

"She has some distinct advantages over you, Kick. First of all, she's not a Catholic, and second, she is a member of the club, so to speak, even though the family is in trouble. David blames the eccentric behavior of the Mitfords on the decline and fall of a fine old family with ancient lineage and lousy investments. He says that it may be the beginning of the end for all of us. The war, he says, is not being fought to make the world safe for aristocracy, and it may, in fact, lead us all down the road to socialism. That's why there was so much opposition to it, at least early on. It was difficult for some members of the ruling class to disagree with Hitler on the subject of Jews and Communists. I suppose that's why your father tried to talk us out of going to war against Germany. Well, I guess it's clear by now that he and Mosley and Chamberlain were dead wrong. Hitler's a madman, a real megalomaniac. We heard that your father got bloody hell from President Roosevelt, and we were not at all surprised."

"I can't defend him, except as a father. Jack and I disagreed with him politically, and I have to admit that sometimes his personal life is embarrassing."

"Well, he certainly gave the London gossips something to talk about. He made no attempt to hide his rather urgent fondness for women. He'd show up at the races with a pair of decorative blondes, and he'd say the most outrageous things. Vulgar, really. Has he always been that way?"

Kathleen shrugged."I don't know, but my mother's not very affectionate, and you know how men are."

"Perhaps she carried her Catholicism a bit too far."

"I think she took it to bed with her."

"It must be the Irish blood. The women pray too much and the men raise hell. Speaking of which, how is Jack?"

"He's in the navy, and as reckless as ever. He had an affair with a friend of mine at the newspaper, Inga Arvad. Blonde and beautiful, and a little older and wiser than him. I think he really fell for her. I know he did. I'm very fond of her, but it was impossible. She'd been married twice already and was working on her second divorce. Imagine, if you can, the look on my mother's face when my father told her that it was serious. Inga was born in Denmark and worked as a journalist even before she came to the States. Somebody turned up a picture of her shaking hands with Hitler, which got J. Edgar so excited that he had his G-men following her around and bugging her bed. Unfortunately, Jack was spending a lot of time with her between the sheets. And, even more unfortunately, he was in Navy

27

Intelligence. He's out of that now and somewhere in the Pacific on one of those neat little torpedo boats. Very glamorous! Inga went off and got married for the third time. I'm sure she wasn't a spy."

"She sounds like an interesting woman," said Sissy.

"She is. I learned a lot from her. She was a real match for Jack, but I can't imagine either one of them married and settled down. Sooner or later I think Jack will probably marry somebody that he doesn't have to think about, and I don't think a wife will keep him from wandering."

"Men like that can be dangerously attractive."

"I know. If he wasn't my brother --"

They had another cup of tea and talked about old friends. "We tried to carry on," said Sissy, " even during the Blitz. Very British you know. Stiff upper lip and all that. The planes came mostly at night, but the restaurants and clubs tried to stay open. Billy had to give up his Cadillac convertible, but he was always ready to go out on the usual rounds, and Sally too. I think the sense of danger made them a bit giddy. One night Billy and Sally and Virginia were en route to the Cafe de Paris, when it became clear that there had been an explosion in the vicinity. Billy told the girls to wait while he investigated. After a while he came back and told them that a large bomb had destroyed the Cafe de Paris, which, of course, we had all thought was as good as a shelter. It seems that the bomb landed on the dance floor and instantly killed Snake-Hips Johnson, all his musicians, and all the dancers. 'It's a bloody mess,' said Billy, to which cool Sally Norton replied, 'Well, then, let's go to the Four Hundred.' "

"How horrible,"said Kathleen. "But how clever. I suppose all our friends were impressed."

"Yes, in a way. She's MI-6, you know. She's never told us what she does for them, just babbles on about confirming military decorations, which we all know is just a routine cover-up."

Kathleen felt a pang of jealousy. "Is it all over between them? Billy and Sally, I mean."

"Oh yes, there won't be a marriage. His parents did not approve, even though she is the goddaughter of Lord Montbatten."

"Good!" said Kathleen with a foxy grin.

"You little devil, you," said Sissy. "Now tell me what your intentions are. If you think that you can persuade him to become a Catholic just because David did, you may have to think again. Billy and David may be cousins, but their circumstances are different and the Duke of Devonshire is absolutely apoplectic on the subject.

"Honestly, Sissy, I don't know what's going on. I'm here because I didn't want to be there. I feel very close to my English friends, including Billy, though sometimes I can't quite remember what he looks like. Isn't that odd? Maybe I've made too much of our old connection. Maybe we were both too young and too romantic. In any case, I've got to do something with my life --."

"Kick, darling, leave it alone? You're only asking for trouble. Your family will never give in and neither will his. Billy is the prisoner of three hundred years of history. The Cavendish clan is ferociously anti-Catholic. Be careful. Don't encourage him, and don't get carried away."

"Don't worry, I won't do anything to make him unhappy."

"I was thinking of you, Kick. You might be tempted to do something foolish."

"Like what?"

"You might give up your faith."

"No, I'd never do that. It's too much a part of me."

"Women in love have been known to do foolish and desperate things."

"I don't think I'm the type. I can't stand unhappiness. Do you think there's something wrong with me?"

"On the contrary, darling. You're almost sensible enough to be English."

"Good! Now, can we go shopping and see what's left of the old haunts?"

That night Kathleen could not sleep, because her mind was filled with visions of destruction. Sissy had taken her on a tour of those places most seriously damaged by the Blitz. They had driven through the East End, an area of docks and warehouses and slums. "It looks terrible, even now," Sissy had said, "but you can't imagine how it looked at the time of the heavy bombing. Everything was on fire. You could see the flames for miles around. Buildings collapsed and thousands died in the rubble. At times it felt like the end of the world."

They had continued on along the Thames past gutted factories and leveled slums. Southwark, Bermondsey, Poplar. They had paused to look at St. Paul's, but from a distance it had not looked significantly different. "It's a bit of a miracle," Sissy had said. "The dome was literally showered with incendiary bombs."

After a brief visit to Whitehall and Westminster, Kathleen had been too tired and distressed to go on. "How about some lunch?" she had said. "I could use a drink."

In her bad dreams that night Kathleen kept trying to cover over the blasted windows and cracks in a structure that looked like the Kennedy house in Bronxville. For every hole that she covered over a new one appeared. There were explosions in the distance. She found a roll of wallpaper and tried to hang it over a broken window. Her mother appeared and said, "What in the world are you doing? Can't you see that it's time for church. Now, take your bath." She tried to explain, but her mother seemed unaware of the devastation as she paused to look at herself in a full-length mirror. She was dressed entirely in black, except for the brilliant feathers in her hat. In another moment the hat became a live bird and she had a coathanger in her hand with which she threatened to spank Kathleen. The next bomb whistled towards them, as though it might be a direct hit, but Kathleen leapt out of her nightmare before it exploded. It took her a while to remember where she was, and then she went to the window and let in the gentle air of the summer night. There was no air raid. In the sky she could see the full moon behind flirtatious clouds, and everything seemed immense and far away.

A few days later Tatty called. "I got my assignment," she said. "It's the Clubmobile and the Eighth Air Force in East Anglia. Just about what I expected. Dad will be pleased."

"Did you ask about mine, by any chance?" said Kathleen.

"You mean you don't know? The girls are all dying with envy. You got the Hans Crescent Club in Knightsbridge, just a block from Harrod's. I hear they transferred somebody named Irene Stark to Londonderry to make room for you. It looks as though your old man can still pull a few strings, even from his political exile. "

"My God, I didn't expect him to go that far, but there's nothing much I can do about it now, is there? I'll call in right away."

"Have you heard from Billy Hartington yet?"

"No."

"Well, you will. He apparently knows that you're here, and everyone I talk to seems to know who *you* are. You certainly left quite an impression - - "

Carved into the stone border over the portico were the words HANS CRESCENT HOTEL. Below these words there were classical columns and a wrought iron and glass marquee, inspired by the predictably unpredictable English weather. Above the words there was a balustrade, from which there was draped an American flag. The Victorian structure was sturdy and spacious and appropriate for its current use as an American Red Cross club that catered to the needs of servicemen on leave. They poured in from military bases all over Britain to spend a few days enjoying the legendary entertainments of London. Uppermost in the minds of the young men who came there were a place to sleep, something to drink, and the companionship of women. At the Hans Crescent Club they could eat, sleep, bathe, and get their uniforms cleaned. There was music and dancing in the evening and such routine recreations as cards and ping pong.

Kathleen was called a program assistant, but she did what all the other girls did -- she played ping pong, jitterbugged until her feet were sore, and listened to the problems of young men who were homesick or frightened. Most of them were polite, and it was not difficult to be firm with those who were not. There were plenty of obliging women in London, and the generous rations of the Yanks made them attractive companions. Her job took more hard work than imagination. The first three days felt like three years and convinced her that God had not, in fact, sent her a new cause to which she could devote herself . Her idea of salvation did not include listening endlessly to "The Boogie-Woogie Bugle Boy from Company C." But she carried on with a smile, because it was so bloody English to do so.

On her second Saturday in London Billy was finally able to come down from his base at Alton to take her out to dinner. His appearance at the Hans Crescent Club was something of an embarrassment, since many of the other volunteers had been denied the opportunity to be posted near the men they loved. She hadn't been thinking clearly. This first meeting with Billy in four years had filled her with anxiety. She had gotten ready too early and kept stepping outside to see if there was any sign of him. The idea that he might not come had just begun to move across the landscape of her mind like a dark cloud when, suddenly, there he was, striding up the sidewalk, tall and handsome in his uniform, moving with the determination of a man and not with the shyness of the boy she once knew. He was, by now, a captain in an armoured division, which meant that he would definitely be involved in the invasion of occupied Europe. True to his class, he would not have had it any other way. Kathleen was very observant and instinctively sensitive to the moods of men.

She stood under the portico, frozen for a moment in her unglamorous uniform, and afraid that he might be disappointed because she was no longer the eighteen-year-old debutante with whom he had once fallen in love. But that thought was cut short by his long strides. He bounded up the steps and embraced her with un-British boldness, ignoring the American soldiers who pausd to look at them. It was her turn to be shy. She drew back and offered him her cheek. He seemed to understand and kissed her politely. "Hello, Billy," she said.

"Hello, Kick, darling. Am I late? "

"Only five minutes, but it seems like four years."

"Were you planning to show me the club?"

"Would you like to see it?"

"Not especially."

"Good! Then take me somewhere, before the ping-pong balls drive me mad."

"How about Claridge's?"

"I guess it will have to do," she said with satirical snobbishness.

They talked their way through some initial awkwardness with the help of a decent bottle of wine and an ingenious boeuf Bourguignon. Billy was recognized by the waiter and a few of the diners who nodded in his direction. "A touch of the good old days," he said.

"Sure beats Spam sandwiches and Beano MacRoosevelt," said Kathleen.

"The war can't last forever."

"Are you sure?"

"I'm not supposed to talk about it, especially to attractive women. You're not a spy by any chance, are you?"

"That's for me to know and for you to find out."

"I have a feeling I can trust you. We're already in training for the invasion. It may come fairly soon. The Germans are suffering colossal losses on the Eastern front."

"Nancy Astor told me that Churchill's strategy is to stall until the Germans and Russians knock each other off. I saw her last week-end. She looks awful."

"She's had a difficult time since all that bad publicity. She ought to retire and be done with it. She'll never survive a general election."

"She's always been very nice to me, except on the subject of Catholicism, but I forgive her for that."

"That's very generous of you. People on the outside rarely understand the long history of the conflict and how entwined with politics it is. But let's not talk about that. Let's talk about you. Tell me how your life has been for the past four years, except for the things that might make me jealous. Your letters were lovely and amusing, but not very revealing."

"Perhaps there's nothing to reveal. Perhaps I am boringly simple."

"In a way I hope you are, but somehow I doubt it. I'm the simpleton. Naive to a fault at times." The gentleness of his smile and the openness of his expression seemed consistent with his self-portrait.

She talked about her family and how she felt about being part of the clan. "Being a Kennedy is not easy," she said. " I love them all dearly but they have a tendency to swallow you up, to own you. It's not an ordinary family. It's something tighter and more demanding, like a tribe. When I was growing up there were so many of us that we were a sort of closed society. We never really became part of any town that we lived in. I wanted to go to the local schools, but my mother sent me off to the Sisters of the Sacred Heart. I guess she didn't trust me to behave myself. And, who knows, maybe she was right. Working in Washington was a revelation. It was fun and exciting. I felt liberated. I made all kinds of friends, including, of course, the notorious and nutty John White. You can be jealous of him, if you want. He made me think about things differently, sometimes in ways I was not prepared for. We were very good friends, but that's all. In any case, the war came and the old gang was dispersed."

"I know what you mean," said Billy. "Most of my friends are in uniform, some of them in faraway places. Some have died or are missing in action. It's very hard to hold on to those days before the war. I wonder if we'll ever laugh that way again. After the war, they say, everything will be different, the twilight of the ruling class, the era of the common man -- that sort of thing. I suppose there's bound to be change, but, damn it all, I don't see why the values that we all cherished can't be preserved. Duty and common decency! I frankly don't understand the appeal of socialism. It seems so awfully drab and functional. Don't you agree?"

She was staring at him with affection and admiration. "Of course, I agree. Now, before the privileges of class disappear completely, see if you can use your influence to get us another bottle of wine."

By the time they got to the Four Hundred Club they were feeling at ease with each other, and Kathleen was convinced that nothing much had changed between them, except perhaps that they had gotten older and more serious. In the old days it seemed that absolutely everything was hilariously funny. She had liked it that way -- a long party with no goodbyes. Now it was all different. People were always going off somewhere. Emotions were intense, compacted like those G.I. rations in tins. The war had ruined the fun. Even the music they listened to, as they sipped their brandy, seemed to be touched by uncertainty and longing. And that uncertainty and longing seemed to be shoving people into one another's arms. Kathleen felt it as Billy looked at her across the table in the soft light or held her on the dance floor. And something in her resisted. She wanted to make fun of all those feelings. She wanted to laugh. During a dance she looked up at Billy and said, "If you get any closer you may have to marry me."

He laughed."Darling, I'd love to marry you, but I'm afraid my parents won't let me. You see I'm going to be a Duke someday and I'll have all those Dukey things to do--" They laughed too hard to go on dancing, and the idea of having still another brandy suddenly seemed like a stroke of genius to them.

They were visited several times at their table by friends who stopped by to kiss-kiss and say "hello" and "welcome back." It was just what Kathleen needed after her long journey and the ping and pong of the Hans Crescent Club. "Darling," she said, "do you think our reunion will make the papers, or is everyone too busy with the war?"

"I really don't know. Perhaps we should behave ourselves just in case. I mean, we wouldn't want to give people the wrong impression, would we?"

"Of course, we would."

"Right. Of course, we would."

They smiled and held hands across the table and whispered like lovers. "How am I doing, Billy Duke?" she said.

"You Kennedys sure know how to get your name in the paper," he said.

In the darkened streets of London there was enough moonlight for them to walk back arm-in-arm. He'd be driving back to his base. She'd be staying in her room at the club. 'They gave me a choice," she said, "between a broom-closet all my own or a bed in a crowded boarding house for Red Cross women."

"You made a wise choice," he said. "But there's not much privacy these days. Where and when are we going to get together? There's so much to talk about. Such difficult things --"

"I know," she said.

"Look, I've got a week-end coming up, but I've promised to spend it with my family in Eastbourne. Why don't you come along?"

"Are you sure they won't mind?"

"Why should they mind? You know them all already, and they're really very fond of you."

'I hear that some people here are angry at my father --"

"Darling, you are not responsible for your father. In any case, as I recall, your parents and mine were not all that far apart politically. And now -- well, now we're all in the war together, aren't we?"

Suddenly, they were in front of the Hans Crescent Club. Billy kissed her good night, gently, not passionately. She wondered in that moment whether or not he had ever made love to a woman. She had not had the courage to ask him, even jokingly. She kissed him back with a bit more warmth than he had offered. And then, her hand against his uniformed chest, as though she liked the texture of the cloth and the feel of the leather, she gave him a gentle push. "Go on, then. It was a lovely evening. I'll be glad to come to Eastbourne with you. Call me when you can."

"Good night, darling," he said.

She watched him walk away with that firm military stride of his until he was swallowed up by the darkness, and it pleased her that he did not look back.

Kathleen was so preoccupied with her private life that her days at the club passed like an old routine. Though she smiled and chatted convincingly, she did not make many friends. Some of the women were in awe of her celebrity, and some resented the special treatment she got. Her arrival made the newspapers, the director's wife gave her a reception, and she had frequent phone calls and visits from dignitaries such as Lady Astor. She was obviously not just "one of the girls." She put in her time, but it was her time off that really interested her.

In her room she had a radio that was always on, and the background noise reminded her of home. There was music and news, and war-inspired programs that gave helpful hints to housewives on how to stretch their rations, and information to gardeners on how to avoid the tomato blight. The war always seemed to be going well, and Vera Lynn would have been made a saint if the troops could vote. When she sang "There'll be blue birds over the White Cliffs of Dover..." the skies seemed to brighten and angels spread their white wings over the troubled world. Kathleen liked the song, but it was played too often.

During her afternoon break she wrote letters and explored her wardrobe for things she might take to Compton Place, the seaside estate of Billy's family in Eastbourne. There wasn't much to choose from. She made a mental note to call Sissy. She washed her hair and considered moving out of the club to some other residence. The close proximity of so many young men might have excited some women, but she found it disturbing, even depressing. They were such boys. Most of them, in fact, were younger than she was. And they smelled of shoe polish and tobacco and something else. That male odor! She remembered it from the dressing room at the pool. She could see her brothers' clothes hanging there. Sometimes from a distance she could hear all of them laughing in the shower --brothers, friends, cousins, members of the tribe. The men! She was jealous in those days. She wanted to be one of them and play their games.

The Sunday before she went to Eastbourne she went to mass alone and prayed for good weather. God obliged her with a glorious summer day and she took it as a sign of approval. Of all the entertainments during her Wonderful Year, what she loved most had been the week-end parties in the country. They made her feel like a character in a Jane Austen novel. But this was wartime, and Billy had warned her that it was to be only a family visit. "A few friends may drop in, of course, and Andrew and Debo will be down. Anne and Elizabeth can't wait to see you. I think you'll find that my little sisters are now quite grown up. My father, on the other hand, is not amused by anything these days, so don't be put off by him. He hates being a duke, and he hates the war. He mucks about in old clothes.Visitors who don't know him often mistake him for the gamekeeper. I think he misses the horses. Most of them were requisitioned for the war."

At Compton Place Kathleen got a warm reception, but she could feel just a hint of hesitation. "Well, here you are back in England," said the Duchess of Devonshire. "We were beginning to think that you would never come back. So many Americans who visit England imagine that they would like to live here, and then one never sees them again."

"We thought the war might keep you away," said the Duke.

"Actually, it was the war that brought me back," said Kathleen. "We're all doing our bit."

"Of course," said the Duchess. "And how is your lovely mother? "

"She's fine," said Kathleen. She waited for someone to inquire about her father, but no one did.

Billy disappeared briefly and returned in civilian clothes that made him look more like his younger self. "Well now," he said, "why don't we try to forget the war and have a look around."

"Too nice a day for indoors," said the Duke." Andrew and Debo went off towards Beachy Head about an hour ago."

On foot and by car they browsed about, stopping at the ancient Church of St. Mary, in the park and in the town itself. "I'm afraid the pier and the promenade may be off limits," said Billy. "There was considerable bombing in these parts during the blitz. But we can drive up the coast a bit and get a good view of the headland. When things were bad, we actually thought the Germans might try a landing along here. When they decided to take on the Russians instead, we were relieved, to put it mildly."

They stopped at a pub and had a long talk about Billy's family. "They're lucky to have a place like this in wartime," said Kathleen.

"Yes, but there have been losses. Many of Father's friends have lost sons -- Halifax, Swinton, Lyttelton. We are always the first to go. The other side of the coin of privilege is duty. Father's worried about me and Andrew. And we are all worried about how the war will change things. There was a wonderful rhythm, you know, in the old way of life. Chatsworth in the winter, Lismore Castle from February to March, the house in London for the

Season, Bolton Abbey for grouse shooting in August and September, Hardwicke Hall for partidge in October. And it wasn't all entertainment. Properties have to be maintained. The social fabric has to be perpetuated. There are births and deaths and marriages. Civic obligations. To an outsider I suppose it all looks frivolous, but it's not. It's history. What do people expect us to do? Once in a while I try to imagine what it would be like to lead an ordinary life, but, honestly, darling, I can't quite picture it. I'm afraid I'm stuck with my heritage, for better or for worse. It's about eight hundred years more difficult than being a Kennedy."

Back at the house there were new arrivals. Andrew had organized a golf match. In the driveway there was a Jaguar beside a mousey little Anglia. Anne and Elizabeth ran up to plead with Kathleen to join them in a game of croquet. "Debo's agreed and you'll make four," said Elizabeth.

The long summer day was filled with activities and quiet interludes. Kathleen enjoyed the peacefulness and traditional grace of country life. The house was pleasant. The air smelled of newly cut grass, and in the distance there were grazing cows and meadows. She played a game of croquet with the girls, and tea was served outside by the Duchess herself. Over drinks and dinner the conversation was lively, due in part to Kathleen's spirited participation and the Duke's fondness for port wine. He told the story of Lord Leconfield's passion for fox-hunting and his refusal to give it up for the duration."You see, we were all ordered to turn our horses over to the local authorities, so that they might be put to use in the war effort. Well, since Leconfield considered himself the local authority, he turned the horses over to himself and went about his business. One day, having ridden a bit in the wrong direction, he saw a small crowd in the distance that was raising quite a bit of noise. He assumed it was a *halloa* and rode off towards the

41

gathering, only to discover that they were attending a local football match. He was furious and shouted at them: 'Haven't you people got anything better to do in wartime than to play football?' And then off he rode after his fox."

Later in the evening Billy and Kathleen slipped away to look at the sea from a high meadow that was fragrant from the recent mowing of the hay. They held hands as they walked and then leaned against a bale. Moonlight shimmered on the water and the thunder they heard was actually the sound of Lancasters raiding the coast across the Channel. "The sound is carried on the wind," said Billy. "Unless it's something closer -- the Wolfpack at work on the incoming tankers."

They listened in silence but heard no more. Kathleen looked up at the sky. "What are those three bright stars in a row?"

"That's Orion's belt. If you follow it over that way you will come to the Pleiades, my favorite heavenly body. They were named for the seven daughters of Atlas, six of whom married gods. Merope, the seventh, married Sisyphus, and because she married a mortal instead of a god, the story goes, she hides her face in shame and is no longer visible to the naked eye. She is called 'the lost sister.' "

"And what does the sky say about us? Is our story written in the stars?" She leaned her head against his shoulder.

"I'm afraid I don't have the gift of prophecy, and I'm glad in a way."

"So am I. Knowing the end always spoils the story. Today is all that matters, they say. And today has been lovely. If only we could make it last a hundred years or so. Am I dreaming the wrong dream? If I am, just wake me up."

"It's just as it was four years ago," he said. "We *are* right for each other, aren't we?"

"I think we are, but I'm afraid that there are too many votes lined up against us. I'd give in gracefully, if only to make my mother happy, but I just can't stand the idea of some other woman sharing your life. It makes me absolutely murderous."

He smiled. "You Americans are very competitive, aren't you?"

"Blame it on my father. He taught us that Kennedys never give up."

"I hope it's true."

"It is!"

"Mr. Churchill preaches the same sermon to the British, but I think what he has in mind is war, not love."

"Well, I don't want you to die for England or for me. I want you alive. And if I can't have you, I will just have to find a way to make my parents miserable forever."

They laughed and he kissed her with polite affection. Then his voice became more serious. "The situation hasn't really changed very much. My family would accept you as a convert, or perhaps even as a Catholic, providing our children were raised in the Church of England. But your family and church would object. And for me to become a Catholic is completely out of the question. You know our history. So there you have it -- the irresistible force and the immovable object."

"Well, I guess we'll just have to throw ourselves into a volcano," she said.

"I'm sorry, darling, but there are no volcanoes in England."

"In that case, why don't we go back to the house and play some bridge?"

And off they went hand-in-hand under the inscrutable stars.

CHAPTER FOUR

It had been a busy evening at the Hans Crescent Club, and the sounds that lingered in her mind threatened to keep Kathleen awake. In her flannel pyjamas she knelt by her bed like a little girl and said her prayers. It was a ritual that she never missed. On this occasion she devoted more time to it than usual, in an attempt to clear away the voices of young men and the reverberations of a trio of military musicians that seemed obsessed with songs about girls -- *Marie, Peg O' My Heart, Lili Marlene* . The collective yearning of the young soldiers annoyed her for some reason, but she prayed for them and for herself, and then she asked God to protect everyone in her family, especially her older brothers, who were now exposed to the dangers of war. Then she said a special prayer for her father, who was still troubled in his heart and mind because of recent events and past sins. And she prayed also for Billy, for his innocence and survival. She did not ask God for the miracle that would make her his wife, but she did whisper a hint to the Holy Mother of God, before saying, "Deliver us from all dangers, oh glorious and blessed Virgin." She made the sign of the cross and climbed into bed. Mother Frances had taught her years ago how to lie on her back with her hands crossed over her breast in case she was called to God in the night. "Precious blood of Our Lord Jesus Christ wash away my sins."

She lay there for a long time but could not fall asleep. In the dull yellow light she caught a glimpse of the framed photographs on the bureau. There was the whole gang at Hyannisport in happier times. And there she was with Jack in a closeup at Palm Beach shortly before their father found a way to get him into the navy in spite of his disabilities. Their smiles reflected the brightness of the sun, and Jack seemed healthy, though he had been sick and was much too thin for his height and the broadness of his shoulders.

She turned out the light and tried once more to fall asleep. She thought of the tombs of saints, the sepulchers in the cold cathedrals of Italy and France to which her mother had taken her, and for a moment she imagined herself as a corpse. She felt a chill of fear and turned over into a foetal position as if to confirm the fact that she was still alive. She often slept that way, her self-embrace a secret pleasure that she could not allow to become truly sinful. She recalled the nameless soldiers who had danced with her that evening, one of whom held her so close that she had been forced to push him away. Some of the girls liked "that sort of thing," as she called it, but she did not.

She turned on her lamp again and thought about her favorite brother. He was like that -- very urgent about sex, always looking for girls, always talking with Lem Billings in that naughty way. When she was young it was an adventure just to overhear them spouting dirty words. A fragment from their college days passed through her mind: *Eddie fixed us up with some girls and we went down to the Cape. We all got fucked at least three times* . He liked bad girls and good girls, but they all had to be pretty. He preferred girls with a sense of humor, but their bodies were more important to him than their minds. There were, however, some about whom he was more serious, some he might even have married eventually. There was Frances Ann Cannon, who got tired of waiting and married John Hersey. She had refused to sleep with Jack, as had Harriet Price, though they both loved him. Charlotte McDonnell had also insisted on keeping her virginity, though she and Jack were practically engaged. Too bad she gave up on him. What a good Catholic match that might have been. He, of course, knew nothing about this new development, since he was on active duty in some remote part of the Pacific. He would be upset when he heard. He always was when a woman got away. Of course, he was never willing to make any concessions to hold on to them. Maybe it was that kind of treatment that aroused them, she thought. What a devil! If she were a man she would probably be just like him. It was so much easier for men. And then, for a moment, she tried to think of "the thing" itself, the forbidden act. As graphic geometry it seemed simple enough, but she retreated from the idea. And then she understood suddenly why Jack and Inga had been so comfortable together. It may also have been love, but it was certainly animal pleasure. Inga had stayed with her for a while in Washington, and it was a real revelation. She knew all about men and she knew all about Jack -- the only woman who ever did. She was a Danish beauty, an actress turned journalist. Breaking up with her was the most difficult thing that he ever had to do, but he had to do it, because she was an embarrassment to his family. The F.B.I. kept her under constant surveillance, in spite of the fact that she had done nothing to deserve such attention. There were other problems, however. He could never have married her, not after two marriages and so many affairs with other men. His family demanded that he marry well, no matter how badly he misbehaved as a bachelor. In the end all would be forgiven. Yes, she thought, it was easier for men. When a woman fell from grace there was no redemption, not in this world anyway. In another moment she was asleep, and the members of her clan stared at her from the photographs on her bureau. "Wherever you are you will never be alone, " her father had once said before kissing her good night.

In the morning she had tea and wrote letters. "Hi, sailor," she said to her brother. "They were playing 'Oh Johnny' at the Khaki Club last night and I thought of you far away in the wide Pacific. Are you sure you're not surrounded by South Sea beauties instead of ugly Japs?" She paused for a moment and then crumpled up the blue sheet of paper and tossed it away. She was annoyed at herself for always being so flippant. "Get serious, Kick," she said, and then started again. She told Jack about her reunion with Billy and their weekend in Eastbourne. She said, "Billy is just the same, a bit older, a bit more ducal...unlike anyone I have ever known at home or anyplace really. Of course I know he would never give in about the religion, and he knows I never would. It's all rather difficult as he is very, very fond of me and as long as I am about he'll never marry. However much he loved me I can easily understand his position. It's really too bad because I'm sure I would be a most efficient Duchess of Devonshire in the post-war world, and as I'd have a castle in Ireland, one in Scotland, one in Yorkshire, and one in Sussex, I could keep my old nautical brothers in their old age. But that's the way it goes. Everyone in London is buzzing with rumors, and no matter what happens we've given them something to talk about. I can't really understand why I like Englishmen so much, as they treat one in quite an offhanded manner and aren't really as nice to their women as Americans, but I suppose it's just that sort of treatment that women really like. That's your technique isn't it?"

At ten o'clock Billy called to say that his schedule had been changed and that there was a good chance for a free weekend. His good news and his cheerfuless lifted her spirits, and her gray future gave way to the brightness of the moment. If she could not be the next Duchess of Devonshire, at least she could escape from the ping-pong wars of the Hans Crescent Club.

They spent a weekend with friends in Yorkshire, and took long walks through a sturdy landscape under billowing white clouds that reminded Kathleen of a child's coloring book or a jigsaw puzzle. On a stone bridge over a narrow stream Billy kissed her, this time with more passion than he had ever revealed before. His face was flushed with boyish yearning, and he had the baffled look of someone who could not define his invisible enemy. "I've always been able to accept what I was supposed to accept," he said, "but I love you Kick, and that's a fact. When you left I thought oh well, marriage and all that. If I can't have Kick, I'll just find an acceptable wife and carry on, but now I simply can't imagine giving you up."

"Then don't," she said.

"I won't. But you've got to help."

"I can only do what I can do. I need my family and I need my religion. You're asking me to give up both."

"Not really. I'm only asking you to marry me. What your family or the Roman Catholic Church decide to do is not your responsibility. After all, we'd be living here with all the heredity advantages of our way of life. Eventually, we would be the Duke and Duchess of Devonshire. Doesn't that appeal to you?"

"Of course it does."

"Then you should insist on some kind of compromise."

"Darling, have you ever tried to work out a compromise with a stone wall?"

His frown dissolved into a smile as she dragged him away from the bridge. A silent crow took off from a nearby tree. "Come on, soldier," she said, "cheer up. The war's not over yet, and neither is the weekend. What are the chances of getting a couple of nags for a morning ride?"

They had other outings that summer, most of them brief. A party at the home of Veronica Fraser Phipps, a visit to the Rainbow Corner Red Cross club near Picadilly Circus to hear Glenn Miller and his New Army Air Force Band, lunch with Adele "Dellie" Astaire, who was married to Billy's uncle. Sometimes she took the train up to Alton and stayed at an inn near Billy's base in order to spend a few hours with him. There were other women there and she enjoyed being among those who were loyal to their men. One day Billy said that his father had once again urged him to make a bid for the seat in the House of Commons that would become available in a few months when his uncle Henry Hunloke resigned. It would mean giving up his commission and being placed in the army reserve. "There is always the risk of losing, of course," he said, "and I might be accused of avoiding active military duty on the eve of the invasion, but at least we would have more time together and perhaps a chance to sort things out."

"Billy," she said, "I don't want you to do that for me. And you shouldn't do it for your family either. You should only do it if you think it is the right thing for you and if you think that you can serve your country better in the government than in the military."

"With you as my wife, darling, I'd be able to do anything better."

"You Englishmen say the nicest things." She encouraged him with a kiss and promised to go home for Christmas and do her best to persuade her parents to be more reasonable. "If you decide to run for office, don't worry about your critics," she said. "Just remember that winners are always forgiven in the long run, and losers are merely forgotten. My grandfather Fitzgerald told us that, and he knew a thing or two about politics."

By the middle of August nothing was resolved, and Kathleen fell into a boring routine at the Hans Crescent Club. She put in her coffee-and-doughnut time, but she did not socialize with the other girls when she had time off. They gossiped about her and sometimes teased her in public: *Are they running out o f husbands in America? Let us know when the marquess is coming for tea. We'll borrow an egg and bake him a cake.*

On the morning of August 19th, Kathleen was rattling away on the old Underwood portable that her brother Joe claimed was his. Her radio provided a soothing background of music and news. Though her own social life had lost much of the glitter that she once enjoyed as a debutante, there were a lot of dramatic things happening on the battlefields around the world. *Messina has fallen* , said the reader of the news,*and Sicily is firmly in the hands of the Allies , after a campaign that has lasted only thirty-eight days. American troops under General Patton entered the city shortly before units of the British Eighth Army.* Kathleen, half listening, tapped out a letter to her father. The sound of the typewriter and the wisp of smoke curling from the cigarette in the ashtray reminded her of her newspaper days. Being a foreign correspondent would have been much more exciting than being a doughnut girl, she thought. *President Roosevelt and Prime Minster Churchill are meeting in Quebec to discuss military and political strategy. High on their agenda is the invasion of France , which both have recently agreed could not be accomplished this year, in spite of the urgent demands of the Russians.* In her letter to her father, Kathleen said nothing about the reputation he had left behind in England, but she did say that she had spent a weekend with Billy's family and stretched the truth a bit when she added that both the Duke and Duchess of Devonshire asked that their good wishes be sent to him and his charming wife. "And since you are both such good parents, I have decided to come home for Christmas, providing, of course, that you can find me a seat on a plane, which will not be easy to do in these perilous times." The neutral tone of the news reader made everything sound routine. *The top-secret German base on Peenemunde Island has once again been bombed by the RAF, in order to impede the development of such new weapons as a pilot-less plane that is rocket-launched. In the Pacific, the Americans have taken another island in the Solomons. John Kennedy, son of former Ambassador Kennedy, recently listed as missing in action when his PT boat was rammed by a Japanese destroyer, is now apparently safe, after he and the surviving members of his crew were rescued from an enemy-occupied island. In a major air raid on New Guinea several hundred Japanese airplanes caught on the ground --*

Kathleen leapt up suddenly, knocking over the chair on which she was sitting. She rushed over to her radio and said "What?" as though she hadn't quite heard the reference to her brother. For a moment she was frozen there as she tried to recover the words that had just been spoken. *Missing in action. Rammed by a Japanese destroyer.* Her heart pounded as visions of violence flashed through her mind. She had seen pictues in the newspapers and she had visited wounded men in the hospital. She remembered the hopeless and helpless expressions on the faces of those who were badly mutilated. Not Jack. Not his style. "If you think you're going to survive, then you usually do." That's what he used to say. Not like George Mead, who had the feeling that he was going to die, and then did, on Guadalcanal, almost exactly a year ago. *Apparently safe.* Did he say that? She wasn't sure. The news reader droned on. She put on her uniform and rushed off to find the morning papers.

On the reading table in the lounge there were assorted magazines, several tabloids and the London

Times . She found a brief reference to her brother in the*Times*. It described the incident as a night patrol of PT boats, whose mission it was to prevent supplies from reaching Japanese positions in the Solomon Islands. The torpedo boat that Kennedy commanded was rammed, either accidentally or deliberately, by a Japanese destroyer. It exploded and sank and nothing was known of the fate of the crew until about a week later when the survivors were rescued. Two men were lost in the encounter.

She wanted desperately to reach her family, but she could not get around the restrictions on overseas calls. By early afternoon several of her friends had seen the report and phoned her about it. Frantic for information about Jack's condition, she went to the London bureau of *The New York Times,* where she was told that the story had made headlines back home. *KENNEDY'S SON IS HERO IN PACIFIC AS DESTROYER SPLITS HIS PT BOAT.* The account was much more compete, and, above all, it said that Kennedy was described as in fair condition. He was also described as a hero, who helped save the lives of three members of his crew who were badly burned. When they finally abandoned the sinking hull of the wooden boat, Kennedy swam for three hours with a seriously injured man strapped to his back and the belt of the man's life-preserver between his teeth. They came ashore on a small island, and for the next three nights Kennedy swam out again into the channel, hoping to make contact with one of the other PT boats that patrolled the Blackett Strait. His efforts failed, but the next day two friendly natives discovered the survivors and carried back a message etched inside of a coconut shell by Kennedy. A rescue party was organized, and, before long, the survivors were picked up.

As the story became more complete, Kathleen imagined how delighted her father would be with Jack's heroic exploits. He had always expected great things from his sons. Too much, in fact. She herself was too shaken by Jack's brush with death to be anything but relieved that he had survived, and she hoped that her father would not make too big a deal of the whole thing. She knew, of course, that he would. And she wondered how Joe would feel about his sickly kid brother's sudden fame. Writing a book was one thing, but heroism in battle was supposed to be Joe's game. It was the old man's scenario, and the whole family had come to accept it. There were bound to be repercussions. She suddenly felt sorry for Joe, and that in itself was a bad sign.

Other people called or wrote to her, Billy came down for a quick visit, and eventually she heard from her parents. Their letters crossed in the mails. Finally, she heard from Jack himself. He was writing from a Navy hospital in the Solomons and sounded embarrassed by all the attention he was getting. After all, he was only trying to get help. Was it because of Joe that he played down the incident, she wondered, or was it because his boat had been sunk and he had lost two members of his crew? She answered him immediately: "Ever since reading the news in all the newspapers over here I have been worried to death about you," she said, and even as she wrote the words she could feel the chill of fear in the very marrow of her being, as if they were inseparable twins.

A few weeks later she heard that Joe was being transferred to England for anti-submarine duty in the Channel and along the French coast. The prospect of having one of her big brothers around delighted Kathleen, even if he wasn't her favorite brother. She talked about this with Billy the next time she saw him. "They're so completely different," she said. "Jack is light and witty; Joe is heavy and serious."

"I remember him as being very much like his father,' said Billy.

"In what way?"

"Very American. A bit rough around the edges."

"You can say that again, but he's really a good guy deep down, and he knows what he wants."

"A career in the military, I suppose."

"No, in government."

"What exactly does he have in mind?"

"He wants to be President of the United States."

Billy laughed. "You're not serious."

"Why not? We're a family of politicians. My father helped to elect Roosevelt in 1936. How do you think he got to be Ambassador to England?"

"Ah, I see," said Billy.

"He even considered making a bid for the presidential nomination in 1940, but his position on the war proved to be unpopular."

"It certainly was here."

"Well, he's paying for that mistake now, but he's encouraging Joe to set his sights on the White House. He's got it all planned. A good military record, a seat in the House of Representatives immediately after the war, then a couple of terms in the Senate, unless there's a chance for the Governorship of Massachussetts. By 1958 he'll be forty-one. If he doesn't make it then, he can try again in 1960."

Billy shook his head in amazement. "You Americans are incredible. The New World mentality, I guess. Everything is possible. That sort of thing."

"Darling," she said, "everything *is* possible."

The theme song for October was "A Foggy Day in London Town." The days grew shorter. The light seemed to be fading, and "the war was always there." But Vera Lynn went on singing, "It's a Lovely Day Tomorrow," and "There's a Land of Begin Again." There was a touch of sadness in all her songs, and sometimes Kathleen cried herself to sleep late at night, lonely for those she loved, exhausted by her job. The war had taken its toll on the home front. Four years of austerity, four years of air raids and casualty lists, of waiting for husbands and sons and lovers, of working harder and trying always to smile. Her friends all looked worn and tense. A friend of Billy's was killed. She went with him to visit the family. It rained that day and for several more days. The machine kept cranking away towards the big event -- D-Day, the invasion. It was on everybody's mind. How many lives would it cost? There was talk of slaughter on the beaches of Normandy.

Joe's telephone call was a bright surprise. "Hello, Kick," he said, his voice a bit loud, as usual. "Just called to say I'm on your side of the ocean, at last."

"Great! Wonderful! Terrific! When can I see you?"

"I don't know. Right now I'm flying out of a mudhole in Cornwall to look for submarines in the Channel. All I've found so far is water. I'll give you a call when I get a break. How's everything going?"

"Swell! The job's a bore, but I get to see my old friends on my day off. I have Mom's newsletter, so I know what everyone is wearing, but what's the real news? How's Dad?"

"Everybody is about the same, except for the family hero, who has been hogging up the headlines. I flew up to the Cape for Dad's fifty-fifth. It was a nice enough party, but all they could talk about was how Johnny won the war. Dad says he loves your letters and to keep them coming. Mom told me to keep an eye on you when I get here and to not let you marry that English boyfriend of yours."

"If I really wanted to marry him, there wouldn't be much she could do about it, or you either."

"Maybe not, but you're still a member of the family, and what you do affects us all."

"Don't worry, I know it's wartime, but I'm not going to do anything stupid. Come to London. I want to show you off. The women here are starving for men like you."

"Good! I hear my old girlfriend Virginia Gilliat is married."

"Yeah, and pregnant too."

"Oh well, you win some and you lose some. Got to sign off now. Duty calls."

One afternoon a couple of weeks later Joe arrived at the Hans Crescent Club, carrying six dozen eggs in a small crate. "I thought I'd surpise you," he said.

"You look terrific," she said, "and I *am* surprised, but I should have smelled you coming."

"I brought these eggs all the way from America as a gift, damn it, and we're going to eat some of them right now, even if we have to throw the rest of them away. So get Cookie to scramble them up and see if you can find some bacon to go with them. I haven't got any time to waste. I've got some important cargo to pick up just north of here and this is an unauthorized detour. I'm due back first thing in the morning. I may squeeze out another night if the weather is really bad, but I'll have to report in."

"Where are you planning to stay tonight?"

"William Randolph Hearst, Jr. offered to put me up."

"You mean you'd give up a cot at the Hans Crescent Red Cross Club for a private room at the home of some lousy foreign correspondent?"

"Why don't you show me around this dump. Maybe I'll change my mind. I see you have some nice-looking two-legged furniture here," he said, ogling a blonde volunteer, whose uniform was containing her bosom with provocative difficulty.

"You're as bad as your brother," she said.

"I taught that kid everything he knows about women. He's still borrowing telephone numbers from me. When he heard I was leaving for England he tried to find out how to get in touch with the two beauties I had been seen with in New York. His spies are everywhere, and I'm not talking about Inga Binga."

The tour of the club was brief, the eggs were edible, and the beer was cold. Joe struck up a conversation with a couple of officers and, before long, they were all playing gin rummy and bridge. The juke box, right out of an American icecream parlor or saloon, played non-stop and included such favorites as Bing Crosby singing "Mexicali Rose" and Frances Langford singing "Harbor Lights." Joe raised his voice, as if to compete with the music, and he became increasingly irritated as Kathleen displayed her usual ineptitude at bridge. Finally, he slammed his cards down and said, "Gee, Kick, aren't you ever going to learn?" She winced apologetically and the two young officers looked embarrassed on her behalf.

The game came to a halt right there, and Joe looked around restlessly as though for a new challenge. "Why don't we go over to the Four Hundred Club and see what's happening. Maybe I'll run into some old connections."

"I don't know if I can get away," she said.

"Sure you can," he said. "Just tell your boss that you've had an urgent call from General Eisenhower. And if that doesn't work, tell him you have a headache. That one never fails, if you're a dame."

The Four Hundred was unusually lively that night, with a solid number of socialites, spiced up by British and American officers, most of them pilots, and topped off by a group of journalists who were celebrating somebody's birthday. "The place is the same, but the faces are different," said Joe. He followed Kathleen around, and she, showing off a bit, introduced him to some of her friends. She addressed the Duke of Marlborough as "Dukie Wookie," and allowed him to kiss her on the cheek. From their table she waved to Pamela Churchill and Ed Murrow. "It looks like Billy the Kid opened a few doors for you in this town," said Joe.

"We used to come here a lot before the war," she said. "It's still the place to come."

They ordered drinks. The band played "Dancing in the Dark," a popular number at the club, where, the dim light laced with cigarette smoke provided an illusion of intimacy. Joe watched the dancers and Kathleen watched Joe. It suddenly occurred to her that she did not know him very well and that she had hardly ever spent any time alone with him. He was five years older than her, and had his own circle of friends. When he went off to Harvard she was only thirteen years old, a pubescent schoolgirl, wrestling with Catholic discipline at Sacred Heart academies.

Before they were interrupted by friends, he turned to her and said, "So what's the story? What's going on between you and Billy? Give it to me straight. Are you thinking of marrying him? Don't worry about your mother. I'm not going to tell her anything you don't want me to tell her. You're old enough to do what you want, but you're still my kid sister, and maybe I can give you some brotherly advice."

She was pleased by his tone of rough affection , and she was encouraged to talk more openly than she had talked to anyone for a long time. There was still that close family bond that made them all a clan apart from the rest of the world. That's what it meant to be a Kennedy. That's what she was trying to explain to Billy one day. "Yes," she said, "I would like to marry him. He loves me very much."

"And do you love him?"

"Yes, I do, in my own way, but I'm not sure that I love him enough to give up everything for him. Does that make sense?"

"Sure, Kick. It makes a lot of sense. Can't you persuade him to wait until the war is over?"

"We've talked about that possibility, but he seems to feel that it will be now or never."

"Maybe he has a feeling that he won't make it, like George Mead."

"Don't even say such a thing. George was afraid. Billy is not. He's a terrific officer. His men would do anything for him. Anyway, I don't believe in premonitions. Do you?"

"I don't know," he said, "but you see all these good-looking guys? More than half of them will be dead by next year. I guess what I believe in is luck. And you can be lucky whether you're Prince Charming or a real sonofabitch. I figure my odds of surviving are as good as the next guy's. Of course, Billy is not a flyer, but those armoured divisions are going to take a hell of a beating when they cross the Channel and hit the beaches."

Kathleen looked down at her hands. "I think his father is afraid for him. He wants him to give up his commission and run for a seat in the House of Commons. There'll be a local election in February."

"Well, if he's smart, he'll jump at the opportunity. Better a live duke than a dead hero."

Joe's words echoed in her mind when she was back at the Hans Crescent Club and unable to sleep. All the talk of war and death reminded her of her father that day in 1939 when England declared war on Germany and he kept saying over and over, "It's the end of the world! It's the end of the world!" Before that day she did not give much thought to politics or world events. She was only nineteen, and, like her mother, was trained to believe that women should mind their own business and let the men worry about the wars and the revolutions.

After that unforgetable day she also became more aware of the differences between Joe and Jack. Joe was physically stronger and her father's favorite. Jack was sickly and her father could not always conceal his contempt for the weak. He once told her that he was against the war between England and Germany because Germany would win and winning was all that mattered. Joe reflected his father's point of view, but Jack made up his own mind. In 1940 he supported Roosevelt for a third term. Joe was the only member of the Massachusetts delegation to vote against Roosevelt's nomination at the Democratic National Convention. Joe was against aid to Britain and said so when he spoke at an America First luncheon. Jack was annoyed at him for refusing to adjust to the political realities. At Harvard Joe was not very popular. He was black-balled from a number of clubs that later accepted Jack, who was not only a better student, but socially more successful. Joe was supposed to be the better athlete, but he never won his varsity letter in football. Jack, at least, got a junior varsity letter by simply hurling himself into the game recklessly and winding up with a bad back. At Choate, Lem and Jack and their friends were the wild bunch known as The Muckers' Club. She remembered how one time all thirteen members were expelled for raising hell. And she remembered the telegram she sent them: DEAR PUBLIC ENEMIES ONE AND TWO ALL OUR PRAYERS ARE UNITED WITH YOU AND THE OTHER ELEVEN MUCKS. WHEN THE OLD MEN ARRIVE SORRY WE WONT BE THERE FOR THE BURIAL.

Now, years later, in another country, this competition between her brothers suddenly became clear. It was Joe who was the bitter one, because it was he who was their father's favorite, and Jack's accomplishments were making it more and more difficult for him to feel that he deserved to be favored. Jack didn't really give a damn. He didn't want to compete with his brother for his father's affection. He was reckless and confident and enjoyed his life, in spite of his beat-up body. That's why she loved him, she decided. That's what the real difference between her brothers was. Joe was loud but not happy. Underneath it all there was a sulleness that worried her. Maybe it was because he felt obliged to be like his father and could not be himself.

These thoughts trailed away into sleep, and just before the curtain of darkness closed around her she remembered another prayer from her convent-school days: *Even in the night have I desired Thee, Lord. Come, Lord Jesus, come.*

The weather turned bad during the night, which meant that Joe could stay over for another day and both of them could accept an invitation from William Randolph Hearst, Jr. to join him for dinner at the Savoy. The legendary hotel on the Strand always reminded Kathleen of her debutante year. She remembered talking to herself in the mirror one day: *Going to the Savoy for dinner, darling. See you later at the Club.* When she was young, being in England was sometimes like being in a Noel Coward play, and it was all "great fun." Now the fun was dampened by the war and the more serious drama of being a grown-up woman.

When they arrived at the Savoy they were taken to a table where Hearst sat with a British officer and three attractive women. The men stood up for a round of greetings and introductions. The officer proved to be General Robert Laycock, head of the British Commandos, and one of the women was his wife Angela. One of the other women was the former Virginia Gilliat, whom Kathleen had already described to Joe as married and pregnant. She was now the wife of Sir Richard Sykes. When Joe was introduced to her he gave her a wink and said to Hearst, "We already know each other." When he was introduced to the third woman, it was instantly obvious that he found her appealing. She had very dark hair and blue eyes that revealed her liveliness. "Patricia Wilson," said Hearst. "Her husband, Major Robin Filmer Wilson, is with the British army in Libya." Joe sat down next to her without waiting for an invitation. The general frowned, but then seemed pleased when Kathleen was asked to sit next to him. Before long they were drinking and laughing and remembering mutual friends. They all seemed to know the same people, and had even taken part in some of the same memorable events of the past, such as the largest party ever given at Blenheim Palace. Just before the war the Duke and Duchess of Marlborough had entertained a thousand guests in such glitter and splendor that the event was often described as marking the end of an era. "If you weren't there," said Lady Sykes, "you were nobody."

Hearst and the general fell into a discussion of the Italian campaign, where the progress of the Allies toward Rome was threatening to bog down for the winter because of the weather and the difficult mountain terrain. The Germans had made a fortress of the old monastery at Monte Cassino, a strategic postion that they were determined to hold at all cost. A series of air raids and frontal assaults by the Allies had all failed. "This could be a terrible embarrassment for Churchill," said Hearst. "His 'soft underbelly' strategy has already been criticized as idiotic. Italy was an impossible battlefield in the first war and it still is. We should be fighting in France not Italy."

General Laycock did not agree. "The Germans have had to make enormous military committments on this front, especially since the collapse of the Fascists and the Badoglio takeover."

Katheen seemed to be listening intently to this disussion, but, actually, she was eavesdropping on Pat Wilson and Joe. Her brother was carrying on another kind of campaign. She had often seen her father behave this way with women. She recognized the predatory focus, the heavy-handed seduction. Even Jack, charming as he was, sometimes was too obvious in the way he circled his prey. Most English women were too reserved to be rushed in this way, but Pat was talking and laughing with considerable confidence and seemed to be enjoying Joe's attention. Kathleen decided from a distance that she was not English, after all, and soon had her suspicion confirmed.

Before the main course arrived, Joe had his arm draped across the back of Pat's chair. "You're not English, are you?" he said.

"How can you tell?"

"You're too relaxed, too friendly. In fact, you've got the hair and complexion of an Irish colleen, and a twinkle in your eye to go with it."

"Well, you're not far off, Mr. Kennedy. I'm Australian, and since Australia was originally a penal colony, an awful lot of Irishmen were sent there. And we all know how prolific the Irish are. I remember the pictures of your family in the papers when your father was here as the American Ambassador. Quite a mob scene!"

"Yeah," he said. "We could always get up a game without recruiting strangers. How about you? Have you got any kids?"

"Three," she said.

"Well, I guess the Major didn't waste much time. You can't be more than twenty-five."

"You Americans are incredibly inquisitive," she said, but Joe persisted until he found out that she was thirty years old, that only two of the children were the Major's, that her first husband was George Child-Villiers, the Earl of Jersey, that they were divorced in 1937, and that she was the daughter of a sheep rancher from Cootamundra, New South Wales, who came to England with her mother to look for a school, but found a husband instead. " I can juggle and tap dance, and, if necessary, carry a tune and speak French. Is there anything else you would like to know?"

"Yeah, what's your phone number and when's you're husband coming home?"

They both laughed a bit too loudly and drew a disapproving glance from the general. It was Kathleen who blushed not Patricia. "The Americans seem to have discovered how to make our women laugh," he said to Hearst in a voice loud enough for everyone at the table to hear. "We've been trying for centuries without much success. I understand that Mr. Kennedy's father also had a sense of humor. He thought the Germans were going to win the war."

"That was a long time ago, Sir," said Joe. "Now we're all in it together."

"Apparently!" he said, and raised his glass. "Here's to all our good men in faraway places."

A raised eyebrow was all that Patricia needed to let him know that she got his point, but she did nothing to discourage Joe's interest in her, and Joe did not seem to think that there was anything wrong with his public flirtation. Virginia glanced in his direction from time to time, but Kathleen did not think there was any trace of jealousy in her expression. Angela Laycock, on the other hand, was amused. When Joe said that he would soon be stationed near Taunton in Somerset, Pat said, "Well, in that case, you must stop by and see us. We have a cottage called Crastock Farm in Woking, which is on the same train line as Taunton. And bring Kathleen if she's free. I can put you up and we can pool our rations for a bit of a party."

Later that night, when Joe took her back to the club, Kathleen said, "I guess you made quite an impression on Mrs.Wilson."

"I don't know about that," he said, "but she sure made an impression on me."

"Do you really want to get involved with a married woman?"

64

"Well, little sister, if you don't approve, why don't you and Billy come down as chaperones. Then we'll all have something that we can't write home about."

CHAPTER FIVE

Kathleen's father arranged to get her home for Christmas, which did not surprise her. Nor did it bother her that no one else she knew would be making the trip. Priority was given to flight crews who had completed thirty missions, and the seats on all the transport planes were filled. She no longer cared what the rest of the staff at the club thought about her. If she had special privileges, so what! She was special. Her brother Jack once told her,"We don't have to apologize for being rich; we were born that way."

The last one she saw before leaving was Sissy Ormsby-Gore, her most reliable friend. She was not only a good Catholic, but she was married to Billy's cousin. Given the darkness of December and the tensions of the time, they agreed that a sinful lunch in luxurious surroundings was in order. Would it be Claridge's or the Dorchester Hotel? "Either one sounds heavenly to me,"said Sissy.

"Make it the Dorchester, then," said Kathleen. "It's closer to Hans Crescent. If I'm late for work again, they are liable to decommission me."

They came to lunch in civilian clothes, Kathleen wearing a Robin Hood hat with an outrageous feather. "If your outfit is a reflection of your inner self," said Sissy, "you may need more than a brief vacation."

"I'm not sure that going home for Christmas is what I need right now, but I'm not going to turn it down. "

"I suppose you'll be getting the usual parental inquisition about your private life."

"Of course!"

"What will you tell them?"

"I would like to tell them the truth, but I'm not sure that I will have the courage to do that. You know, sometimes I'm actually afraid of them. God knows what sort of a person they think I am. From the time I was old enough to be aware of men my father has investigated the background of any man who showed the slightest interest in me. Sometimes he even consulted the F.B.I."

"How peculiar!" said Sissy, fingering the cool glass of her daiquiri.

"I used to think it was normal. I was even rather pleased. You know, 'daddy's little girl' and all that. When I got older, I realized it wasn't exactly par for the course. But every time I go home, it's two giant steps backwards, and there I am, 'daddy's little girl' and my mother telling me that if I wear the wrong clothes I won't go to heaven."

"My, my, we are upset, aren't we?"

"I always feel that they know exactly what I'm doing, even if I lie to them, even if they are thousands of miles away." Kathleen looked around the elegant dining room as though she half expected to see her father there, trying to make a deal *to buy the joint.* He had taken her to lunch there when she was eighteen years old, and he had said that she could have anything her heart desired, even if he had to buy the joint to get it for her.

"You're just feeling guilty, Kick. We all do when we disagree with our parents. Billy's feeling the pressure, too. David saw him recently and thought he looked terribly worried. He let himself be talked into this election, and now he's worried about what his regiment will think. On top of that he's afraid he might lose you. The last time you two were separated it was for four years. This time, he told David, it might be forever."

"I also urged him to get into this election," said Kathleen, "and now I'm sorry I did. It was terribly selfish of me. I promised him I would have a serious talk with my parents. I mean, we're practically engaged, even though our wedding is impossible. What a mess!"

"I hate to agree with you," said Sissy, "but it really is a mess. You could not have chosen a more difficult family into which to marry. Over three hundred years ago, Robert Cecil, one of Billy's ancestors, prevented the marriage of the Prince of Wales to the Spanish Infanta because she was a Roman Catholic. His family has opposed home rule in Ireland for centuries. The Irish Republicans hate them. In 1870 the Eighth Duke of Devonshire was made secretary of state for Ireland. In 1882 his brother succeeded him. The day after he took office he was killed by the I.R.A. in Phoenix Park. Billy Cavendish does not have to go to France to be shot; he can be shot in Ireland, or even Boston."

"They wouldn't have to shoot him in Boston; they could just bore him to death," said Kathleen. "So, what am I supposed to do now? Kiss my family goodbye? Tell the Church that I find it inconvenient to be a Catholic?"

Sissy hesitated. "Well, as a matter of fact, you could, and many women would, but, in the long run, you might be sorry."

"I never challenged the authority of the Church, but John White once told me that even if I wound up damned for all of eternity I would probably have a lot of interesting company. Do you suppose they play bridge in hell?"

"Darling, that's probably what hell is all about -- being scolded forever for playing the wrong card."

They laughed and ordered another drink.

In Palm Beach, Kathleen became a Kennedy again, moving with her restless clan through games of tennis and Monopoly and random social gatherings, "distracted from distraction" by the people who came and went, leaving little trails of news and gossip behind them. There was rarely the time or inclination for a sustained discussion of any kind. Rose faded in and out to make announcements about Christmas concerts and church services, or to deliver little lectures on such subjects as modesty, poise, and a proper education. It occurred to Kathleen one day that she had never taken her mother by surprise, had never, in fact, seen her in those personal moments when, half-dressed or off-guard, she might seem to be just like everyone else, a real human being. She was, in this respect, like the nuns in her Catholic schools, hidden in their robes, reserved for Christ.

These thoughtful moments were few and were often shattered by the younger children and their friends. Her brother Teddy was only eleven years old. Jean was fifteen. But the beach and the sea were consolations, and the Florida sun soon drove out the prolonged chill of the English winter. Some of the young men who were part of their crowd showed up on the beach, home from college or on leave from the service, but the one person she had secretly hoped would be there was not. When they last heard from Jack he was in a hospital in Tulagi, with a pretty good chance, he thought, of being shipped back to the States, but not before Christmas.

She did, however, get to see Nancy Tenney, whose husband was a Navy pilot in the Pacific. She was pregnant and asked her old friend Kathleen to be the godmother. Kathleen was so pleased that, for an hour or so, she thought she might be able to give up her impossible English dreams for a more ordinary American life.

Everybody asked about Joe. Her father asked several times. She told him what she could, but he never seemed quite satisfied. "Is he all right?" he kept saying. "How does he look?"

And then it was all over, and she had failed to do what she had promised Billy she would do.

The next time she saw him he was talking to a small group of farmers from the auction platform of a cattle market. Without his uniform he looked

69

younger and less important. Everything marked him as the gentleman candidate who was trying to persuade his rural constituents to vote for him. She had driven up to West Derbyshire in a borrowed Austen, and, with the help of Elizabeth Cavendish, was planning to suprise Billy after this brief local appearance in Bakewell, where he had his campaign headquarters.

Kathleen watched from a distance under a heavy January sky. She sat in a pony cart with Elizabeth. The cart sported the colors of the British flag and was drawn by a pony named Poppet. On the seat in front of Kathleen there was a stack of leaflets, held down against the wind by a stone. She read one of them: *A vote for Hartington is a vote for Churchill. Support the Conservative party for victory in war and peace.* Kathleen wore a raincoat over her Red Cross uniform and turned up the collar because of the chill in the air. "Are you sure you don't want to sit in the car?" she said to Elizabeth. It's liable to rain any minute."

"I'm afraid I can't," she said. "You see, the pony cart is our way of showing the voters that we are conserving petrol. It's all part of the political game. We have to seem to be sharing the problems of ordinary people, but, of course, everybody knows who we are."

Kathleen was amused. "I think we could teach you a thing or two about campaigning. You're too low key. You need more noise to stir people up, maybe a brass band or a big drum. You have to make the voters feel good, as if the circus has come to town." Elizabeth gave her an innocent and dubious look, as though she were being lured away from school for some illicit fun.

A man twice Billy's age stood beside him on the covered platform. He looked like an undertaker in his black overcoat and fedora. In a deep voice and a local accent he said that it was his pleasure to introduce Lord Hartington, "who would like to explain why it would be to your advantage to have him as your representative in the House of Commons."

A few portly men in woolen caps and muddy boots provided scattered applause. Some of the others waited silently, their hands in their pockets revealing vests and watchchains. There were not many young men among them, but there were some women, in plain coats and kerchiefs and heavy country shoes. The ground was soft and the air a bit sour from the cow barns.

Billy seemed confident as he spoke, and his voice carried easily beyond the small crowd to the pony cart where Kathleen and Elizabeth sat. "My opponent," he said, " is running as an Independent Socialist and has the support of an organization called the Common Wealth, not to be confused with the British Commonwealth of Nations, which is currently cooperating to win a war against the German aggressors in Europe and the Japanese imperialists in the Pacific. Mr. White and his Socialist colleagues claim to be deeply concerned about the economic problems of the post-war era. They seem to have overlooked an immense technicality. The war is not over! We have a long way to go and many sacrifices to make. Anyone who promises you prosperity before it is paid for is leading you up the garden path..."

Afterwards they drove off in the pony cart, Billy looking all legs and arms and a bit ridiculous, but ruddy from the weather and animated by the excitement of suddenly finding Kathleen there. "I knew it, I knew it, I knew it," he said, echoing the bumpy rhythm of the cart on the dirt road. "I knew you were here. I could feel it."

"Are you sure your little sister didn't tell you? She's too honest for her own good."

"I didn't. I swear I didn't," said Elizabeth over her shoulder as she held Poppet's reins and failed to slow him down for a puddle.

They all laughed and Billy put a protective arm around Kathleen and kissed her impulsively.

Later, at Chatsworth, they sat alone by a fire in one of the guest cottages. Billy explained about the school that was being accommodated in the main house. "Our private quarters are reserved, of course, but you can imagine the noise. The place is crawling with energetic young girls."

"Lucky you!" said Kathleen.

"They're a bit too young, I'm afraid, but some of them are very pretty, and will, eventually, be even prettier."

"You're trying to make me jealous," she said, playing the little game.

"Yes, but I can see that I'm not doing a very good job."

"I'm not the jealous type."

"I used to think that I wasn't either, but whenever I thought of you in Florida, lying around on the beach or cavorting with all those athletic friends of your brothers -- well, I have to admit that I caved in a bit to the old green-eyed monster. But it must have been a pleasure for you to get away from all this. After all, America is not directly involved in the war. No air raids or invasion threats."

"I was too distracted to enjoy it. I kept wishing you were there."

"And I kept wishing you were here. This election campaign has had me on edge. It would have been good to have you nearby, to feel your support."

"Well here I am, and I will be happy to address the masses on your behalf. I've learned enough from my grandfather to get a one-legged dwarf elected."

72

"How about a tall, two-legged soldier with a slightly receding hairline and an Irish-Catholic American girlfriend?"

"Now, just a minute, Hartington," she said. "I can't perform miracles."

"Speaking of which, did you manage to talk some sense into your family?"

She looked into the fire for a moment and then at Billy. "You're going to think I'm an awful coward," she said.

"It's not your fault if they refuse to be reasonable, but I was rather hoping that they would be kind enough to assure you of their love and loyalty no matter what decisions you make about your personal life. I feel I have that assurance from my family, though obviously we disagree on the subject of a mixed marriage."

"You don't understand, Billy. "I lost my nerve. I didn't even have the courage to bring up the subject, and, of course, they avoided it. I think they were secretly hoping that I had lost interest in you."

He looked troubled. "Perhaps you have."

"Don't say that, darling. You know it's not true."

"Maybe it's not, but it begins to look as though they have found a way to keep you in line. All I'm asking is that you make up your own mind. And what they are saying is that if you assert your will, they'll withdraw their love. They're playing God with you, and a Roman Catholic God at that, to whom nothing matters more than blind obedience. Sometimes I think that my ancestors were right after all when they broke with the old church. What we need in this world is a god of love, not a god that strikes terror in your heart."

"Maybe it's the fear of eternal damnation that keeps us honest," she said.

"Oh, damnation be damned. I personally think that it is the height of arrogance to think that we

73

can know what God's will is. And the prize for arrogance goes to the Vatican with all its earthly power and wealth. How dare they claim that everbody is wrong but them. If you were born in India you'd probably be a Hindu. The conflict that we are involved in has nothing to do with theology and everything to do with family relationships and social conventions. I'm looking for a solution in this world, not the next one. My soul, if I have one, I leave to God, if there is a God."

"Please, Billy, don't talk that way. Don't be angry. It's not my fault that I was not born in India or that I was born a Catholic. I can only believe what I was taught to believe." Standing beside the fire she looked like a scolded schoolgirl. "But I have had my secret doubts," she said, "and another secret that I have not wanted to tell you, because it frightens me more than my doubts about the Church."

"Perhaps this would be a good time to tell me, whatever it is."

There were shadows under her eyes, as though she had been crying in some private and invisible way. "From before I came here I knew that if you wanted me I would not be able to refuse you, no matter what the price. I never told that to anyone, and I even tried for a while to keep it from myself. But don't ask me to pay the whole price right away. Give me a little time."

"And what if we should run out of time?"

"We won't. Better the registry office than nothing at all. I want to be your wife, Billy. I want that more than anything else in the world."

He took her in his ams and comforted her. "I'm sorry I lost my temper, Kick. It was wrong of me. I was afraid that your family would persuade you to give it all up, even, perhaps, find a match for you. Some fabulously rich robber baron from Boston or New York."

She leaned against his shoulder. He stroked her honey-brown hair and kissed her gently. "I don't want a robber baron, Billy," she said. "I want an MP from Derbyshire, so you'd better win."

"Yes, ma'm. I'll do my best, ma'm," he said with his boyish smile.

They joined Billy's family for dinner. The other guests included the local party organizer and a man sent up from London, who kept referring to Prime Minister Churchill, as though everyone in the room were hard of hearing. Kathleen was introduced to them and to Billy's uncle, Henry Hunloke, whose resignation resulted in this by-election. Hunloke's opponent in 1938 was the same Charles White who was now opposing Billy. His father had the distinction of having been the only one to defeat a Cavendish in the past two hundred years, and the pugnacious alderman was determined to follow in his father's footsteps. In an aside to Kathleen, Elizabeth Cavendish said that the potbellied socialist looked like Porky the Pig, and the two young women laughed behind their hands. The Duchess looked at them and smiled, as though she were pleased by the effect that Kathleen's arrival was having on her children.

After dinner the men retired to another room to talk politics in an atmosphere of cigar smoke and brandy. The ladies sat in the adjoining room and talked about more dometic things. When Billy's mother spoke to Kathleen she was warm and friendly, even appreciative. "It's really a pleasure to have you back. Things have been altogether too serious around here, what with this election and all. Poor Billy is doing his best, but I don't think he's been very happy. Today, however, he has been absolutely beaming, and I give all the credit to you. Incidentally, I knew you were coming. You must never ask Elizabeth to keep a secret. She's just awful about such things."

Elizabeth blushed. "Well, I can't help it," she said. "Keeping a secret is like trying not to laugh in church. Once you think about it, you just do it, whether you like it or not." Elizabeth was several years younger than Kathleen. She was only a child when they first met in 1938; now she was an attractive young woman.

From where she sat Kathleen could hear the men talking in the next room. The gathering reminded her of similar gatherings at home, strategy sessions in Hyannis Port or Bronxville or Palm Beach. The women had always been excluded, and it never occurred to her that there was anything wrong with that. Politics was the smelly business of smelly men. That's how she remembered it from her childhood -- fat perspiring faces, woolen suits and whiskey smiles.

The man from London, whose name she did not catch, was talking with an air of great authority, representing as he did the governing party and the prime minister. "We're getting a great deal of attention in the press,"he said. "Too much, in fact. They are trying to use this by-election as a barometer for the post-war general election and Churchill's popularity. The Socialists are claiming that the old man has served his country well as a war-time leader, but is not equipped to deal with economic recovery and other domestic issues. We disagree, of course, but we've got to demonstrate in this election that our party can hold the line. To lose a seat such as this one would be a disaster. Our opponents know this and are apparently throwing everything they can into this campaign. History tells us that we can not lose here, but the press seem to think otherwise. Sir Richard Acland and his Common Wealth group have hired about a hundred professionals to get out the vote for Charles White, and they are turning this election into a nasty, muck-raking contest. Young William here is being attacked as a pampered aristocrat who knows nothing about the workers, and as a soldier who gave up his commission in the Coldstream Guards in order to avoid military combat. A ridiculous insinuation, but one that may have to be countered in some way. My message, in brief, gentlemen, is that you have got to win this election. It is not an exaggeration to say at this point that the whole world is watching."

Kathleen retired early and took with her that ominous statement: *The whole world is watching.* And what if he should lose, she thought. What would Billy do? The very idea of defeat frightened her. She had lived all her life with her father's doctrine that winning was everything. Defeat was a kind of death. Would Billy be called up from the reserve and rushed suddenly into combat before they could find any resolution to their problem? She fell asleep in her cold bedroom, wrapped in these cold thoughts. She tried to pray but could not, as though she had already been cast out of the faith that had nurtured her.

Something woke her in the middle of the night. When she opened her eyes she saw Billy sitting beside her on the bed. "Did I startle you?" he said.

"No," she said. "I was hoping that you would come. I left the door unlocked."

"It wouldn't have mattered," he said. "I have a key. I had to see you." She reached for the bedside lamp, but he touched her hand. "No," he said, "let me light a candle. I'll only stay for a few minutes and then you can go back to sleep. I don't want you to think --"

"Stay as long as you want. You know I trust you, " she said, lifting herself to lie back against two pillows. Her long-sleeved flannel nightgown was buttoned to her neck and her hair was dissheveled. She watched him light a single candle on the mantlepiece of the small fireplace where the embers still glowed. The candlelight made visible the portrait of a woman in an oval frame. "Who was she?"

Billy looked at the portrait. "A great aunt of mine. I only knew her when she was old."

"She was very beautiful when she was young."

"Yes, a whole biography in two sentences and one picture. Life is very strange. Very swift and very perilous."

He came back to the bed and sat down. "I see you're wearing your Irish sweater," she said.

"Does it make me look Irish?"

"No, it makes you look more English than ever."

"I went to bed but got up again. I put on whatever was there. It's very comfortable, very soothing -- like you." He sat down beside her and brushed a few strands of hair from her forehead. "All that political talk was very upsetting."

"Why?"

"Because I seem to have gotten myself into something much more complicated than I thought it would be. I've been told this evening that the future of the Conservative party may be decided right here in West Derbyshire, and that the burden is squarely on my shoulders. Those are high stakes."

"Yes, Billy, but the higher the stakes, the greater the victory. Winning here would make you a political hero."

"Would it?" He sounded unconvinced. "Or would it mean that the party had to come to my rescue because I am young and inexperienced and unable to persuade the voters that I understand their everyday problems?"

"And do you understand their problems?"

"Of course! At least, I like to think I do, and I have to say I do." He hesitated and frowned. "On the other hand, it's obvious that I do not share all their experiences. I'm not a farmer or a worker, and I'm not poor. Neither are Winston Churchill and Franklin D. Roosevelt. Many of the greatest leaders in your country and mine have been wealthy and well educated. They devote themselves to the service of their country not for profit but because they believe that improving the quality of life for everyone is a noble endeavor."

"Why don't you say that, when you make your next speech, instead of falling into Charlie White's trap when he says you don't know how to milk a cow. Tell him that there are no cows to be milked in the House of Commons, but plenty of difficult economic and political decisions to be made. Tell them that if they want someone who knows how to milk a cow to represent them then they should elect a milkmaid."

"That's really very good," he said. "Perhaps I should hire you to write my speeches."

"I'm not much of a writer, but I'll be glad to come up on week-ends and make the rounds with you, unless you think my presence would be an embarrassment."

"Your presence, darling, would be an inspiration. Please come."

"And when people ask you who I am, what will you say?"

"I'll say you're the woman I love."

"I don't think that's a good idea," she said.

"Why not?"

"Well, for one thing, because you would sound too much like the Duke of Windsor, and for another, you'd probably lose the votes of those who hate the Irish and the Catholics, and those who think my father is a traitor."

"My God, you've got it all figured out, haven't you?"

"In my family we learned mathematics by studying election returns. So if I do come up and follow you around, I'll be with Elizabeth, and you can say that I am a friend of hers."

"If you insist, but you *are* the woman I love, and I wish I could tell that to the whole bloody world, and those who don't like the idea can just -- just'shuffle off to Buffalo.' I'm sorry. Did I say something vulgar in American English?"

"You certainly did, from the song by the same name." She laughed and her face seemed illuminated by something other than candlelight.

"Did I every tell you that you have a wonderful way of laughing?" he said.

"No."

"Well, I'm telling you now. It's a laugh that rewards the person you're with. It makes him feel that his mere existence delights you. It's innocent but seductive, full of warm promises. I'm not the only one who knows this. You have other admirers."

"Who? Tell me."

"Why should I? You might be tempted to amuse them."

She took him by the front of his sweater and pulled him toward her in a tough-guy gesture. "If you don't tell me, I won't ride in your pony cart anymore."

And then, suddenly, he kissed her. She put her arms around him and returned his kiss with warm but unparted lips. "And do you have admirers, too? Is Princess Elizabeth giving you the eye?"

"As a matter of fact --"

"Well, you just tell her that she can't have you until I'm through with you, which will be never."

"That's a long time, darling," he said. "Never is forever."

She suddenly seemed cold again and held him close. "It's hard to think about."

"Perhaps I should go now," he said, without moving away.

"Don't go," she said. "I promise not to seduce you. Just stay until I fall asleep. We can pretend that we're married."

"If we were married, I'd probably keep you awake."

She smiled. "Well, for now you can rub my back. It helps me to relax." She turned over and hugged her pillow. She felt his hands move over her shoulders and then slowly down her body, almost to her hips, and then up again, firmly, slowly. She felt warm again, and soon the steadiness of his touch lulled her to sleep. She did not hear him leave, but in the morning he was gone. She lay there for a long time, wondering about whether or not she desired him and whether or not any of the women she knew had slept with him.

Kathleen came up for the next few weekends and followed Billy around from village to village, from agricultural fairs and marketplaces to tea parties and club meetings. She admired him from a distance, standing under an umbrella in a crowd or sitting in the back row of a chilly town hall. He held his ground and defended himself well against the ruthless accusations of Charlie White and his "hired bullies from the West Country, who preach revolutionary garbage, instead of laying out a sensible post-war plan."

He offered his hand democratically to both men and women, but some of the women responded with a curtsy and a shy *Your Lordship,* and some of the men looked apologetically at their earth-soiled hands and nodded their heads. When he leaned over to chat with a small child, the lad retreated into his mother's arms. "You must have looked awfully tall from his point of view," said Kathleen later. "Anyhow, kids don't vote, so don't worry about it." She was chewing gum and doing her little Mae West routine to cheer him up.

81

With increased press coverage the crowds grew larger and more vociferous. They were stirred up by the professionals and by the importance of the outcome of the election. It made them feel more involved and more inclined to voice their opinions openly. The once docile supporters of the Cavendish tradition now seemed to have minds of their own and complaints that were rarely made public. Provoked by the intensity of the contest and by personal attacks, the Duke himself joined the fray with several emotional speeches and the appeal for loyalty: *Don't let the old side down!* Even Billy's mother made public appearances on his behalf, about which Billy had mixed feelings, since he was being accused of being the hand-picked candidate of an autocratic ruling class.

Inevitably, the paths of the candidates crossed, and the excited crowd joined the debate with shouts of criticism or support. On the last market day in Bakewell both candidates were there, along with a score of reporters and a newsreel camera crew. Charlie White hammered away at "this young heir of a dukedom, this candidate of the Palace on the Peak, who, on the eve of the great invasion of Europe, has chosen to abandon his comrades and find personal security in the House of Commons. He knows nothing about the common people. His hands are not soiled by common labor. He is not one of us --"

Angered by these remarks, Billy leapt to the platform and shouted to the crowd. "I refuse to stand by when I am attacked in this ruthless and unethical way. Where is your common sense? Can't you see that this is organized muck-raking and slander?"

The crowd's response was mixed and loud. "Where is your uniform?" shouted one man.

"I especially resent my opponent's attack on my patriotism and military record. I have served in the army for five long years, and I have seen major action in Europe. How dare he suggest that I have not been a good and responsible officer, a leader of men."

He was interrupted by applause, and then the applause gave way to a shouting duel among the partisans in the crowd. "Give up your pony cart, Hartington, and get yourself a tank," said a gruff voice. "Be quiet you rabble-rouser and let the man speak," said a stout farmer. "If the shoe fits, let him wear it," said another man."

Billy raised his voice another notch. "I may not be perfect, but you can be damn sure that if the shoe fits it was not made by Charlie White." This remark drew a wave of laughter from the crowd, since Charlie White was a cobbler's son and often boasted of the fact. "To put it in plain language, my opponent is a liar, who will say anything to win this election. He does not know the meaning of the word *decency* , and he may even have trouble spelling it."

"Let him have it, Billy!" shouted a woman from somewhere in the crowd. Heads turned but the woman could not be identified. Only Billy knew who she was.

The next day the voters went to the polls to cast their secret ballots in an election that most newspapers described as "too close to call." By the following day the counting of the ballots at the Matlock Town Hall was completed, and Billy and his family went there to hear the official results. They proved to be devastating. Billy was defeated by the wide margin of sixteen thousand to eleven thousand. From a balcony the candidates spoke to the crowd. Charlie White was a graceless winner, who continued his attack though the battle was over. Billy spoke more briefly and was clearly shaken by the outcome. He said that he was disappointed that he was not given the chance to prove himsef in the House of Commons, and that his plan now was to return immediately to active duty in the army. "I will give myself entirely to the defense of my country. I will fight for you, perhaps die for you. God bless you all!"

Standing behind him, with his family and friends, Kathleen held back her tears, as her mother had taught her, but inside of her there was an invisible tempest of anger, love, and admiration. At that moment, she could have killed on his behalf to avenge his defeat.

CHAPTER SIX

The following weekend Kathleen and Billy joined Pat Wilson and Joe at the Crastock Farm cottage, recently dubbed "Crash-Bang" Cottage. Once the house of the gardener for an estate in Woking, it now served as a safe haven for Pat and her children and a weekend retreat for her friends. It was ideally located. There was a factory nearby, where Pat could contribute part-time to the war effort, and London was near enough for her to keep up with the social adventures of the circles in which she moved. She was an outgoing person who did not like being alone for too long, especially with three small children. The prolonged absence of her army husband created in her a more specific need, one that Joe Kennedy seemed willing and able to satisfy.

The stuccoed cottage with its shingled roof sat pleasantly among trees and bushes that were already announcing an early spring. The gardener had done his job well, and a chorus of birds sang their approval at dawn each morning. They sang also in the wooded glen behind the cottage.

The weekends at "Crash-Bang" were not like the weekends at the grand country houses that Kathleen enjoyed during her debutante year, but in their own way they were just as enjoyable. There was the old tennis court that they managed to make playable. And there was an element of surprise in their meals, since they never knew in advance what each person was able to beg, borrow, or steal for the occasion. In the evening they played cards and listened to the gramophone. Sometimes Kathleen smuggled recent American records out of the Hans Crescent Club, recordings by Harry James, Benny Goodman and Tommy Dorsey.

On this particular weekend, "to lift Billy's spirits after his defeat," Joe produced a bottle of

French Champgne. "Don't ask me where it came from," he said. "I have sworn by all that is sacred not to tell."

"That's a lot of swearing," said Billy.

"Damn right!" said Joe.

It was Friday evening. The children were in bed, there was a friendly fire in the fireplace, and the ladies were consulting in the kitchen about how to make a coherent dinner out of the odds and ends that confronted them. On the back burner of the stove there was a pot of water patiently boiling away. It would become "Survival Soup" if all else failed. On the counter there were the inevitable tins of Spam and beans and grapefruit juice. There was also a wedge of cheese, four eggs, a jar of pickled onions, a large pork kidney and a pair of local lake bass. Fresh vegetables were scarce this time of year, but Pat had stocked up on potatoes and carrots in the fall and they had kept well in the cold weather.

"What shall it be?" said Pat, "Charles deGaulle bisque or Cassino Casserole?"

"We'd better use the fish before they go bad," said Kathleen.

"They're awfully small."

"We can fill up on potatoes and Joe's corny jokes."

"I've already had my fill of those," said Pat.

"He's not beginning to bore you, is he?"

"Not at all. In fact, he's pleasantly crude at times, like the sheep ranchers of Cootamundra, but he's as honest as the day is long -- and rather interesting at night." She raised a naughty eyebrow.

"You're as bad as he is," said Kathleen.

"Worse," said Pat. "I'm married; he's not. But this is wartime, darling, and we also serve who only lie there and wait."

The boys heard them laughing and Joe called out: "What's going on in there? Bring some glasses, we're going to pop the champagne."

Joe made the first toast. "Here's to Billy, who lost an election but will win the war. May he return, like MacArthur, when it's all over, and give 'em hell in the House of Commons."

"By then the place may be full of Charlie Whites," said Billy.

"You're right," said Joe. "The biggest problem in the post-war era is going to be the spread of Communism. Sometimes I think old "Blood-and-Guts" is right when he says that the real war won't be over until we march into Moscow."

"That may be going a bit far," said Billy, "but we will have to find a way to make our message clear politically. I could have done a better job in this election."

"You did just fine," said Kathleen. "In hard times it's always easier to promise the people prosperity than to tell them the truth."

"Perhaps the best policy," said Pat, "Is to tell them only what they want to hear."

Kathleen wondered what Pat planned to tell her husband when he returned, but she said: "In that case, I am happy to announce that we are having Porterhouse steaks for dinner."

"You're a bigger liar than Charlie White," said Billy.

"Does that mean I'll be elected?"

"Darling," he said, "you have already been elected -- by me." He put his arm around her and kissed her on the cheek. On the gramophone Edith Piaf was singing *La Vie en Rose.*

Reality was fishcakes, mashed potatoes and carrots, topped off by a mousse improvised from G.I. chocolate bars and evaporated milk. When the champagne was gone, they opened a bottle of wine that Billy had "requisitioned" from his father's carefully guarded wine-cellar at Chatsworth. Before long they were singing *I Think of You* along with Frank Sinatra, the vocalist for Tommy Dorsey's orchestra.

Over real coffee, compliments of the Hans Crescent Club, they turned to the one thing that was not rationed -- gossip. So many of the people they knew were involved in wartime romances that at times "love for the duration" seemed an acceptable concept. But there were also legitimate marriages, some of them too hasty to be taken seriously. "I give it six months from the day the war ends," said Pat of one such marriage, "unless she's pregnant, in which case I give it a year."

"Patricia!" said Kathleen in a harsh voice that sounded so much like her mother's that she startled herself.

"I'm sorry, darling," said Pat, "was I being disgusting?"

"No, but you're giving away a secret."

"You mean she actually is --"

"Well, yes, but --"

"But what?'

"Apparently her husband is not the father."

"Oh, how delicious!" she said.

Billy looked amused but disapproving. "Did it ever occur to you rumor-mongers that at this very moment some of our so-called friends are probably talking about us in this same way? We're all very vulnerable, you know."

"Well, I hope they're enjoying themselves as much as we are," said Pat. "Anyway, you Kennedys should be used to that sort of thing. Your names are always popping up in the newspapers. What is it about you people that is so intriguing? Plenty of people with money are never mentioned. Kathleen rides a bicycle to her Red Cross job and her picture is featured in *The Daily Mail.* And Jack has an accident in the Pacific and beomes a national hero."

"My theory," said Billy, "is that Americans like people with good teeth, and the Kennedys all have marvelous Hollywood smiles. Some day Joe will probably smile his way right into the White House."

"Well, he certainly had no trouble smiling his way into *this* house," said Pat.

"We shouldn't make fun of my kid brother," said Joe. "He's had a hard time and he's done a good job."

"He came home with a bad back and a touch of malaria," said Kathleen. "Inga wrote to tell me that he came to see her in L.A. and that he was depressed and disillusioned about the war and women and the world in general. There was very little of the old feeling between then, she said, but they had a long, friendly talk and she interviewed him for*The Boston Globe*. . He kept telling her that he did not want any of that hero nonsense in the article, because the real heroes were the guys who died out there. I like Inga very much, but she sure didn't wait around nursing a broken heart. We all thought that she had married Nils, but it turns out that she was just living with him. Now, it seems, she's got a new boyfriend, a Jewish doctor, who is an officer in the army. She's a columnist and a script-writer in Hollywood and doing great. With her looks and talent I'm not surprised."

"So what will Jack be doing now?" said Pat.

"I guess the war is over for him and he'll need time to recuperate and think about the future." Kathleen caught the look on Joe's face. She recognized it as the wounded expression he always had when Jack was the center of attention. Suddenly, he stood up and said, "Come on you guys, get out the cards. I'm feeling lucky tonight."

Kathleen and Billy could have had separate bedrooms, but they chose the one that had two beds. Joe teased them about it. "We could string some barbed wire between the beds if it'll keep you honest," he said.

"I don't think that will be necessary," said Billy. "I'm sure I'll be able to defend myself if I'm attacked in the night." Kathleen punched him playfully and dragged him off to bed.

Through the old walls they could hear the muffled voices of Joe and Pat, and they lowered their own discreetly. Billy stretched out on his bed without undressing, as though he were waiting for Kathleen to go first. "What are you staring at, soldier?" she said.

"My future wife, I hope," he said.

"Well, until the future gets here, how about turning around and giving a girl a little privacy."

"I'm sorry, darling. I didn't mean to embarrass you. On the other hand, it would be a pleasant kind of intimacy. It would make me feel that you trusted me."

"I do trust you, Billy. It's just that -- well, in the Catholic schools I went to we were not even allowed to see ourselves undress.We were never fully naked, even in the shower. I know it all sounds absurd, but to this very day I avoid looking at myself in the mirror unless I have something on. Once I'm in my nightgown, it's different. I feel comfortable. I'm afraid I may be one of those silly wives who needs a little time. Please don't laugh at me. I've thought about it a lot and I'm sure we'll be all right."

"That was an awfully good bottle of wine that I stole from my father," he said, "but don't worry, a promise is a promise." He turned away and faced the wall.

She took off her clothes with an occasional glance in his direction. When she was completely naked she glanced over her shoulder at the full-length mirror and saw herself standing there. A little wave of excitement sent a chill through her body as she reached for her long flannel nightgown. In the moment before she slipped it on she was tempted to ask him to turn around, but then decided not to.

90

When they were both in their beds like a married couple, she said, as though completing a sentence that she had started earlier, "Besides, I'm sure you know what a woman looks like after five years in the army."

"Oh my, that *must* have been a good bottle of wine," he said. "It's aroused your curiosity."

"You don't have to tell me if you don't want to."

"Well, as you say, darling, I've been in the army for five years. And before that there was Cambridge. There were the occasional naughty parties and brief encounters."

"How about Sally Norton?"

"She was very good company at the 'Caff,' but I think it would have been a loveless marriage. I never really wanted anyone but you."

"That's very sweet."

"It's also very true."

"In that case, why don't you climb over the barbed wire and join me? It's the least we can do while we're being virtuous."

They held each other without speaking and were amused by vague hints of passion in the next room. "If my parents only knew --" she said.

"They'd probably approve," he said. "After all, Joe's a man, and he doesn't have much to lose."

"Why is it that women are always at risk and men have nothing to lose? When my brothers come home after their wild adventures, my father gives them a wink and a chuckle. If I had the same adventures, my father would kill me, and my mother would forgive him."

"But do you really want that kind of freedom?"

She thought for a moment. "No. Sometimes I think I don't want any freedom at all. I think how wonderful it must be to give yourself completely to the man you love."

"What a terrific idea," he said. "Perhaps we can start right now. I can't think of a more convenient time." He drew her closer to him and kissed her. She yielded, but only because she could tell that he would not go any further.

After a few minutes she drew back a bit. "In the books they say that there is a point of no return for lovers. I think it must be true." She found a cigarette on the night table. He joined her. There were no longer any sounds from the other room. "Do you suppose they're sleeping?" she whispered.

"Probably," he said.

"Is that what lovers do?"

"Yes."

Suddenly, she frowned and seemed deep in thought. "I think I'm going to write to my parents soon and tell them the truth. We can't go on like this. Anyway, I think they already know and are only waiting to hear it from me. Last month I asked my mother's old friend Marie Bruce to write to her to suggest that we might be a good match, if the religious question could be resolved. So far my mother has not answered. It's a very bad sign. Her silence is worth a thousand words."

"In that case, you really don't have much choice. You've got to tell her how you feel."

"Perhaps I can ask them to help me get a special dispensation from the Church. They are on very good terms with Cardinal Spellman, and when the Pope was still Cardinal Eugenio Pacelli, they were selected to ride with him from New York to Hyde Park to visit President Roosevelt. In the newspapers they called us one of the most important Catholic families in America. We had a special invitation to Pacelli's coronation in Rome in 1939. All of us except my brother Joe were there. It would be terrific if some loophole in Church law could be found to allow me to remain a Catholic in good-standing.

"That might be asking an awful lot," said Billy.

"If anybody can do it, my father can, but my mother might just buy herself a black outfit and consider me dead."

He stroked her hair and she felt like a child in his arms. She did not always like to be touched, but his hands were gentle and she felt secure. They listened to the lonesome drone of a distant airplane in the night sky. It came closer and then started to fade.

"Where is the devil?" she said sleepily.

"What do you mean?"

"At school they used to tell us, *Where two are together the devil loves to make a third.*

"There's no devil here, darling," he said.

"Are you sure? Have you looked in the closet and under the bed?" She was remembering, suddenly, how Joe had told the younger children a scary story. For weeks she could not sleep until she was sure that the horrible monster in the story was not hiding in her room.

"I'm sure he's not here, and if he shows up, we'll just chase him right back to hell."

She slipped into a reverie and heard the voice of one of the older nuns at Noroton: *The only thing God wants is the thing you are afraid to offer.* It was the voice of the nun who had also told her that breaking away from the Church was a kind of mutilation of one's soul. She had felt that word *mutilation* as if it were a razor sliding across her flesh.

She drifted into sleep and into the security of her childhood. She was in the room over the garage at Sancy Falvey's house, which was just behind her house in Hyannis Port. Nancy Tenney, who lived next door, was also there. They were all about ten or eleven years old. The room was their private club. They were hanging up pictures of movie stars, and she boasted about all the famous Hollywood celebrities her father knew, including Gloria Swanson. They were putting on stolen lipstick and laughing at themselves in the mirror. She was startled by the sound of her mother's voice calling her from across the back yard and across all those years: *Kathleen!* Two precise notes: *Kath-leen!* It was dinner time. Everything was done on a strict schedule. No excuses were acceptable. With wads of toilet paper she cleaned her mouth and ran for home, her heart pounding. Every evening at the dinner table her father insisted on detailed reports of their activities. She did not always tell the truth. During the day he kept an eye on them from his "bullpen," the terrace outside his bedroom, where he often worked all day. If he saw any of them sitting around idly, he would shout at them like a general: "Go do something!" He frightened her friends. She tried to explain to them that he was really very nice when you got to know him, but they were not convinced. When he was away, as he often was, her brother Joe took over and shouted at them in his father's voice. He was the godfather of his own little sister Jean, though there was less than thirteen years between them. In her dream she confused her brother and her father. They were sailing and Joe was yelling, "Come about! Come about. Let out the line, Kick! For Christ sake, when are you going to learn?" And then, suddenly she saw Jack's smiling face and they were at a dance at the Wianno Yacht Club. She was thrilled to be dancing with him, and she was absolutely sure that every girl in the place was jealous of her, even though she was only his kid sister. The music turned into the sound of a ping-pong game. Her sister Eunice emerged from the dancers wearing a nightgown and looking skinny and pale. She sang out to her: *Puny Euny can not sleep. She lies awake counting sheep.* Her mother appeared, all dressed in black. She said, "Please don't flush the toilet tonight; your sister has insomnia." Jack drove up in a convertible and she jumped into the seat beside him. He drove recklessly through the town and then up the highway, going faster and faster, until the car was completely out of control. She tried to scream but she could not. An attack of asthma took her breath away. She thought she might drown.

She rose desperately from the depths of her dream, and, gasping for air, she found herself in Billy's arms. "It's all right! It's all right," he was saying. "You must have been having a bad dream.

She looked around and finally realized where she was. She caught her breath and let out a sigh. "Are you sure I'm awake? Sometimes I feel like Alice in Wonderland."

"We all do these days. So many things happening all at once!"

The only one who seemed solidly anchored in reality was Joe. At breakfast they argued over the portable typewriter and everything seemed normal again. "I did not give you the damned typewriter," he said. "You borrowed it."

"It was not yours to give," she said. "I was supposed to get it after you graduated from college, which was a long time ago."

"Where did you get that stupid idea?"

"Now, now, children," said Pat. "As soon as the war is over there will be plenty of typewriters. Let's talk about something really important. What kind of an omelet shall we make with our precious eggs?" In her bright floral dress, against the morning light of the kitchen window, she looked calm and beautiful and motherly. Her little blond flock flitted in and out like playful birds pausing to drink at a fountain. "Billy will be back any minute with Mrs.Ward's fresh cream." Kathleen looked from her to the brother-father man who sat at the table as though he owned the house and everybody in it. They had made love in the night and now they were as easy with each other as a husband and wife.

She could not imagine the future that would separate them.

Later, she said to Joe, "Pat's a terrific woman. Are you in love with her?"

"Maybe," he said, as though she had no right to ask him questions such as that.

"Don't you ever think about what's going to happen?"

"What's the point?" he said with his tough-guy smile. "None of us will have a future until the war is over."

"I guess you're right, but I hate it. I wish it was all over so that we could get on with our lives."

"Well, you might have to get on with yours right now. I think the cat's out of the bag. I had a letter from Dad the other day. He says that your old editor Frank Waldrop is absolutely sure that you intend to marry Billy. What have you been telling him?"

"The only one I said anything to was Inga Arvad."

"Well, that was a clever thing to do. Why didn't you just put an ad in the *Times-Herald?* She probably told Waldrop -- and Jack."

"What else did Dad say?"

"He said I should try to stop you from doing anything foolish."

"And do you think I'm being foolish?"

Without softening his tone, he said, "Look, Kick, I know how you feel, and I'm going to back you up a hundred percent. I didn't feel that way when I first came over because I thought it would hurt the family, but now I see things differently. Life is full of tough decisions. It's no picnic, and it's not a Catholic school for girls either. I haven't lost my faith or anything; I just don't think the world can ever be as perfect as the Church would like it to be. I mean, that's the whole point isn't it?"

She put her arms around him and kissed him before he could push her away.

CHAPTER SEVEN

It was raining when Kathleen dropped the little blue V-mail air-letter in the A.P.O. box at the Hans Crescent Club. She had written to her parents in the middle of the night and left the letter unsealed until she could re-read it in the morning. She listened to it fall, as though it were a bomb, but it made no sound at all. She lingered at the box for a moment and then found a secluded corner where she could have a cup of coffee alone and watch the drops of rain run down the window like tears.

Some days later she sat by the same window, in dusty shafts of morning sunlight, reading telegrams from home. The campaign to stop her from marrying Billy had begun. Every day brought new messages from her family and the friends and clergymen whom they enlisted in their cause. Kathleen had set no date for announcing their engagement, but everyone knew that it had to be soon, because everything now pointed towards a spring invasion and the long-awaited second front. It was mid-March and the fields in Derbyshire were aleady plowed for the new crops.

Both Joe and Billy reported increased activity at their bases. More planes were assigned to submarine patrol, and there were more raids on the U-boat ports and all along the Channel shore. Billy described the new tank-carrying landing craft and the daily arrival of other American equipment. "If the Germans had any bloody sense they would quit now," he said, "and save themselves a lot of death and destruction. They can't possibly win, even if the rumors are true about a secret rocket bomb being developed in the underground factories of Peenemunde." She remembered her father's prediction that bombs would fall again on London, and, suddenly, she was afraid that his prediction would come true. Maybe the Nazis had secret weapons, after all. And maybe they still had a chance to win the war. Why else would they go on fighting? The possibility heightened her anxiety about the more personal blitz of letters and telegrams that was aimed at her. Her father and mother were determined to stop her, and, since they loomed larger than life in her mind, she half believed that they, too, had a secret weapon. Perhaps it was guilt. They accused her of willfulness and disobedience, of complete disregard for the laws of the Church and the feelings of others. Her mother would be crushed. Her family would be shattered. As the first to marry, she would set a horrible example for her sisters and brothers. Joe would lose the Catholic vote if he went into politics. And she, of course, would rot in hell, along with any children she might have, since she would have robbed them of their religion. They tried every form of persuasion and even asked friends in London to try to talk some sense into her.

One day Kathleen said to Billy, "My mother may be right. Perhaps I am hopelessly willful. Even the nuns at school warned me about this. For Catholics, willfulness is a really big sin. I could actually wind up in hell just for that, let alone marrying you."

"Don't worry, darling," he said. "If you go to hell, I'm going with you. Heaven wouldn't be heaven without you." He looked distracted and older and different in a way she could not name. Was he keeping something from her, she wondered.

And then he was gone for two weeks, under special orders, and Joe was unable to leave his base at Taunton. There were rumors of unusual troop movements. Some of the men on leave at the Hans Crescent Club were suddenly called back to duty. "This may be it," one of them said to her as he paused under the portico to thank her. He was an intelligent looking pilot in the 8th Air Force and seemed to know what he was talking about.

In a near panic, she sought out her friends. Sissy Ormsby-Gore managed to calm her down. "I talked to David just a couple of days ago," she said. "He thinks it's very unlikely that anything will happen until the middle or the end of May, when weather conditions are more reliable. He thinks that these rumors may have been started on purpose -- part of a war of nerves to unsettle the Nazis."

Then they talked about Kathleen's personal war. "I shouldn't tell you this," said Sissy, "but you look awful. Your family is being very difficult and their tactics are a bit heavy-handed, but perhaps they are right. Perhaps you *are* making a mistake that you will regret later and for the rest of your life."

"I don't want to give up my religion," she said, "but the Church is making it impossible for me."

Sissy laughed. "That's a very strange view of the Church. It wasn't established for your convenience, only for your salvation. In any case, I think it is very inconsiderate of Billy to force the issue this way. He seems perfectly willing to have you make all the sacrifices. The only concession he and his family have made is to accept a woman with Irish blood, and there's not much you can do to change that. Besides, they will insist that you are American, removed by several generations from Ireland."

"It was my choice to go ahead on his terms," said Kathleen.

"I'm not sure that he should have allowed you to make that choice. If he didn't have the courage to do what was necessary to have you as his wife, he should have had the decency to give you up and spare you all this torment. I mean, the Duke of Windsor gave up his throne for the woman he loved, and she was considerably less virtuous than you. It was not easy for David to become a convert so that we could be married. There was plenty of resistance, but it was his choice. If he had decided against the marriage, I would have been miserable, but I would have understood. I'm sorry, Kick, but I think that Billy is faced with the same kind of choice. It should not be up to you. You are a woman and a Catholic. Let *him* choose!"

Kathleen suddenly looked helpless, her eyes deeply shadowed and blinking, as if to hold back tears. "I can't!" she said.

"Why not?"

"Because I want him, damn it! I want to be part of his life here in England. I don't want to go back to America. I love my family, but I will never be able to be my true self there. Don't you understand?"

"I do, Kick. I really do, but I can only speak out of my own convictions. In the long run we all have to make our own decisions, no matter how much advice we get. And whatever you do, I'll always stand by you as your friend. You know that, don't you?"

"Of course. And if I don't take your advice, it's only because I'm a stubborn fool who doesn't know when to quit."

In her desperation she turned to Lady Astor, knowing full well that she considered the Catholic Church a menace to free thought and accused it of being involved in all kinds of conspiracies. She felt at home with her fellow American, the sixty-six year old Member of Parliament, who once said of her that she could be the next Nancy Astor if she played her cards right.

They had a private lunch in that part of Clivedon that was not given over to a war-time hospital. Nancy shook her head sympathetically when Kathleen described the barrage of telegrams that her decision to marry Billy had provoked. "Family conflicts are extremely painful," she said. "The accident of birh often links us with people with whom we have very little in common. When I first met you before the war I thought that you were not at all like the other Kennedys. I was not the only one who felt that way. We all adored you. When I saw you and young Hartington together it looked like a perfect match. It wasn't long before the rumors of an engagement began to spread and the newspaper people were circling around like jackals. So you will have the press to put up with in addition to your parents and the Catholic Church, but I say, get on with it, Kick. Marry him and don't worry about what anyone else thinks."

She felt vaguely encouraged as she made her way back to the club, but by the time she arrived she realized that Nancy had not really solved her problem. Ignoring the whole world was not as easy as it sounded. In fact, ignoring her mother was virtually impossible. Her father, at least, had agreed to talk to Cardinal Spellman to see if a compromise could be worked out. He had always been that way."For every problem there is a solution," he used to say, whereas her mother always got her way by threatening to withdraw her love and by laying her misery on your doorstep.

She went to confession on Saturday at the Church of the Immaculate Conception on Farm Street in Mayfair. It was not easy for her to sort out her sins. Her failure to obey her parents troubled her. Surely, she could "honor" them without being absolutely submissive to them. Or could she? She did not ask the invisible priest, but in a moment of impatience she thought, "You need the mind of a lawyer to figure that one out." Then she confessed that she was often impatient, that she questioned the authority of her parents, and that she sometimes used unacceptable language. She hesitated and added, quickly and in a lowered voice, "I am also planning to marry a non-Catholic." As soon as she said it, she was sorry, because it suddenly occurred to her that planning to commit a mortal sin might be as serious as actually committing it.

There was a pause in the usual ritual. She could feel the presence of the priest behind the partition in the confessional. He cleared his throat and said, calmly, "You may want to consult Father D'Arcy about your plans." And then he slipped back into his more routine role.

She knew Father D'Arcy, and had already thought about consulting him. He was a Jesuit of considerable reputation, having assisted in the conversion of Evelyn Waugh and several other literary figures. A few days later she sat in his book-cluttered office and described her dilemma. He had a pleasant smile that put her at ease, and in his eyes she could see the quickness with which he undertood the full scope of her problem.

When she had bared her mind to him and was most vulnerable, he revealed himself as a true Jesuit, a scholar with missionary zeal, willing and able to defend Church law and the authority of the Pope. "Whenever I talk to young women who are in love and on the brink of marriage," he said, "I feel at a distinct disadvantage. Their emotions are very intense, and they are driven by certain earthly desires that are more persuasive than logic or faith. Part of the miracle of life is that it is self-perpetuating. It is difficult at your age to think of any stage but this, and marriage and children seem like the ultimate fulfillment. There is, however, another dimension to life, which should never be forgotten. Time passes swiftly. We grow old. We die. Our souls pass from these brief blossoms to a garden that is eternal. You must never lose sight of this progress, no matter how urgent your immediate needs may be. You must never do anything in this life that will jeopardize your eternal life with God. It is simply not worth it. As a good Catholic, I think you know all this, but as an attractive young woman it is easy to be swept away by strong feelings. The cumulative wisdom of the Church is great in these matters, and it provides you with clear guidelines. These are not arbitrary rules. They exist for your protection. What does your catechism say about marriage? 'It is a sacrilege to contract marriage in mortal sin, or in disobedience to the laws of the Church, and instead of a blessing, the guilty parties draw down upon themselves the anger of God.' Your case is very simple. If you want to be a Catholic in good standing, if you want to make a true confession and receive communion, you can not marry a non-Catholic. The Church will not perform the marriage, and any other ceremony that you participate in will not be recognized as a true marriage, even if it is, in the secular sense, legal. You will find yourself living in sin without any hope of redemption. And if you are the first to die, you will be doomed forever, a high price to pay for a moment of earthly joy. Your only hope for salvation would be the death of your partner while you are still alive and able to repent and receive absolution."

The chair in which she sat felt, suddenly, like a black hole into which she was about to fall. She felt a surge of desperation that made her raise her voice. "But is there no special dispensation for people who are innocent and honest and in love?"

"None that I know of," he said. "And now I see that I've made you angry because you can't have what you want. And your anger makes me suspect that, in addition to love, there may be more material considerations. Many young women dream of Prince Charming, because the prince is not only handsome but wealthy, and such a marriage would certainly mean a life style that is glamorous and full of earthly delights." He shook his head. "Perhaps now you understand why I find it so difficult to advise young women in love. So often they do not understand their own motives."

"If I were arrogant enough to think that I understood myself completely, I wouldn't be here,"

103

she said. "Thank you very much for your time. You've given me a lot to think about."

When neither Billy nor Joe could make it to Crastock Farm for the second week in a row, she decided to go down alone. Without the men around, she and Pat felt closer and talked more freely, especially after a little brandy.

They lingered at the table after dinner and Kathleen told Pat about her visit with Father D'Arcy. "I suppose he was sympathetic," she said, "but I had the feeling that he thought women were rather dumb."

"If he's a good Catholic priest, he can't know a hell of a lot about women," said Pat.

"But he sure knows a lot about hell. He sounded like my mother, full of doom and gloom. God, I'm so sick of doom and gloom, I could just give it all up."

"Why don't you?" said Pat.

"What do you mean?"

She shrugged a shoulder. "I mean, give it up, quit the Catholic Church." She was leaning back in her chair, her face flushed from the brandy, her hair still disheveled from bedtime story-telling. She was bold and beautiful, a woman who was not afraid of life, who had married twice and born three children. Kathleen suddenly felt like an inexperienced schoolgirl compared to her. "How can I do that?" she said.

"I guess you just stop going, or else join another church. It never seemed all that important to me, but maybe Australians are not as serious about religion as the Irish."

Kathleen was intrigued. Pat was talking about religion as frivolously as she might talk about shopping for a pair of shoes. "Do you really think I'm too serious about all this?" she said.

"I think your normal instinct is to be light-hearted. You're full of energy and fun. That's why

104

the guys all like you. But when it comes to religion, you get confused and miserable. I suppose it's all tied up with your mother and those convent schools she kept sending you to. What I really think is that, underneath it all, you're not a very convinced Catholic. I don't think it's something that you've thought through for yourself. It's just something you inherited. And if you didn't think that it would kill your mother, you'd probably be just as happy in the good old C of E."

"Well, it would certainly make Billy and my future in-laws happy, but as far as my mother is concerned, it would be the worst possible solution. It's one thing to be rejected by the Church and quite another to do the rejecting. She would take it personally, as though I meant to reject *her*. I don't suppose it would kill her, but it sure would make her miserable and furious. She would never forgive me."

"Well, damn it, Kick, let her be miserable and furious, but don't let her ruin your life. Don't let her tell you what to think. If you want to be a Catholic, be a Catholic. If you want to marry into a prominent Anglican family, then go all the way and please yourself. If it's serious conviction that is holding you back, all right, but don't let your mother hold you back. You're a grown up woman now."

"Maybe you're right. Maybe I should talk to someone before I lose my mind completely or just cave in and go home. There's a Father Torbert, an Anglican monk. Somebody gave me his name. I wrote it down, but I never got in touch with him."

"Talk to him. It can't do any harm." Pat reached across the table and touched her hand in a sisterly way.

Kathleen smiled. "I wish I could be more like you."

"I'm not sure that would help," said Pat. "I'm better at giving advice than taking it. I've got a few problems of my own."

"I know. What are you going to do?"

She shrugged her shoulders and reached for the brandy. "Nothing right now. I don't think Joe can afford to get serious. Neither can I, really. I've got a husband, and Joe's got big political plans that do not exactly include a twice married woman with three children. How would your parents feel about something like that?"

"It would probably kill them both. After all, I'm only a girl; Joe is going to be President of the United States someday."

They laughed and had another drink.

Kathleen paid several visits to Father Torbert without saying anything to Billy, but news filtered back to his family through Lord and Lady Halifax, who had made the recommendation in the first place. Billy's parents were pleased with her willingness to seek Father Torbert's advice, and they began to talk as though a better solution would be found in the future, even if a registry office marriage was all they could expect in the present.

When Billy got his next pass, he went to Eastbourne and took Kathleen with him. His family greeted her warmly, and his mother was especially attentive, as though Kathleen had come home with a good report from school. They were careful, however, not to mention Father Torbert. They would leave that to Billy.

In the morning the sky was overcast. Billy came down for coffee wearing his uniform and carrying a gift-wrapped package under his arm. "My mother has asked me to deliver this to one of the servants who has just had a baby. She's been with us for several years and we are all very fond of her."

"Where is she?" said Kathleen.

"She's staying with her mother just a few miles from here. Her husband is in the Navy."

"Not a very convenient time to have a baby."

"I guess she didn't have that in mind when she said goodbye to him."

"It must have been a long goodbye."

" Why don't you come along? We'll pack a lunch and make an outing of it."

"They say it's going to rain."

"Darling, in this country there is no such thing as a reliable weather forecast. Besides, if it does rain, there's an old inn nearby which is sometimes called The Blind Eye."

She smiled at him with mock suspicion. "You're not trying to lead me astray, are you?"

"Well, as a matter of fact, I thought we might rehearse our honeymoon, just in case we don't have one."

"Once you guys put on a uniform you're all alike. When do we leave?"

He leaned over and kissed her. "Right now!" he said.

It began to rain shortly after they left and continued steadily until they reached the house they were looking for. En route they passed through a military check point and saw other evidence of the much talked about preparations.

"What a dreary place," said Kathleen when they pulled up in front of the gray timber and stucco house, which seemed to be sinking into the soft ground. "Why did you have to come here in person? Couldn't you have sent the gift?"

"I suppose so, but my mother thought it might be nicer if one of us could stop in."

"Do you mind if I wait in the car?" she said.

"Oh, come on, Kick," he said. "it's not all that bad. Besides, if we ever become the Duke and Duchess, we'll have to look in occasionally on the people who work for us."

107

"Births, deaths, and weddings," she said, as though she were mulling over her future responsibilities. "All right, but let's make it brief."

They only stayed five minutes and chatted with the girl's embarrassed mother, who could not persuade them to take a drop of whiskey against the rain. The old man who looked on had apparently had a stroke and could not speak, but his eyes followed the bottle. The week-old baby was barely visible under the blanket in the antique crib.

"What a horrible way to live," said Kathleen, staring through the windshield wipers into the dismal weather. "What will she do if her husband doesn't come back?"

"Oh, I suppose we can manage something. She's a good strong girl, the kind of servant you can depend on for forty years or so."

She sat there without speaking for a minute or two, as Billy's last remark passed through her mind like a slow cloud. She wondered whether or not he thought of *her* that way, under all the talk of love. *A good strong girl you can depend on for forty years or so .*

They were stopped at a crossroad by a soldier in rain gear that made him glisten in the dull, late-morning light. When he bent over to look into the half opened window on the driver's side, he could see that Billy was a captain and gave him a quick salute. "I'm afraid you'll have to take the detour, Sir. Heavy equipment coming through here any minute now. Go a mile and a half north and then left after the railroad crossing."

"Well, we're in luck," said Billy, as they drove off. "This is the road to The Blind Eye." Are you up for a drink and some early lunch?"

"Sounds absolutely fantastically wonderfully marvelous," she said, making fun of his kind of English.

"Okay, kid!" he said, and she burst out laughing.

Under the sagging beams of the low-ceilinged room they sat at the table closest to the fire. The other tables were unoccuppied, but a few local farmers with weathered faces stood at the bar and glanced occasionally in their direction. "How about a toddy for the chill and a kidney pie for the tummy?" Billy said.

"I do!" she said. "You may now kiss the bride."

He gave her an innocent peck on the cheek, and the men at the bar suddenly pretended to be minding their own business.

"How do you know about this place?" she said.

"I heard it was a good place for a soldier to bring his girl."

"Is that why we're here?"

"Of course not. I just wanted to get away from my family for a bit so that we could talk. Tell me about Father Torbert. Has he been at all helpful?"

She looked down at the tumbler, on which she seemed to be warming her small hands. "He tried his best to be," she said. "I hope I didn't hurt his feelings."

"Why? What did you do?"

"Nothing, really. We talked about a conversion to the Anglican church. It all seemed rather easy. He had me convinced for a while that the two churches were really one. He said that, historically, the split was fairly recent, and that, in any case, there was nothing in the Bible about an infallible Pope. The Archbishop of Canterbury, he said, provided a more humanistic leadership. Suddenly, I felt like a little girl who was being lured by a stranger into a large, black automobile. I pulled back. I said I wasn't sure I could go through with it. He suggested compromises. He said that under certain conditions I could remain a Catholic and be married in an Anglican church. I didn't know whether or not the conditions would suit my priest, I told him, but I was sure they wouldn't suit my mother, because she was determined to have her grandchildren raised as Catholics. He said it was possible to work out a compromise in which the sons would be raised in the Anglican Church and the girls in the Roman Catholic Church. I didn't much like that idea either."

Billy frowned. "When you went to see Father Torbert, we all assumed that you were serious about converting. Now it turns out that --"

"I *was* serious. I was desperate, in fact, because I had just heard from my father that Spellman was unable to help us. But then I just couldn't do it. Maybe in time --. I think that the registry is our best bet. Things may change. My family may get more used to the idea, or the Church might become more lenient. Since you will be away a good deal, perhaps living in sin won't be quite so sinful."

"Darling, nothing you do can be sinful. Don't worry so much about the priests. They'll have a little explaining to do also when the time comes. Right now we will do what we can do and be done with it. After the war -- well, maybe we'll have a second honeymoon someday."

When she smiled at him there was a special light in her eye. Under the table he took her small hand in his and held it until it was no longer cold. "I do!" she said, as though she were trying out her courage for the brief service in the Chelsea Register Office.

CHAPTER EIGHT

Joe Kennedy drove the borrowed jeep along Kennsington High Street to Prince's Gate, slowed down as he passed the American Embassy, and then went on to Sloane Street and Hans Crescent. He was a handsome figure in his newly pressed uniform, and on his face there was a look of determination. It was the fourth of May, and nature was trying to assert itself with sunshine and a seductive breeze. He was a man with a mission. The announcement of the engagement of Kathleen and Billy had just been made, and there were things to do. He had come up from Taunton by train and had already met with the solicitor for Billy's family to discuss the agreement that Kathleen would raise her children in the Anglican Church. His firmness had prevailed and they agreed that a verbal promise would suffice in lieu of a formal document. Now he hoped to pick up his sister's belongings at the Red Cross club before the newspaper men got on to the story that an Irish-American Catholic was going to marry into the anti-Catholic family that crushed the dreams of Parnell for Irish independence. Joe shook his head. They'll be roasting Kennedys in the bars of Boston tonight, he thought.

When Joe drove up to the club he noticed only one civilian among the many servicemen who lingered under the portico or chatted in groups on the sidewalk. The man was so obviously a reporter that he made no effort to hide the fact. He wore a dark suit. The strap across his vest supported a 35mm camera that made a bulge under his jacket. He came right up to Joe and said,"George Sims, London *Evening News* . May I have a word with you, Mr. Kennedy, about your sister Kathleen's forthcoming marriage?"

Without stopping, Joe said, "Sorry, George, no comment on that."

111

The reporter stayed with him and persisted as they ascended the stairs together. "Can you give us a date, sir?"

"No comment!"

"How do your parents feel about this marriage?"

"No comment!"

"Is it true that your sister has given up her religion to marry the man she loves?"

Joe stopped and jabbed the smaller man with his forefinger. "Look, George, I said no comment and I mean it. Don't force me to say it again." He left the reporter standing there as if his shoes were suddenly glued to the porch.

By the next day the papers were full of speculations and rumors, especially since the members of both families were refusing to be interviewed. The only person they could actually quote was Adele Astaire Cavendish, who said that it would be a pleasure to have another American in the family, but that pleasure was not officially expressed by the Duke of Devonshire, whose private secretary fended off the press with the usual "no comment." They wanted to know when and where the wedding would be held and what kind of a ceremony it would be. Had there been a religious conversion? Would the Kennedys be permitted to make the trip in spite of the war-time travel ban?

It was May 5th and the wedding was scheduled for Saturday May 6th, at ten o'clock in the morning at the Chelsea Register Office. Most of the preparations were being made at the home of Marie Bruce and at the townhouse of Cavendish relatives in Eaton Square. Joe caught up with Billy and Kathleen at Marie's house, where they were discussing a new dress that was literally going to be made overnight for the occasion. Joe pulled a fistful of ration coupons out of his pocket and donated them to the cause, compliments of the British squadron to which he was attached. Kathleen broke into a bright smile and said to the others, "Isn't he the best brother a girl ever had?" In Joe's glance she could see that he had not forgotten that Jack was her favorite brother, but he also looked pleased. Besides, he was playing the father in this drama, just as Marie was playing the mother. He would give away the bride, and sign as a witness along with the Duke of Devonshire.

Joe was carrying several newspapers with him, and they took time out to have a look. "Listen to this," he said, reading from the London *Evening News:*" 'Parnell's ghost must be amused by this union of a Cavendish and a Kennedy. '"

Billy interrupted him. "Parnell, of all people, would not be amused. He would not have confused one's politics with one's private life. Besides, he was a Protestant. What idiots these reporters are!"

"In this piece," said Joe, "you guys are described as the family 'that wrecked Gladstone's Home Rule Bill,' and we are described as 'one of the great Home Rule families of Boston.' That's news to me. I always thought of myself as a third-generation American with a degree from Harvard. We haven't lived in Boston since we were little kids."

"Don't pay any attention to the newspapers," said Marie. "They're not interested in history or religion or anything, except controversy and conflict. We've got more important things to do and very little time in which to do them. They'll have to work through the night to get the dress done. And I may be able to persuade Claridge's to make us some kind of a chocolate cake for the reception if I slip the head waiter a few pounds."

Billy went off to Eaton Square to confer with his parents, and Joe took Kathleen to a small restaurant where they were not likely to be recognized. He had something to say and he got right to the point. "Look kid," he said. "This is it. If you have any doubts about what you're doing, you'd better tell me now. Don't worry about hurting people's feelings or anything like that. Just be sure you want to go through with it."

"I'm sure, but I've already hurt a lot of people, haven't I?" she said. "Mother especially." She unfolded a piece of paper and handed it to him. "This cable came early this morning. She sent it from the hospital."

He read the first part aloud and then finished reading it in silence: " 'HEARTBROKEN. FEEL YOU HAVE BEEN WRONGLY INFLUENCED--' "

"I guess she's trying to blame it all on your evil Protestant friends, and maybe me too. She just can't believe that you made this decision yourself. And then she pulls this hospital routine, as if she's sick and you're to blame. We know that she's not sick. She's there because she doesn't want to talk to anybody, especially the press. She worries too much about appearances. She's afraid that her Catholic friends are going to accuse her of not bringing you up right. I've already written to her to tell her not to worry so much about what other people think. 'The hell with them,' I told her in plain English. And as far as your soul is concerned, I told her that you've got a far better chance than me of seeing those pearly gates. Mother and I understand each other, and I don't mind giving it to her straight from the shoulder."

"I'll write to her after the wedding. I didn't really expect her to give me her blessings, but I was sort of hoping that Dad would."

" I'm sure you'll hear from him sooner or later."

Over coffee she said, "I've always dreamed of having an enormous wedding, maybe even in St. Patrick's Cathedral. Mother and I used to talk about it. She must have had it all planned out from the bridesmaids to the lingerie, ever since Peter Grace first got serious about me."

"You would have made her and the Pope real happy if you had married that guy," said Joe.

"I couldn't get serious about anybody. I was only seventeen. Peter was twenty-three and already out of Yale." She smiled nostalgically. "Remember that party his brother Michael gave for his friends from Notre Dame? He was always trying to show up his older brother, so he dared Peter to tackle this huge fullback. Poor Peter couldn't back down, because he was trying like crazy to impress me. Anyhow, there was this long hall, and they gave the Notre Dame guy the ball, and he came running down this hall like a train. Peter not only tackled him, but he broke the guy's leg."

"Yeah, I remember hearing about that," said Joe. "Pretty heroic. Any decent Catholic girl would have married him on the spot. What more could she want -- an heir to a fortune and a vicious tackler!"

"I was playing the field in those days," she said.

"You sure were. We could never figure out why all those guys were interested in you. I mean, you weren't that good looking."

"Maybe it was because I wasn't afraid of them. I never felt shy around boys, so I guess they felt more at ease. And I always did my share of the talking, if not more. Some girls just stand there looking pretty and expect the guy to do all the work."

"You can say that again. Maybe that's why I always liked the older ones instead of those dumb teenagers. Jack was the same way. Look at old Inga Binga. She was a real talker, and smart as a whip."

"That's probably why you like Pat Wilson."

"Yeah," he said, sounding suddenly wistful and distant. "Too bad we all fell in love with people we couldn't marry. You're the only one who's doing something about it. It's that stubborn streak of yours. Remember when we all used to go to the movies? Sometimes four of us wanted to see a movie, but you wanted to see something else, usually some dumb comedy or musical. You'd always get your way. There was just no sense in arguing with you. You wouldn't give in for anything. I guess that's why you're marrying Billy. You know what you want, and nobody is going to change your mind. I admire you for that."

'Well, I hope the voters of Boston don't blame you for your kid sister's stubbornness."

"Frankly, Kick, I don't give a damn what the voters of Boston do. I'm not planning to run for mayor. In fact, I may not run for anything. Maybe I don't even belong in politics. Maybe Jack's the guy who's got what it takes."

"Don't say that, Joe. You're going to make a terrific candidate. Besides, brother John's a physical wreck right now. He doesn't know what he's going to do."

"Poor Johnny Hero!"

"Don't be nasty."

"He was just in the right place at the right time."

"You'll have your turn. You're a great guy and you're going to do great things."

He smiled. "You sound like the old man."

A shadow crossed her face. "I wish he were here to tell me that everything is all right. He doesn't have to agree with what I'm doing. He just has to assure me that I haven't lost his love. A few words right now would make a big difference. What they're doing to me is not fair. I'm not a child any longer."

"I guess they haven't figured that out yet," said Joe. He looked uneasy, unaccustomed to the role of comforter. He glanced at his watch. "We have to go. I have to get this jeep back before they court-martial the guy I borrowed it from."

He delivered Kathleen to Eaton Square, and then stopped briefly at Victoria Station, from which he sent a cable to his father: "THE POWER OF SILENCE IS GREAT."

The next morning they all gathered at the Chelsea Register Office, a drab red brick structure that looked and smelled like all such public buildings. Kathleen held on to Joe's arm as he led her quickly past reporters and a curious crowd. She wore her new pink dress, which was completed at dawn after an all-night effort of three people, driven by the determination of Marie Bruce. The color of the dress was echoed in the blue and pink of her hat and veil. She also carried a bouquet of pink camelias that were sent by the Duke from Chatsworth. At the snug neckline of her dress she wore an old borrowed diamond broach, and she carried an old gold mesh bag, newly decorated with sapphires and diamonds. Though it was a hasty wartime wedding, she held to the traditioin of "something old, something new, something borrowed, something blue."

They were led into a small room, where Billy and his family waited, and where several bunches of pink carnations struggled to introduce some color into the functional dullness of the place. Kathleen succeeded where the flowers almost failed. The expression on her face was a blend of genuine joy and distant sadness. She did not seem at all afraid or shy or awkward. There was, in fact, a hint of triumph in her whole appearance, as if she wanted the world to know that, cathedral or no cathedral, this was her wedding, her achievement, her passport to a new and wonderful life. Billy wore his Cold Stream Guards uniform, and was accompanied by his mother and father, his sisters Elizabeth and Anne, his aunt Lady Salisbury, and his best man Charles Granby, whose father was the Duke of Rutland. With Kathleen there were only her brother Joe, Marie Bruce, and Lady Astor. "Two stand-ins for your mother," was Billy's earlier comment. "She must be a formidable woman, indeed."

Joe gave away the bride. The ring that Billy put on her finger was an old family heirloom. Joe and the Duke of Devonshire signed in the necessary place, and the "forbidden wedding" became part of the history of one of England's oldest families and part of the web of controversy that surrounded one of America's wealthiest families. They left the Chelsea Register Office in a shower of petals, instead of the traditional rice, which the war had made scarcer and more essential than flowers. They paused only briefly for the photographers, and their smiles were not very convincing.

There were two hundred people at the reception given by the Duke and Duchess of Devonshire in the house in Eaton Square, but Kathleen was preoccupied with those who were missing, until someone handed her a cable from her father. For the first time that day her hands trembled. She turned aside for privacy and read: "WITH YOUR FAITH IN GOD, YOU CAN'T MAKE A MISTAKE. REMEMBER YOU ARE STILL AND ALWAYS WILL BE TOPS WITH ME." The message was like a blood transfusion. It brought a flush of color to her cheeks, and she greeted her well-wishers with a warmer smile. Across the room she could see Joe looking in her direction, as though he had been able to read in her expression exactly what had happened.

And then, after the handshakes and kisses, the champagne and chocolate cake, they were off to catch the train to Eastbourne for an abbreviated honeymoon at Compton Place, unaware that the military orders that would separate them were already being secretly prepared.

Not all the messages and newspaper accounts that reached them at Compton Place were congratulatory or full of affection; some were critical and even downright nasty. Evelyn Waugh, famous for his wicked wit and for his conversion to Catholicism, blamed Kathleen's sinful decision on her "heathen friends" and her anxiety about the inevitable invasion. Some of the newspapers referred to the enormous popularity of Kathleen in her debutante year and her future as the "first lady of the realm after royalty." Others were obsessed with the strange movements of her mother and the obvious rift in the Kennedy clan. They reported that Rose Kennedy left a Boston hospital, dressed completely in black, still refusing to comment on her daughter's marriage.

For a few days, however, Kathleen and Billy were lost in a world of their own. One morning they sat like naughty children on a bed littered with letters and clippings. They were more playful than passionate, and clearly pleased that the physical requirements of their marriage had been satisfied. Now they could get on with the really important part, which was simply enjoying each other's company. Suddenly, Kathleen lifted the blanket and sent all the pieces of paper flying into the sunlight that filtered through the white curtains. "Who cares what they all think," she said. "We've done it. We've actually done it! Against all odds."

"Isn't it wonderful," said Billy. "I feel rather heroic."

"You should," said Kathleen. "We've won!" She bounced out of bed, drew back the white curtain and welcomed the world as though it were the first day of her life. Her naked body was clearly outlined through her nightgown. Billy sat on the edge of the bed and watched her. He was a lanky figure in baggy pyjamas, his hair in comic confusion. Kathleen turned around to face him. "We've won," she said, "and no one can ever hurt us again."

119

CHAPTER NINE

It was early June and the days were long. Billy went to and from the base at Alton on a motorbike. When he returned in the evening the sun was still shining, and the clouds that tried to obscure it were tinted with gold as they moved like a dream across the sky. Sometimes it rained briefly, and the vapor that rose from the fields and rooftops became an eerie diffusion of light over the landscape.

Kathleen wrote letters by an open window in their room as she waited for the sound of his motorbike. A month had passed since their wedding day and there was still a large pile of unanswered mail on the round table that she used as a desk. Each day new letters arrived from friends, some of whom had just heard about her marriage. There were letters from the whole gang at the *Times-Herald*, including Inga Arvad, JohnWhite and Frank Waldrop. Her mother, however, did not write to her, though she wrote to Joe. In her own letters Kathleen described the Swan Hotel and the other army wives who played the waiting game. She said that she had taken a flat in Mayfair but preferred to be with Billy, who had been given the unusual privilege of spending his nights off the base. She said that they were very happy, but that they lived at the moment in a kind of limbo. With her father she was serious, but with her friends she was often amusing. To John White she wrote: "At the moment I am living in a pub, but don't worry, things will get better and I've been in worse places (mainly with you)."

She looked up from her writing and stared out the window. It was later than usual, and she was suddenly afraid that Billy might not come, that he might already be in a military convoy under secret

120

orders. But then she heard the familiar sound of his motorbike and rushed downstairs to greet him.

They had supper at the hotel, and then walked out into the fading light of the evening. There was a dark red glow in the sky where the sun had gone down, and Billy remembered how, during the Blitz, one could see the red glow over London from a great distance. "It's their turn now," he said. "Berlin is burning. It's the beginning of the end for them."

"You sound very serious tonight," she said. "Have you been told --"

"We know that the plan is in place and that it is called Operation Overlord. It is a chess game now. Nobody knows exatly where and when it will all begin."

"But do you think it will be very soon?"

He hesitated: "Yes, but I don't think we will go in until a beachhead is established. That may give us another week or two, depending on how well prepared the Germans are."

They paused to watch the red glow dissolve into darkness. The distant sound of military engines was an intrusion upon the silence of the night, but they took refuge in the stars and held each other close in the ruins of an old church. "We should have been married here, among these stones," he said. "God would have been our witness, and we would not have had to deal with his bickering agents."

They stood there for a while, studying the constellations. Then she said in the voice of a small-town girl: "Billy Cavendish, you better come back to me, and I don't want to hear any excuses."

"Yes, ma'm," he said with a smile.

The next morning Billy left shortly after dawn. Kathleen had a cup of tea and then rode her bicycle along a narrow lane into the countryside to pass the time and to look for wildflowers to replace those that were wilting in the white vase on her writing table.

She was back by nine o'clock and joined two other army wives with whom she sometimes had breakfast, a childless woman of thirty-five and a pale girl of nineteen, recently married and pregnant. A little after nine thirty the music on the radio was interrupted and a BBC voice said: "We have a special report from Supreme Allied Headquarters. Allied naval forces, supported by strong air forces, began landing Allied armies this morning on the northern coast of France..." For several moments the three women looked as though they had turned to stone. Then Emily began to weep into her handkerchief as the news was repeated. Kathleen picked up her flowers and went upstairs to be alone.

Billy's regiment did not leave for another week. In their last hours together they talked about the good times they had had and tried not to think about the war. "I know it's been five weeks," she said, "but it feels like five minutes. It doesn't seem fair to have waited so long and paid such a high price for just five weeks."

"It's been the happiest time of my life," he said. "I can't even imagine getting through one day without you." Shortly before he left he scribbled a note in her diary: "How beastly it is to be ending things. This love seems to cause nothing but goodbye. I think that that is the worst of it, worse even than fighting."

He left before dawn, and she cried herself to sleep. When she woke up, the room at the Swan Hotel seemed oppressively empty. She decided to go into London immediately and then on to Eastbourne to stay with Billy's family for a while.

It was the twelfth of June. On the train she stared blankly out the window at the changing landscape that went by under clouds created for a child's coloring book. A middle-aged woman sat opposite her reading an Agatha Christie novel. She glanced at Kathleen from time to time, as though she were about to ask her if she was all right. But she said nothing, and, after a while, she left with a nod and a motherly smile. The incident was nothing really, but Kathleen felt strangely comforted by the expression on the woman's face.

On the way to her flat, she stopped at the Church of the Immaculate Conception on Farm Street. She lit a candle and prayed for the safe return of her husband. Many candles were already burning, and she wondered how many of them were for men who had gone off to war. She liked the familiar shadows of the cool interior and the fragrance of incense. Though she could not make a true confession without intending to give up her "sinful marriage," she attended church regularly, wherever she happened to be. As she knelt at the feet of the crucified Son of God, she could not bring herself to feel any remorse for what she had done or any desire to change things, though Father D'Arcy's description of eternal damnation still haunted her. Wasn't it possible for God to overrule the Church? She remembered a term that her brother Jack once used when he was having doubts about his faith. "I can't accept divine injustice," he had said. "How can the innocent be punished?" That was how she felt as she knelt and prayed. She could not make a sin of her marriage. It was a true marriage. Surely God could see that. How could Father D'Arcy be so sure that she would burn in hell for all of eternity? She was startled by an old woman who appeared beside her. She wore black and her hands trembled as she lit a candle. For whom, she wondered, was the old woman praying?

She spent the rest of the day alone and read the newpapers in the evening, as though it were her wifely duty to be well informed about the war. The maps in the newspapers made vivid the scope of the invasion. Five thrusting arrows pointed at the northern coast of France from Cherbourg to Caen.

123

Each represented an invasion force and was given a military code name: Utah, Omaha, Gold, Juno, Sword. It sounded like a game, she thought, a game of arrows and little flags and dotted lines.

In bed she thought about who she wanted to see in London before going down to Eastbourne. Sissy perhaps, especially since David was now home for a while. Pat Wilson and Joe, of course, if it could be arranged. She was not very good at being alone. She drifted off, at last, still troubled by the maps that tried to turn reality into a game.

She had a dream in which she was eighteen years old again and a guest at an enormous country house. She was lost in the labyrinth of high hedges. Someone was calling to her from another part of the labyrinth: "Kath-leen! Kath-leen!" Was it her mother? She began to run, but every path she followed turned into a dead end. She tried to retrace her steps, singing *One two, button my shoe, three four, knock on the door.* Suddenly it was raining and her white confirmation dress was splattered with mud. *Rain, rain, go away,* she sang. *Come again another day. Little Johnny wants to play.* The sky grew dark. The distant rumble of thunder was like the growl of an immense beast. *Eternal damnation,* she thought, standing in the jaws of darkness. She was being swallowed alive. Then the sky was blasted by an explosion that made her sit up terrified and wide-eyed. Was it part of her dream? Was it real? She heard no airplanes, no gunfire. For a few moments everything was very quiet. Then came the sickly sound of the wailing siren. Then another and another.

She got out of bed and went to the window without turning on a light. There was a glow in the distance so enormous that it looked more like an eerie dawn. She rushed to the night table and found a match. She struck it and looked at the clock. It was just after midnight. She was confused.What was happening? Had she died in her

124

sleep? Was this the beginning of her personal hell? She heard an echo of herself saying, *Forgive me Father for I have sinned.*

When she was fully awake she knew that it had to be an air raid, in spite of the strange silence. She dressed quickly in order to be ready for whatever might happen next, but what happened was too unfamiliar for her to deal with. First there was the silence, except for the sirens. Then there was a rushing, wheezing sound, as though the night itself were breathing and coughing. It was impossible to tell where the sound was coming from. Suddenly, it stopped, as though the mysterious machine, whatever it was, just disappeared. Fifteen seconds passed in twice as many heartbeats and ended in another explosion, this one further away than the first.

She put a torch in her bag and went down to the street. An air-raid warden was directing people to a nearby shelter. "What is it?" she said.

"Some sort of rocket bomb," he said. "Go to your shelter and wait for the all clear."

The next day everyone knew what it was. The BBC described it as "The V-1, Hitler's Vengeance rocket," a pilotless craft with a jet engine and a ton of explosives, one of the so-called miracle weapons that the Germans had been developing in top-secret, undergound locations. Kathleen remembered her father's warning that more bombs would fall on London before it was all over. Her memory of his panic combined with her own anxiety about Billy, and she felt herself in the grip of fear and confusion. She wanted to call everyone she knew, and, at the same time, she wanted to hide in the closet like a child. She felt dangerously alone. She was the outcast of the Kennedy clan, an exile in a world at war. She pulled herelf together and picked up the phone. There was no dial tone. She dialled a number, but nothing happened. It was dead. The radio droned on, describing the death and destruction caused by the new weapon. She remembered Billy's account of an old friend of theirs who cracked up during an air raid and went screaming hysterically through the streets of London. Suddenly, she went to the closet, dragged out a suitcase and stuffed it frantically with whatever clothing was at hand. She had to flee, as though from the vengeance of God.

The train to Eastbourne was crowded with people who were leaving London because of rumors that the raids would continue and that the Germans were about to reveal an even more terrifying weapon, already referred to as the V-2. There were many women and children on the train, and somewhere nearby an infant cried with such desperation that the sound became unbearable and threatened to shatter Kathleen's nerves.

There was no one to meet her at the station, since she was not expected for several days. When the antique taxi rumbled up to Compton Place, it was Elizabeth, watching from an upstairs window, who first noticed it. She ran through the house and out the door to greet Kathleen, her summer dress a blur of wildflowers against the garden greenery. "We were horribly worried about you," she said, embracing her new sister-in-law.

"I'm all right," said Kathleen. "It's good to see you, good to be here."

At dinner they talked about the new attacks on London, and Kathleen told them about her experience. "At frst I had no idea what was going on," she said. "There had been an explosion of some kind. From the window I could see the glow of a large fire. Before the sirens started there was an eerie silence. No planes, no anti-aircraft fire. Then I heard this weird coughing engine, not at all like an ordinary motor. It came closer and then suddenly went dead, just like that. It took about fifteen seconds for the thing to explode."

Billy's father looked agitated, his face a map of all his concerns. "Damn it," he said, "our intelligence people have known about these weapons for a long time, and they've known exactly where they were being built and how they would be launched. I don't know why those sites haven't been bombed to pieces by now."

"Easier said than done," said one of the guests, a retired major, who had served in the RAF in the First World War. "They're too deep and too heavily protected by concrete bunkers. We've dropped hundreds of tons of explosives on them, without much effect. We need a new kind of weapon, perhaps something like their pilotless buzz-bomb. We need some sort of remote control from the ground or another aircraft. I have it from a source very close to General Spaatz that the Americans have been at work on the problem for some time. They refer to the project as 'Aphrodite.' The goddess of love! I'll be damned if I know what she's got to do with it."

The Duke frowned. "It's been a long time since Greek, but didn't Paris choose her as the most beautiful of all the goddesses, which had something or other to do with the Trojan War? In fact, I think she was in love with Ares, the god of war, though she had children with quite a few Olympians."

"Well done!" said the Major, "But it's not the sort of thing one would expect Americans to know."

"Why not?" said Kathleen. "We know how to read. My brother Jack is even an author. Right now, however, he's flat on his back in the Chelsea Naval Hospital."

"Poor lad!" said the Major's sturdy wife. "We've heard all about him, of course. He's quite a hero. Was he badly wounded?"

"He wasn't actually wounded," said Kathleen, "but he came home with malaria and a bad back, both of which he's had before. He's scheduled for a spinal operation next week."

"How dreadful for you to have so many problems so soon after your wedding. A brother in hospital, another chasing submarines, and your husband about to be sent to France. And here you are, thousands of miles away from your family. You must miss your mother."

Kathleen said nothing, and for a moment there was an awkward silence at the table. "She has us," said Elizabeth, "and it's lovely to have another sister."

"I consider myself very fortunate to be here," said Kathleen. "And I have some very good friends in London."

"But surely you won't be going back there very soon," said Mrs. Hunt. "It must be awfully dangerous."

"I'm still a Red Cross volunteer, though I've given up my regular assignment."

"I think we can persuade her to spend the summer with us," said the Duchess."

Kathleen gave her an affectionate smile. "It won't take much persuasion. You've all been wonderful to me."

"It won't exactly be a holiday, my dear. As Lady Hartington you will have certain responsibilities. We can talk about all that tomorrow."

That night Kathleen and Elizabeth sat up late and confided in one another. Elizabeth was now old enough to be a real friend. "We felt terrible about your mother's reaction," she said. "It was difficult for all of us, but especially for you, of course. I'm sure there will be some kind of a reconciliation eventually."

"I suppose so," said Kathleen, "but sometimes I'm glad I'm not a Kennedy anymore. I have such a sense of freedom. I know it sounds horrible to be saying this, but it's true. I got to the point where I just couldn't deal with my mother any longer. She seems so uncompromising, so demanding and, at the same time, so distant. In any case, I want to be part of your family, and I hope that your parents will accept me, in spite of the fact that they did not approve of our marriage. I know that it was painful and embarrassing for them, especially the drab civil ceremony. There's bound to be some resentment, but here I am, and I will do my best --"

Elizabeth interrupted her with a sisterly hug. "Well, I for one have no resentment. I used to pray that you and Billy would get married, because I knew from the beginning that you were perfect for each other. Maybe I was too young to understand how serious the religious problem was, but I was not too young to see how much he loved you. You've made him very happy."

By the end of the week almost a hundred of the strange robot bombs were fired at London. Though they traveled at close to four hundred miles an hour, some were shot down. Those that got through exploded wherever they fell. There were no targets. There was no strategy, just vengeance and destruction. Three thousand people were reported killed, and many more were injured.

At Compton Place they listened to news reports and worried about friends in London. In a radio speech, Prime Minister Churchill assured the country that this new peril would be dealt with swiftly and severely.

Kathleen canceled a trip to London and lost herself in letter-writing and long walks. The peace and quiet of the country made it difficult for her to believe that people were dying in London and that young men were being slaughtered on the beaches of Normandy.

One morning she returned from a walk to find Billy's father in his favorite old work clothes, puttering in the flower beds. He seemed lost in his thoughts and did not notice her. She knew that he was worried about his son, though he kept such concerns to himself. And she knew also that under his sometimes rough exterior there was an appealing human being. Instinctively, she greeted him with a bright and brazen smile. "Hi, Duke!" she said.

He looked up, startled for a moment, before his face eased into a smile. "Oh," he said. "Good morning! That's the first cheerful voice I've heard around here in days."

"Sorry for the informality," she said. "Just an old habit. We don't have people with titles in America."

"No, no, it's quite all right. Unless there are other people around, of course. I rather like it."

"In that case, you can call me Kick, even if there are other people around."

"I prefer Kathleen. You're awfully cheerful this morning."

"We were brought up not to be got down by bad times. My father doesn't believe in mourning and moping around."

"Yes, it's always better to be doing something, isn't it."

"Of course! Maybe you'd like to come for a walk sometime."

"Oh, well, I --" He looked flustered. "I suppose I have things to do. I'm supposed to be a very important man around here. But, well, perhaps --. In any case, why don't we have some tea. I must say you have a very nice way about you, Kathleen. I've always thought that."

"Good!" she said, taking his arm as they walked towards the house.

CHAPTER TEN

When Joe invited Kathleen to spend a weekend with him and a few of his friends at the Imperial Hotel in Torquay, she accepted without hesitation. It did not occur to her that her brother might be showing her off as well as sharing in the special attention that was usually paid to members of the ruling class.

The next time they gathered at the Crastock Farm cottage, Pat Wilson was full of questions. "How was your weekend at Torquay?" she said.

"Terrific," said Kathleen.

"I can't tell you how jealous I am. You had Joe and half the Navy air force at a beautiful hotel in Devon, and I had some refugees from the buzz-bombs in London, a couple of girls from Rainbow Corner. Their flat was wrecked and the Red Cross was looking for a place to put them up. They called here, hoping to get you."

"I'm glad I was away."

"I'm sure you were, but since it was only for the weekend, I said they could stay here. There are times when my generosity borders on stupidity."

"You're occasionally too generous, but never stupid. We were away and you don't like to be alone."

"Right as rain, as usual, darling. If they were a couple of American Navy officers, I wouldn't be complaining."

"Ah, so you really were jealous."

"Of course," she said, unpacking the usual contraband and pausing to examine the label on a bottle of wine.

"Well, if it will make you feel any better, Joe and I really missed you and good old Crash-Bang Cottage. It's too bad you couldn't make it. Anyhow, it wasn't half the Navy air force, just a couple of officers from the base at Taunton."

"My friends were really wowed by the treatment Kick got from the hotel staff," said Joe. "It was 'My Lady' this and 'My Lady' that. When you come from Nowhere, Nebraska, you only see that kind of thing in the movies. It was a real treat for them, and Kick was the perfect Lady Hartington, except for the chewing gum and a few four-letter words. We had a hell of a good time."

"Like old times," said Pat wistfully. She finished unpacking the provisions. "Quite a haul this weekend," she said. "What's the occasion?" She looked up at Joe. Something in his expression made her frown. Kathleen glanced from one to the other.

"Why don't we open the wine?" he said. He loosened his tie and took off the jacket of his uniform. There was visible perspiration on his forehead. "Pretty warm weather for the land of fog and drizzle."

"We have our moments in the sun," said Pat. She looked cool in her white, loose-fitting dress, against which her hair was very dark and her eyes very blue. When she handed him the bottle of wine, she stood very close to him and said, "You're going away, aren't you?" Her voice was subdued, but her feelings were revealed in the sudden stiffness of her body.

Joe took the wine and pretended to look at the label. "Not exactly," he said. "I'm being transferred to another base."

"Which one?" said Kathleen.

"Fersfield," he said. "A joint Army-Navy attack unit."

"Did you know about this when we were in Taunton?"

"More or less, but it's a secret mission, and I'm not allowed to say anything about it."

"You must have volunteered," said Pat.

"I did."

"I don't understand," said Kathleen. "You told the whole family that you'd be flying a few patrols

132

beyond your quota and then you'd be heading home. They're all going to be very disappointed, especially Dad. He's already talking about a big reception."

"He'll understand when he finds out what it's all about."

"What *is* it all about?" said Pat.

"I want some action before I quit this war; that's what it's all about. Do you know what it's like to spend 1700 hours in an airplane staring down at the sea, without spotting an enemy submarine? It's incredibly boring and frustrating. If I had it to do over again I'd go for the fighter planes and carrier duty. When I enlisted, it was the U-boats that were grabbing all the headlines. Every day there would be pictures of freighters and tankers going down, sometimes in a sea of burning oil, the few survivors blackened by the flames and scarred forever. I thought I could do my bit by nailing a few of those Nazi subs, but it didn't work out that way. It was the armed convoys that did the job. Meanwhile, in the Pacific, the aircraft carriers have come into their own and stolen the show."

"I thought the little darlings of the fleet were those torpedo boats," said Pat.

Joe shook his head angrily. "It's all a lot of glamour and bullshit," he said. "Anybody who knows fighting ships knows damn well that those PT boats are the most useless and vulnerable vessels in the whole bloody Navy. They couldn't sink an enemy ship if it was parked in a bathtub. They run on gasoline and they're made of wood. A couple of hits from a .50 caliber machine gun and they go up in flames. I'm not taking anything away from Johnny. He looked after his men when his boat went down. But what the hell was he doing, sitting there in the path of a Jap destroyer? The only thing those PT boats have going for them is speed and maneuverability. Why the hell didn't he use it? So now his story is in the *New Yorker* and John Hersey, who once stole his girlfriend, has paid him back by making him a legend in his own time, while I go out on twelve-hour tours and stare at a thousand miles of water. Now do you understand why I volunteered for this mission?"

"But is it dangerous?" said Pat.

"Every time you go out with a payload it's dangerous," he said. "It's a short hop, and, if all goes well, it may mean the Navy Cross. You don't expect me to go home with just a European Campaign medal."

"You'll get more than that," said Kathleen. "You were already written up in the *Boston Globe* a couple of months ago."

Joe smiled sardonically. "Some headline-maker: KENNEDY'S SON CHAFES AT HUNTING U-BOATS. "

Pat relented. "All right, sailor," she said, "you're a big boy now. I suppose you know what you're doing."

"Don't worry," he said, "I'm not going to do anything crazy-- not as long as I've got someone like you waiting for me."

She smiled. "So when is this mysterious event taking place?"

"I'll be training at Fersfield for a few weeks, but they haven't set a date for the mission."

"Will you be able to come down on weekends?"

"I'm afraid not, but I'll find a way to call."

"If you don't get free until August, you can reach me at Virginia Sykes's estate in Yorkshire. The kids and I are invited to Sledmere for the month. And you too, of course, any time you can make it."

"I'll try," he said, "but right now I can't promise anything."

She raised her eyebrows and shrugged a fatalistic shoulder. "Well," she said, "in that case, we might as well open the wine."

134

The next morning Joe slept late and Kathleen woke up to the sound of birds and children. Before she was fully awake she imagined that Billy was with her, but the impression was short-lived. She opened her eyes to confirm that she was alone, and then could not close them again, could not crawl back into her dream. There was sunlight at the windows, and the fragrance of flowers filled the room.

She had a cup of tea with Pat, who did not seem to mind that her children were romping about outside in the damp grass in their pyjamas. It reminded Kathleen that Pat was a country girl and an Australian, refreshingly relaxed compared to her English counterparts.

They chatted quietly against the background of the morning news report on the BBC. Roosevelt had been nominated to run for an unprecedented fourth term. The Germans were in retreat on the Russian front. And Col. von Stauffenberg was named as the leader of a group of officers who attempted to assassinate Hitler. At a reference to Normandy they looked up and listened more attentively. *After an eight-day siege, forces under the command of General Omar Bradley have taken St.Lo. Meanwhile, in the flatlands south of Caen the British and Germans are locked in a fierce armored battle...*

"Do you have any idea where Billy is? said Pat.

"No," said Kathleen, "but he'll be all right. I know he will."

"Of course, he will," said Pat.

"But I wish he'd be more careful. He's so determined to prove himself."

"It's the curse of the oldest son, who is always struggling too hard to measure up to his father's expectations."

Kathleen sipped her tea slowly, as if to let the remark sink in. "I guess Joe is like that. Dad's boy.

Always trying to prove how tough and successful he is."

"But he's twenty-nine years old, Kick. Time for him to grow up. There is a limit to what we can do to keep our parents happy. You had the guts to stand your ground, why doesn't he? He's so damned busy trying to please his old man that he has no idea what he's really like as a person. He doesn't want to be the President of the United States any more than I want to be the bloody Queen of England. Underneath all that Kennedy hoopla he's a lovable, ordinary, down-to-earth guy. Even all this womanizing is just a contest between him and Jack, spurred on by your father, who, in plain language, is a dirty old man. Don't be offended, Kick. I'm only saying what everbody already knows. When I took up with Joe, I thought he was just another handsome playboy, and that the chances of a serious involvement were nil. And now -- well, now he's in love with me. He clings to me. He calls me almost every day. In fact, I think he stayed on here because of me. I know that sounds awfully egotistical, but we've spent a lot of time whispering in the dark in one another's arms."

"If he stayed on because of you, then why did he volunteer for this secret mission?" said Kathleen.

"I'm not denying the rivalry with his brother, but deep down I suspect that he knows he can't win. Jack is not only a hero and the author of a best-selling book, but a real Don Juan, witty, handsome and heartless. It will be a shattering experience for Joe to lose his position as the favorite son. And if he loses me, he won't have anything to fall back on. I think he's quite desperate and I don't quite know what to do about it."

"Is there any chance that you two might stay together? I mean, get married?"

"We've talked about it, but it seems impossible. Your family would never accept me, and I just can't imagine being that cruel to my husband.

Robin's a good man. He would understand a wartime affair but not a divorce. And then there are the children, of course."

"But do you love Joe?"

She hesitated and stared into her empty teacup. "I'm trying not to." When she looked up, there were tears in her eyes. Kathleen reached out to touch her hand, but Pat squared her shoulders, as if to scold herself for being a silly woman. "It all started out as a lot fun," she said, "but now it's turned into risky business for all of us. Robin might lose me. I might lose Joe. And Joe might lose -- everything."

On Sunday morning Joe and Kathleen went to church. The stained-glass windows, illuminated by sunlight, reminded Kathleen of other times and other places. Even though she could not receive Holy Communion, she found it a comfort to sit there and watch the familiar and simple drama of the Mass, the reenactment of the great sacrifice: *This is my body; this is my blood.* From time to time she glanced at her brother, as though she wished she could read his mind. His expression in church was usually a mixture of reverence and impatience, but this time his inward gaze seemed fixed on something far away, something just outside of his comprehension. His lips were slightly parted. His hair was neatly combed. In that moment she felt sorry for him, because it seemed to her that he might feel the impact of his confusion without ever being able to understand it. Suddenly, he turned to her with a brotherly smile and said: "You're the one who should be going up there, not me." And then he made his way to the altar for the Holy Communion.

On the way home she said, "I bet you're really going to miss Pat when this is all over."

He seemed to wince before he answered, and then he said, "There's no point in wanting something that you can't have." Before she could pursue the matter, he changed the subject.

After a couple of weeks at Fersfield, Joe was ready for his secret mission, but he was troubled by certain rumors that kept him awake at night. One moning he woke up at dawn, having slept only a few hours. Careful not to disturb his bunk mate, Jim Simpson, he stepped outside the wooden barracks and looked up at the hint of light in the eastern sky over the flat lands of Norfolk. It would have been a wonderful morning for a walk, if it were not for the smell of fuel and the whining sound of cold engines on a distant runway, where the silhouettes of aircraft all in rows suggested a cemetery.

He wore his leather flight jacket against the morning chill and walked slowly towards the hangar that housed the B-24 Liberator that he had volunteered to pilot. From a fringe of reeds came the sudden flutter of birds. It was an ordinary morning sound in the country, but it startled him in this strange landscape with its corrugated steel structures, its concrete runways and barbed wire fences.

He paused outside a ready room and looked at the names chalked on a blackboard. Through a window he could see the men -- fighter pilots ready to scramble to take on attacking aircraft. A loudspeaker echoed in his mind: *All sections scramble! Forty bandits approaching, angels one-five!* His breathing quickened. He loved the sound of action. But this was just a memory. The Spitfires were still on the ground, becoming more and more visible as the light expanded over the airfield. Further on, the ground crew were working over several Hurricanes. One man dragged a long belt of machine-gun bullets from a wooden crate. In the mist he looked as though he were wrestling with a snake.

138

The ready rooms were kept staffed around the clock. The Luftwaffe still made its presence felt, in spite of serious losses and diminished production. Joe had been to Germany just before the war. He was impressed then and he was impressed now by the intelligence and determination of the Germans. In his briefing he had been warned that there was always the possibility of a sudden attack on Fersfield. "If they get wind of what we're packing into that Liberator," his C.O. had said, "they'll try to hit us on the ground for sure. And wouldn't that be a pretty mess? Ten tons of TNT can rattle a lot of tea cups and window panes."

Joe's plane was housed in a special hangar in a restricted area that had its own checkpoint and patrol. The men on duty knew him and did not ask for his I.D. He paused before the open hangar and gazed into its yawning and shadowy interior, as though he were reluctant to step from the light into the darkness. Two mechanics went by with a nod and climbed up a ladder onto the wing of the bomber, which sat there, passively, like a huge beast being prepared for an ancient sacrifice.

The only thing that was absolutely certain about the project they called *Anvil* was that the B-24 that carried the explosives would never return. The plan was to pilot the beast into formation. It would then become a drone, controlled by two Venturas, referred to as the "mother" planes. They would be flanked by two B-17 bombers and protected by sixteen Mustang fighters. Once the "mother" planes had complete remote control, the pilot and co-pilot would bail out. The Liberator and its escort would then proceed across the Channel to its target on the French coast near Calais. The B-24 would be guided like a flying bomb into what was believed to be a major launching site for the devastating V-1 rockets. It would be the largest single explosion in the war, and it was expected to destroy a facility that had survived scores of conventional air raids. Even as preparations were being made, V-1's were falling on London and, more recently, on the troops in the Normandy invasion. The Navy Cross for the pilot of the mission was not just a private speculation, it was a guarantee from the highest military authorities.

Joe stood there for a while, his hands thrust into the pockets of his flight jacket. In one of the pockets was the crumpled letter he had just received from his brother Jack, who had written to him from the Chelsea Naval Hospital to urge him to come home now that he had completed his ten additional missions. In a letter to his parents Joe had described his new assignment as "nothing to worry about," but obviously his brother could see though the assurance.

Joe looked back towards the morning sun. The mist was clearing over the fields and runways. Suddenly, he turned away and headed for the canteen. He needed a cup of coffee. In another hour or so, in spite of official restrictions, he'd find a way to get into the village to call Pat. She would be up by then.

Joe carried his brother's letter around for a couple of days and then wrote to him on the 10th of August. He insisted that there was no reason for the family to get all excited about his staying on for another mission. He wasn't contemplating marriage, nor was he planning to risk his neck. He described the mission as "interesting" but "secret," and that was that.

But he was in a talkative mood and rambled his way through several subjects. He accused Jack of violating their brotherly agreement not to go out with the other guy's girls. Then he commented on John Hersey's PT 109 story in the *New Yorker* and said that he had shared it with the whole squadron, all of whom were very impressed. But he couldn't figure out how he got rammed by that destroyer."Where the hell was your radar?" About his social life, he boasted that he had planned to spend his leave at the estate of Lady Sykes (a former girlfriend) in the company of another beauty (unnamed), but "gave it up for this job," which wasn't quite true. What he was unable to say was that his mission was scheduled for August 11th, and that he had already promised Pat that he would come up to Yorkshire the following day.

On the evening of the 10th, Joe said to Jim Simpson: "It looks as though the deal is on for tomorrow. Why don't we get together and cook up a mess of bacon and eggs. And not a word to anyone! I'll provide the eggs if you slip into the company mess and pick us up some butter and bacon and a little coal for the stove."

Jim was a country boy from Texas who couldn't have been more impressed with Joe if he was Clark Gable himself in the role of Rhett Butler. More than anything else, he wanted to be Joe's co-pilot on the Anvil mission, no matter how dangerous it was. "I don't give a damn about the arming circuitry," he said, his mouth full of bacon and egg sandwich and leaking butter down his chin. "We'll be bailed out of there long before anyone pushes that button."

"Who have you been talking to?" said Joe.

"I haven't been talking; I've been listening," said Jim. "Earl Olsen is all in a flutter because they won't postpone the flight so's he can work on the arming panel circuit."

"Why didn't he say something to me?"

"Maybe somebody upstairs told him to keep his mouth shut. He says the Navy brass is pushing hard to upstage the Army on this project. Their official opinion is that the drone is ready to fly. Maybe they're right. Maybe Olsen is having a case of the jitters. We're the ones who should be worried. He'll be on the ground."

"You're jumping the gun, Jimmy. They haven't named the co-pilot yet, but I think it's going to be one of the senior men."

"Like Bud Wiley, you mean."

"I wouldn't be surprised."

"You didn't ask for him, did you?"

"I didn't ask for anybody. I believe in the luck of the draw. And, who knows, kid, you may live to thank your lucky stars. In the meantime, I've got a treat for you." He brought out a bottle of bourbon and a box of Cuban cigars.

Jim shook his head and smiled. "Where do you get all this stuff?"

"Friends in high places," said Joe.

They drank whiskey out of water glasses and puffed away on their cigars like a pair of hoboes on a freight train imitating the rich. After a while Jim frowned and said, "Are you sure you want to go through with it?"

"Believe me," said Joe, "I've thought about it from every possible angle, until I'm tired of thinking. My job is to keep quiet and obey orders, and that's what I'm going to do."

The next day the weather accomplished what Olsen could not. The flight was postponed for twenty-four hours, and would go on August 12th, weather permitting. Joe was annoyed because he had already told Pat that he would see her in Yorkshire on the 12th, and now it might be difficult to get a message to her.

That afternoon Olsen showed up, looking damp from the rain and worn down by his gnawing sense of responsibility. "I have to tell you this Joe," he said. "That system is still not working right . You could be risking your neck on this mission. Why don't you talk to the skipper? See if you can persuade him to give us more time."

Joe refused. "My job is to fly the airplane. Nobody can tell me how to do that and I can't tell anybody else how to do his job. This is the Navy, Oley, and that's the way it is. Thanks anyway for leveling with me. I appreciate it."

No one in the Anvil project was allowed to leave the base that day, "for any reason whatsoever." It was a special order and it was to be strictly obeyed. Twice he asked for special dispensation and was refused. He was furious. Maybe Jim was right, he thought. Maybe there *were* flaws in the system that had to be kept under wraps. After supper he avoided the canteen and brooded in his bunk. It would serve the bastards right if he just pulled out of the whole deal at the last minute. But he couldn't seriously consider doing that. Finally, with the night coming on, he decided to give it one more try. He located his C.O. and said, "Look, I just want to pedal down to the phone box and call my girl. I'm supposed to meet her in Yorkshire tomorrow and there will be a hell of a balls up if I don't reach her tonight. You know how women are."

His man-to-man appeal worked. He was given one hour, no more. If he was not at the canteen by 2200, he'd be put on report. He took off down the narrow road towards the crossroads at South Lopham. There was a slightly closer phone box, but he was sure they would be queued up for that one. The wet road was barely visible in the dull light of the torch taped to the handlbar, and the rain sounded heavier than it was against his borrowed poncho. The headlights of the cars that came along the road were blacked out, except for cat's eyes slits. He felt a strange urgency about getting in touch with Pat, but he was beyond logic at that point. He had to reach her or someone who could give her his message.

When he arrived at the red phone box there was no one there. He fed the phone from a fistful of coins, but got nothing but static. Finally, an operator answered and he gave her the number. She tried to get through twice and then reported trouble on the line. Before she could hang up, he gave her Kathleen's number in London. The familiar voice of the housekeeper answered. "Lady Hartington is not here," she said. "Would you like to leave a message?"

"Yes," he said, in an overly loud voice. "Tell her to get in touch with Patricia Wilson at the home of Lady Sykes. I was due there tomorrow but will be delayed a day. And take this note for my sister: "I am about to go into my act. If I don't come back, tell my dad -- despite our differences -- that I love him very much.""

In spite of the rain, he was sweating when he left the phone box. He stood there for a few minutes and felt the blood draining from his flushed face. Then he got on the bike and made his way back along the narrow road, his sense of urgency now gone, as though the phone call he had just made was more important than the mission he was about to carry out.

The next morning Joe and Jim walked to the mess hall under a clear blue sky that confirmed the flight even before they saw the written order. Take-off was scheduled for six P.M., and Bud Wiley would be the co-pilot. "I sure wish I was going with you," said Jim. "We could smoke a couple of them Cuban cigars on the way down after we pop the chutes."

"Don't worry, Jimmy, we'll get around to that. Keep an eye on my stuff."

"You bet!"

"And if I don't come back --"

"You better come back. I'm planning a party and you've got to be there."

After breakfast Joe went out to the hangar to check out the plane. He watched the ground crew carry the boxes of TNT into the belly of the beast. The interior of the B-24 had been stripped down to make as much space as possible. "I ain't never seen anything like it," said an old master sergeant, scratching the back of his neck. "It's a flying ammo depot."

In the briefing room that afternoon the mission was rehearsed in detail, using the code names that were chosen for radio communications. Joe's plane was *Zootsuit Black,* and one of the "mother" planes was *Zootsuit Red*.

When it was almost take-off time, Jim and some of the other men gathered at the plane to wish Joe good luck. He leaned out the window and yelled something to them that they could not hear over the sound of the propellers. In another few minutes he was taxiing into position on the runway.

The take-off was routine, but the men on the ground lingered until the B-24 was almost out of sight. In the cockpit Bud Wiley gave Joe a confident nod. He was a senior officer who had been on the project for a long time. "All in a day's work," he said, and Joe gave him a thumbs up.

They could see the town of Diss on their right and a scattering of smaller villages. They were heading east towards Southwold on the Channel. At the designated checkpoint Joe turned control of the plane over to *Zootsuit Red* with the code words "Spade Flush." With a minor adjustment the B-24 was right on course. "A-Okay," said Bud Wiley. Twenty minutes into the flight they could see the Channel dead ahead.

"Looking good," said the radio man in the mother plane. And then, almost immediately, the sky was torn by two enormous explosions and there was a vast hourglass of white heat and shock waves that scattered the formation and shook the ground at a place called Newdelight Wood near Blythburgh. Where once there was an airplane flown by two men there was now nothing but a cloud of dust and vapor, its shadow moving like a diaphanous shroud over the landscape.

CHAPTER ELEVEN

Four days later Kathleen was on her way home aboard an Army transport plane, leaving behind one nightmare and flying toward another. Like everyone else she was in uniform. Hers was the light blue summer outfit of the Red Cross. The woman beside her was a veteran Army nurse, who needed only a glance to recognize the face of tragedy. "Had a hard time, honey?" she said in a voice toughened by battlefield experience. Kathleen nodded, as though it would have been too much of an effort to speak. Her eyes were deeply shadowed and evasive. The unread magazine that she held was clutched so severely that its cover was damaged. "Well, don't worry about me," said the nurse. "I'm not going to chew your ear off. I've got a hell of a lot of sleep to catch up with. If I'm not awake by the time we reach Gandor, give me a poke." She turned away and bundled herself into a vaguely foetal position.

Kathleen leaned her cheek against the cool glass of the small window. The plane struggled upward through a sea of clouds and occasional turbulence, its propellors throbbing in her ears. They levelled off in a white-blue sky without horizons, and she closed her eyes against the glare and tried to sleep, but the voices of the men kept her awake. They were going home, some of them for good. When her eyes crept open, she saw strands of drifting cigarette smoke and a boy standing in the aisle with the armless sleeve of his uniform stuffed into a pocket. She closed her eyes again quickly to avoid being talked to. It was like crawling into a dark hole, not like the childhood experience of snuggling into the fluffy comfort of her bed, except that she had always been afraid of the dark. Now the darkness was more than the absence of light, it was the ruthless crow of death, pecking at the eyes of

146

her very existence. They were a family devoted to life; now one of them had died.

In a half-sleep she remembered the phone call from the RAF. The man's voice was gentle, fatherly, perhaps the voice of a clergyman. "We tried to reach you at the home of Lady Sykes in Yorkshire...." From the moment he started to speak, she suspected that something was wrong. Her heart was poised to leap and run. "Is there anyone with you? I'm afraid I have some bad news. It's about your brother...." He went on, his human voice strangled by the wires through which it had to travel. He was *terribly sorry*. Was there someone he could call for her, someone with whom she might stay? Her chest tightened. Her mouth went dry, and she had to steady herself against the edge of the table. When she spoke it seemed to her that her voice was coming from across the room. She heard herself thanking him and insisting that she would be all right. But she wasn't. After a while the phone began to ring, and the slow process of accepting the death of her brother began.

That night Joe's friend Mark Soden called from the base. He was kind and consoling, and she tried to sound brave. But then he told her that there were some things that Joe had wanted her to have in case he didn't come back: his victrola and radio, his Zeiss camera, and the Underwood typewriter. Suddenly, she burst into uncontrollable tears. Later, she wrote to Mark and apologized. That typewiter, she said, would always make her "think of that hard-talker Joe." And, in spite of his rough ways, "he was the best guy in the world."

The transport plane droned on. She slipped into the darkness of sleep for a while. When she woke up she heard the hefty army nurse snoring quietly like a hibernating bear. Her thoughts turned to Pat and then to her own family. She could imagine her mother all in black, praying in the cave of her religion, but she could not picture her father. She assumed that he would find a way to carry on, but she knew that inside he would be devastated. What would she be able to do to comfort him? What could anybody possibly do?

Logan Airport was a mirage in the summer heat, the air visible over the baked Tarmac. She had left the Army transport in New York for a commercial flight to Boston, where, she was warned, the press would probably be waiting for her, that corps of reporters that for years had been encouraged, perhaps bribed, by her ambitious father to cover the comings and goings of the Kennedy clan. She had seen the evidence already of their continuing curiosity in a day-old copy of *The Boston Globe*, dropped carelessly on a nearby empty seat: EX-ENVOY KENNEDY, CRUSHED BY SON'S DEATH, REMAINS IN SECLUSION. She had turned away to fix her attention on the drab landscape that was rushing up to meet the plane. From her days on the staff of the *Times-Herald*, she remembered John White's joke about yesterday's newspaper: *good for nothing but wrapping fish.*. He had complained often about the kind of writing that had the life expectancy of a fruit fly. That moment of nostalgia helped to hold back the tears that she was afraid would embarrass her when she stepped off the plane.

The plane taxied to a stop, and the passengers shuffled along the narrow aisle. One by one, they descended. In the distance, up a ramp, she saw the crowd, not all of them waiting for her, she hoped. She recognized the animated jostling of the press. Then she saw a gaunt figure coming down the ramp. She hesitated. She could not believe that it was her beloved brother. He called out to her: "Hello, Kat!" She smiled briefly and then ran into his arms and wept. The photographers took pictures and asked questions that she did not hear. John held her for a moment and then whispered something to her that made her square her shoulders and face the crowd. Together they walked back up the ramp and through the crowd to a waiting car. She noticed that he walked with difficulty and that the look on his face was not a smile but a grimace. His face was all bones, and his skin was yellow from malaria. In his tired eyes she could see that he was in constant pain. "You shouldn't have come," she said.

"I wanted to," he said. "I had to. It wasn't easy to convince the doctors at the Chelsea Naval Hospital. They want me back tomorrow."

"What are they doing to you, Johnny?" she said, holding his hand with both of hers.

"Who the hell knows! But listen, Kick. About Joe. It's hard now, but it will be all right. We're all together now."

"How's Daddy?"

"Not so good. Broken. He'll need time. Be careful with him. Don't say anything. You know how he is. Just go about your business. He wants everybody to keep busy."

"And Mother?"

"She's remarkable, as usual. As solid as stone."

"Is she?"

"You know what I mean."

"Yeah, I know what you mean."

The house looked the same, but it did not feel like just another summer in Hyannis Port. Kathleen could actually feel the gloom as it wafted like invisible sadness from room to room and across the lawns of their childhood. The brothers and sisters who greeted her with hugs and kisses did not come running and shouting, full of the old energy and joy that made them wrestle and argue even as they laughed. Their welcome was orderly and quiet, as though they had been scolded by the harsh reality of their brother's death. Kathleen noticed the thinness of Eunice's arms and the confused look in

149

her eyes, as though she were still wrestling with unresolved personal poblems, in spite of her recent graduation from Stanford. Pat at twenty and Jean at sixteen had the Kennedy habit of smiling, no matter what the occasion. Behind those smiles Kathleen could see that they were nervous and awkward. In that moment, in the very act of embracing them, she suddenly wondered whether or not they had been forced to share their mother's disapproval and anger over "the forbidden marriage." Bobby, not yet nineteen, presented himself in his Navy cadet whites and said, "Dad wants us to carry on."And Teddy, at fourteen, was too shy to say anything at all.

There were no tears. She knew that it would be that way, because that's the way her father wanted it. They were all good soldiers in the Kennedy army, and though she wanted to be like them, to be one with them all again, she knew that she wasn't.

Her mother appeared, composed and theatrical in black. It was the moment about which she had worried most. She had dared to hope that Joe's death would bring them closer, but there was nothing in the formality of her greeting that might be interpreted as forgiveness or real affection. She desperately wanted her mother to take her in her arms, she wanted to weep with her mother for the lost son and brother, but all she got was a little lecture on bravery and the healing power of prayer.

She did not see her father until later. She was alone when he came down from his room, the others having gone off to keep up the pretense of summer as usual. The moment she saw him she could see that Jack was right. He was broken inside, as though a mirror had been shattered in his mind. And in that moment she realized fully just how much Joe had meant to him. In the wake of his own political failures the Ambassador had made Joe the heir apparent of his hope, the keystone of his dreams of glory, and it occurred to her that Joe's death might actually mean the death of her father.

When he held out his arms toward her he seemed feeble, like a beggar torn between desperate need and faltering pride. His anguish was written in his face, which was no longer the face of a robust man of fifty-six. There were lines and visible capillaries and shadows under his bloodshot eyes. He had obviously been crying, and he seemed to be once again on the brink of tears. In a last ditch stand to maintain his dignity, he talked in a voice that was loud but lacked its usual strength. "How's my girl?" he said, his pale lips quivering. "We've lost Joe, but we must not give in; we must keep going." He held her, but she had the feeling that it was she who was keeping him from swaying or falling. "Your brother was a hero. Don't you ever forget that. He was a hero and his story has to be told."

"Don't worry, Daddy," she said. "We all know what a hero he was. The whole world knows."

He could not get out another sentence. He stepped back, his eyes blinking rapidly to fend off the tears. He recovered long enough to say, "Got to rest now. Got to get things back on track. Talk to your mother. Make it up with her. Go to church or something --" His voice trailed off. He walked away unsteadily and then climbed the stairs back to his room.

She found Jack at the beach, leaning against an old rowboat and staring out to sea, as if he were searching for the line between sea and sky that the summer haze had obscured. "They've all gone sailing," he said. "It seems strange, but it's just as well. Remember all the trophies we used to bring home?"

"Yeah," she said. "We were unbeatable."

"I'm not much of a sailor now; just an old wreck."

"In that case, why don't you come with me. I'm going to church."

"St. Francis Xavier?"

"Yes. It's still Sunday and I haven't been to mass. Please come. Unless you'd rather not be seen with your outcast sister."

"Well, now that you've got mansions in England and castles in Ireland, I guess I don't mind."

She laughed for the first time since she heard the tragic news. Arm in arm, they walked back towards the house.

By the time Kathleen woke up the next morning, Jack had already left for the hospital, and her mother had gone off to church , as usual. Jack had finally talked to her about his medical problems. He had to go back into the Naval Hospital for an operation to relieve the pain in his back and legs. The operation on his spine had been a miserable failure, and there was a festering wound where a metal plate had been used. She had tried to sound encouraging, but she could see that his suffering was wearing him down, even as he was being celebrated as a national hero.

There was no one left at the table when Kathleen appeared for breakfast, all the others were gone, afraid that the Ambassador would scold them for "moping around." She had coffee and toast and read about herself in *The Boston Globe* : "Kathleen Kennedy, last of her family to see Lt. Joe Kennedy, Jr. before he died... arrived here from London by plane yesterday to join her family -- her first visit since her marriage in May to Lord Hartington...." Much was made of her new title and the fact that she would one day be the Duchess of Devonshire. Under normal circumstances, she would not have minded being talked about that way, but she knew that such stories in the paper would only make her mother more bitter and reduce the chances of a reconciliation.

She put the paper aside and went for a long walk on the beach to avoid being dragged into the vigorous activities that had been scheduled for the clan to keep them from thinking about their dead brother. In the old days she had been as active and competetive as the rest of the gang, but now she needed time to think.

She walked in mid-morning sunlight, wearing her old civilian clothes and a pair of tennis shoes that reminded her of happier summers. The water was soothing and the sand was wet and clean where the tide had run out. If only life were like that, she thought, washed clean by the tide. She picked up a smooth white stone, studied it for a moment and then carried it with her as she walked. It felt solid and good in the palm of her hand. Offshore, a small fishing boat went by, its outboard motor humming leisurely, an old man in waders at the tiller, his chin thrust forward and his white hair swept back.

Down the beach she saw another woman. She was walking alone and pausing from time to time to make odd gestures, as though she were scolding the water or the sky. The morning breeze played in her gauzy white garment. It was a while before she recognized the woman as Nancy LLoyd, whose husband, a fighter pilot, had been killed in the Pacific in June, leaving her with an infant girl. Nancy was a close friend, and, like Kathleen, just twenty-four years old. Several people had written her about Nancy's tragedy and her sad state of mind, her outbursts of anger and incoherence. Kathleen had hoped to see her, sooner or later, but now she hesitated. If Nancy had not heard about Joe's death, she did not want to be the one to tell her. Kathleen watched her drop to her knees and stretch out her arms, as though she were about to be crucified by the invisible forces of the world. Perhaps she was simply praying. In any case, she had come down to the shore to be alone, and Kathleen decided not to disturb her. She turned and walked back up the beach, without stepping in the footprints she had left in the wet sand.

She went on in the opposite direction for a long way, thinking about all the young men who had died in the war and all the women who mourned for them. It was all so hateful and cruel and stupid. She sat against a piece of driftwood until her anger dissolved into tears.

By the time she got back to the house, the clan had gathered for lunch. She excused herself and went to her room. There she found a telegram from overseas. Since it had no official markings, she assumed it was just another of the scores of condolences that had followed Joe's death. She opened it and read: MAJOR ROBIN WILSON KILLED IN ACTION. POOR PAT. Her vision blurred before she could see who the sender was. The flimsy piece of paper fluttered silently to the floor, and she threw herself on her bed and buried her face in her pillow, as if to shut out the horror of it all. "Oh, God!" she sobbed. "Why are you doing this?"

She was still on her bed when her mother came into her room. "Are you all right, dear?" she said.

Kathleen sat up quickly, as though she had been caught doing something indecent. She tried to deny her tears with a smile. *Kennedys don't cry!* "I'm fine," she said.

"Was there bad news in your telegram?" said Rose.

She followed her mother's gaze to the piece of paper on the floor, and then stooped to pick it up. She folded it several times and hid it in her fist. "It's all right, Mother, really it is."

"Well, obviously, it's not, my dear. You've been crying."

"I'm sorry," she said. "I just came from the beach. I ran into Nancy Lloyd."

"Oh, that poor girl! Did she go on about her husband?"

Kathleen hesitated at the lie, like a horse who stalls at the jump, but she could not think of any way to talk about Pat Wilson without involving Joe. "She looked very upset, worse than I imagined she would be."

"It was a terrible shock, and, having just had a baby, she was especially vulnerable. She needs our prayers."

It was impossible for Kathleen to focus on Nancy. All she could see was Pat and her children in the sunlit cottage where, so recently, they had all laughed and sang and shared their contraband. "I'll stop around and see her," she said, "but I'm very tired right now."

"Well, try to sleep a bit," said Rose, retreating toward the door and then pausing. "Incidentally, what *was* that telegram all about?"

"Nothing, really. Just a London friend, who was worried about me because I left so suddenly. Nobody you know."

"I see. One of *those* people."

Kathleen did not feel the impact of her mother's remark until she was gone. Then she realized that it was a reference to those friends in London who had encouraged her to marry Billy Hartington. But she was too exhausted to be angry. *Poor Pat! Poor Joe!* It was all so damned ironic. If only they had decided earlier to make a life together. If only Robin had died before Joe.

Jack was sent home to recuperate, and by Labor Day he was feeling well enough to have some Navy friends over for the weekend. The prospect of a party lifted Kathleen out of her gloom. She had grown impatient with death and needed a taste of life. With Jack and his friends around it would be a lot easier to believe that life was worth living. They had been there in the water in the jaws of death, and every minute that they spent together was a celebration of their survival and of life itself.

"But what about Dad?" she said.

"He keeps telling us to carry on. Wait until he sees how my buddies carry on. It might lift his spirits."

"It's worth a try," she said, "as long as they don't get carried away. Who are you inviting?"

"Red Fay and Barney Ross, of course. Bernie Lyons, Lennie and Kate Thom, Jim and Jewel Reed. We decided to include the two wives, in spite of the fact that Kate's more than a wee bit pregnant. She won't be much good for touch football, but maybe she can crew for Eunice in the big race. Everybody's got to take part."

"What about you, Slim? What can you do in your condition.?"

"The only thing I can do is not on the agenda."

"Very funny!"

"Let's see, there's tennis, golf, football, sailing, water polo, softball, horse shoes, ping pong, charades and monopoly. Maybe I'll just be the ref this year."

"The old Kennedy summer olympics! Did you warn your friends?"

"No, and I didn't warn them that cocktail time means one drink before dinner."

"They're not going to like that."

"That's Dad's rule, and I'm not going to ask him to change it, but, just between you and me and the kitchen cupboard, I happen to know where there's a bottle of Scotch."

"You wouldn't dare."

"Of course not, but I thought maybe you --"

"Forget it!"

"Nobody would notice if you drifted into the kitchen from time to time."

"Yeah, but what if someone else drifted in at the same time. I'm in enough trouble around here."

"Good point, Kick! We'll talk about it later."

Saturday was a riot of competitive activity, to which Jack's friends added the sports of joke-telling and bitching. "I had never been in a boat before," said Kate. "How was I to know where the jib was? It's a good thing we won the race. Eunice would have forced me to walk the plank if we lost."

Kathleen joined the boys for a round of golf at the Hyannis Port Country Club, where they disregarded all decorum and laughed their way from hole to hole. At one point Red Fay walked up to some women who were taking their time on the fairway and said: "Excuse me, ladies, the Marchioness of Hartington would like to play through." Kathleen blushed and promptly sliced the ball into the woods.

When they gathered for a drink before dinner, Jack had to warn them that there was a house rule against more than one cocktail. "Sorry about that," he said. "Dad has strong convictions about booze."

"I thought he had a lock on the distribution of Haig and Haig," said Bernie.

"He's not even here," said Red Fay.

"He'll be down for dinner," said Jack.

"What a revolting development," said Barney Ross. "Why don't we run down to the local gin mill. The women and children can stay here and sip lemonade. We'll be back in a flash or two."

"Wait a minute," said Jack. "Maybe I can fix you up. I'll send Kick into the kitchen. She knows where the bottle is. Then you can go in one at a time for a refill. But make it quick."

One by one they drifted away, but only two of them returned. Jack went inside to see what was going on. He found Red and Barney and Kick, hushing each other and trying to stifle their laughter. Right behind Jack, Bobby appeared. "I

157

know what you're doing," he said in his boy scout voice. "I'm going to tell Dad."

"Get lost!" said Kathleen.

Bobby retreated helplessly. Nobody believed for a minute that he had the guts to say anything.

They came into dinner feeling pretty good. Kathleen was amused by Red Fay's remark to Jack: "Your sister's a swell gal. Too bad she's already married."

The Ambassador made his appearance at the head of the table and immediately took over. In his blazer and ascot and wing-tipped black and white shoes, he looked like his old self, but Kathleen could see that he was "carrying on" with considerable difficulty. He went immediately into his routine of checking up on everyone's activities. He asked everyone at the table for a detailed report. He wanted to know who won and who lost and what the score was. Some of Jack's friends thought he was joking, but when they tried to add to the joke, they could see that he was dead serious. Kathleen was embarrassed by his performance. She was Lady Hartington and he was treating her like a child. Jack's friends were battle-scarred veterans, and they were puzzled by the whole ritual.

Everyone was relieved when it was over. The conversation took a livelier turn, the veterans leading the way with anecdotes and jokes that eluded Rose and annoyed Joe. After dinner Joe disappeared without saying anything. Kathleen knew that he was going back to his room, and she knew, instinctively, that the presence of all these tough young sailors made him think of his dead son. She was tempted to follow him, but her mother stopped her with a glance.

The last scheduled event of the day was an after-dinner movie in the Ambassador's "little cinema," with its professional furnishings a reminder that he was once in the business. Rose, who was not fond of those memories, slipped away

158

quietly to escape the noise and laughter. The film was "The More the Merrier." with Jean Arthur, Joel McCrea and Charles Coburn. It was a comedy about a working-girl in wartime Washington, and it reminded Kathleen of all her old friends at the *Times-Herald* . It was difficult for her to believe how much had changed since she boarded that troopship for England just a year and a half ago.

After the film, Jack and his friends drifted out to the lawn to catch the last light of a spectacular sunset. It deepened into orange and gray and focused their attention , as though it were a campfire settling into embers. Facing the sea, they smoked and remembered the good times and hard times that they had had together. A mysterious silver flask appeared, which they passed around as though they were performing a private communion service. Kathleen noticed how the men had arranged themselves around Jack, and how forceful his presence was, though he was painfully thin. In the dying light, the bones of his face gave him a dramatic look.

They reminisced quietly, at first, but each anecdote seemed more amusing than the last, until they were laughing out loud and singing and clapping their hands. Barney Ross recalled how two native scouts were afraid to help him and Jack when they stumbled upon them on Olasana Island. "They thought we were Japs. We kept showing them our white skin. Christ, if Jack was as yellow then as he is now, they would never have picked us up."

In the gathering darkness, they forgot how close they were to the house. Suddenly, they heard a loud voice from an upstairs window. It was Mr. Kennedy, and he was in a rage. "Jack," he shouted, "don't you and your friends have any respect for your dead brother? You get in here! You're making a nuisance of yourselves with the neighbors."

"Sorry, sir!" said Jack, as though he were speaking to a superior officer. When his father was no longer at the window, he apologized to his friends: "I guess we'll have to keep it down." But the party was over, and they all knew it.

Kathleen was furious with her father and embarrassed on his behalf for making such a fool of himself, but she said nothing for fear of making matters worse. When Bobby came out of the house and said, "Dad's awfully mad," she turned on him and said, "Stop trying to scare our guests." In English terms, she thought it was inexcusable for her family to air their personal feelings that way.

The next day her mother took her aside for a little talk. "You must understand, dear, that your father is still in a state of shock. And you must not imagine for a moment that either one of us has gotten over the earlier shock of your marriage. We are civil to you because we love you, but forgiveness is out of the question. It was wrong of you to put your personal happiness before the happiness and harmony of your family. Your eternal soul is in jeopardy, and so is Joe's for encouraging you, even though we admired him, in a way, for standing up for his sister. Furthermore, we do not believe that what is done can not be undone. We have talked to some important churchmen about the possibility of an annulment and --"

"No!" shouted Kathleen. "I don't care who you've spoken to. There will not be an annulment. I love my husband, and that's that. Now, if you want me to leave, I'll make arrangements in the morning."

"Nonsense!" her mother said. "We want you to stay as long as possible. You are a Kennedy, and these are difficult times. We need you here. You're a great comfort to your father."

"I'm sorry, Mother. We're all feeling the strain, I guess. Of course, I'll stay. But couldn't we get away a bit? It would be good for Dad to get out of the house. Why don't we all go to New York? We can see the Fall fashions and maybe a few shows."

Rose smiled, her perfect teeth a reflection of her perfect string of pearls. "That might be just the thing," she said. "I really miss my shopping trips to Paris, but New York also has a great deal to offer. I'll talk to your father in a day or two, and we'll see."

Later that day Jack and Kathleen walked down the beach together, in defiance of the Kennedy doctrine that vigorous physical activity was next to godliness. "It's like being at summer camp around here," said Kathleen. "Why do they go on treating us as children?"

"I don't know," said Jack. "Maybe they haven't grown up yet. They have this retarded idea that they can control our lives forever."

Kathleen laughed. "I never thought of it that way. They actually seem to need us more than we need them."

"Without us they would only have each other, and, let's face it, they haven't been the happiest couple in the world. I think there is a kind of emptiness in both of them. They've had a lot of bitterness and frustration to deal with. Dad turned to women and money; Mother turned to God and Bergdorf Goodman's, and they both live through us. Look at Dad and Joe."

"Yeah," she said, "and you're next on the list."

"That's what I'm afraid of. I'm thinking of going away for a year or so -- you know, to recuperate, in more ways than one. I've got to make some decisions about my life before Dad tries to make them for me. Mother has tried to do the same with you, and she's furious because you got away. You don't know how lucky you are."

"I do know," she said. "And I can't wait to get back to England. I'll have a good life there with Billy."

"The way things are going, the war will be over soon. Paris has been liberated, General Bradley

161

is about to set foot on German soil, and Montgomery is rolling through Belgium. Billy may be in the streets of Brussels right now, sitting up there on his tank and catching kisses and flowers from a lot of pretty girls, who are yelling *vive la liberation* and *Fifi loves the R.A.F.*"

"I don't know if he's in Brussels, but he's mentioned some other places in his letters. After that big battle at Caen, they've been moving very fast, sometimes without much opposition. Dieppe, Abbeville, Douai. He loves playing the liberator. He says that when he sees what those people have been through, he is deeply moved. Helping them is a wonderful experience, and he wishes I were there to share it with him."

"Well, the adoration part is okay," said Jack, "but I don't think you'd like the accommodations."

"If you're suggesting that I'm a spoiled brat from a rich family, you're probably right, but I miss my husband anyway. He says he amuses his men by playing the aristocrat on the battlefield. He has an orderly named Ingles, who helps him with his personal appearance and his social life, which consists mainly of serving his guests good rum in crystal glasses, as they sit among the ruins."

"Sounds as though he has a great sense of humor."

"He does."

"Well, after the war, we'll have to get together for a good chin wag, in one of your castles."

"You won't be so sarcastic, Johnny Boy, after you actually see those estates," she said, taking his arm affectionately and noticing how thin it felt through the long-sleeved shirt.

Kathleen's father was persuaded to come along on the shopping trip to   New York, and the change of scene lifted his spirits, as did the mild and sunny mid-September weather. He stayed, as usual,

162

at the Waldorf, at 50th Street and Park Avenue, and, as usual, Rose and the children stayed at the Plaza, at 59th Street and Fifth Avenue, at the Southeast corner of Central Park. They had made these separate arrangements for so long that the children no longer bothered to ask why.

On the stationery of the Plaza Hotel, Kathleen wrote to her friends in London. To one of them she said, "New York has a liberating effect on me, in spite of the tall buildings and the rush of traffic. If it weren't for all the guys in uniform, you wouldn't even know that there was a war on. When you're in New York you can't possibly run out of things to do. Dad has fixed us up with tickets for *Oklahoma* and *Fancy Free*, the ballet by Jerome Robbins and Leonard Bernstein. But the feature attractions will be Bonwit Teller, Saks Fifth Avenue, and Bergdorf Goodman. And, if I can hide it from my mother, I plan to buy a copy of *Forever Amber* ."

On their second day in town, Kathleen arranged to do some shopping on her own at Bonwit Teller, but agreed to meet Eunice for lunch. She loved walking on Fifth Avenue. London, by comparison, was a drab and wounded city, where it was almost impossible to get anything that was not an absolute necessity. In New York the shops were well stocked, and one might imagine that the world of high fashion had not even broken stride for the war. The Paris designers were not represented, of course, but others had taken their place.

At Bonwit Teller's Kathleen saw a number of things that appealed to her, and she took her time making her choices. Suddenly, there was Eunice, looking over her shoulder, more than a bit early for lunch. "I'm not finished yet," said Kathleen.

"I was just curious to see how you were doing," said Eunice.

Kathleen stared at her for a moment and realized that something was wrong with her. She looked pale and distracted. "Aren't you feeling well?" said Kathleen.

"I'm all right," she said. "Why don't you show me what you bought?"

"You're not all right. What's going on?"

"Daddy wants to see you."

"What do you mean he wants to see me?"

"I guess he has something to tell you."

"Did he say what it was about?"

"No. He says he wants you to come to his hotel right away."

Her heart paused, then seemed to sink. Her mouth went dry. She didn't dare to think what it might be that he had to tell her. What could be so ugrent? "Is Mother all right?"

"Yes, she's fine. Why don't we just go to Daddy's hotel and talk to him." Eunice seemed to be cowering as she spoke, and her voice faded to a near whisper.

"All right!" said Kathleen, and they walked together in silence all the way from 57th Street and Fifth Avenue to the Waldorf, about eight or nine blocks. They walked through crowds, past luxurious window displays and Rockefeller Center, but Kathleen was no longer aware of anything around her.

When they reached the carpeted corridor and Kathleen saw her father standing in the doorway of his suite, she knew what it was all about. She wanted to turn and run, but her feet kept moving forward. She saw it in the way he moved, then she saw it in his eyes. Then, as he closed the door behind her for privacy, she heard him say it: "Your husband has been killed in action. God help us all!"

She stood there for a moment, her eyes cast down, as though she were watching a small white stone sink slowly into a deep pool of water. Then she slumped into a chair and wept, as her father stood by, his hands making gestures of helplessness in the air, his lips white and trembling.

Back at the Plaza she stayed in her room alone until evening. She came to the table at dinner time, because she knew her father wanted her to, but she was unable to bring herself to speak or eat. She had the look of someone whose spirit was utterly crushed. "Is there anything we can do for you?" said her mother.

Kathleen shook her head, and then said "No."

"Will you come to mass with me in the morning?"

Again she said, "No!"

Later that night her father tried once more to talk to her. "If we can't help you, Kick, maybe somebody else can. A friend maybe. We'll call her for you. We'll explain things and ask her to stay here with you for a while."

"Patsy White," she muttered. "John's sister. She's Patsy Field now."

Her father winced. "You know how we feel about those people, but if that's the friend you want --" It was midnight when he dialled Patsy Field's number.

She arrived the next day and found Kathleen sitting on the floor in her room with clothing scattered all around her and her mother standing over her saying: "God doesn't send us a cross heavier than we can bear."

When they were alone, Kathleen spoke her grief to Patsy Field: "I never thought that God would do such a thing to me. I went to another country. I made a new life for myself. We were as innocent as children. There were times when I thought I did not really love him, but I did, I did love him, I did. He made me feel so needed. I would have done anything for him. My mother must have prayed day and night for this to happen. Now, they're both gone -- the sweet man I married and the brave man who stood up for me at my wedding. My husband and my brother."

And in her diary she wrote: "So ends the story of Billy and Kick. I can't believe that the one thing I feared most should have happened... Life is so cruel."

PART TWO

THE FATAL AFFAIR

CHAPTER TWELVE

The Fall of 1944 was creeping toward winter. The days grew shorter, the clouds grew darker, and the rain was a cosmic reflection of Kathleen's personal tears. *The dark night of the soul,* she thought, as she walked along the narrow cliff path and looked seaward toward the distant and invisible battlefield that had claimed the life of her husband and ruined her dream.*The dark night of the soul.* Father D'Arcy had used that phrase. "Despair is destructive," he had said. "it is a kind of self-pity that drags us down, deeper and deeper into the dark pit of alienation from God. It is seductive and addictive, because there is a kind of perverse pleasure in seeing oneself as the victim of destiny, which can only lead to a rejection of God. And it is this rejection that is the dark night, in which we feel totally abandoned and alone. After the wound and the anger and despair, there can only be one way to go. The next step is a true confession and a holy communion. Once you are forgiven and embraced and at one with God, your soul will mend and your life will be renewed by comfort and joy." He had persuaded her to come back to the Church, but she was still waiting for the "comfort and joy."

She stood by a crumbling stone wall and watched the grim clouds sweep across the troubled sea. There was no horizon, only a gray veil of rain. She carried an umbrella, but she did not open it. The cold drops fell on her hair and face, and she wanted to stretch out her arms to the darkness in a gesture of complete surrender. Suddenly, she thought of Nancy Lloyd, standing that way on the beach, and she understood something that she could not have understood on that sunny day in Hyannis Port. To lose one's husband was a kind of surgery from which some women never recovered.

She looked down at the black rocks against which the heavy waves destroyed themselves. Her vision was blurred. For a moment she swayed uncertainly, then, suddenly, she took a deep breath, snapped open her umbrella and started back along the path.

She had left the house of her in-laws because it was full of the war. News broadcasts interrupted the music. The Duke lunched with other men who had lost their sons, and they healed themselves with drink and rage and dire predictions of the end of Western Civilization as they knew it. The last thing she heard as she escaped unnoticed was that the British were advancing on Cologne. It meant nothing to her except more death and destruction. For her the war had ended with the single bullet that had pierced her husband's heart, and she fled from the description of his death provided in letters by survivors of his company. Each news broadcast brought back the picture of him lying there outside the farmhouse that was overrun by the Germans.

Back at the house Elizabeth was waiting for her. "Where have you been?" she said. "You shouldn't go off like that in the rain."

"It wasn't raining when I left."

"Look at you. You're sopping wet. Where's your mac?"

"I'm sorry. I had to get away from all that war talk."

"Well, they're all gone now and Father's having a nap." She took the umbrella and stood it in the corner of the hallway near the kitchen. "Look at your hair. Come on, we'll go up the back way and get you out of those clothes."

She allowed Elizabeth to unbutton her tweed jacket and skirt and to wrap her in a warm robe. "I'm not a child," she said.

169

"Of course you are. We all are -- at times." She handed Kathleen a large towel. "What you need now is a hot toddy. I'll be back in a minute."

"You're very sweet, Liz," she said, "but sometimes I wish you didn't look so much like Billy."

She smiled girlishly. "There's not much I can do about that, is there," she said.

When she came back, Kathleen was lying on her bed against two large pillows. The other bed in the room was being used by Elizabeth, because Kathleen was unable to sleep alone since Billy's death. She had always been afraid of the dark, but that childhood fear now bordered on panic.

"While you were gone we heard some good news," said Elizabeth.

"If it's about the war," said Kathleen, "I'd rather not hear it." She warmed her hands on the steaming mug and lifted it to her lips. The aroma of the rum seemed to soothe her.

"No, no, it's about the Red Cross. They've been awarded the Nobel Peace Prize."

For a moment Kathleen looked pleased, but then she said, "Pretty soon all of us, dead or alive, will have awards. Even my father, I hear, got some big deal decoration from the Vatican. I don't know what for. His children's war record maybe."

"Come on, Kick," said Elizabeth. "You mustn't be so bitter. We were all devastated by my brother's death, but life must go on. The Nobel Award was a wonderful thing for the Red Cross, and you were part of it. You should go back to work for them. It would be good for you to do something like that at a time like this."

"I'm sorry, Liz. You're absolutely right, and I have thought of it. I really hate myself for being such a weepy mess. I never used to cry at all and I never thought I would. It's just so uncontrollable at times."

"You don't have to apologize, Kick. Every woman needs a good cry from time to time. It's only

170

natural. I don't know why your parents made such a fuss about it. Now you're all backed up and the dam has burst."

Suddenly the two of them laughed. "My God, what did you put in this toddy?" said Kathleen.

"Lots of rum," said Elizabeth, and they laughed again.

Kathleen had not followed the presidential campaign very closely, because of her distance and distractions, but her friend Inga never failed to provide her with commentaries and gossip. "Well," she wrote, "Mr. Roosevelt has done it again, no thanks to your father, who is still sore because F.D.R. hasn't given him a job in the government. He even threatened to endorse Dewey, my colleagues in the press tell me, but that would not have made much sense for a Boston Democrat. I heard that he and Harry Truman crossed paths and swords at some gathering in Boston, and he said: 'Harry, what are you doing campaigning for that crippled son of a bitch that killed my son Joe?' Truman's response, they say, was unprintable. In any case, if your brother Jack plans to run for office, I hope he has the good sense to put some distance between himself and his father. But he won't have to worry about the women's vote, will he? We are all for him. What does he have that makes him so irresistible?"

Encouraged by Elizabeth and most of her friends, she returned to the Red Cross as an occasional volunteer, and in other ways tried to recover her emotional balance. There were good days and bad days, but not a glimmer of the old spontaneous joy most of the winter and spring. The worst day was April 12, 1945. The sudden death of President Roosevelt was to her, and millions of others, like the death of a father. She had been a girl of twelve when he was first elected. Her British friends called to say how sorry they were, as though he were, indeed, her father. How ironic, she

171

thought, when she imagined that her own father might actually be celebrating.

But soon there came the good news that made all the difference. Jack, who had been covering the UN conference in San Francisco for the Hearst papers, was coming to England to cover the June elections. From that moment on she could feel the flush of life again. Not even the celebration of Victory in Europe Day a couple of weeks earlier had done that for her. It had been, in fact, a bit depressing, since it was the day that she and Billy had once dreamed of. But now she was alive. She bought new clothes and an old Austin 7, a lucky find in all that wartime austerity. And she thought of all the girls to whom she might introduce that amusing and lusty brother of hers, that naughty sailor, who had lost his boat and become an American hero.

It was the last day in May. London was bathed in sunshine, as if the very sky had been liberated by the end of the war in Europe. It would be the first post-war Season, and the grand old town was stirring like an ancient sleeping beauty whose wardrobe needed mending. Behind the wheel of her Austin 7, Kathleen made her way through the noisy traffic, challenging taxi cabs and lumbering double-decker buses as if she were driving a Rolls Royce. She was on her way to the Grosvenor House hotel to meet her brother and his pal Pat Lannan, who had gotten them a room through a friend of his who was the head of the London bureau of the *Chicago Tribune.* They were two rich young adventurers in the world of journalism, and they would be at the very heart of things, following Churchill around during his bid for re-election. The reunion with Jack and the promise of action excited her.

She announced herself rather arrogantly to the hotel staff and enjoyed their prompt response. "Lady Hartington is here for Mr. Kennedy," said the clerk on the telephone, while the assistant manager stood by stiffly to see that she was properly served. The old days are not dead yet, she thought, as she was led to the lift.

In the spacious room Jack took his sister into his arms and kissed her. She held him tight and closed her eyes for a moment, as if to savor her joy. "Boy, am I glad to see you, Johnny," she said. "You feel like a bag of bones, but you look great."

"You lost a little weight yourself, little sister," he said.

"Well, what did you expect? I didn't get cut in two by a destroyer, but it was something like that."

"It was a bad year all around, but things are looking better."

"Well, *you* sure are, after all that Arizona and California sunshine. You look like a movie star. I hear you raised hell on the Coast."

"Don't believe everything you hear, even if it's true. Come on, we'll order up some breakfast and swap some dirt. There's a lot to talk about, not the least of which are those girls you mentioned in your letters."

She looked around at the large room with its high ceiling, its heavy drapes and deep carpets. "It's not Chatsworth," she said, "but it's not the usual reporter's flophouse either. Not bad! I see you've unpacked." She nodded towards the scattering of clothes on the floor."

"Who are you to lecture me on neatness? It was never your strong suit."

"I followed in your footsteps and tripped over your shoes. Incidentally, where's your partner in crime?"

"He's looking for an adapter for his wire recorder, a fantastic piece of equipment. He's planning to record everybody who's anybody in this election."

The breakfast was wheeled in like an MGM prop and laid out on a small round table complete with a white tablecloth and two roses in a vase. "I couldn't eat a thing this morning,"she said, "and now, all of a sudden, I'm starving. Do women often react to you that way?"

"Yeah," he said. "My arrival seems to increase their appetite for some reason."

She laughed and helped herself to the scrambled eggs and bacon. "So give me the inside scoop on Hollywood," she said. "I'm sure there were things you couldn't say in writing."

"There's not a hell of a lot to say. Hollywood is a party and somebody is always getting laid, but in the end it's kind of depressing. I gave them a good performance, in spite of the fact that I was a walking catalogue of medical disasters. When I finally got back from the Pacific in December of '43, I was practically a basket case. Two operations later I was even worse. I had a terrible back, chronic colitis, and recurrent malaria, but it took the Navy until November '44 to decide that I was unfit for active duty. And it took the Retiring Board another month to decide that I should be honorably discharged, effective March, '45. They couldn't think of anything else to operate on, so they sent me home for an indefinite period of rest and rehabilitation. I went out to Castle Hot Springs, Arizona to see what I could do to salvage my wrecked body. Dad had already decided that I was going into politics. He knew before I knew, and he expected me to get into shape. He was like a coach. He kept sending me expensive cuts of meat and other foodstuffs to build me up. And he sent me all kinds of books and reports to read, as if I were prepping for an exam. Behind the scenes he was already making deals and pulling strings. You know how he is."

"I sure do," she said. "I suppose he means well, but once he's got a plan, it's almost impossble to turn him down."

"Yeah, he takes over and you become part of his dream. In my case it was even tougher because of Joe's death. He was really knocked off his pins by that, and I felt that I couldn't let him down. But had I known then what I know now, I might have felt differently. He was very secretive about the whole thing. I only found out recently what it was all about."

"What did he do?"

"It was his cousin Joe Cane who first suggested the scheme. He figured that old James Curley was in enough legal and financial trouble to shake him loose from his Congressional seat in the 11th District. He was scheduled to run for re-election in the Fall of '46, but they persuaded him to run instead in the Mayor's race this Fall in Boston. Dad apparently paid him $12,000 outright and made other arrangements to bail him out of his troubles. He and Joe Cane virtually guaranteed Curley's victory. It's kind of ironic, since he was the son of a bitch who ended grandpa Fitzgerald's career as mayor over thirty years ago. Jesus, it's like stepping on a pile of horse manure to jump on the horse. I never thought I'd have anything to do with that Boston crowd of political bosses."

"That's pretty lousy," said Kathleen. "Maybe it's not too late to change your mind."

He took a deep breath. "I'd like to tell them all to go to hell, but what am I going to do? This is Dad's way of doing business, and he doesn't seem to think there's anything wrong with it. I can't hurt him. I just can't do it -- not at a time like this. Besides, I learned something about myself in San Francisco. I really enjoyed covering the United Nations, the big political arena. History was being made and I was there. I met a lot of interesting and important people, including your great admirer Anthony Eden. The whole atmosphere suited me, and I made up my mind then and there that I would make a career of public service."

Kathleen paused thoughtfully over her food for a moment. "Do you really think that Dad can get you a Congressional seat?"

"I don't think he can buy it outright, but with his money and my charm, who knows? In the eleventh district all you have to do is win the Democratic nomination. The rest is easy."

"Well, look at it this way, Curley's a crook and doesn't deserve the job anyway. You can run as the new breed, the young war hero, the post-war politician."

He smiled and his teeth looked very white against his sun-darkened skin. "I ought to hire you as my campaign manager."

"I don't think the widow of a Cavendish would be very popular with your constituents," she said. "Tell me more about your wild trip to the wild West."

"I guess Castle Hot Springs was good for me in a way, but it was truly boring, a place where self-panickers go to die. Too many old folks and not enough young women. That kind of deprivation gives me severe headaches."

"I guess when you say you have a headache the girls better watch out. With women it's just the other way around."

"Unfortunately!" he said. "Anyway, there was no action, so I did a lot of reading and eating and sun-bathing. By the time I met Pat Lannan, I was feeling a lot better. After a while we went to Phoenix for a little distraction and stayed at the Biltmore, which was designed by Frank Lloyd Wright. It was terrific looking, but a little too dressy for us cowboys, so we went over to the Camelback Inn, where we met James Stewart, also just out of the service. We also ran into John Hersey and his wife, my old girlfriend, Frances Ann. By the time we left Phoenix, my headaches were gone, but my back was killing me. I thought of checking into the Mayo Clinic, but after a while I felt better . Both Pat and I were fed up with the dull atmosphere at Castle Hot

Springs, so we took off for California, where I planned to look up Inga. Pat knew Walter Huston from somewhere, which was a great introduction into a whole Hollywood way of life. We met Gary Cooper and Olivia de Havilland and Sonja Henie--."

"I heard that you got pretty cozy with her."

"Well, let me put it this way," he said, "I think I know now why they keep her on ice."

"So you fell right in -- to Hollywood, I mean."

"I had a good time, until the shock of Roosevelt's death, and then, all of a sudden, it was back to reality. Dad was at it again, and I had this call from Louis Ruppel about going to San Francisco to cover the birth of the United Nations for the Chicago *Herald American*. And now here I am, chasing down the Churchill story." He paused and fixed his eyes on her. "Now let's talk about you, Kick. You always put up such a brave front, but what's the inside story? What are you doing? What are you thinking?"

"For a while I wasn't doing much of anything," she said. "I used to think I was pretty tough, and I really wanted to be, but I turned into a weeping willow. I came back last September for the memorial service at the little church near Chatsworth, and everything was so sad and beautiful that I guess I sort of caved in. Billy's family was very good to me, but we were all in the same boat. He was such a sweet and wonderful man that our sense of loss was just terrible. The papers were full of praise for him, which, in a way, only made matters worse. There were constant reminders. People kept coming around and calling. I even wept when I went to see Father D'Arcy. I made the necessary act of contrition, but I had to tell him that I could not honestly say that I was sorry that I had married Billy. That didn't seem to matter to the Church, since I was no longer living in sin. In my bittterness I said to Father D'Arcy, 'I guess God has taken care of the matter in His own way, hasn't He?'

I think he was annoyed, but he didn't say anything."

"The power of a woman's tears," said Jack.

"I wasn't looking for sympathy," she said. "I just wanted him to know how I felt. I was trying to be honest. Besides, some of my Anglican friends had heard a rumor that Mother believed that God had doomed Billy and Joe for taking part in the sinful marriage, and that those tragedies were God's way of giving me another chance. I didn't dare say that to Father D'Arcy or to anyone else, because I didn't dare believe it. She couldn't possibly have said something as horrible as that, could she?"

"I hope not," said Jack, "but, frankly, I wouldn't be surprised. Sometimes she spouts Catholic Doctrine without thinking of all the implications. She's no theologian, that's for sure. Personally, I think she exploits the ideas that suit her own needs. She was the one who was furious, not God. And maybe she was the one who really wanted revenge."

"Maybe you're right. I sometimes feel that she will never forgive me, even if the Church does. But why?"

"Don't you know, Kick?"

Kathleen shook her head. "I really don't understand."

"Because you were the only one of the children who had the guts to stand up to her and to beat her in a head-to-head battle of the wills. Besides, you were a girl, and that just made it worse. She had tried to assert herself when she was young and she had lost. To see you succeed only added to her bitterness. She herself must have once dreamed of a Prince Charming, of mansions and castles, only to find herself married to an Irish businessman, for whom she mothered nine children, while he chased showgirls around the movie studios. Dad's got his good points, but he's no Prince Charming."

"I hope you're wrong, Johnny. I hope it's just a matter of time before she accepts me as I am. I hate to say it, but I need her. I need all of you -- my family. Some of you think that I deserted the Kennedys for my husband's family and country, but it's not true. I love you all, and I want to be on good terms with you, including Mother and Dad, but I also have to lead my own life in my own way. Is that asking too much?"

"I don't think so, but it's not that simple. Maybe in order to keep a family together we all have to sacrifice some of our individuality. In any case, Mother and Dad are hoping that you'll come home. And I don't mean for just a visit."

"I've been thinking of doing just that. I've been thinking about it for months. I can stay on here, of course, but it won't be the same now that Billy's gone. And since I did not produce an heir, I won't have much of a role in the Cavendish family. Andrew has become the new Marquess of Hartington, and he and Debo will someday become the Duke and Duchess of Devonshire. I will still be called Lady Hartington, but a widow without an heir is like a maiden aunt, a dependent on a small income. I'm too young to settle for that. Of course, I could buy a house in London and play the merry widow. I could lure prominant politicians and intellectuals to my salon and seduce the husbands of all the women I hate."

"You mean, you'd give up touch football on the lawn for the high life in London?"

"I might, but in the meantime the Season is upon us and the invitations are beginning to pour in. You have no idea how many people are waiting to see you."

"Tell me all about it."

"Well, there's Baby Carcano and her sister Chiquita, now married to Jakey Astor, and Virginia Sykes and, of course, Pat Wilson --"

"Ah, yes, the beautiful Patricia Wilson. Is it true that Joe was in love with her?"

"He hated to admit it, but I think he was. Anyhow, if you can behave yourself, I'll ring her up and see what we can arrange. Your friend Lannan can make a fourth."

"Incidentally, I hear you have a car now."

"What about it?"

"I'd like to borrow it. I've got to chase Winnie around for the Hearst people. You can come along if you want."

She beamed. "Are you sure?"

"Sure!" he said."Bring your camera. You might as well make yourself useful."

It was easy to become sentimentally attached to Kathleen's little Austin. It had all the charm of an arrogant puppy that did not know when to quit. Though it rattled and squeaked and its windshield wipers had given up, it carried on. Jack was at the wheel and there was a smile on his face as he raced up the King's Road, honked his way around Sloane Square and headed north on Sloane Street towards Hyde Park, where Churchill was scheduled to address an outdoor gathering. Kathleen glanced over her shoulder at Pat Lannan, who was folded into a back seat that was designed for a child or a dwarf. "Are you all right?" she said.

"I don't know," he said. "Can you live after your heart stops? Tell your brother that this is not a Grand Prix event." The car veered to the left and narrowly missed a taxi. Lannan's head disappeared and then bobbed up again. "Hey, Jack, keep to the left for Christ's sake. This is England."

"If you insist," he said. "I hear the whole bloody country is moving to the left."

"Which reminds me," said Kathleen. "I talked to Barbara Ward. She wants to take us over to Lambeth to see Herbert Morrison, the Secretary of the Labour Party."

"Terrific!" said Jack. "I could use an interview with him in the next piece I file for Hearst. Maybe Pat can record it."

"Sure!" said Lannan, "as long as we survive your lousy driving."

"My friend Hugh Fraser would also like to be recorded," said Kathleen. "He's running for a seat in Staffordshire. I promised him that we would pop up and take in one of his appearances at Stone or Stafford."

"Christ, that's a hundred and fifty miles from here," said Lannan.

"We'll take the train," she said.

"Good!" he said.

"And, oh yes, I also promised Alistair Forbes that we would look in on one of his campaign gatherings. He's a dear friend, a poor-as-a-churchmouse distant cousin of F.D.R."

"You've got more damned friends," said Lannan.

"Actually, he's more than just a friend. He says he's in love with me."

"Everybody in this country seems to be in love with you," said Jack.

"That's not my fault," she said. "I like Englishmen and they like me. I don't know why."

"What's wrong with us American men?" said Lannan.

"She thinks we're a bunch of fumblers and gropers," said Jack.

"I never said that."

"You did so!"

"Hey, keep to the left," shouted Lannan.

There was a sullen sky over the restless crowd that waited for Churchill to appear. The flags were limp on the platform and there was a sprinkling of hand-held signs, some of them featuring the V for Victory that had become the Prime Minister's trademark. It was not a colorful crowd. Wartime restrictions had kept their clothing drab and austere. A preliminary speaker droned on, applauded mainly by the men who sat on the platform behind him. After a while, there was a stirring to the right, and a path was cleared for Churchill and his modest entourage. He waved his hat to the crowd, revealing his bald head. He was greeted by a loud confusion of sounds: cheers, applause, questions, shouts of disapproval and even booing. The sounds were sustained not so much by enthusiasm as by conflicting attitudes.

"They seem to have mixed feeling about the old boy," said Lannan.

"I can't believe it," said Jack. "In the States we have the impression that he is the most beloved man in Britain. I certainly thought he was. In fact, I've already filed a story with my editor, in which I predict that he will be returned to office on the strength of his personal popularity, even if his party loses some seats."

"That may yet happen," said Kathleen, "but I wouln't bet the farm on it. The war in Europe has been over for a month now. It's been six years of sacrifice and the average person doesn't want to be told that there are more hard times coming. Somebody ought to tell Winnie to lay off the doom and gloom or he's liable to lose this election."

"You sound like your old man," said Jack.

"Maybe you will, too, when you become a politician."

"Kick's right," said Lannan. "You've got to promise them a rosy future or they won't vote for you."

"I'm not going to promise them anything that I can't deliver," said Jack.

Churchill waited in the dull light of the late afternoon, a short, round-shouldered man in a dark suit, a man of seventy who was suddenly slipping into history. Kathleen's eyes drifted to a sign that read *Our Time Has Come*. It gave her a sudden chill, though she had no idea whose time it was that had come.

When it was quiet enough to speak, the great man performed his miracle with the English language. There were some people in the crowed, no doubt, who applauded him for his brilliant syntax and imagery, and there were some who felt romantically attached to the old British Empire, but there were a lot more people who were disappointed because, in lieu of a plan for the future, all the old guy had to offer was a warning about Communism and the potential treachery of the Soviet Union.

Later, in a crowded and smoky pub, they talked about Churchill's chances of winning. "I wrote you about the swing to the left," said Kathleen. "Don't you remember? I wasn't making it up. All my political friends have been talking about it."

"Well, if it's true, then Churchill is doing the right thing," said Jack. "Communism is a menace to the free world, and it's his duty to say so."

"Come on, Jack," said Lannon. "Nobody in his right mind likes Communism, but anti-Communism is not enough of a political platform for this election. People want to hear about economic recovery, about the bright prospects for the working class. They are being told by the Labour Party that they spilled their blood to save the country and that they deserve a bigger share of the wealth than they had before the war. I wouldn't be at all surprised if the Conservatives lose. Maybe they would have been better off with Anthony Eden or some other younger leader."

"Poor Tony's got an ulcer," said Kathleen.

"Another Englishman hot for my sister's body," said Jack, lifting a lecherous eyebrow.

Their suite at Grovesnor House soon became a gathering place for their friends, especially Kathleen's promising young politicians. One day, as they lounged in the increasing disorder of the place, Pat Lannan said to her, "Where do these people all come from? I mean, how did you and your brother come to be so well connected? Your father wasn't exactly a popular ambassador."

"I think it's just easier to get a handle on English social life," said Kathleen. "It's just one big club, and anybody who matters is in it. Once you're accepted -- well, that's it. From the beginning they seemed to accept both of us. And then, of course, I married Billy Hartington, and Jack wrote a book about why England slept and almost lost the war. I don't know. I think we're both atuned to the way they do things here. Besides, I like the men and Jack likes the women."

And then, as if on cue, in walked Pat Wilson, looking more like a summer bride than a divorcee or a widow. "It's an absolutely fabulous day outside," she said. "What are all you bookworms doing in here?"

Jack was unshaven and barefooted and his wrinkled shirt-tails were hanging out. He stepped carefully over a heap of newspapers and Lannan's recording equipment and gave Pat a quick embrace. Kathleen watched them and wondered whether or not they had made love yet. She thought of it as something that was inevitable, not in spite of the fact that Pat had been his brother's lover, but because of it. And because they both were a bit reckless by nature about such things. At thirty-two Pat was in full bloom and dressed for the Season. Kathleen felt a moment of jealousy, but it passed when Pat kissed her and said, "Why don't we sneak away from these children and have a bite of lunch?"

"Can't do it," said Kathleen. "All sorts of people are coming over. Hugh Fraser is bringing his speech to be recorded. And William is coming over to talk to Jack, who has just finished reading his new play. They've become great friends." She was referring to William Douglas-Home, who had spent time in a mlitary prison because he had refused to order his men to attack a German-occupied French town from which the civilians had not been evacuated. During his year at Wakefield his only visitors had been Angela Laycock and Kathleen.

When Hugh and William arrived, Lannan was still working on his recording machine. Before he got the thing to work properly, two more people arrived. One of them was the brilliant young foreign editor of *The Economist* , Barbara Ward; the other was a tennis celebrity named Kay Stammers, with whom Jack had "connected" in a bar a few nights earlier.

Lannan finally triumphed over his machine. "Listen up," he shouted. "Hugh Fraser is going to read his speech now, and the rest of you can be the crowd. Try to sound interested and enthusiastic."

"Are we for him or against him?" said Jack.

"Shut up and cheer!" said Kathleen.

Pat Wilson eyed the tennis player. "Jack's latest conquest, I gather," she said to Kathleen.

"She doesn't mean a thing to him."

"I don't suppose any of us do, but he's still great fun to be with."

The London Season, sparked by the end of the war in Europe and by an early election, turned into a series of wild parties. At one such affair a young lord was rumored to have gambled away almost two hundred thousand pounds in a single night. The gossip columnists feasted on the exploits of the young aristocrats, and hardly a week went by without an engagement or a lavish wedding, one of the earliest of which made Sally Norton the wife of Bill Astor, Nancy's oldest son and heir to the estate. It seemed to Kathleen that almost everyone she knew in England and America had now found a mate, and she did not like being among those who had lost their husbands in the war. She was often invited to take part in gatherings that honored wounded veterans or the widows of those who had not returned, but now that the season had started, she could look forward to a few lively weekends in the country, accompanied by her handsome brother.

The weekend at Hatley Park, the estate recently acquired by Jakey and Chiquita Astor, promised to be tame and pleasant, a chance for everyone to see old friends. Jack had met Stella and Anna Carcano (Baby and Chiquita) on a trip to South America in 1941. Though he was only in Argentina for two weeks, he managed to carry on a passionate romance with Baby Carcano, the older of the two daughters of the Argentine ambassador to Vichy France. "She's going to be real happy to see you," said Kathleen, "especially since you're still a bachelor. She's been nuts about you for years."

"Yeah, these hot-blooded Catholic girls are very interesting," he said, "but they can also be very possessive."

"On the other hand, you wouldn't get any complaints from Mother and Daddy."

"Sometimes I think Dad was match-making when he sent me down to visit the Carcanos, a family with two beautiful daughters and a ranch the size of Rhode Island."

"You're going to have to reconsider your bachelorhood, sooner or later, Brother John, if you expect to get anywhere in politics."

"I suppose so," he said, "but in the meantime I might as well enjoy myself. Who else is going to be at this weekend shindig?"

"William for sure, who is still depressed because most of his friends have not forgiven him for following his conscience instead of his military orders; Nancy, maybe, who is depressed because she is about to lose her seat in the House of Commons;

186

and Sally Norton now Astor, who will be smiling like the old canary-eating cat."

The weekend was quiet but not boring. Nancy Astor lectured her family and friends on the evils of alcohol, and then, as if to prove that no one was perfect, she had an enormous drink, after which she bundled Kathleen to her bosom and consoled her once again for the loss of her husband. "Such a beautiful young man. Such a horrible war. And now the socialists are going to take over and dismantle the British Empire. I have a good mind to go back to America. Why don't we do that, Kick? Why don't we leave this bloody country to the Communists and go back to good old America?"

"I just got the same advice from my parents," said Kathleen. "My father is convinced that England has had it."

"Well, without me in the House of Commons, I really don't see any hope at all for the country."

There was plenty of amusing chatter, but Kathleen's conversation with William Douglas-Home was personal and serious. If he had had his way, she would have been his wife, and they would already have celebrated their fifth or sixth anniversary. As they walked in the garden he said, "Do you remember how, one day before the war, we walked in another garden? It was at Hever. And do you remember how, standing by the fountain, you promised to marry me?"

"Oh, William," she said, "you're so poetic. Even your memory is poetic. I didn't promise you anything of the sort."

"Then why did I have the impression that you did?"

"I don't know. I was probably either teasing you or flirting. Women are allowed to do that sort of thing. Besides, I was very young and not very serious about marriage. It was all just a lovely game when I was a debutante, and I suppose I broke some of the rules. But you were very sweet, and I was very impressed. We were all rather innocent in those day; now I think we're both a bit disillusioned. The war has made us bitter. It may take us a long time to recover, if we ever do. I believed in my marriage, and you believed in your act of conscience, but, in a way, we are both damaged people. I honestly don't know what I should do now."

"Neither do I," he said, "but it won't be politics. What I did was inexcusable, even though I was being true to myself. I realize now that when you are in the military you do not have the luxury of making independent moral distinctions. On the other hand, I'm glad I don't have the blood of those French civilians on my hands."

He had a tormented look on his face. She took him firmly by the arm, as if to lead him away from his dilemma. "Let's not think about it now," she said. "It's such a marvelous morning. Let's take a walk. Let's have a look at that donkey. Chiquita says it's perfectly safe to ride him."

"I've never been on a donkey," he said. "It sounds rather childish."

"It's good to do something childish once in a while," she said. "We all take ourselves too seriously."

In a few minutes they were laughing at the big-eyed beast and taking turns climbing on and jogging around the paddock.

Back at the house they had coffee, and through the window they could see Jack and Baby Carcano disappear through an arch in the tall hedges of the garden.

That night Kathleen called her brother "Don John" and teased him about his adventures. "You sure don't waste any time between women," she said. "From Pat Wilson to Kay Stammers to Baby Carcano. How will you ever find time to run for political office?"

188

"It'll take a tight schedule," he said with an arrogant smile.

"Don't you ever get serious about women?"

"My desire is serious."

"I'm talking about love."

"Women are always talking about love. I think they invented the idea to hang on to their men. And somebody -- Nietzsche, I think -- said that a man can never possess a woman's soul. What I really believe, Kick, is that it is man's nature to be free, and that it is woman's nature to try to put an end to that freedom."

"Not all men and women are alike."

"No two bananas or grapefruits are either, if you look at them closely enough. I personally think that women are more attractive from a certain distance. Sex is risky for men because it gives women ideas."

"Is that why you've always got one foot out the door?"

"I suppose so. But, don't worry, sooner or later I'm going to have to settle down if I want to get anywhere in politics."

"And what sort of a wife do you imagine you will have when you settle down?"

"Catholic,"I suppose. "Healthy and well educated. From a good family. And willing to accept certain conditions."

"Such as?"

"She will have to agree to respect my privacy and my freedom ."

"Sounds like the old song: 'I want a girl, just like the girl who married dear old Dad.' "

"That's not what I had in mind."

"But that's what you'll get if you can't treat a woman like a human being."

"It doesn't have to be that old Irish-Catholic battle between the men and the women, does it? Can't a woman allow a man his freedom without hating him?"

Kathleen frowned for a moment. "Do you really think she hates him?"

"I don't know. I can't figure her out. I guess she resigned herself to the situation years ago and has just been doing her duty every since. That's what I mean by the Irish-Catholic mentality. There's a lot of hostility in the marriages, especially in the women. Maybe because of all the children they have been forced to bear."

"They can blame the Church for that. The husbands are only doing what comes naturally."

"You sound like Inga. She was the only woman who ever agreed with me on this subject. Maybe I should have married her."

"That would really have been a kamikaze marriage. Can you imagine running for political office with a wife who was twice divorced and suspected of being a spy?"

He laughed. "I guess what I need is a woman like you, Kick. Witty and liberated -- a good sport."

"Forget it, Johnny," she said. "If I were married to you, I wouldn't treat you the way a sister does. But I might let you have a little fun now and then."

"That's what I call a good sport! Maybe that's why so many guys fall in love with you. You had your pick before the war, and even now --"

She stopped him with a glance. "Don't say it, Johnny. I'm not ready to talk about getting married again."

"It's been almost a year."

"I know, but I still have to sort things out. I thought at first I would just stay here indefinitely, but now I'm not sure. Maybe I should go back to the States, rejoin the family, make a life."

"That's what everybody back home hopes you will do."

"I know! Mother and Dad keep hammering away. In every letter and phone call they remind me that I am an American and a Kennedy. Maybe they're right. I don't know. What do you think I should do?"

"I can't tell you what to do, Kick, but, personally, I can't imagine living out my life in a foreign country, no matter how much I like to travel. I'd always feel like an expatriate, never completely a part of the place. You may not feel that way now, but in the long run you might. And by then it might be impossible for you to come back and start again. If I were you, I'd give America another try. You still have a lot going for you there, and you're still young."

"You know, Johnny, for a guy who is so reckless and irresponsible, you sometimes make a lot of sense."

Baby Carcano suddenly appeared at the terrace door, as though she were silently presenting herself to Jack. "The call of the wild," whispered Kathleen. Jack smiled and shrugged his shoulders apologetically and then was gone.

CHAPTER THIRTEEN

"Here's to peace and prosperity," said Pat Wilson, "or whatever the hell they've promised us now that the war is over."

"To whatever the hell," said Kathleen. Their champagne glasses touched with a clink over their table at the Dorchester. Though the war in the Pacific had suddenly ended with the dropping of the atomic bomb, they were both feeling a bit nostalgic and moody in the wake of Jack's departure. He had taken off for the States two weeks earlier, a few hours before the blast that demolished Hiroshima, He had been to Ireland and Paris, where he joined James Forrestal, the Secretary of the Navy, who was on his way to a summit meeting in Potsdam, Germany. It was an opportunity arranged by his father, but it was abbreviated by a recurrence of old ailments that sent him back to a London hospital, and from there to America.

"What exactly is wrong with that brother of yours?" said Pat. There was a note of impatience in her voice, as though she were talking about one of her children. "He always seems to be ailing from something or other."

"Nobody knows for sure," said Kathleen. "Bad back, bad stomach, sudden bouts of fever."

"I don't usually like men who are sickly, but there's something special about Jack."

"Is it his sense of humor, or should I guess again?"

"Now, now, Kickie, it's a bit early in the day for playing games. I found Jack very amusing and very handsome, but a bit boyish otherwise. It was great fun being seen in public with him, and I am sure he will be very successful in politics, but in private he's a bit strange and aloof. I don't know exactly how to explain it. He's the man that no woman will ever get. Maybe that's why we're all fascinated by him. In the long run, however, most of us marry bankers and other more reliable types."

"I suppose Joe was more reliable."

"Under the right circumstances, I think he would have been quite devoted. I might even have taken a chance with him, but that's all water under the bridge, and life goes on."

"Do you think you'll ever marry again?"

"I don't know. It's always possible for a woman to explain two husbands, but a woman with three husbands is liable to be considered frivolous."

"Well," said Kathleen, "you do give the impression sometimes of not being very serious about life."

"Do I? That's odd. I sometimes feel that life is not very serious about *me* . But let's not talk about men, darling; let's talk about you. What is all this nonsense about giving up and going home?"

"It's only for a visit. I promised to go in April and put it off until the summer, and now the summer is almost over. Sooner or later I have to go."

"Oh, come on Kick, you know it's not just a visit. Your family will do everything in their power to get you to stay. And they may succeed. You're very vulnerable right now."

"I know, so I've decided to buy a house. There's this lovely little place in Smith Square."

Pat smiled, her lipstick moist with wine. "How marvelous! When can I see it?" She lifted her glass.

"This afternoon, if you've got time."

"I certainly do, and here's to wonderful times in Smith Square. Perhaps you're one of us, after all."

It was October before the house business was setttled and she gave in to the constant urging of her family. By then she was sure that they had ulterior motives for wanting to see her, motives perhaps that went even beyond her mother's obvious need to exert her power over her children.

At the airport she gave a brief statement to the reporters who monitored the movements of newsworthy people. She was going home for a visit. It was that simple. No, she was not leaving England for good, and she was not at odds with the Duke and Duchess of Devonshire. No, she was not planning to remarry. And no, her trip had nothing to do with her brother's political career.

Aboard the plane it was a relief to sink into anonymity. She had been away for over a year, and, as the Pan American DC-4 headed out to sea over a bank of clouds, she tried to picture her family and wondered how much they had changed. Bobby was trying to make his mark at Harvard in the shadow of two older brothers, both of whom were war heroes. Little Jean was suddenly a college girl, a freshman at Manhattanville, with a roommate namd Ethel Skakel. Pat had just graduated from Rosemont, and Eunice was working for the State Department in Washington. They all seemed to be moving ahead, spurred on by the family conviction that the Kennedys were winners and had to excel. They would all, of course, get behind Jack as soon as his campaign began. The idea excited her, and she wondered where she might fit into that effort. Her father still dreamed of having a son in the White House, but she couldn't think that far ahead, and she couldn't honestly imagine her skinny, lecherous, twenty-eight-year-old brother as President, even if she squinted the eyes of her mind.

Her father was at LaGuardia Airport to meet her, beaming like his old self, hugging her for the cameras, and telling the reporters that his daughter had come home to stay after her wartime service with the Red Cross in battle-scarred London. "Don't overdo it, Dad," she said, stiffening in his embrace and then turning to confront the photographers

194

with a smile. The reporters asked her questions, which her father answered for her, as though she were a child.

In the car she was angry at him. "Why did you tell them that I was home to stay?"

"Well, aren't you?" he said.

"It's only a visit. I haven't made up my mind about anything else."

"Gee, kid, I'm sorry. Your mother and Johnny both gave me the impression that you were thinking of coming home for good now that your husband's dead. I mean, you haven't got any real family over there. What's the point --"

"The point is that I like living in London, and I told my friends and in-laws and the press that I was only going to the States for a family visit."

"All right, all right, so maybe I jumped the gun, but don't you realize how important it is to give the public the impression that we are a happy and united family, that whatever differences we had over your marriage have now been reconciled? We owe it to Johnny to keep up appearances. That boy is going to make history."

She was hardly unpacked in Hyannis Port before the perpetual motion machine that was her family swallowed her up. She was swept off to football games and reunions, to luncheons and fund-raising dinners for veterans and the Red Cross, to the theater and movies and shopping adventures in New York. With Jack about to toss his hat into the political arena, her father's blood was up, and there were frequent visits from the old warhorses of Boston, including her grandfather Honey Fitz, who, at eighty-two, was still ready to give a speech or sing endless choruses of "Sweet Adeline." She had very little time to herself and no one with whom she could carry on a personal conversation. When she was feeling depressed or confused she would call her old friend Charlotte McDonnell Harris in Rye, New York.

When John White called to say that he was working for Polaroid in Boston, she was delighted. The moment she heard his voice she could tell that he had not changed a bit. "There's no point in my coming out there," he said. "Your father hates my guts. So why don't you come into town?"

At lunch she noticed that he even looked the same, and then she realized with a jolt that it was only two and a half years ago that she had left her job at the *Times -Herald* and gone off to London to work for the Red Cross. "God," she said, "so much has happened in the past few years that it seems like forever since our newspaper days."

"There's been a war," he said. "It does funny things to your sense of time."

"It's done funny things to my sense of everything," she said. "When I am in England, America seems to fade into a dream of childhood, one of those nasty dreams in which there is a nagging riddle that can't be solved. And when I am here, England is the dream."

"You seem to be having trouble staying in touch with reality," he said. "If you would like to lie down under the table, perhaps we can get to the root of the problem."

She laughed, and, suddenly, it was as if no time at all had passed and nothing seemed very serious. She remembered him playing fortune teller with a towel wrapped around his head in the basement apartment he called "the cave." He was always like that, always turning life into a joke. Perhaps that was why they had never become lovers, she thought, in spite of the feeling of closeness that made them such good friends. "Is it true that you've broken off your engagement to Nancy Hoguet?" she said.

"Yeah," he said. "I didn't mind being engaged to her, but as soon as I was discharged from the service she expected me to marry her. I guess I got cold feet. It was fun while it lasted.We exchanged some sizzling letters. Maybe all love affairs should be conducted by mail."

Kathleen laughed. "I hope you never get serious, John," she said. "It will make you considerably less charming."

They talked their way through a bottle of wine, remembering old friends and adventures. She described her dilemma and asked him what he thought she should do.

"My advice to you, Lady Hartington," he said, "is to go back to England and stay there. The problem between you and your parents is never going to be resolved. Stop coming home to fiddle with the knots." For a moment he actually looked serious, but then he broke into a smile and said, "You can take me with you if you want. I always thought I'd make a great court jester."

For weeks she had been hoping to talk with Jack privately, but he was always off somewhere or busy with other people. At last there was an opportunity and she did not let it go by.

It was a mild early-November day. There was touch football on the lawn. Bobby was home for the weekend, and some local friends had stopped by looking for a game. Eunice and Jean and Teddy joined in, but Jack watched from a wicker chair on the porch. Kathleen came in from a long walk on the beach and sat down next to him. "Why aren't you out there playing ball?" she said.

"I've got a bad back," he said. "What's your excuse?"

With a toss of her head and an affected British accent she said, "Oh, I've outgrown all that childish nonsense, darling. Since I've been living in England I've taken up more sophisticated pursuits."

"Like what?" he said, playing her little game.

"Like donkey-riding, pub-crawling, and back-stabbing," she said, removing her kerchief and unbuttoning her tweed riding jacket.

He laughed, and then, for a moment, seemed caught up in the action on the lawn.

"Where are Mother and Dad?" she said.

"They went off in a bit of a huff -- in separate directions, of course. Dad's probably up in his study keeping an eye on his tribe, and Mother's probably gone off to church to scold God for not being more cooperative."

"What were they arguing about this time?"

"About you, of course."

She blushed visibly. "And what did they have to say?"

"Dad was saying how glad he was to have you back, and how important it was for you to get your picture in the papers with the rest of us, so that the world could see what a big, happy, wonderful family we are. And Mother was hoping that you would not beome involved in my election campaign. In fact, she thought it would be a good idea for you to go on a religious retreat to purge yourself of arrogance and protestant contamination. She thinks that you have been very rude to her and that you might be a political liability."

There was a flash of anger in her eyes. "And what do you think, Johnny? Do you think I'm a liability?"

"Of course not, Kick. I saw you charming those English politicians. You'll always be popular, wherever you go. I don't think anybody is going to make an issue of your marriage. After all, you married the man you loved, and he died in the war as a hero. If a few idiots have a problem with that, they can vote for the other guy. I'll win without them."

"Thanks, Johnny. I knew you would say that, but maybe it would be better if I stayed away."

"Why?"

198

"Because no matter what you think, you won't be able to change their minds. Daddy treats me like a PR opportunity, and Mother has never really forgiven me. My marriage to Billy was politically inconvenient as well as a religious embarassment. Maybe they're right. Maybe I am a liability, and perhaps Mother has good reasons not to forgive me. After all, I am disobedient and stubborn and arrogant, and, God forgive me, sometimes I hate her."

"But not really," he said. "I think I know how you feel."

"No, not really," she said in a lowered voice. "I want her love, but, Christ, what does one have to do to get it?"

Suddenly, the game on the lawn broke up, and a herd of young people came galloping toward the porch.

She brooded in her room for half the night before deciding to confront her mother. She did not know when or where, but, sooner or later, they had to have an honest conversation. Meanwhile, the level of activity continued to increase as Jack's political circle expanded to include old college and Navy connections, as well as experts recommended by his father, who took it upon himself to enlist the services of a public relations firm.

It was like old times for Rose, who once stood beside her father on campaign platforms because her mother was too shy to appear in public. Now it was her bachelor son who needed a woman to stand beside him, and the attention she received made her seem younger and more lively. Kathleen admitted to herself, but to no one else, that she was jealous. She remembered how she was forced to remain in the background when Billy made his bid for a seat in the House of Commons, and now it was happening again.

Her involvement in her son's political career sent Rose to the fashionable shops of New York to refurbish her already elaborate wardrobe. With the end of the war there came dramatic changes in style, and she was determined to be up-to-date. Kathleen accompanied her on one of these shopping trips, and, as usual, they stayed at the Plaza Hotel.

It was here one night that Kathleen, breathless with anxiety, said to her mother, "Why are you excluding me from everything that has to do with Jack's campaign?"

Rose was taken aback, but, still glowing with the exitement of the day, she seemed genuinely affectionate. "Oh, my poor child," she said, "you mustn't feel that way."

"But Eunice is quitting her job in Washington to help out, and you've got plans for everyone else in the family except me. How do you expect me to feel?"

"You'll be doing your bit by showing the world that you are once again a part of this family, but we don't want you to do anything that will remind people of your past. Don't you understand?"

"No, Mother, I don't understand. I have a past and I am not ashamed of it. I did nothing wrong."

The glow disappeared from Rose's face. "My dear girl," she said, "how can you stand there and insist that you did nothing wrong when you deserted your family in wartime, disregarded the feelings and convictions of your parents, violated your religion, and jeopardized your brother's political career?"

"Johnny was not in politics at the time."

"I was not thinking of him; I was thinking of Joe."

"Joe knew what the score was and he encouraged me to follow my heart. If he were here and running for political office, he wouldn't hide me in the closet."

"We're not trying to hide you in the closet. We want you to be seen as a good Catholic young woman who is loyal to her family. Why should we remind people of your wartime adventures and your connection with an English family that for hundreds of years denied the Irish their independence. From the time I was a little girl I have heard the story of the assassination of Lord Frederick Cavendish in Phoenix Park. Billy's grandfather was his brother, and Billy's father was a Freemason, and Freemasonry was condemned by the Church. Perhaps you are too young to know all these things. Young people have a way of losing touch with their heritage."

"Since when are you and Dad such Irish patriots?"

"I'll thank you not to use that tone of voice with me, young lady. Now just you stop for a minute and think about things. As your mother, did I not give you my love and my best advice? I was not trying to make you unhappy, Kathleen; I was trying to prevent this sort of situation."

"I'm sorry, Mother. I know I was disobedient and all that, but when are you going to forgive me and forget the past?"

"That's exactly what I've been trying to do, but you don't make it easy. You've made your confession and your holy communion, but I'm not convinced that it was a true confession. And if it was not, then I fear for your immortal soul. For God's sake, when are you going to come to your senses? When are you going to put the needs of your family before your own selfish desires? I did. Why shouldn't you? I gave up things. Plenty of things. I have devoted my life to this family, and all I get from you is this -- this seething resentment."

Kathleen felt a surge of tears but she held them back because it would be a sign of defeat. She took a deep breath and walked across the room. Then she turned around and said,"I'm sorry. I didn't mean to get carried away, and I didn't mean to suggest that you have not been a good mother. I guess I was just upset because I was being left out." She took a step forward to approach her mother. She waited, but Rose did not move towards her. She simply composed herself and forced a thin smile.

"All right, my dear," she said. "And now that you've gotten a few things off your chest, perhaps the air will be clearer and we will be able get on with the things that we have to do. Why don't you get some sleep? I'm sure that in the morning we will be friends again."

Kathleen nodded and went to her room. And there, when the light was out and everything was quiet, she allowed herself the luxury of tears.

The next day she got up early and went for a long walk alone. New York looked wonderful in the crisp autumn air and sharp sunlight. It was alive with post-war activity and optimism. The shops were full, and the "new look" designs of Chistian Dior were all the rage, a lavish rebellion against wartime austerity.

She walked south on Fifth Avenue from the Plaza to the Waldorf. She had gone that way often as a child when the whole family was taken to the city. Until she was older, she never thought there was anything odd about her father and mother being at separate hotels. She remembered those days in the pre-Christmas season as times of dazzling lights and crowded shops and rides on the double-decker Fifth Avenue bus that went uptown along Central Park.

By the time she got back to the Plaza she had decided to return to New York on her own. She had to get out of her parents' house, and a prolonged visit to New York would be just the thing. She had done it often enough in the past, and it would not seem unusual to anyone, except perhaps her mother. When she told her, however, her mother surprised her with a smile of approval and no reference to their recent disagreement. "An excellent idea," she said. "It will do you good. You have a lot of friends in New York that you haven't seen in a long time." Afterward she wondered about her mother's reaction, and finally decided that she considered it a good solution to an awkward situation.

The next time she called her friend Charlotte, Kathleen was at the Chatham Hotel. "I just couldn't take it anymore," she said. "I had to get out."

"How did your mother feel about that?" said Charlotte.

"I guess she'd rather see me in a convent, but New York will do. I really couldn't tell whether or not her feelings were hurt. Since that argument at the Plaza we've both been rather polite and cautious with one another. We smile a lot. She probably doesn't want to say anything provocative at this point because she's afraid I might just go back to England."

"I guess you are going back, then, sooner or later."

"Yes, but for how long depends on certain things."

"Does that mean you've got someone special there?" said Charlotte.

"In England? No, just friends."

"What about New York? Anyone interesting?"

"What makes you think that I am looking for someone interesting or special, Mrs. Knowitall?"

"Because I'm just as Catholic as you are, and we were all brought up to think about our immortal souls and finding a husband."

"I'm tired of thinking about my immortal soul," said Kathleen.

"Ah, so who is he? Come on, confess. Is it anyone I know?"

She hesitated. "Do you remember Winston Frost?"

"Of course. He was that handsome friend of John White's."

"They went to college together," said Kathleen.

"His name pops up from time to time. He's a cafe society regular from an old Virginia family that lost their money. I remember him as tall and blonde with a charming smile. About thirty-five."

"That's right. He's a lawyer, distantly related to Page Huidekoper. I can't get too serious about him, but he's great fun to be with, and he says he's crazy about me."

"Aren't they all? What kind of perfume do you wear anyway? I'd like to order some."

Kathleen laughed and fell into her adopted accent. "Charlotte, darling, you're a married woman. You can stop worrying about being seductive."

"You know, Kick, that's the first time I've heard you laugh since you got back from England. I suppose we can thank Winston for that."

"Oh, he's amusing enough, but it's really being in New York on my own. It makes me feel giddy, as if I've leapt over the convent wall or something. Anyhow, do come in for lunch or whatever, and if you bring Richard we'll make it a party."

"With Winston, you mean?"

"Why not?"

Staying away was not exactly an act of vengeance on Kathleen's part, but she took a certain amount of secret pleasure in feeling that her mother might think it was. Rose responded by calling her frequently to describe in detail every reception and speech in Jack's campaign. One day she said, "In the old days, you know, they wanted me up on the platform, but they didn't want me to say anything. I suppose they thought it was not suitable behavior for a young woman. Politics was all men and cigar smoke. The other day at the VFW hall in

Brighton I gave a little talk, and, frankly, I think I got more applause than John. Sometimes I think he's a bit too serious."

In December she failed to show up for the commissioning of the destroyer that was to be called the *Joseph P. Kennedy Jr.* Young Jean was enlisted to do the honors. Her father was annoyed at her for missing the event, though he and Jack were basking in the sun in Palm Beach and also missed it.

During the Christmas holidays, her father took her aside and said bluntly: "I don't like this guy Winston Frost who you've been seeing in New York. I hear he's a playboy who likes to associate with women who have money."

Kathleen felt as though she had been punched by a truck driver. There was nothing gentle or understanding in her father's tone, even when he said, "I'm thinking of you, kid. Do yourself a favor and drop him before things go too far."

After the shock came anger. "How can you talk like that?" she said. "You don't even know him."

"Oh, I know him all right. I know his type. He's a smooth-talking son of a bitch with fancy manners and no money. I checked him out."

"Who did you call, the F.B.I.?"

"I don't need the F.B.I. The guy's got a reputation, and it's not all good. He spends a lot of time in night clubs."

"He's a bachelor. He likes to go out at night. Besides, he goes to the best clubs, The Stork and The Twenty One. He knows a lot of important people, and they seem to like him very much."

"I suppose the horses like him too. I hear he spends a lot of time at the race track."

"He comes from Virginia. It's an old tradition and he's very knowledgeable. I've been to the races with him. It's great fun."

Her father grumbled and relented. "Well, I said what I had to say. The last thing we need in this family is another problem marriage."

"I'm not planning to marry anybody. I have lots of friends in New York, and some of them are men. I'm twenty-five years old. I've been married and widowed. I'm not your little girl anymore."

"Yes you are," he said. "You'll always be my little girl." And then he gave her a kiss, for which there was no refutation.

When she saw Winston Frost again she could not keep herself from thinking about her father's comments. She looked at him across their table at *Le Valois* and wondered whether or not he was too good to be true. He had the fine features of an English aristocrat and the shoulders of a fashion model, on whom anything would look chic and expensive. He seemed to belong to a world of candlelight and champagne. The appreciative glances of other women had never displeased her. She took them, in fact, as compliments. But now, with the worm of suspicion nibbling at her heart, she heard herself say, "I love it when other women look at you, and I hope they die of envy, but how have you managed to ecape them all these years?"

He smiled disarmingly. "You know, I was wondering when you were going to get around to asking me that. Practically every woman I have ever been out with has wanted to know why I'm not married. It makes me feel a bit like husband material instead of a human being. My usual answer is that I have not found the right woman, which is a terrible cliche, but, in my case, absolutely true. But I have a more practical reason. My family doesn't have any money. Well, not the sort of money they used to have. And I like to live well, as you know. It's taking me time to establish myself. If I marry a wealthy woman, I'm probably going to be accused of living off her, and I'll be damned if I'm going to put myself in that position. But I have some good opportunities now, and I am sure that, in due time, I'll have something substantial to offer. And when I do, darling, you will be the first to know."

Her suspicions dissolved, and she reached across the table and touched his hand.

In the months that turned late winter into early spring, she grew accustomed to him, and though she dared not call it *love* , she felt more at ease with him than she had ever felt with any man except her husband. She trusted him, and he did not take advantage of her moments of weakness. She was glad that neither of them felt any urgency about marriage, though the possibiity assured her that he was honest. And he had given her the weapons to defend him against the telephone assaults of her parents. They called constantly to warn her that her friend was a notorious playboy, and she fended them off with the argument that appearances were deceiving. He was misunderstood by people who did not know him as well as she did, she said. And, in any case, she was not ready to marry again.

But then one day her father called to say that he had talked to his friend Walter Winchell, who had provided him with proof positive of Winston's duplicity. "He is being kept by a woman whose name I don't even dare to mention on the telephone, but I will give it to you when I see you, which I hope will be soon."

Kathleen was plunged into confusion. She struggled to deny her father's accusations, but she knew him well enough to know that this time he was probably right. There was that certain hateful note of triumph in his voice. In tears she called Charlotte to tell her what had happened. "I know it's not true," she said. "I don't want it to be true. He's not a playboy. He explained everything months ago. There are no other women in his life."

207

"How do you know?" said Charlotte.

"I just know!"

"Why don't you just ask him bluntly?

"I can't do that. If I ask him, it will mean that I don't trust him. And I want to. If I can't trust him, then it will never work. I believed him. I believed every word he said. Oh, God! I don't know what to do. Why are people so bloody awful?"

"Why don't you get the name of the woman your father is referring to?"

"Because if I ask for it, he will know that he's beaten me. And I don't want to give him that satisfaction."

"So what are you going to do?"

"I don't know. I just want to disappear. I just want to pack up and leave. I have a house in London. I have friends I can trust. I have Billy's family. They've been very kind to me, very understanding. Why can't my own parents trust me? What do they want from me anyway?"

"Oh, you poor darling! Why don't you come up here for a few days? It will give you time to think."

"That's very sweet of you, but if I think about it anymore, it'll drive me nuts. I've just got to clear out."

Charlotte hesitated. "Maybe you're right," she said. "Maybe that's the best thing to do under the circumstances. But how sad it is! How cruel!"

Kathleen's voice faded into resignation. "The same old bloody tune," she said. "Only the words are different."

CHAPTER FOURTEEN

Her charming little townhouse at 4 Smith Square was waiting for her when she returned to London. The moment she set foot in it she knew that she had done the right thing. Her flight from America and her family was not a reckless impulse. She was simply coming home. Though she had never really settled into the white Georgian house with its small but cheerful rooms, she suddenly realized that it was perfect for her and that, above all, it was *hers* . She savored the idea: her house, her very own house! And she had a life of her own to go with it. She was Lady Hartington, the widow of a war hero and the daughter-in-law of the Duke and Duchess of Devonshire. In America she was nothing -- a naughty little girl who was an embarrassment to her parents. Even now she could hear them *explaining* her to their friends.

By the time Nancy Astor came around to see her she had a number of new acquisitions to show off -- antiques and works of art, silver and porcelain -- some of them on loan from Chatsworth, some of them purchased at recent auctions. Nancy paused at an exquisite tea and coffee set. "If this is what I think it is," she said, "it must have cost you a pretty penny."

"The price was not pretty, but I had to have it."

"I know how you feel, my dear. I heard there was a Chamberlain's Worcester set at Christie's that went for nearly a thousand pounds."

"Yes, I know. This is it."

"Oh my, we have been naughty, haven't we?"

"It's a shameful luxury in a time of austerity, but I couldn't resist."

"Nonsense, dear girl. The war is over. The Labour Party is in power. Let Mr. Attlee worry about austerity. I think you have a right to pamper yourself a bit after all you've been through. You've done an absolutely marvelous job on the house. I'm sure you'll be very happy here. There's nothing like a house to settle a woman's emotions and organize her time. And what a lovely location you have. Just a few minutes from the Houses of Parliament. You'll have Hugh Fraser and all those other young MPs dropping in. They say that a house is never really furnished until there's a man in it, but few of them prove to be more interesting than a Hepplewhite chair. So be careful, Kathleen. Young, attractive widows excite the interest of married men, and inspire suspicion in married women."

While Kathleen was settling into her house and trying on new clothes that would suit her new image, the outside world seemed to be doing, more or less, the same thing, rearranging its global furniture and absorbing new ideas. Her friends were full of talk and post-war politics. They argued about the dismantling of the British Empire and about Churchill's new crusade against Communism. In a speech in Missouri he said, "an iron curtain has descended across the continent." His conservative friends on both sides of the Atlantic picked up the phrase and condemned the Russians as ruthless aggressors. Released from wartime restrictions, workers everywhere went on strike. They shut down coal mines and steel mills, railroads and docks.

"The whole bloody world is moving to the left," said Evelyn Waugh at one of Kathleen's dinner parties. "The barbarians are at the gates."

"You mustn't let your gardener hear you talk that way," said Pamela Churchill. "You might wind up pruning your own roses." She was twenty-six years old and six months into her divorce from Randolph Churchill, Winston's only son. She was as famous for her beauty as Randolph was for his drinking and his abusive behavior. Everybody loved her and nobody loved poor Randolph.

It was May, and this dinner party was Kathleen's modest contribution to the celebrations that marked the first anniversary of the end of the war in Europe. She had taken seriously the advice of Lady Astor, who had said on her first visit, "Now that you have this house, my dear, you must think about entertaining. It's not Clivedon, of course, but you have some very interesting friends and you might become the charming hostess of a lively salon. You don't want to be merely a prominant war widow, appearing at endless fund-raising affairs for crippled veterans."

Kathleen needed only a cook and a housekeeper, since the house in Smith Square was not very large. On this occasion there were only eight people for dinner, "a good number for conversation," Nancy had told her. "Larger groups tend to break up into smaller groups, which is a bit frustrating for those of us who are compulsive orators." Nancy also said that she hoped to be invited to dinner sometime, but only if there were not too many Catholic guests. "I know you have a lot of Catholic friends," she said, "and when I find myself surrounded by them I tend to get a bit hostile."

Nancy was not there the evening that Laura and Evelyn Waugh came to dinner, along with David and Sissy Ormsby-Gore. They were members of an influential circle of Roman Catholics that now claimed Kathleen as a regular, but she was careful not to be swallowed up by them. Her other guests that night were Pamela Churchill, Hugh Fraser and Richard Wood, the son of Lord Halifax. It was no secret that Richard was courting Kathleen, in spite of the fact that he had lost both legs in the war. He got about awkwardly with a cane, but once he was seated at the dinner table one tended to forget all that. He was intelligent and witty, the rich and

211

lively sort of Englishman Kathleen might very well have married at this point in her life.

"To the Empire," said Evelyn Waugh, washing down epigrams with his wine. "To India. It's been a bit like having Helen of Troy as a mistress. Sooner or later, you know that her own people will come and take her away, and maybe even kill you in the process."

"It's sad," said David. "I'm afraid the world changes, and at a time like this it changes very rapidly. Colonialism is out; Communism is in."

"Yes, but Communism will create the next colonial empire," said Waugh. "And at the heart of it will be Russia, China, and India, with more than half the population of the world. England will be a little man in a bowler hat standing in the rain waiting for a bus."

"My brother Jack agrees with you," said Kathleen. "He's standing for a seat in our House of Representatives, and he rides around like Paul Revere, warning people about Communism."

"Then he's bound to win his election," said Hugh Fraser. "It's the perfect formula. First you frighten the people and then you offer to save them from the dragon. In the real world, however, things are a lot less theatrical. We've got a lot of mundane problems to solve, such as housing and health care."

Before long the big questions of the post-war world seemed too immense to deal with in such a modest diningroom, and the talk inevitably turned to matters more personal -- to wartime anecdotes and social gossip. "When Lieutenant Colonel Robert Laycock was recruiting officers for a commando unit," said Waugh. "quite a few of us decided to sign on, including Randolph, Peter Beatty, Philip Dunn, and King Dandy himself, Peter Fitzwilliam. The White's Club crowd, unfortunately, turned the unit into a refuge for playboy soldiers. The indolence and ignorance of the officers was remarkable. When they were in training at Largs on the Scottish coast, some of them stayed at the Marine Hotel, where they were joined by their wives or girlfriends. It was one long party for all of them. They blundered through their training exercises like a bunch of irresponsible schoolboys. One night Peter Beatty was instructed to bring his landing craft ashore at three o'clock in the morning. He never showed up. When he was asked why, he said, 'It was dark. I couldn't see my watch.' Incredible! Absolutely incredible!" He looked across the table at Pamela. "Those friends of Randolph were all scum. And the worst of the lot was Fitzwilliam, because he was so bloody charming. He could talk anybody into doing anything. They all adored him. He was their hero."

"Randolph's judgment was at its worst when it came to picking friends," said Pamela.

Kathleen remembered listening to other stories about the eighth Earl Fitzwilliam, but she couldn't remember actually meeting him. Billy's brother Andrew was another of his admirers. His name came up frequently in connection with horse racing. And hadn't she, in fact, just been asked by Olive Fitzwilliam to chair the committee for a ball honoring the Commandos? She would have to check the stationery again.

Pamela lingered after the other guests left, as though she had something special that she wanted to talk about. She was quite beautiful, sitting there in the soft light, sipping her wine meditatively, her lips red and moist. Kathleen had always admired her for the way she charged into life, even though she had to disapprove of her complicated affairs with men. Her wartime affair with Ed Murrow had finally come to an end in New York, when he told her that he could not give up his family for her. But then there was Averell Harriman, who had just arrived in London to replace Gil Winant as the American ambassador. Pamela's involvement with him went back to 1941. Even her incidental lovers had excellent credentials. To Kathleen she seemed worldly and daring, while she herself held back, attracting men but always keeping them at a slight distance.

"Well, Miss Pamela Digby," Kathleen said, "what's going on now in that wild, wild life of yours?"

"Please don't call me that. It's a horrible name. It has a kind of damp smell about it, don't you think? Like an old house in Dorset after a long rain."

"You weren't upset by Evelyn's nasty remarks about Randolph, were you?"

"Not at all, but sometimes I feel sorry for the silly old sot. I should never have married him. I was only nineteen. He proposed to me the day after meeting me for the first time. I suspect that he was mainly interested in a broodmare to produce an heir. And maybe I was looking for a passport to a new life, but things always turn out to be more complicated than they seem."

"That's all water under the bridge," said Kathleen. "The last time I saw you, you were all excited because Averell was back in London, and it would be like old times."

"Well, since then, his wife Marie has decided to close her gallery in New York and join him after the summer."

"But she's got a life of her own. They've been more or less separated for some time."

"It's the embassy people. They want her here. They're afraid that there's going to be a scandal now that I'm divorced and seeing Averell more openly."

Kathleen frowned. "You wouldn't actually marry him, would you -- I mean, if he were free?"

"Why not? We get along very well. I think he's a wonderful man."

"But he's thirty years older than you."

214

"Twenty-nine!" she said, and they both suddenly laughed. Anyhow, I talked to Lord Beaverbrook -- Max. He said he'd give me a job in the New York office of the *Daily Express* if I wanted to clear out. He thought it might be the smart thing to do."

Katheen refilled their glasses and shook her head. "You know, Pam, I really envy you sometimes because your life is so romantic, so unconventional, but I don't think I could deal with your probems. Mine are much more ordinary."

"Darling, there is only one problem, and we all have it. A woman needs a husband."

"Yes, but I'm trying to find my own, not somebody else's."

Again they laughed, and the color in their cheeks confirmed the truth in the wine.

"So, who will it be, my little chickadee?" said Pamela. "Not Richard Wood, I hope."

"In spite of the obvious problem, it's not completely out of the question. He's intelligent, witty, rich, and English."

"Kathleen, what are you thinking? I hate to sound cruel, but the man has no legs!"

"It may not matter as much to me as it does to you. I'm not as interested in -- in *physical* things as you are."

"What's the matter, honey? Jesuits got your tongue? The word is *sex*. God, you can't even say it. I hope you can do it. Someday you're going to find out what I'm talking about, and if you're married to Richard, you're going to wish you weren't."

Later, lying alone in bed, Kathleen thought about what Pamela had said. She was right, of course. It was all this business of being a noble war widow that was getting in the way. Confronting herself in the night, she had to admit that personal sacrifice was not her cup of tea. Poor Richard! At her request he had struggled through the two volumes of Fulton J. Sheehan's *Apologetics and*

Catholic Doctrine only to decide that he could never, in all good conscience, become a convert, though he would oblige the church by allowing his children to be raised as Catholics should he and Kathleen ever decide to marry. At the time, she thought she was disappointed, but now she felt relieved.

The ball to honor the Commandos was held at the Dorchester in June. It was one of the high points of the first post-war Season, which was beginning to recover the glitter of the good old days. Many of the themes were war related. There were fund-raisers for veterans' groups, for the wounded and the dead and their devastated families. It was the duty of the ruling class to show their appreciation to those whose sacrifices saved England from defeat, as though the nation was still the private property of the rich.

Kathleen was a frequent guest at these events. At the gathering for the Commandos she was a member of the committee. Her duties kept her very busy. The presence of Princess Elizabeth had attracted a large crowd of "significant" people to the Dorchester. The music played, the jewelry glittered, taffeta rustled on the dance floor. Kathleen wore a pink gown with diamond adornments. She was slimmer than usual and her hair was longer and done in the popular pageboy style. She was endlessly complimented by men and women alike as she managed introductions and provoked conversations, only to smile and excuse herself in order to attend to new arrivals. Many of the people she greeted she already knew and almost everyone was aware of her tragic losses in the war -- a brother and a husband within a few weeks.

Then, suddenly, someone took her by the arm and said, "You must come and meet Peter Fitzwilliam. He's been paying you compliments from across the room, and he insists on being introduced, though, of course, he knows who you are." It was a woman's voice, and it may have been Virginia Sykes, but for a moment everything became strangely indistinct, and she found herself staring at a very tall man with broad shoulders and ruggedly handsome features. His formal attire could not hide the ease and confidence with which he moved. She blushed at the intensity of his gaze and the deep, slightly breathy quality of his speech. Though he was only telling her how pleased he was to meet her at last, she felt as though he were telling her a secret that she must guard with her life. And then her small hand was lost in his, and she felt herself being led away from the person who introduced them.

The orchestra was playing "The nearness of you," and they were dancing before she was aware of what was happening.

Peter Fitzwilliam came from the wealthiest Anglo-Irish family in Britain and had inherited his title as the eighth Earl during the war. He had estates in England and Ireland. Wentworth Woodhouse in South Yorkshire was generally considered to be the largest mansion in all of Europe. He was the only son in a family with four daughters and was raised by a proud father and a house full of adoring women, who led him to believe that he could have anything that he wanted. He saw no point in self-discipine and he had nothing but contempt for authority. He had been a captain in the Grenadier Guards, but in his quest for excitement and adventure he had joined the commandos and distinguished himself as an officer aboard the *Hopewell*, a torpedo boat that made a daring run through enemy waters to Sweden on a top-secret misson. He loved speed and danger in all forms and satisfied his passion with fast cars and horses, with gambling and women. His nickname was "Blood," and he lived up to it in everything he did.

When it came to business, he was aggressive and calculating, and he acquired more land at a time when some of the leading families were forced to sell. His favorite acquistion was the Grange in Newmarket, which he developed into the most important breeding and training stable in England under the name of Rockingham Stud. His early marriage to Olive "Obby" Plunkett had already linked him to the fortune of the Guinness family inherited by Obby's clergyman father, Bishop Plunkett.

Peter was admired for his wartime exploits, but not for the excesses of his personal life. His marriage was rumoured to be a disaster. His womanizing and his wife's drinking kept the gossips busy. He was only thirty-six, but the pace of his life sometimes made him look older and a bit world weary.

It was in this man's arms that Kathleen danced, and she knew full well who and what he was. That knowledge excited her as much as the physical nearness of the man himself. She felt his large hand against her back, but his touch was surprisingly gentle. She had to look up to see the expression on his face.

"Do you do this sort of thing often?" he said, his eyes intense, his voice detached, as though he didn't much care what he said.

"What sort of thing?"

"Oh, you know, fund-raising dances. That sort of thing. War widows and orphans."

"I do my bit," she said. "My husband --"

"I know. I know all about that -- and about you."

"I suppose you do," she said, feeling herself blush. She had forgotten for a moment how tribal they all were. Fitzwilliam and Randolph were carousing friends. Pamela had married Randolph and was a childhood friend of Hugh Fraser. Billy and Andrew loved horse-racing and admired Fitzwilliam, who now led her around the dance floor as though he were a trainer breaking in a filly.

"Wouldn't it be nice to be total strangers meeting for the first time while crossing the Atlantic aboard the *Queen Mary*?" he said. "These charity balls are getting to be a bit incestuous. Since I've heard all about you, I imagine that you have heard certain things about me, but don't believe everything you've heard. I am much maligned, especially by my friends. But that's neither here nor there. Since we both know the same people, why haven't we met before?"

"When the war broke out, I was sent back to the States. I was there for four years before I joined the Red Cross and got an assignment in London. By that time you were probably in the thick of it."

"I suppose so," he said. "Still, it's rather amazing how just an ocean and a war can keep people apart."

She caught a hint of amusement in his eye, and the hand that held her became a bit firmer. She resisted politely.

"Sorry," he said. "I love to dance, but I'm afraid I'm not very good at it."

"Nonsense! You're very good, and you know it. But now I have the feeling that duty is calling me, and that your wife is probably watching *you*."

"How refreshingly blunt you are, Lady Hartington."

"Please don't call me that," she said. "Call me Kathleen."

"Of course, and you can call me Peter." Suddenly he looked around irritably, like a caged animal. "Look," he said, "this sort of gathering is not my cup of tea. I have a feeling that we have a good deal in common and that we might enjoy some civilized conversation, but not in this setting. So how about lunch? Saturday. Noon. The Ritz. Don't say no."

She hesitated for a moment, and then she said, "All right. Saturday. Noon! And here comes the committee. If you want to escape, I'll cover for you."

"Right!" he said with a smile. "You can tell them that I've gone off to see how many martinis they've put in the Olive."

She was still laughing as she watched him move with graceful determination through the crowd towards his wife Olive, who was part of a cluster of women around Princess Elizabeth.

On Saturday Kathleen was not surprised to find Peter at the Ritz without his wife. The day after the Commando affair it occurred to her that something as ordinary as having lunch with a man like Peter might prove to be risky business, but she decided not to call it off. She also decided not to mention the lunch date to Pamela, or anyone else for that matter. And then she scolded herself for acting like a nervous old maid. Finally, she argued that there was absolutely nothing wrong with meeting Peter Earl Fitzwilliam for lunch at the Ritz. Such a meeting could hardly be described as a secret rendezvous. In fact, they would no doubt run into friends there. It all sounded rather nice.

She made it a point to be ten minutes late, and when she arrived she could tell that he had been there on time, if not a bit early. His glass was half empty. As soon as she entered the room he stood up. He was an imposing figure, standing there alone by his table in the slanting sunlight that filtered in through the white gauzy curtains. She followed the headwaiter, who addressed her by her title. She was pleased. Peter took her gloved hand and gave her an abbreviated bow that made her smile. "Don't you look nice," she said.

"I'm supposed to say that about you, and it's true. You look lovely -- Kathleen. I understand that some people call you Kick."

"A bit rustic for the Ritz, don't you think?"

"An unusual nickname," he said. "Dare I ask where it came from?"

"Kid stuff," she said. "One of my sisters had trouble pronouncing my name. I don't really mind."

"I think I'll wait until I know you better. I spend a lot of time around horses."

"And how are your horses running these days my Lord?" she said in her parody of British English.

"Do you always make fun of the men who take you to lunch?" he said.

She watched the waiter pour the champagne. "Sorry, it's an old family habit."

"What is?"

"Nastiness! It is a form of affection in the Kennedy clan. My brother John is a master."

"I read his book about how England slept while Hitler planned to conquer the world. Is he the one who is getting into politics?"

"Yes, he plans to be the President of the United States."

"Isn't he a bit young for that sort of thing?"

"In America you only have to be thirty-five to be President, and he's already twenty-nine."

He caught the sparkle of humor in her eye and laughed. "I have a feeling that everything I've heard about you is true."

"And what exactly have you heard?"

"That you have a very special quality that makes people feel good, especially men."

"Who told you that?"

He shrugged. "Everyone. It's your reputation. As mine is bad, yours is good. It's Beauty and the Beast all over again."

"How flattering for both of us, but it's too early in the day for games. Why don't you just tell me something about your horses or maybe your wife."

"You know, I had it all planned out," he said. "If you asked about Olive, I was going to tell you that she pleads prior engagements and sends her apologies, but now that you have completely disarmed me I'll tell you straight out that I preferred to have lunch alone with you and that I planned to do my best to impress you."

She stared at him for a moment and then smiled. "I'm impressed!" she said. "Now can we eat?"

"Of course!" He nodded toward the waiter. "I understand that you Americans are very fond of eating," he said.

"I suppose we are. But then we don't have to eat English food, do we?"

"And who can blame you? Even the English avoid it, if they can afford to. But the good restaurants never serve it."

She glanced at the menu. "What do you suggest?"

Without hesitation he said, "The dilled blanquette de veau. Just perfect for a perfect day in June. And a bit of salmon mousse beforehand to keep the champagne company."

"I like your way of dealing with decisions," she said. "Very definite. Very swift. You've just simplified my life enormously."

"Do I detect a bit of irony in your tone? You mustn't let me bully you into anything. I've been told that I have a tendency to do that."

"By whom?"

"By a number of people, but especially by my wife, who I do not think has a very high opinion of me."

"I can't imagine why. You seem to have such a high opinion of yourself that you're not likely to be wrong."

"I suppose it depends on one's point of view. In any case, we needn't waltz around the subject. It's common gossip that we have our problems. She drinks, and I am less than a perfect husband."

"Less than perfect? I don't believe it. How ordinary for a man of your stature. But you're always with her in public. Keeping up appearances, I suppose."

"Olive and I have been married for thirteen years. We were both very young and it was wild times before the war. Things are different now. There were the usual wartime infidelities, but afterwards we never got back to the good old days. A kind of permanent distance has settled in between us. We still care for each other, but something is missing. Love, I suppose."

"Don't tell me that you're the romantic type."

"Why not?"

"I don't know. You're too tall. You move too fast on sea and land."

"He who hesitates is Hamlet."

"Exactly! And he drove Ophelia mad. Love takes a lot of time, and you seem to be in a hurry."

"You don't exactly come across as a sentimentalist yourself," he said.

"I never met a woman who was not interested in love, but I guess I'm not very gushy about the hearts and flowers part. The Kennedy kids were always kind of rough. If you liked somebody, you tried to beat his brains out on the tennis court."

"Olive was like that -- always impatient, easily bored, a real daredevil. During one week-end party she went dashing down the hallway into a plate-glass door. If you look closely you can still see the scars. Poor Obby, always in a hurry. And no sooner did we get where we were going than she wanted to go off somewhere else. She's still full of energy, but sometimes I think she's lost her sense of fun."

"You make her sound old. She can't be more than thirty-five."

"She was eighteen when I met her."

"Nobody is eighteen forever." A photograph of her parents flashed through Kathleen's mind. It was a summer place somewhere a long time ago. They were very young and her mother was smiling and alive. "So how serious is all this?" she said.

"What do you mean?"

"This thing with your wife. It sounds as though you're not getting on too well. Is that what you're trying to tell me?"

"Not really. I just assumed that you've heard the usual rumors --"

"Of course I have, but if you're trying to give yourself an excuse for having lunch with me, forget it. You don't need an excuse, unless you have more than lunch in mind, in which case, the next time we meet it better be in a crowded room."

"How about the roaring crowd at the races? I'll have some runners going at Newmarket. Obby will be there, of course. Why don't you join us?"

"I'd love to. Can you guarantee me a winner?"

"I've got two very promising entries -- Golden Girl and Light o' Love."

"I'll try to bring you luck."

"What more could I ask for?" he said with a sly smile.

"I'm sure you'll think if something," she said.

White clouds billowed in the blue sky over the racecourse at Newmarket and over the fenced meadows of the horse farms that surrounded the old town. Since the early seventeenth century there had been racing on the heath, where there was an ancient earthwork known as Devil's Dyke. It ran five miles from Reach to Wood Ditton and probably formed part of the boundary between the old kingdoms of East Anglia and Mercia. Another part of the past was the large training stable known as The Grange. Peter had acquired the property at the end of the war and named it after the Marquess of Rockingham, an ancestor of his who had commissioned the painting of Samson, believed to be the world's largest Thoroughbred. "I'll show it to you when you come to Wentworth Woodhouse," said Peter to Kathleen.

Olive lowered her binoculars and said, "We don't go there very often. They have been digging coal on the land under some new resolution by that bastard Shinwell."

"The Minister of Fuel and Power," said Peter. "They've torn up about two thousand acres of the estate."

"It's a bloody mess," said Olive. "We spend most of our time now at Coolattin Castle in Ireland or Grosvenor Square in London. Wentworth Woodhouse is a major disaster. Peter is thinking of donating it to the National Trust." She had the tight look of a tense woman with her thin eyebrows linked by a frown and her small mouth made smaller by the cupid-bow style of her lipstick. In spite of the tension, however, there were flashes of youth and beauty, and a bird-quick eye that did not seem to miss much. Though the weather was mild, she wore a fur jacket and tam, a nice complement to Peter's tweedy horse-breeder's look. They had drinks in their box, and friends came and went with greetings and handshakes.

Kathleen had her share of little recognition scenes. Virginia Sykes waved to her from a distance and mouthed a message that she did not quite understand. She was with a group that included the Duchess of Kent, whom Kathleen had met at Sledmere, the Sykeses' Yorkshire estate.

"Isn't that Seymour Berry?" said the sharp-eyed Olive.

"It must be," said Peter. "That's his father there, old Camrose. But who's the lovely little clinger hanging on to his arm. Never saw her before!"

Olive looked at Kathleen through cigarette smoke. "Wasn't there some sort of rumor about you and Seymour? Something about an engagement that never materialized."

"We've been friends, that's all, and still are," she said. "As you can see, he's got plenty to amuse him right now."

Olive squinted through her binoculars. "I don't think I know her. Do *you* Peter?"

"No, no, of course not," said Peter, a bit defensively.

Olive looked over the binoculars and gave Kathleen a wise old smile.

There was enough sunshine to cause a mist to rise from the damp turf. Peter insisted that they go down to the paddock before the next race to have a closer look at Golden Girl. "The ground's a little soft for her," he said. "She has rather small feet. Ellen Victoria goes well in the yielding ground, but she may not have the stamina for the distance. Our horse can run all day, but she has a tendency to tuck in behind the males, especially in the spring."

"Do you think she's going to win?"

"She's at four to one, not a bad price in here. Take a chance."

The handler walked Golden Girl over to the rail. Peter talked to her affectionately: "Hello, old girl. How are we doing today? What do you say we win this one for Kick."

"Who's Kick?" said Olive.

"Me," said Kathleen.

"You have my sympathy. As a child I was called Hobby Horse. It's been shortened to Obby."

The other horses in the paddock were paraded past them. Kathleen could feel the heat of their bodies, and in their eyes she could see a hint of excitement.

It seemed hours of small talk before the race got underway. Kathleen wondered whether or not Olive recognized her husband's flirtation with her. Was it possible that he did this sort of thing often and that it was only a harmless amusement on his part, a bit of extra female companionship at the races? Olive seemed confident to the point of indifference.

They watched the race from their box, with the help of binoculars and champagne. Sundown took the early lead and did not yield it until the last half mile. From the middle of the pack Golden Girl moved up along with three other horses. They all went by Sundown who was tiring badly. Ellen Victoria seemed out of it but came into contention with a burst of late speed. She had a long stride and actually seemed to enjoy the soft going. With a furlong to go she went by Golden Girl and opened up five lengths by the time she crossed the finish line. "Got it!" shouted Olive, waving her winning ticket. "I should have warned you never to listen to Peter," she said to Kathleen. "I never bet on the horses he picks, and I never tell him what my choice is until the race is over."

Horse racing was a part of the social calendar of the London Season, but only the true aficionados could find time to attend all the major events from Cheltenham to Ascot. Peter Fitzwilliam was passionate about the sport and followed it in Ireland and England and even on the Continent, where he numbered among his friends such racing enthusiasts as the Aga Khan and Marcel Boussac.

"One of my favorite events is the Grand Prix de Paris at Longchamp," said Peter when he met Kathleen for lunch again at the Ritz. "And afterwards there is Aly Khan's annual ball at the Pre Catelan restaurant in the Bois de Boulogne."

"How elegant!" she said. "Since I haven't been invited, I guess I will just have to settle for the nags of Newmarket."

"Would you like to be invited?" he said. He had a way of looking down at her, like a schoolmaster who was trying to help her find the right answer.

"By whom?"

"Does it matter? I can probably arrange for a friend to take you."

"No thanks. I have plenty of friends of my own, some of whom, I am sure, would be pleased to take me."

"Well, I don't suppose it would work anyway. As soon as Olive saw you there she would assume that I had arranged it."

"Why would she assume that? She has no reason --"

"Not yet, but I think she has decided that you are not as harmless an acquaintance as she first thought you were. She's pretty sharp. She picks up vibrations."

"From you maybe, but not from me. I'm not about to cause any problems between you and your wife."

"I think she has the feeling that I rather like you. Women have a way of knowing these things. In Olive's case female intuition is coupled with paranoia. She hasn't actually said anything, but she has begun to drink a bit more than usual. A sure sign of anxiety on her part."

"Well, Mr. Peter Blood, my advice to you is to stay home and comfort your wife, so that she will feel secure and confident. You might even be rewarded for your efforts."

"You sound like the advice-to-the-lovelorn column in the tabloids," he said. The color in his face deepened, as though a momentary cloud of anger had passed over the landscape of his mind.

"Sorry," she said, "I didn't mean to be critical. Your private life is your own business, and I can tell that things are difficult. I have to be careful not to be drawn into your problems, because I rather like you, too. If you were not married--"

"What then?"

"Well, then things would be different." She looked away, as though she were nervously trying to avoid his gaze. And then she let her eyes drift back to his. They seemed to be pleading silently for her to take the next step. She heard herself breathing as though she had run towards him from a great distance and had suddenly stopped."

"I'm sorry if I've imposed on you," he said, "but I felt from the moment I saw you that we were secret friends who could confide in one another without all the usual preliminaries. It happens that way sometimes. A certain instant compatibility."

"Yes, I know," she said, her voice fading into a whisper.

"But I suppose I became too personal too soon. Perhaps I was overexcited. In spite of all my acquaintances, I tend to be something of a loner. Meeting you was like meeting an old friend in a crowd."

"I didn't mean to hurt your feelings, Peter."

"And I didn't mean to sound like a man on the make who has just told you how awful his wife is. It's a bit embarrassing."

"But Peter, you *are* a man on the make, and you *have* just told me how awful your wife is. What am I supposed to do now? Should I feel flattered or insulted?"

"I don't know. How *do* you feel?"

She hesitated. "I feel that there is a certain sadness in you, and I am drawn to you because I would like to do something to make you happy. Or, at least, to make you laugh. But I am afraid that you will simply treat me the way you have treated the other women in your life. Not because you're malicious, but because you have that old male need for conquest -- like my brother and my father."

"When I first met you, I warned you that I had been pampered by women all my life, beginning with four sisters and a mother. When I become interested in a woman, I expect a response. I'm not asking you to be one of those women. I'm asking you to be my friend."

"You mean like a sister?"

"That may be going a bit too far."

"Why?"

"Well, if I should happen to kiss you one day -- purely by accident mind you -- it would be rather incestuous."

She laughed. "Oh, you impossible man. I don't believe that you have ever been serious for one moment in your entire life. Why don't you just go off to Paris and have a wonderful time with your horsey friends and then , when you come back, come to dinner at my house and tell me all about it. I have a wonderful new Hungarian cook. She and her sister look after everything. I'm lucky to have them."

"I'll ring you as soon as I get back."

"And pick a horse for me in the Grand Prix, will you. I'll give you the ten quid when you come back."

"Can I trust you?" he said.

"Yes, Peter," she said, "you can trust me."

A few days later Pat Wilson called to say that Kick had been seen at the Ritz in a very cozy tete-a-tete with a tall handsome man who could not have been anyone other than Peter Fitzwilliam, judging by her informer's description. "Well, was it or wasn't it? And what are you up to, you sly devil, you?" said Pat.

"It was, and we were having a business conversation about a horse."

"I bet you were, darling. He's got quite a track record."

"Oh, Patricia, clean up your thoughts and tell me what the hell you've been up to."

"Nothing special. Shopping for washables at Marshall and Snelgrove. Saw Pamela yesterday. She's off to Paris to be the guest of Aly Khan at a big bash of some sort. She sure gets around."

"She certainly does," said Kathleen, feeling a twitch of jealousy.

"I really just called to ask you for dinner. Can you come tomorrow.?"

"I'd love to," said Kathleen.

"Good! And you watch out for that scoundrel Fitzwilliam. He's not to be trusted."

Peter came back from Paris looking painfully dissipated. He had the kind of full face that always seemed about to collapse into jowls, and he frequently had the expression of a man who was confronting danger, even though he was only sitting at a table at the Savoy. One could easily imagine him as one of his own warrior ancestors who could trace their lineage back to the Norman Conquest. "I'm afraid one thing led to another at the Pre Catelan, and it was dawn by the time Elie de Rothschild's chauffeur was delivering me to my hotel. Three days of French exuberance was just too much for me. And then, on top of everything else, I squandered your ten quid on a horse named April Song who had more beauty than speed. In short, my dear, you lost and I have an enormous hangover."

"What would you like, then, a hair of the hound?" she said.

"Yes, something long and cool with a lot of gin in it. I hope this is not going to be a dinner party. I seem to have forgotten half of my vocabulary."

"Gin and tonic," she said to Ilona. "Don't worry, Peter, it's only us. I decided that it might be a bit risky to invite anyone else."

"But why?"

"Because I wasn't sure that I could get undistracted enough to be a good hostess."

"That's a bit cryptic for my crippled brain. Do you mind translating it into basic English?"

"If you're fishing for compliments, you've come to the right person. I had a little trouble getting you out of my mind, so I suppose I missed you."

231

"Good! I was hoping you might."

"Did you run into Pamela at the party?"

"Very briefly. She went by in a blur, hotly pursued by Prince Aly Khan. Actually, I couldn't tell who was the pursuer and who was the pursued. But I think it all worked out rather well, unless I was seeing double."

"When I heard she was going to Paris I was annoyed," said Kathleen, "maybe envious, maybe jealous. She charges into one adventure after another with such cheerful abandon. Why can't I do that?"

"Perhaps it's your Catholic upbringing. Those Irish priests can scare the hell out of anyone. Pamela doesn't have that problem."

"She certainly doesn't. The fact that a man is married doesn't mean a damn thing to her. I don't think I could ever feel that way."

"Well, then there's not much hope for us, is there?"

"According to the church, even the hope would be sinful."

"Sounds like a serious case of indoctrination."

"It was. I believed it all. I still do, but maybe with some reservations now."

Ilona called them in for dinner. She was a sturdy refugee with a motherly manner. Peter looked at the label on the wine bottle and then filled their glasses. "My own faith is a lot shakier than yours, I'm sure, but I always enjoyed the rituals. Did I ever tell you about my my wedding?"

"No, you've been kind enough, thus far, to spare me the details."

"It was in 1933. You must have been all of thirteen years old. Obby insisted that it take place in Dublin at St. Patrick's Cathedral. My father, who was fond of massive entertainments, sent two shiploads of his tenants from Yorkshire to Dublin. The whole thing was a great festival. The bride wore blue, and I was so naughty that I nearly missed the whole bloody thing. And then, horror of horrors, the procession was held up to allow a funeral to pass. There is no event more inauspicious than that. The marriage was declared 'doomed' by the superstitious peasants, but we went off and celebrated our carelessness from the Riviera to the Caribbean. When Juliet was born two years later, we settled down, more or less. And then there was the war --"

"And then there was the war," she said, her voice a soft echo of his.

"It was awful for you, wasn't it?" he said.

"Yes," she said. "I don't believe I have ever really forgiven God for killing my husband and my brother. I know it sounds absurd and sacrilegious, but that's how I feel."

"What do you say when you go to confession?"

"I say, 'Forgive me Father for I have sinned. I have doubted the goodness of God in times of affliction.' "

"I don't mean to sound cynical, but that's probably all they want to hear."

After she cleared away the dishes and put out the coffee and brandy, Ilona and her sister retired to their rooms on the third floor. The candles lingered on in the stillness of the room, flickering slightly when the air was gently moved by their voices. "It's late," she said. "You ought to be going."

"I wish I were staying," he said, leaning back wearily in his chair. In the dim light his eyes looked sad and his mouth looked surprisingly soft.

"Don't say anymore, Peter. You know how I feel." She stood up and waited for him to do the same.

"Will I see you soon?" he said.

"I don't know," she said. "I need time to think about all this. I feel as though we are about to step off a cliff or something. I'm frightened."

He took her by the hand and drew her close to him. She resisted for a moment, and then allowed him to put his arms around her and hold her against his chest. She shut her eyes and took a deep breath. He kissed the top of her head, as though he were comforting a child. She looked up and he kissed her gently on her forehead, her cheek and then her unparted lips. "No," she said. "It would be too easy to lock the door and keep you here. But I'm not Pamela or Pat. I don't know what I would do. I've never felt this way before. You'd better go. Please go." She paused for two quick breaths. "But come back."

He let her slip out of his arms. "I will," he said. She saw him to the door. He kissed her good night. When he was gone, the room seemed terribly empty. She poured herself a brandy and sat at the table. When there was nothing left in her glass, she put out the candles and went upstairs to bed. The sheets were cool against her warm body, and she conjured up the scent of this man who wanted to be her lover. She tried to imagine him there beside her and it was all too easy.

In the morning she scolded herself in the mirror, holding her toothbrush the way Sister Agnes held the wooden pointer with which she tapped the blackboard or the maps of the world that came down like shades in the classrooms of the convent of the Sacred Heart. She had been sent to Noroton at the age of thirteen because her mother was worried about her interest in boys. Some of them had actually called Kathleen at her home in Bronxville. She smiled as she recalled the look on her mother's face, and she spoke to her in her mind:*I'm a big girl now, mother, and you can't send me away to school.*

CHAPTER FIFTEEN

A whole week went by without a word from
Peter. She had canceled a lunch date with Evelyn
Waugh and a shopping trip with Pat Wilson. Both of
them had warned her about that "debonair devil,"
that "lady killer," and she was in no mood to be
lectured again. She stayed in and wrote letters. It
was July and the sun was shining, but she wasn't
interested.

She thought of her family and wondered
whether or not the usual summer vacation at
Hyannis Port would be turned into a summer of
campaigning in Boston for Jack. She tried to conjure
them up from recent letters. There was Eunice
giving her heart and soul to her brother's
campaign for Congress. *Puny Eunie thinks she's
Joan of Arc.* She had said that once to Jack, who had
laughed and accused her of being jealous. She could
see Jean and her roommate Ethel Skakel ringing
doorbells and handing out campaign literature,
while they schemed to divert Bobby's romantic
interest from Pat Skakel to Ethel, her younger
sister. She could see her mother, beaming with
pride, and perfectly dressed, as she stood among
dignitaries on the platform of a political gathering.
And, finally, there was Teddy, bringing up the rear,
doing his bit at fourteen. How incredibly young
they all seemed! Here she was in London, having
been married and widowed, having met the Queen
and dined with Members of Parliament, and having
been courted by a fifty-year-old statesman and
pursued by a married nobleman. Was it just the
Kennedys, she wondered, or were all Americans that
way, eternally childish? For a moment she felt
mature and superior, and then, suddenly, she felt a
pang of nostalgia for her younger self, for the fun
and games, the noise and laughter, even the rules

and punishments of their old summers at Hyannis Port.

She was sitting at a small table by the window, her pen poised over the writing pad, a few tears dampening her cheeks. The view was lovely but a bit austere. A taxi went by, a woman walked her dog. No one frolicked in the surf, and no sleek sailboats ran before the wind. She reminded herself that it was possible to fly home for a summer visit, but almost immediately she decided that Christmas would be soon enough. Jack's election would be over by then, and maybe things would get back to normal.

Her housekeeper Elisabeth brought in the mail and put it on the writing table. "Is Ilona to make lunch?" she said with her Hungarian accent.

"No, tell her not to bother. I will probably go out."

"Yes, madame," she said, lingering just long enough to indicate that she was aware of Kathleen's sadness.

Kathleen gave her a quick smile as if to assure her that it was nothing serious. Then she looked at the mail. There were only two personal letters, one from her mother and one from Peter. She took a deep breath, as though she were able to do so for the first time that day. The note from Peter was very brief: "My incredibly busy week is no excuse for not calling, but now I have something to look forward to. I'll be back in London by Wednesday. Think of something wonderful to do."

She had been trying to gather together enough anger to tell him that she did not think it was a good idea to go on seeing him this way, because if Olive found out, she would assume that there was a lot more going on than there really was. She had rehearsed letters and phone calls, but she could never quite do the deed. And now this little note completely disarmed her. She felt that if he walked through the door at that moment, he could ask her for anything and she would be unable to refuse him. She was falling in love, even though they had never *made* love. She had insisted on that as a condition of their continuing to see one another. He called it the "Kathleen Doctrine," and often teased her about it. She tried to tell him how important it was to her. He laughed, as though it were only a matter of time. To herself she described him as "a lover at the the gates," and she was determined not to be the "other woman" in his life, the mistress who made his marriage bearable.

She opened her mother's letter and found the usual duplicated family news roundup, but attached to it was a short personal note in which her mother said that she and Eunice hoped to make a trip to Paris sometime in the fall, in which case they would stop in London, of course. With Peter threatening to become a serious part of her life, Kathleen had mixed feelings about her mother's plans to visit. Now that she had a house of her own, she was obliged to put her up and arrange dinners and other entertainments for her. Good Lord, she thought, was there anyone in her new circle of friends that her mother could possibly approve of? Her mind went blank

When Peter came for dinner, she told him about the letter from her mother. "If she's going to Paris for the fashions," he said, "it won't be until September. Plenty of time. Obby may be going too.. Maybe they can travel together. Now wouldn't that be an amusing scene for a playwright?"

"I don't think my mother would approve of Obby," said Kathleen.

"I can't imagine why," he said. "Just because she's an alcoholic, adulterous Protestant doesn't mean she's all bad."

She laughed. "Don't be naughty. Just help me make up a guest list that does not include you or your wife or anyone who drinks too much or women of questionable virtue or people who are liable to say nasty things about Catholics."

237

"I guess that rules out old Nancy Astor, and just about anyone else I know, except maybe your friends the Ormsby-Gores and that repulsive convert Evelyn Waugh. I suppose you could scrape together a meeting of the Kathleen Kennedy Catholic Society and talk about virginity and the menace of the motor car."

"Very funny, Fitzwilliam, but not very useful. Have you got any other suggestions?"

"Yes, but they're liable to get me tossed out of the club."

She got up and went to him. From behind his chair she draped her arms over his shoulders. "Come on, Captain Blood," she said, "smoke your cigar in the sitting room. I'll send the Hungarians to bed."

"Why don't we let the Hungarians smoke the cigars while we --"

She shoved him playfully. He reached out for her and pulled her onto his lap. His kiss and his touch were passionate, and she let herself sink into his long embrace. She liked being on his lap and feeling the strength of his arms. "God, I've missed you," he whispered.

"And I've missed you, God help me!"

"Why is it that you Irish Catholic women always cry out for God's help when you're in a man's arms?"

"Because all men are beasts, haven't you heard?"

"All too often, but it's not true. Some of us are gentlemen."

"If I could believe that, I'd ask you to spend the night."

"You're in a nice, devilish mood. Is it a full moon or something?"

"I wouldn't be at all surprised."

"Why don't we go up and have a look out your bedroom window?"

"Because you're not to be trusted."

Suddenly, he stopped smiling and held her away from him by both arms so that she could see the expression on his face. "I know you've heard a lot of bad things about me, Kathleen, and most of them are probably true, but trust me when I tell you that I am dead serious about us. Do you think I would be here now if I weren't?"

"I don't know, Peter. I don't know what to think. When you're here I always seem to be sending you away, and when you're away I always seem to be waiting for you to call. Maybe there's something wrong with me."

"It's easy enough to find out."

"No, darling, not here, not tonight."

"Perhaps we should go away for a few days. Somewhere in the country."

"Yes, let's get away from London. Let's spend some time together somewhere doing ordinary things. Perhaps after my mother's visit."

"I know some lovely places," he said.

"Don't tell me," she said. "I like surprises."

The Royal Garden Party at Buckingham Palace at the end of July was the culminating event of the Season and could not easily be avoided. Kathleen saw Peter there, but only from a distance. In August anybody who was anybody went off to the country or the continent. Obby insisted on a trip across the Channel to Le Touquet, described as "Mayfair on the French coast." Kathleen consoled herself with a trip to Sledmere in Yorkshire, where the guests of the Sykeses would include Hugh Fraser, Pat Wilson, and other people in their lively circle. The rest of the summer dissolved in a series of distractions, and she found herself staring at September as though it were an uninvited guest.

Kathleen was nervous about her mother's visit. She had the house cleaned from top to bottom, she bought theater tickets, she invited some people to dinner, and she warned Peter to stay away. As soon as she put down the phone she realized that she rather liked having this secret to keep from her mother.

And then they were there -- her mother and Eunice, her family, her past, her childhood. It all came in with the baggage, with the hugging and kissing and the harsh American accent. "So this is your house," said her mother, taking it all in before handing down her verdict. "I see you have some Chippendale."

"On loan from my mother-in-law. She's been very generous."

"But not generous enough to give you the furniture outright."

"It all belongs to Chatsworth, and when they do the renovations it will all go back there. During the war the house was used by a school. I must have written to you about that."

They paraded upstairs, the Hungarians helping with the luggage. When they had seen it all, Rose declared the place "really charming," and Eunice echoed her mother's judgment that it was just right for one in Kathleen's circumstances.

At lunch they talked about Jack's campaign and his victory in the Democratic primary. "It was a landslide, an absolute landslide," said Eunice. "He should win hands down in November. Johnny's working hard and holding up pretty well."

"Eunice has given him a lot of support," said Rose. "She's very good at that sort of thing. Your father said the other day that if she were a man she'd be the first Catholic president."

"Oh, Mother --" said Eunice, a sudden touch of color in her pale face. "I wish you would stop telling people that. This is 1946. I don't see anything wrong with a woman running for poltical office."

"Are you planning to?" said Kathleen.

"Not right now, but who knows? I'm only twenty-five."

"It's not easy for a woman," said Rose. "If she gets married and has children, as we are all expected to do, then she doesn't have the time or energy to run a campaign and hold elective office. On the other hand, if she doesn't get married then people think there's something wrong with her. They may even suspect her of not being entirely feminine, if you know what I mean."

"You don't have to spell it out, Mother; we know what you mean," said Eunice, as though the remark was aimed at her.

"And how about Dad and the rest of the tribe?" said Kathleen. "How are they doing? I sure do miss everybody."

"And everybody misses you," said Rose. "Your father sends his love, and Johnny wants to know if your in-laws are going to let you keep that castle in Ireland."

"Oh, brother!" she said.

In her letters Rose had often said that she looked forward to meeting Kathleen's London friends, but Kathleen did not look forward to such an encounter. After all, these were the friends on whom her mother had once blamed her original defection and sinful marriage. The people who came to dinner the following night were either good Catholics or benign non-Catholics who avoided controversy. Among her more reliable guests were Father Martin D'Arcy and Countess Birkenhead.

The conversation was low-key, high-ground, and inoffensive. The food was French with an Hungarian accent. In some circles the dinner party would have been described as a *success*. Rose talked about the recent canonization of Mother Cabrini and about Eunice's interest in becoming a nun. Father D'Arcy smiled at Eunice and nodded his approval. Kathleen drank the wine that was in her glass and accepted a generous refill. Then she raised her eyebrows in her sister's direction, as if to say, "What the heck was that all about?"

When everyone was fully engaged in eating and talking, Kathleen got up and went into the kitchen. Her absence was hardly noticed. She made her way upstairs, her recklessness fueled by wine and her mother's queenly performance. In the privacy of her bedroom she dialled Peter's number at Grosvenor Square. She did not expect him to answer the phone himself, but when he did, she said, "Hello, Peter, it's me."

"What a nice surprise?" he said. "I thought you had a houseful of people tonight."

"I did. I do. Are you alone?"

"Not exactly. Obby's asleep in her chair with a copy of *Queen Magazine* in her lap. Poor thing!"

"I shouldn't be calling like this, but I was sitting there at the table with all those people, thinking that the only person I really wanted to talk to was you. Say something sweet and then good night. I think I love you."

"Be careful what you say; I'll be crashing your party. I love you, too, Kick."

"Good night, darling."

"Goodnight!"

Her heart was pounding as she descended the stairs. *I must be mad*, she thought. Her mother was the first one to notice her return, and her glance lingered, as though she suspected something.

When dinner was over, the men stayed at the table for port and cigars, and the women retired to the small sitting room on the first floor. "Well, my dear," she said to Kathleen, "for a widow you seem to be enjoying a very pleasant way of life here in London, but what have you been doing for the Church?"

Kathleen looked stunned. She glanced at some of the faces that were turned in their direction. Her mother repeated her question in a more accusative voice, and Kathleen mumbled something about

242

putting in time once a week at the Central Office. Her mother relented, as though Kathleen had offered up the Catholic Charities instead of the Central Office of the Conservative Party, where she was a volunteer. It all happened very quickly, a flash of anger followed by a smile, but she felt the humiliation of having been scolded in her own house as though she were a little girl. And why, she wondered, did her mother wait until there were only women in the room to give in to her feelings of resentment?

No reference was made to the incident during the balance of the visit. Rose gave the impression that she had forgotten all about it, or, in fact, had never said anything that she considered offensive. Shopping forays and social commitments did not leave much time for serious conversation. Kathleen promised to come home for Christmas and a bit of the winter season. Rose smiled, waved goodby, and boarded the boat-train to Paris. How she loved to travel, thought Kathleen, remembering all the goodbyes of her childhood and feeling the threat of tears. Her mother was always going somewhere, sometimes with a few of the children, sometimes alone, hardly ever with her husband. Paris, Rome, the Riviera, South America. She was a mysterious woman, Kathleen thought, as the train pulled out of the station.

It was another month before Peter could arrange a trip to the country. They were walking in Hyde Park after lunch on a fall day that had a hint of summer in it. "I've got to go up to Milton to have a look at our foxhounds," he said. "We'll be out in the field soon. Why don't you come with me or join me there on the weekend? From there we can head north and do whatever we please. Obby will probably go back to London."

"Billy's family want to go up to Hardwick Hall before the partridge season ends, and they want me to go with them," said Kathleen. "I'd hate to disappoint them. Billy and I had a terrific time there once in the long ago and far away. It's a fond memory for all of us. Besides, I don't think I should be seen with you too often."

"Darling, it's only a fox hunt, a lot of people thundering around on horseback, trying to catch a scrawny little animal who kills chickens. Besides, I plan to invite only my most disreputable friends, those who don't mind breaking the rules. Sometimes it can be very exhilarating. Obby will feel right at home. You should have seen her in her roaring youth. The original minister's daughter who went wild."

"I bet you were just as bad," said Kathleen.

"We did everything at top speed. It's a wonder we didn't kill ourselves."

"I suppose you knew lots of women."

"No. I only took them to bed. I didn't know them. You're the only woman I've ever known."

"You're such a charming liar, Peter."

"Perhaps the truth is over-rated," he said. "In any case, I don't lie to *you*, Kick."

She slipped her hand into his big coat pocket and held his hand. She remembered how she and her father walked this way in the cold weather when she was a child. "I've only been fox-hunting once," she said. "I rooted for the fox."

"How American of you! But do come to Milton and meet some of our friends."

She hesitated for a moment and then gave in. "All right," she said, "but only if we can go off alone afterward. I'm getting tired of people. On the way back you can leave me at Hardwick Hall, and I can make up lies about where I've been and how I got there."

244

The day of the hunt was filled with ambiguities. The weather seemed unable to make up its mind, but the sun made an appearance and peeked through the curtains of Kathleen's room. She lay awake among pillows and blankets. Like the weather she was unable to make up her mind. Was it a good idea to come to Milton, after all, to see Peter among his friends and coupled with his troubled wife? Her compassion for Obby was modified by jealousy, but she admired her for playing the sophisticated hostess with a certain fatalistic panache. It made her feel, by comparison, like a boring widow with the limited experience of a schoolgirl.

She propped herself up on the pillows and thought about this place and these people. She was one of nine guests staying at the house, and others would join them at the meet. Most of the people at dinner were about ten years older than her. It seemed to her they drank and smoked an awful lot and laughed at almost anything. Her father would have hated this crowd, she thought. They were not at all like the Kennedys and their friends. And such strange noises in the night! What in the world were they up to? She suddenly remembered a man appearing at her door, saying, "Sorry, wrong room, unless you'd like some company." Was it that naughty game that Pat once described to her as "musical rooms, a game of chance encounters for the rich and bored." She wondered whether or not Peter and Obby slept in the same bed or even the same room. She was reluctant to ask, and he said nothing on the subject.

She heard voices in the courtyard and, further off, the sound of dogs. It was time to get up. Draped over the back of a chair she saw a scarlet coat with a dark green velvet collar. It had belonged to one of his sisters, Peter had explained. And her horse was to be Nimrod, who had never yet thrown a lady.

By the time she came down, the place was full of activity inside and out. "Pretty exciting!" she said to Peter.

"Come and meet your horse," he said, leading her out.

Peter looked very handsome in his hunting outfit and even taller than usual. The scene outside seemed to her noisy and disorganized. He tried to sort it all out for her. "I am the Master of the Hunt and the host, but the dogs are controlled by our huntsman, who is assisted by two whippers-in. We've sent out a couple of earth-stoppers to close up old burrows and other potential hiding places. We should get five or six miles out of the fox before a kill is made. Sometimes we mark the trail with blood, so that the hounds will not be distracted by stray scents and lured away from the covert where we suspect there is a fox. We start here with the meet, a gathering of hounds, huntsman, and followers. We are served refreshments, as you can see. When I give the command, one note of the horn will be sounded and the hounds will move off to draw the covert. When the fox is found, you will hear two notes of the horn, the distinctive cry of the hounds, and the shout of 'Tally-ho.' That's when the hunt begins and off we go. When the fox is seen, there will be a high-pitched holloa. If he's killed, we take the brush, mask and pads as trophies and let the dogs have the body. They have to be rewarded with blood; otherwise, they will lose their incentive to hunt."

Peter rode beside Obby, and Kathleen dropped back beside a lean old military type who gave her a salute and a smile. It had been a while since she had been on a horse, but the feel of it soon came back. She had forgotten how much she enjoyed it. The lane skirted a patch of woods and followed a stone wall to a gate that opened onto a series of fields. From the high ground the fields sloped away into the mist, and off in the distance there were the dark humps of hills. The landscape reflected the light and shadow of the sky. It was a wonderful view, she thought, realizing in that moment, how much she missed the country.

She felt the strength of the horse she rode, though he was not a huge animal. His walk was regular, and at a trot she posted easily. At the sound of the horn the riders broke into a gallop across the furrows of a harvested field. She held on with her knees and she could feel the yielding of the soft earth. Then they reached the stony slope of unworked ground and the footing was firm. Nimrod proved to have good running speed, and before long she was on the heels of Peter and Obby. The yelping of the hounds and the sting of the fall air was exhilarating, and she lost herself in the driving effort of the hunt, the sound of all the horses, the flash of green meadow, the turbulence of the sky, and the fragrance of rich, turned up earth. Then, suddenly, her horse shied and reared, as though something frightening had crossed his path. She held on long enough to jump clear, but rolled forward when she hit the ground. She stood up immediately, and Nimrod came back to her, as if to apologize. As she took the reins she could see Peter riding back for her. She waved him off and shouted, "I'm all right." By then he was dismounting. About the same time, one of the grooms with the second horses also arrived.

Peter looked at Kathleen and then at the horse. "No harm done," he said to the groom. "We'll be along in a few minutes."

There were a few earth stains on her borrowed coat and her eyes were bright with excitement. When they were alone, Kathleen said, "Something happened back there."

"Maybe it was a cat or some other small animal," said Peter. "Could have been merely a shadow. Let's have a look." They walked their horses back forty yards or so, close to an ancient wall that was nearly completely covered with weeds and vines. In the high grass Peter found a coil of fencing wire. "Here's the culprit," he said. "Nimrod must have caught sight of it at the last minute. He might have been tripped up if he hadn't seen it. So I guess you're rather lucky, after all." He looked around. "And here we are, all alone. Fortunately, I have an emergency flask of brandy. Let's step into the forbidden forest and have a nip, and then we'll be on our way."

They followed a narrow path and came to the ruins of an ancient church and a graveyard where the stones were so eroded by time that the inscriptions were gone. "What a gloomy place," she said.

He passed her the flask. She took a sip and made a face. "Strong!" she said.

He took his turn and smiled. "It warms the chest," he said, "and 'the secret places of the heart.' Don't ask me where that line is from. Something left over from my university days. I've never been very romantic, but I do believe that we all have secrets, even some things that we hide from ourselves."

"We Catholics know all about that sort of thing," she said.

He stood close to her as she leaned against a pile of crumbling stones that once was a wall. "This place reminds me of death," he said.

"Death is awful," she said. "So final."

He put his arms around her. She could smell his warm, brandy-scented breath. She raised her face to his to invite a kiss, and when he kissed her she closed her eyes. "Ah," she said, "you do that very well, Fitzwilliam. And I like the way you ride. He kissed her again, more passionately, and slipped his hand inside her coat to feel the softness and warmth of her breast.

"I've always wanted to make love in a graveyard," he said.

"If your wife rides back this way to look for you, we're liable to become the new tenants of this place. Let's go, before anything stupid happens." She took him by the hand and led him away.

When they stood by the horses again he shook his head and said, "What am I going to do about you, Kick? I can't have you and I can't let you go."

"All I need right now is a hand up to get back on this horse," she said.

He obliged her and then gave her horse a whack on the rump that sent him galloping off with Kathleen hanging on for dear life. They raced their way back to the hunters, who were still in pursuit of the wily fox.

Two days later they woke up in one another's arms in an old inn in the Cumbrian Hills of the Lake District. They had registered the previous afternoon as Mr. and Mrs. Reginald Fox of London. That evening in the bar Kathleen revealed to the innkeeper that Mr. Fox was, in fact, the Reverend Fox, but did not wish to advertise the fact while on holiday. This was their fifth wedding anniversary, she explained, whereupon the innkeeper bought them a drink and shared their secret with his pudding-faced wife.

It had all happened very quickly and very naturally. Restless Obby had taken off suddenly for London on her own, and they left discreetly for "somewhere," to escape the oppressive visibility of their usual lives. When they were safely in bed, naked under the heavy quilts, Peter said to her, "I can't tell you how much I enjoy being the Reverend Reginald Fox."

"And I can't tell you how much I enjoy being his wife," she said. "Thank God you're not a Catholic priest!"

Warmed by whiskey and excited by their adventure, they made love without thinking about it, until Kathleen, struck by a physical revelation, let out a cry of pleasure and held on to her lover as though she were suddenly in danger of falling from a great height. After a while, Peter whispered, "Are you all right, darling?"

She was trembling and breathless, but she smiled to reassure him. For a while she seemed incapable of speech, but then she said in a very soft voice, "If I'm dead, don't wake me up," and soon she was asleep in his arms.

When she opened her eyes in the morning he was still asleep. The large room was filled with sunlight and smelled pleasantly of the previous night's fire. In the fireplace, one smouldering log still showed signs of life. She looked around as though to assure herself that her memory was not just a dream. They had come there like the wind in a fast sportscar with a strapped down hood. A Morgan, she thought. And they had kept the top down until they looked like Alpine skiers and had to stop at a tavern to thaw themselves out.

From the very beginning she'd known that they were going to make love, but she had no way of knowing beforehand what the experience would be like. It was not just the liquor, not just the weakening of one's defenses or the overcoming of one's inhibitions; it was something deep down and high up, something that animals and angels do. It was as if their bodies had been made into flesh from the same mud and their souls created by the same breath of God. For the very first time in her life she felt completely alive.Wherever he touched her, life followed; whatever he did to her was done for the first time. And afterward she knew what it was to be completely naked and without shame.

He had his back to her, and, leaning on her left elbow, she studied him, as though she were committing him to memory. She was no longer afraid. She had given herself to him, and instead of falling from a high place, she found herself soaring upwards on invisible wings. Everything would be different now, she thought. Everything!

CHAPTER SIXTEEN

Early in December Kathleen got into a taxi in Smith Square and gave the driver the name of the restaurant at which she was meeting Sissy Ormsby-Gore for lunch. The invitation reminded her that she had been neglecting her friends, especially her Catholic friends, who were not likely to find her relationship with Peter acceptable. She was in love and she was afraid that it might show in her face or that she would simply announce her happiness to anyone she talked to, perhaps even total strangers. She noticed the gray hair of the taxi driver, and the folds in the flesh at the back of his neck. Winter was in the air and there was a threat of rain, but she didn't care. When she got out of the taxi, the old guy held the door and gave her a wink. "Now there's a pretty smile on a dark day," he said. She was pleased and dropped an extra coin in his hand, but as she walked towards the restaurant she thought, *If I can't keep it from a taxicab driver, how am I going to keep it from Sissy?*

It didn't matter. As soon as they were seated at a table, Sissy said,"I had a special reaon for inviting you to lunch today. I might as well tell you what it is."

"I think I know," said Kathleen.

"And do you know what people are saying, my dear?"

She took a deep breath. "Frankly, I don't give a damn what people are saying. I've never been so happy in my whole life. Never!"

"Not even with Billy?"

She hesitated. "It was different. Everything was different with Billy. We were very young, very innocent. I feel all grown up now. I feel like a woman."

"You may feel like a woman, but you sound like a schoolgirl with a crush on an older man."

"Oh, come on, Sissy, at thirty six he's hardly an old man."

"Maybe not in years, but in experience--. I mean, doesn't it bother you? All those other women! And what about his wife?"

"What about her? She's impossible. Even Peter's mother thinks he should divorce her."

"Did it ever occur to you that you may be contributing to their difficulties by seeing Peter?"

"On the contrary,"said Kathleen. "It has occurred to me that I may be helping to keep this marriage together by allowing Peter to have both of us."

Sissy touched the pearls of her necklace as though they were the beads of a rosary. "Do you know what you're saying, Kick? Listen to yourself. I can't tell you how to live, but as your friend and as a Catholic I can warn you that these new friends of yours, including Peter, are, morally, a very risky crowd. Their sexual arrangements are sometimes bizarre. Obby might very well tolerate you in order to keep her husband, but you don't really want to be the mistress of a married man, do you?"

Kathleen looked distressed. She glanced around the restaurant as though she were just becoming aware of her surroundings. Then her eyes returned to Sissy, and she seemed lovely sitting there across the table. Fine features in a saintly, oval face. "It doesn't have to be that way," she said. "Peter wants a divorce."

"We've heard that rumor for years, Kick, but he and Obby keep turning up in the newspapers, dancing at a hunt ball or dressed to the limit at Ascot. They do a pretty good job of keeping up appearances for a couple on the brink of a divorce. Besides, do you know how difficult a divorce would be? There would be financial complications, family conflicts, legal difficulties. Adultery is the only argument one can offer, and if Obby refuses to cooperate -- well, that certainly would be a mess. Can't you see the headlines in the newspapers? Notorious philanderer accuses wife of adultery! Good Lord, Kick, you don't want to be part of all that."

Kathleen watched the waiter serve her food as though he had just materialized from another realm. When he was gone, she said in a subdued voice: "We love each other, and I know there must be a way."

"You're not suggesting that you will be able to marry this man and still remain a Catholic?"

"Why not?"

"I'm not even going to try to explain. If you want to know *why not*, speak to Father D'Arcy."

"Perhaps I will, but I'll be leaving soon to visit my family in Palm Beach."

"And what are you going to tell them?"

"I don't know. Lies probably." She smiled, and Sissy laughed outright.

That week she could not go to confession, nor did she attend Mass on Sunday. Sissy's warning echoed in her mind. Christmas seemed to be approaching through darkness, and then there was a dusting of snow, just enough to give a ghostly look to the world. She cried in the night and asked God to help her find a solution to her life. "Please don't let your priests push me out of the Church."

With a flicker of hope in her heart she went to see Father D'Arcy. In short order he doused that little flame. "No, no, no!" he said, standing at his desk as she sat in a chair with her head bowed. "No, you can not be married by the Church, nor can you have any kind of marriage with this man that will be accepted by the Church. You can not expect us to put our seal of approval on things that you do in this condition of spiritual confusion. Give it up, Kathleen! Do not lend yourself to adultery. Do not come between this man and his wife. Go home to your family in America and stay there until you have had time to put your feelings and your soul in order. Pray for guidance and forgiveness!"

She nodded submissively, but when she was outside she wanted to scream and curse at the murky sky.

The night before her departure, Peter came for dinner. She told him about Sissy and Father D'Arcy. "I thought you seemed upset," he said. "I can understand your talking to Sissy, but I don't know what you expected to hear from Father D'Arcy. He works for the Church and his boss is in Rome. You're lucky he didn't excommunicate you on the spot."

"At this point I'm not sure it matters," she said.

He watched her as she rotated her wine glass meditatively. "I wish you weren't leaving tomorrow," he said. "Why don't you spend the holidays here for a change? After the way they treated you last year, who would blame you? You have your husband's family here, and they are very kind to you. They would be delighted if you stayed. And so would I, of course. Besides, if you go away, you may never come back. What would I do then?"

"I don't know. What did you do before we met?"

"Don't be bitter," he said.

Suddenly, she burst into tears, and he reached out to comfort her. "I'm sorry!" she said, rubbing her eyes with the back of her hand and laughing as suddenly as she had cried. "I hate to tell you what crazy thoughts run through my mind."

"What is it? Tell me."

"Women are awful. I'm awful. I was just thinking how much I hated everyone in your life before I met you. My heart is rotten with jealousy. Get me a straight jacket. Lock me up. Of course, I don't want to go. And, of course, I will come back. And, of course, everybody will tell me that I'm wrong. Am I wrong? Tell me I'm not."

They were standing up, and she was leaning against him, as if to lose herself in his arms. "You're not wrong," he said. "Go, if you must, but think of me, because I will be doing everything I can to set things right for us. And watch out for that Jesuit priest of yours. He's liable to get in touch with your parents."

"He can't do that," she said. "I talked to him in confidence."

"You were not in the confessional."

"It doesn't matter. He's a priest --. Anyhow, I don't care. I would like them to know; I'm just too much of a coward to tell them."

"It's just as well you don't tell them yet. They might find a way to keep you there. You father might have your passport lifted. I hear he's good at that sort of thing and that he's an old friend of J. Edgar Hoover, the head of your Gestapo."

"I don't want to think about it," she said. "Come upstairs and help me to not think about it." She smiled over her shoulder as she walked towards the stairs.

On the eve of her departure she decided that she was glad to be going away. The weather was awful, and she was tired of the gossip and scandal, the admonitions of friends and relatives. There were times, she thought, when the Old World was like a damp mausoleum, and America was like a breath of fresh air, a new world focused on the future and not bogged down in the past. Before she fell asleep she thought of her brother, who was now a Congressman. In a couple of weeks he would be taking up his duties in Washington and playing a real part in the making of the new world. By comparison she felt useless. She had no career, no husband or children, no direction in life. She didn't even have Peter. Her parents would probably ask her to come back home for good. Perhaps she would consider it, she thought, as she closed her eyes.

In Palm Beach she marveled at the eighty-degree temperature and cloudless blue skies. The breeze that wafted through the palm trees felt as though it came from tropical places further south. Though she had done her share of traveling, she suddenly felt as though she had seen too little of the world. Perhaps it was London that made her feel a bit claustrophobic. The city that she once loved now seemed shadowy and incestuous because she and Peter had become the subject of so much talk.

They were all in Palm Beach for Christmas, except for Joe, of course, who was always mentioned, and Rosemary, who was rarely referred to. Ethel and Pat Skakel were also there. Bobby was interested in Pat, and Ethel was interested in Bobby. Kathleen was given a warm greeting, but the center of attention was Jack. A close second was Eunice, who had just been appointed the executive secretary of the Justice Department's new project on juvenile delinquency.

There was a tree and there were presents, but Christmas was not very convincing in such a warm climate. When Kathleen opened her gifts she said the usual things until she came to the present from her mother. When she saw it she laughed so hard that she could not explain why she was laughing. It was a beautiful fox furpiece. "Mr. Reginald Fox," she said at last, smiling and misty-eyed.

"What in the world is so funny?" said her mother.

"Sorry!" she said. "We were on this fox hunt in Peterborough, and I fell off my horse."

"I don't get it," said Eunice.

"The man who helped me up was named Reginald Fox."

"That's funny," said Jack.

"Yeah," said Eunice, "but not that funny."

"Who do you know in Peterborough?" said Rose.

"I can't remember. We were just there for the hunt."

"Who's *we?*"

Kathleen looked flustered for a moment.

"It wasn't by any chance Peter Rabbit?" said Eunice.

"I went up with Debo and Andrew. Our host was a friend of theirs. Fitzwilliam, I think." She held up the fur piece as though it were a trophy. "It's lovely, Mother, really lovely!"

Later Kathleen and Jack walked on the beach. There were sunbathers and swimmers. "It doesn't seem right," she said. "I prefer the New England landscape for Christmas."

"Give me the sunshine anytime," said Jack.

"So, how was it?" she said. "The election, I mean."

"It wore me out, but now comes the really hard part; I have to do the job. I felt like a hero until it was all over. Now I feel like a guy who has to go to work every day. Eunice and I are going to share a house on 31st Street in Georgetown. I guess you remember that old neighborhood."

"I sure do. I miss those days at the *Times-Herald.* Frank Waldrop, Inga, Page, Betty Coxe, John White. You were still in that old apartment before they transferred you to Charleston. We had some good times."

"Do you ever hear from John White?"

"Once in a while."

"That guy was crazy about you."

"He was crazy, period."

"For a while there I thought you were going to marry him."

"I thought about it, but I figured it would be a fifty-year feud. Besides, every time he got engaged he managed to talk himself out of the marriage. Or maybe I was the one who talked myself out of it. I don't know."

"Incidentally, he's back at the *Times-Herald*, and he's going to do a piece on Eunie in that column that you and Inga sometimes wrote."

" 'Did You Happen to See --' "

"Yeah, that's it. She's getting a lot of press coverage, and she probably deserves it. I hope nobody tells them that her job was the only string attached to the money Dad put up to fund a national bureau for juvenile delinquency."

"Daddy Warbucks strikes again," she said.

"He means well. He gave me a lot of help in the campaign, and he had the good sense to keep a low profile. Anyhow, we'll be moving in next week. Why don't you come up and visit us?"

"I can't imagine you two in the same house. Who's going to pick up all the dirty clothes and the hairy hamburgers rotting behind the couch? You'll have roaches before you know it."

"No we won't. We're taking old Margaret with us to be our housekeeper."

"She has my sympathy."

"And I think Bill Sutton is going to move in and be my assistant. But, don't worry, there will be plenty of room for you, unless you've been spoiled by mansions and castles."

"Not bloody likely, though it's nice sometimes to be called Lady Hartington."

"How about we compromise and call you Lady Kickie Poo?"

She poked him with her elbow and he flashed his Hollywood smile. "How about we call you John Juan?"

"So, tell me, Lady H, how's your love life over there in the land of lords and faggots?"

"My love life is none of your business."

"Ah, so there is one. Come on little sister, tell your big brother."

She turned serious. "There is something, but I can't tell you about it now. Maybe before I go back. Don't say anything --"

"Of course not! But if some guy is giving you a hard time, tell him your brother has friends in high places."

"I don't think it would impress him."

Jack raised his eyebrows. "In that case, *I'm* impressed."

It wasn't until Jack and Eunice left for Washington that Kathleen's parents focused their attention on her. First it was her father, still smiling with satisfaction over the accomplishments of his children. His receding hair made him look older than fifty eight, but his trim figure still gave him that tall, distinguished look, that distinctively American look of success, complete with the winning smile. "Johnny and Eunice are going to make their mark in Washington," he said. "They're going to stand that town on its ear. Naturally, I wish it was Joe who was going off to Congress, but, you know, in some ways, Jack's got more political sex appeal. The women are crazy about that guy."

"He must take after his old man," said Kathleen.

He smiled at her, his face framed by one of the arches of the Spanish style house. They were drinking lemonade at a table by the pool. "My kids are all good-looking, all winners!" He said, and then he hesitated, as though he might be thinking of the two who were missing. She could see his eyes behind his spectacles, zeroing in on her. He wasted no time. "You know, Kick," he said, "I don't think living in England is such a hot idea. Why the hell don't you just come home and make a life here with us? We've had our bad innings, but the war is over now and we're back on track. Things are going to be pretty exciting from now on."

"I can see that," she said, "and it's very tempting to be a part of it all, but I can't quite imagine what I'd be doing. I'm not in politics, and I don't have Eunie's dedication to causes."

"You can start by finding yourself a good husband," he said.

"I had a husband!" She could hear the hint of accusation in her voice. "I'm sorry. I guess I'm not ready to think about that."

"Maybe we can get you a job in Washington."

"Sure, I'll start as a secretary. How about Secretary of State?"

"What are your qualifications?"

"Transatlantic diplomacy and typing."

"I give up! You'll never be serious about a career, but you're still my favorite girl."

His tone was less convincing than it used to be, but she could tell how strongly he felt the bond of flesh and blood. His children were, for him, literal extensions of his own being. She realized, suddenly, that her independence was almost as devastating to him as his son's death.

Her mother was more elusive than her father. She kept disappearing, and whenever Kathleen inquired about her, she was told the same thing: "She's probably gone to church."

One Sunday, Rose insisted that Kathleen accompany her to Mass. Afterwards, she seemed to be in the mood to talk. "You didn't go up for Holy Communion."

"No," said Kathleen. "I just didn't get to confession."

"Was there any problem?"

Kathleen hesitated. "No, Mother, no problem. Just laziness on my part, I guess."

"Well, you can't afford to be lazy about something as important as that. In any case, I've been meaning to have a talk with you."

261

"About what?"

"About your plans, of course."

"I don't think I have any plans, Mother, except to enjoy my visit and go back to London."

"Your father told me that he talked to you and that you were thinking of giving up London. I think that would be very sensible of you. We have heard from some of our old friends in London that you are now associated with a rich and reckless crowd that is raising eyebrows. Why didn't you introduce us to some of your more *intimate* companions?"

"If you mean *men,* Mother, I can assure you that there are some in London, and that some of them are my friends. And, yes, I do have a social life. I may even marry again someday. At the moment, however, I don't think I'm in a position to do so."

"What is that supposed to mean?"

She rolled her eyes toward the innocent Florida sky. "It means, Mother, that there are not very many men in London who are both interesting and available. I think the war had something to do with the shortage. Those who survived do not have to marry widows. It's a matter of supply and demand."

"You might find it easier in America. You have a lot of friends here. And, of course, we might be of some help."

"That's very nice of you, Mother, but I'm not a debutante anymore. I don't need a chaperone."

Rose frowned. "That's not what I meant. Why do you have to be so antagonistic?"

"Because it *is* what you meant. You think I made a mistake the first time and you think that you can keep me from making the same mistake again."

"And what's wrong with that, may I ask?"

"Nothing, except that it's my life, and I 'd like the privilege of ruining it in my own way."

Rose's face tightened with anger. "Well," she said, "I can see that there is no point in talking to you right now. Someday you may see things differently."

During the rest of her visit, Kathleen was sometimes tempted to apologize to her mother and to confide in her, but she did not. She was also sometimes tempted to rush back to London on an impulse and fling herself into her lover's arms, but she did not. She traveled to Washington D.C. and New York in order to extend her time in America. She wanted Peter to believe that she could do without him, though she herself knew that she could not. It was early spring before she returned to London.

CHAPTER SEVENTEEN

She traveled east into the dawn and tried to escape from her unresolved problems into random reveries. She felt alone and strange and far away from everything. Always there was the sea, the sailboats of her childhood, the feeling of the captured wind in those wonderful races that meant everything at the moment. And then she was looking for something, digging in the sand with her small shovel. Her brother was a shadow on the sand. He helped her to dig, using the big shovel and turning up shells, clams with tails. "Little boy clams," he said. And then she was a big girl and she was running and running and running, and Johnny caught her in his arms and threw her down on the grass. And then he picked up the football and threw it to Joe. She limped back to the gang and they started again. "Everybody out for a pass," said Joe.

By the time she reached her house in Smith Square she was very tired. She got a warm greeting from her Hungarians, who assured her that the house was in order. "There is much mail and some telegrams," said Llona.

"And some telephone calls this morning," said Elisabeth.

"Anything important?" said Kathleen.

"Friends who said they welcome you home. Their messages are with your mail on your desk. And one who said nothing."

She knew instantly who that one was. She wanted to say, *Where is he?* but she kept the thought to herself and went upstairs. She felt the beating of her heart and she felt her mind suddenly focused on that one thought, that one person, as though all the fragments of her life had coalesced there in that simple question: *Where is he?* She wanted to know.

She wanted to be there. She wanted to call him by his nickname. *Blood!* How awful! She had never used it, but now, suddenly, it seemed to make sense. *Blood.* He was her lifeblood. *Where is he?*

She turned to her desk. There might be something there, a letter, a telegram. Sometimes when he was away he would send her a message, a brief sentence or two, just a reminder. That was all she needed. And then there it was, at the very top of the pile, as though the Hungarians knew. At times she was sure they did but dared not say anything. How could they?

She opened the telegram. His voice leapt into the room: EVERYONE IN LONDON STARK RAVING MAD STOP HIDING OUT AT MILTON SOLO STOP HOW CAN I LURE YOU TO THE COTTAGE STOP INCREDIBLE LOVE.

She knew it would be pointless to lie down. She would not even be able to close her eyes, but how could she even think of jumping in her car and driving a hundred miles to see him. It was a disgraceful, sinful, awful thing to do, she thought, and then she did it!

The ordinary world on an ordinary day sailed by in the form of mailmen and children and horse-drawn milk wagons in the city, grim factories on the outskirts, and lorries lumbering on roads that led to the rolling meadows of the countryside. Her Austin was as ordinary as a car could be, but in her mind she was driving in a private Grand Prix event, leaving the slower traffic in the dust and turning the slow lorries into dying dinosaurs. Her adventure, of course, was not visible to the police or anyone else, though she cursed with impatience the drivers who stood between her and her destination.

Three hours later she was at the cottage near Milton. It belonged to one of Peter's old friends. She had never met him . He was never there. *On His Majesty's Service somewhere,* was all that Peter would ever say. There was no telephone.

It was late afternoon. It was March. The wind swept the clouds across the sky, and shy buds had begun to appear on the trees. She could not remember the name of the music that ran through her mind over and over again. Was it Glenn Miller? Was it "A String of Pearls"?

Sycamores lined the lane and ivy covered the old bricks of the two-story cottage. Before she even parked the car she could see that the door was open and Peter was standing there in cap and scarf and woolen jacket, as though he had just returned from a long walk. She leapt out and ran to him. He held out his arms and she was home again, safe and warm, like a wanderer who had been traveling among strangers in foreign places. Their kisses were like sipped wine or the savorings of a feast. There would be time now and they would be alone.

Inside, there was a warm fire in the stone fireplace. Peter brought in drinks. "I never told you this," he said, "but the reason Richard doesn't come here anymore is that his wife died and he was broken-hearted."

"How awful," said Kathleen.

"Yes." He hesitated. "She committed suicide."

"But why?"

"Nobody knows. They seemed very happy together. She was young."

"How strange! To me it is such an inconceivable thing to do."

"Of course, darling; you're a Catholic. It's a mortal sin."

"That's not why. It strikes me as such an admission of defeat, and I guess I was not trained for failure. Not winning for us was a form of death."

"Maybe death is a form of not winning," he said. "And everything else is a game of run for your life and beat the devil."

"Don't you believe in God?"she said.

"I don't think it's a question of God's existence; I think it's a question of his attitude. I

266

mean, something had to set in motion all this nonsense, but what if God's purpose is less than pure, or just plain confused!"

"Don't talk that way, Peter. Come sit by the fire. We'll never know what God's purpose is, so just tell me about *your* purpose. Is it less than pure?"

"Why did you stay away so long?"

"I was trying to decide whether or not I could trust you."

"And what did you decide?"

"I decided finally that I wanted you whether or not I could trust you. Tell me why you came here?"

"There was a terrible scene in London. We had a very important invitation to Buckingham Palace. It doesn't happen very often, even for a countess, and Obby was in a panic. She tried to fortify herself with a drink or two and wound up dead drunk. I had to make her excuses, but I don't think anyone was convinced. It was all very embarrassing. Now the rumor-mongers are at work again, saying that I have driven my wife to drink by carrying on with other women, one of whom is believed to be Lady Hartington."

"And who are the others?" she said.

"There are no others. Not anymore. I'm sorry about all this. Obby is very careless about what she says. She's at Grosvenor Square now, and I just couldn't stand to be there with her any longer. I'm convinced that our marriage is over."

"Perhaps if we didn't see each other things might improve," said Kathleen.

"After you left for the States things actually got worse," he said. "In any case, I don't want to give you up. I need you, darling. We need each other. I refuse to be responsible for Obby's behavior. There must be a way to arrive at a settlement for her and Juliet. I'm going to ask my lawyers to look into it. With your help I think I can do it this time. What we do then will depend on you."

267

"If we are going to stay together, Peter, we will have to get married. I'm not very good at being the other woman, and I can't stand living in the moral shadows. I want to be a legitimate part of society. I want to be able to hold my head up in my adopted country. Do you think we will ever be able to do that?"

"I suppose some people would go on talking, even if we were married. And, of course, there's your family. Even if they accepted me, which is not likely, they might not accept my religion. Well, I'm not going to change that, and I'm not going to impose Catholicism on my children. I am bound in these matters by strong traditions that affect a lot of people. You will have to deal with your family, and I may not be able to help you very much, except to prove to you in other ways that I love you. You will be told, of course, that these are promises made to you by a scoundrel and a liar."

She leaned against his shoulder, and the light of the fire illuminated her face. "I don't care," she said. "I will probably believe you even if you lie to me."

"I think that's the highest compliment I've ever been paid in my entire life," he said, and she could tell that he meant it.

The London Season took further strides towards the glitter and style of the good old days, though everyone knew that something would be permanently missing. The gray top hats and morning coats were back at Royal Ascot. Princess Elizabeth became engaged to Philip Mountbatten, and a great wave of old-fashioned jubilation swept through Britain and the Empire. In the backwash and undertow, however, the monarchy was attacked by the left as an archaic extravagance that was an insult to the working people in a modern democracy.

For Kathleen a temporary order was restored in her life after her mad dash to the country to find her lover. After several days of peace and privacy with Peter, she could easily imagine a lifetime with him. She was convinced that those who described him as a scoundrel did not know what he was really like or how profoundly unhappy he was with his difficult wife. They could not know what stifled affection there was behind his rough facade or how gentle he could be, even when he was driven by desperate passions. She knew! And together in bed they shared the secret that all lovers have -- the mystery of a compatibility so complete that it could only be described as finding one's self in another person. She believed that in some high sense they belonged to one another, and this belief protected her from the accusations of society, self, and church.

The days went by like dreamy sailboats seen from a distance. Spring advanced from the shy appearance of daffodils to riots of roses and rhododendrons. Peter assured her that he and his lawyers were in complicated negotiations with Olive, who was determined either to discourage him or take him for everything he was worth. "I never thought that she was going to make it easy," he said, "but this is beyond anything I imagined. She has even hinted that she may name you as the corespondent if she is forced into the courts. What she wants is a private settlement, in which she remains my wife but allows me my freedom."

"No, Peter," Kathleen said, "that would never work. You know how I feel about living in limbo like that. Sooner or later, it would destroy us both."

He agreed, and the legal maneuvers went on, while they settled into a routine of seeing each other whenever and wherever they could. Meanwhile, his public life with Obby seemed strangely untouched, in spite of all the rumors about a possible divorce. The aroma of scandal excited the press, who covered their activities more closely than ever. It troubled Kathleen to see their pictures in the papers, dancing together at the Derby ball or looking "fabulous" at Ascot. "These are things we have to do," he explained, and Kathleen renewed her vows of patience after a few tears of disappointment.

Though she was tempted to be defiant, she found herself staying away from much of the social activity. She had to make an exception of the Independence Day garden party on the lawn of the American Embassy. There were two thousand guests but Mrs. Lewis Douglas, the wife of the new Ambassador, had urged her to attend in a personal letter, in which she also suggested a more private meeting. Kathleen continued to see friends in smaller gatherings, and her in-laws were kind enough to give her the impression that they knew nothing at all about her connection with the Eighth Earl Fitzwilliam. It was her sister-in-law Elizabeth who revealed their secret. "Of course they know. They've known for some time, but they have a great deal of respect for personal privacy. They are not very fond of Peter, and they don't want to hurt your feelings. Andrew likes him, but he has to admit that a woman would have to be a bit of a gambler to marry him."

"What about you?" said Kathleen.

"Oh, I think he's wonderful -- handsome and dashing and dangerous. The sort of man you read about in novels. You know, the hero who dies at the end and proves that he loved honor more -- that sort of thing."

"Don't say that! Don't talk about death."

Elizabeth comforted her. "I'm sorry, Kick. I was only joking. I'm sure he's not the rogue they make him out to be. I think he's very attractive. He's got a wonderful sad look in his eye."

270

"Do you think Billy will forgive me for this?" she said.

"I'm sure that he will, if it's what you really want."

Kathleen hesitated, but then she said in a firm voice, "It is. I know it is."

A few weeks later Olive called her to suggest a meeting. Kathleen did not consult Peter before agreeing to see her; in fact, she invited her to tea that very afternoon. As soon as she hung up she had a moment of panic. She almost called back to cancel her invitation. Instead, she told Llona to arrange a special tea for the Countess Fitzwilliam. "And we will not want to be disturbed," she said. The expression on Llona's face was all the comment she needed.

By five o'clock she thought she was ready. She had spent an hour finding the right clothes to wear and checking herself in the mirror. The idea was not to look threatening, she decided. She chose black to emphasize her widowhood. Olive, on the other hand, tried to look like the betrayed wife. They knew each other, of course, and did not need elaborate greetings.

Olive lit a cigarette and got right to the point. "Now isn't this a fine mess we've all gotten ourselves into," she said. "Don't worry, I did not come here to accuse you of stealing my husband. He doesn't need stealing; he's always ready for a little fun. And you're not the first woman he's talked out of her knickers."

Llona came in with the tea. "Would you prefer something stronger?" said Kathleen.

"Tea will be fine," she said, "but after I've said what I came to say, I'll probably need a drink."

"I suppose I will too," said Kathleen, and they both smiled as though they were members of the same club and were about to close ranks against a common enemy.

271

"I suppose you know that Peter has asked me for a divorce," said Olive.

"Yes," said Kathleen, "but I haven't asked him to do that. In fact, I've offered to stay out of the way, if a reconciliation is possible. He's assured me that it isn't."

"My dear girl, Peter could convince a woman that he was Jesus Christ and still wind up in bed with her. What I came here to tell you, Kathleen, is that the man is not to be trusted. We've been through this divorce routine before. Some women will not give in until he proves he's serious. Don't you see? It's all part of the game. And I'm part of the game, too. He wants me to believe that he is capable of leaving me. Underneath it all, he knows damn well that he and I were made for one another, for better or worse. I know what I'm talking about. We'll go on fighting, but he won't leave me. He'll have his women, and I won't be able to leave him. Maybe we've already died and gone to hell, but that's the way it is. Now, I'll have that drink, if your offer is still good!"

Kathleen was stunned. It was as if her mother had found her tongue and talked honestly about her relationship with her father. They, too, were hopelessly bound together, and not only by the chains of their religion. She suddenly understood that strange impasse, but she refused to believe that it was true of Peter, even though she was chilled by Olive's recital.

They had drinks and Kathleen explained her own position. "I had no intention of becoming involved with a married man. He told me that his marriage was over. Other people seemed to have the same impression."

"When it comes to marriage, what the hell do other people really know?" said Olive, holding out her empty glass. "There are things that go on at night in the bedroom that can not even be discussed

272

in broad daylight, and will never make sense morally or otherwise."

"I'm afraid I've had very limited marriage experience," said Kathleen, "but I'm sure that people who are married a long time have a special intimacy and understanding. For a long time I refused to become involved, but then --"

"Yes, I know all about it."

"What do you mean?"

"I mean, he gets drunk and boasts about his conquests."

"To you?"

"To me, to his friends--"

"I don't believe you. Why should I? You'll say anything at this point."

"I'm not trying to be cruel, Kathleen. I'm trying to warn you. You are walking down the garden path, and if you look down you'll see the footprints of a lot of women who have been down that path before you. I will admit that this time it seems a bit more serious, and, obviously, I'm worried and upset, but ask yourself what you would do in my place. What would you do?"

The very thought horrified her, and she could feel herself turning pale as she tried to envision herself standing there like Olive, pleading with the other woman to let her keep her husband, her lover. "No!" she said firmly, as if to dismiss the vision and everything that Olive was trying to tell her. "No, no, no, it's not going to be that way."

"Well, then how is it going to be, darling? Do you expect me to step aside and give the bastard his divorce on a silver platter? And do you expect him to walk away from all that Guinness money I inherited? I doubt that he will, unless he hopes to get his hands on some of your Kennedy money."

"He's got plenty of money of his own," said Kathleen with a sudden flash of anger. "He doesn't need yours or mine. And I don't think this conversation is going to do either one of us any good, so why don't we drop it? I didn't meant to hurt you. I'm sorry. Why don't you and Peter just work out your own problems, and I'll go somewhere and stay out of the way."

"I didn't mean to sound so vindictive and awful," said Olive. "He brings out the worst in me, I'm afraid. Sometimes I wake up in the morning and I promise myself that I will be sweet and ladylike and reasonable, and then, by five o'clock, I've turned into the Wicked Witch of the North."

Kathleen's mouth was dry. She kept seeing herself in Olive's position. She stood up and said, "I'm glad you came by. You've given me a lot to think about."

At the door Kathleen had the impression that Olive wanted to kiss her goodbye, but they simply shook hands and smiled politely. Back inside, Kathleen poured herself a strong drink. She could feel her hand shaking as she lifted the glass to her lips.

CHAPTER EIGHTEEN

In August, Kathleen retreated to Lismore Castle in southern Ireland. Of all the Cavendish estates it was her favorite, "the most perfect place in the world." The Duke and Duchess, knowing how she felt, allowed her to use it as though it were her own. Whenever she was there, she was reminded of her girlish dreams -- to be the chatelaine, the mistress of a castle. For a while, the dream was true. Had her husband lived, it would have been true forever, though sometimes, as she walked through the haunted countryside at Lismore, she wondered whether or not she had outgrown her youthful and romantic longings. She was a woman now and had discovered a whole new world of desires. She was a woman and a widow. She had a lover and a dead husband and two families. She found it difficult to define herself and her place in the world.

Lismore Castle was part of her image of herself as a member of an aristocratic English family, not as a descendent of Irish peasants. Like her mother and father, she preferred to distance herself from those poor Irish immigrants who settled in America.

When her Congressman brother came to visit her at the end of the summer, she was breathless with excitement and insisted on taking him on a tour of the place in spite of his bad back. "Isn't it wonderful?" she said. "Of course, there's not much left of the original from the days of King John in the twelfth century, and it's more a mansion than a castle now, having passed through the hands of the Church, Sir Walter Raleigh, and the Earls of Cork. It did not become the property of the Duke of Devonshire until 1753. It was the fifth Duke who built the bridge across the river, and the sixth Duke who fell in love with Gothic revival and gave it this look around 1850. I love it. Don't you?"

"It looks like a Hollywood set for one of those old historical romances," said brother John. "Errol Flynn and the Virgin Queen! If I didn't have a bad back, I'd be tempted to slide down that bannister. I wonder how many of the old drunken dukes gave that a shot on a rainy Irish night."

She held his arm on the ramparts and looked down the steep rocks into the Blackwater River. The air was warm and misty, and the river mirrored the trees along the bank. "Do you ever stay here alone?" he said.

"You know me, Johnny. I don't like to be alone, but sometimes it's been a comfort. I've had a lot to think about."

"Castles are supposed to be full of ghosts. Maybe you're not alone, after all. It's pretty damned splendid, but I think I prefer Washington, the city of single women and cherry blossoms, not to mention the Congress of the United States."

"I guess you really like it."

"Yes, I do. I really do. The legislative process is boring, but, otherwise, it's like Don Juan heaven. With all the distractions, I'm not sure I'm going to get any work done."

She smiled. "Are you being bad?"

"Sure!" he said. "How about you?"

Her smile turned into a frown. She looked away towards the river. "I don't think so, but almost everybody else does. I was going to tell you in Palm Beach, but then I decided not to. I don't want Mother and Dad to know -- not yet."

"I take it you've got a serious boyfriend," said Jack. "So what's the problem this time?"

"I never thought of him as a boyfriend. It sounds so high-schoolish."

"He's not that fellow who lost his legs in the war?"

"No!" She squared her shoulders. "He's the Eighth Earl Fitzwilliam. Anglo-Irish and Protestant."

"Not again?"

"It's even worse this time. He's married and he has a twelve year old daughter."

Jack shook his head. "No wonder you've kept him a secret. Is there anything else wrong with him?"

"He drives too fast, he drinks too much, and he chases women."

"He better have a lot of redeeming qualities?"

"He was a commando in the war. He's a wonderful, forceful, witty man, and --"

"And I suppose he's great in bed."

She blushed. "Well, yes, in fact. he is."

"I'm sure Mother will be happy to hear about that -- and all the rest. Now, get serious, Kick. Why in the world would you even mention this guy to her?"

"Because Peter and I are planning to get married, that's why."

He looked at the stone he was holding in his hand and then threw it into the river with a sidearm motion, as though they were on the beach in Hyannis Port. "Honey," he said, "you and Peter may be getting married, but there is no way in the world that your mother is going to accept that marriage. And I'm willing to bet that she will be able to keep Dad and the rest of the family in line. She can be pretty formidable at times."

"How about you?"

"Offhand, I don't like the idea either, but only you know what will make you happy. Besides, I don't even know the guy."

"You'll meet him soon. I've invited him over. He's got a castle in Ireland too. At Coollattin, about a hundred miles from here, en route to Dublin."

"Terrific! You can play *my castle or yours.* What a cozy way of life you've got here! But what about all these other people you promised to introduce me to, like Anthony Eden and Pamela Churchill? Do they know about all this?"

"Of course. And they all know Peter. In fact, the whole ruling class is like an extended family. They don't all approve of our affair, but most of them understand the situation."

As they followed the path along the river, she told him about Peter and Olive, about their families and fortunes and their difficult marriage. "He was already determined to end it before he met me."

"That's what they all say."

"But it's true. Everyone knows that they've been at odds for years."

"It doesn't matter. They will still blame you for breaking up the marriage. One of the things I've never understood about the Church is how they can say that a Protestant marriage is not valid and at the same time say that you have committed a sin if you contribute in any way to the break up of that marriage. Anyhow, Kick, you're in big trouble. You're already doing something sinful, and even if Peter gets his divorce, your mother and the mother Church will never sanction your marriage to him. You won't convert and he won't compromise. Why don't you just change your name and start your life over again? Forget your past and your family. Join the English church, marry your English lord and hang out with the Duke and Duchess of Windsor in Monte Carlo and Bermuda."

"Don't be cruel, Johnny. I love Peter. I didn't really know what love was all about before I met him. He feels the same way, and he is determined to rearrange his life so that we can be together. He thinks it can be done, and I believe him."

He took her hand and looked into her eyes. "It's the real thing, isn't it?" he said.

"Yes," she said. "Haven't you ever felt that way?"

"I guess I've been close enough to it to know what you're talking about, but maybe I was too young or too scared to go all the way. It must be a wonderful feeling, but I also think you're a fool to let yourself get into a predicament like this."

"When it all comes out will you stand by me?"

"Sure, Kick! I'll just tell them what I think. It's a personal decision and it's yours to make. I don't think it's up to the rest of us to pass judgment on you. I'll accept whatever you do." He smiled. "I think a woman in love has a perfect right to make an idiot of herself. Of course, the rest of the gang is going to give you a rough time. You'd better be prepared for that."

She took his arm and kissed him on the cheek. Then they started back towards the gatehouse and the stone bridge. The castle walls loomed before them, one wall covered with green moss, another with reddish ivy. The clouds had thickened and there was a sudden chill in the air.

A few days later Lismore Castle was as lively as a townhouse in London or a country house in Derbyshire. The most distinguished of Kathleen's guests was the fifty-year old Anthony Eden, who, as a young man, resigned from his position as foreign secretary to protest the appeasement policy of Prime Minister Chamberlain. His personal affection for Kathleen was an old story by now. Her other political guests included Tony Rosslyn, Hugh Fraser and Charles Johnson, all Members of Parliament. The Irish writer Sean Leslie and the irrepressible Pamela Churchill made a considerable contribution to the liveliness of the scene. "I have been warned," said Sean Leslie, "that Pamela is a spy for Lord Beaverbrook. I, therefore, expect to be paid, in advance, for anything I say that is even remotely quotable."

"Well, so far you haven't made a farthing," said Pamela, with her round-faced, self-satisfied smile.

Jack took to Anthony Eden immediately. In a room with tapestries and books and sunlight slanting through tall leaded windows, they talked about the Marshall Plan and other post-war issues. Independently, they reported to Kathleen how pleased they were to have had this opportunity to exchange ideas. "Your brother has a first-rate mind," said Eden. "He ought to have a bright future in American government."

"My father has already decided that he's going to be President," said Kathleen.

"For once your father may be right," he said.

At dinner they made plans for golf and tennis and horseback riding, but Jack, pleading a bad back, said that he was hoping to visit the ancesctral home of the Kennedys, a place called New Ross. "It's on the River Barrow in County Wexford, about fifty-miles from here. But it was about a hundred years ago that the first Kennedys emigrated to America, and in time they lost touch with their relatives in the old country."

"The place is crawling with Kennedys," said Sean Leslie. "Some of them are bound to be relatives, but if I were you, I wouldn't go around announcing myself as a rich American. You'll wind up down at the pub with more cousins than you bargained for."

"I tried to talk Kick into going with me, but she says she couldn't care less about her peasant ancestors."

"Why should I?" said Kathleen from the other end of the table. "They probably don't even have plumbing yet."

"She's got a point," said Hugh Fraser. "I've been through that part of Ireland. It's very poor. Sod houses, that sort of thing. Pigs and chickens and children, and a lot of mud. I'd personally find it very embarrassing, driving up in that huge station wagon that she had sent over from the States."

"I happen to like my car," said Kathleen. "It's very useful on these awful roads."

"But is there enough petrol in County Waterford to keep the thing going?" said Sean.

The next morning Pamela joined Kathleen for coffee. "Your brother asked me to go along with him to New Ross. Personally, I'm not in the mood for visiting the wretched of the earth, but it beats playing golf. And don't worry about Jack. He's too young and too scrawny for me. Not my type. But he does have a nice light in his eye. I'll give him that. And Hugh says that he has a very good sense of humor. We'll see!"

When they arrived back that evening, Jack was full of excitement as he told them about his great adventure. Pamela made it clear that she did not share his enthusiasm. "We actually found my ancestors," said Jack. "It was a glimpse of the old Ireland, and the way things were when the Kennedys left."

"Now I know why they left," said Pamela.

"So, do they have a bathroom?" said Kathleen.

"They haven't got anything except lots of children," said Pamela.

"That's not the point," said Jack. "It's the continuity. We all like to know where we came from."

"I thought it was only the aristocracy that was interested in that sort of thing," said Tony Rosslyn. "I mean, a hundred years is nothing, really. This castle, for instance, was built about seven hundred and fifty years ago. A lot of Englishmen can still trace their families back to the Norman Conquest in 1066."

"Well, we don't have much of that in America," said Jack. "We just haven't been around that long, and when you cross the ocean and settle in a new world, I guess history has a way of getting lost. Anyhow, I had a good time, and afterwards I took a bunch of the kids for a ride around town in the station wagon and they were delighted. I guess they'll be talking about our visit for a long time."

Kathleen wondered briefly whether or not Pamela and Jack had made an amorous detour somewhere, but she decided that they probably had not. Jack looked a bit on the pale side, and there was just a hint of petulance in Pamela's voice, as though he hadn't tried anything and she was disappointed, even though she wasn't very interested to begin with.

Peter Fitzwilliam made a brief appearance during Jack's visit, and Jack had to admit that the ex-commando was quite an impressive and charming fellow. "There's something refreshingly earthy, maybe even vulgar, about him. A man's man, I'd say, and the kind of person for whom a woman might wreck her life. But maybe that's the kind of man you need. And, who knows, maybe he needs a woman like you to settle him down."

"I think so," she said. "I think I can keep him happy for a long time."

"He's not at all like Billy, is he?"

Kathleen hesitated. "No," she said, "not at all."

"Do you want me to say anything when I get home?"

"No, I'd rather do it myself. I'll be in Palm Beach for part of the winter. As soon as we are sure that Peter's divorce will go through, I want to announce our marriage. Once it's a certainty, I don't think I will be quite so frightened. I will have to take the consequences, whatever they are."

"I'm not going to try to talk you out of it. You know what you want, and you're not going to give it up for anything, are you?"

"No, not for anything," she said. "I'm in love, and I'm happy. I won't let anything ruin it for me this time. Not even God!"

Jack shrugged. "Who knows! Maybe he's on your side, in spite of what the Church says."

CHAPTER NINETEEN

Sometimes things seemed so ordinary in London that her affair with Peter felt like a fantasy, a recurrent dream in which she stepped through a door into a different world. Sometimes the sun would be shining and she would be walking along Sloane Street with, maybe, Jane Kenyon, and they would be talking about where to shop and where to have lunch, and the very sound of the traffic was like the music of reality, compared to the strange sounds in the shadowy world in which she and Peter struggled with their problems and urgent desires.

Reality was a movie matinee with Sissy Ormsby-Gore. One Saturday they saw *Open City*, and another time it was *Brief Encounter*, which made her weep. There were newsreels and radio reports and headlines. The real world seemed to be moving by at three times the speed of her private drama. India and Pakistan were given their independence. Elizabeth and Philip were married in Westminster Abbey. Ghandi was assasinated. War and violence were refreshingly real. At night, when she walked through that dark door into her dream of paradise, Peter was forever standing there at a window, looking into the distance over a moonlit landscape. And he was saying, "It won't be long now. These things take time." And then he would hold out his arms to her and she would go to him and they would make love in a dimension populated by just the two of them.

She seemed to be forever waking up and finding him gone. There would be sunlight, street noises, and voices telling her that someone called or that her mother was planning a trip to Paris. She met her mother there at the end of September, and they were both surprisingly happy to see one another, as though they had missed something in the past that they were now trying to recover. They went to the fashion shows. The models were like mannequins in motion, their faces fixed for all of eternity in female expressions of absolute confidence. Together they went back to London for a fortnight. They talked about Jack's health problems. He had fallen ill in London and was attended by Lord Beaverbrook's doctor, an arrangement made by Pamela. Dr. Davis called it Addison's disease, a failure of the adrenal glands that could prove fatal. John was back in America, improving in spite of the diagnosis.

Christmas came and went. She did not go home. She visited her in-laws, who were so kind and considerate that she considered staying with them. She tried to imagine playing her widow's role forever, and maybe eventually being matched with an elderly peer. There would be no children, of course, no complications. She walked in the woods and wept as though those were the last trees left on the planet and she were the last woman. Her sudden sense of loneliness attacked the very marrow of her bones and she was in physical pain, but only until she saw her lover again and slept in his arms.

He kept assuring her that everything was going to be all right. Sometimes he was furious; sometimes he was sad. "Obby's a pathetic wretch," he said one night, when he himself had been drinking. "It might have been easier for me to love her, if she hadn't been so full of self-pity and self-hatred. Sometimes I'm afraid she's going to kill herself." Kathleen caught herself hoping for a moment that she might, and then spent half the night trembling, saying prayers for forgiveness.

January seemed to go on forever, but near the end of the month he surprised her with flowers and said, "We've arrived at a settlement. I've given her just about everything a woman could expect. She and Juliet will be very comfortable. My mother is very pleased and gives us her blessings."

His announcement caught her off balance. Suddenly, she was shoved onto a stage, where it would be her turn to perform. Her mother and father were waiting in the wings. "Are you sure?"

"Absolutely, darling. It's been a nightmare and now it's over. You can go to America and talk to your family. If they would like to meet me, I'm sure something can be arranged. As soon as you get back we can work out the details." He gathered her into his arms, as though his bear-like embrace was intended to provide her with a new home and a new life. It was the firm grip of a man who always got what he wanted, and it made her feel both helpless and secure.

To please Peter, she had been staying away from her Catholic friends, many of whom could not accept his reckless pursuit of pleasure, but once her plans to visit her family in Palm Beach were firm, the person she most wanted to see was Sissy Ormsby-Gore. She had a lot to talk about, and she wanted a point of view more objective than her own or Peter's.

Sissy and David invited her to have dinner with them the night before she was scheduled to sail. She arrived in a state of nervous excitement, overdressed for the occasion and talking as though she had been starved for listeners. "You look marvelous," said Sissy, referring to her chic black dress and double string of pearls. "And where did you get that hat?"

"In Paris, the last time my mother was here."

"I'm afraid that our modest dinner is not going to measure up to your outfit. And look at your hair! It's longer. It makes you look very sophisticated. Where's that good old-fashioned American look of yours?"

"When I get back to the States I'll probably put on a sweater and a skirt and my penny loafers, It's Peter who likes me to dress this way. He's forever heaping gifts on me and asking me to buy some clothes that are worthy of them."

David cleared his throat diplomatically. "So, how does it feel to be going home, Kick?" he said. "A bit nervous-making I suppose, considering the circumstances."

"I know now what those young soldiers felt like at the Hans Crescent Club during the war," she said. "I feel as if I'm shipping out at dawn for the front lines."

"You are in a way," said Sissy.

"Except that your chances of survival are not as good," said David.

"If I could just count on my family, I would take my chances with the Church and pray for some sort of compromise in the future. If I can convince my parents that Peter and I are determined to be married, maybe they will just accept the inevitable."

"But your mother will only accept what the Church accepts," said Sissy. "And you really can't condemn her for trying to be a good Catholic."

"No, but she sure can condemn me for being less than perfect. Sometimes I get the feeling that she uses her religion to condemn me for something else."

"For what?" said Sissy.

"I don't know," said Kathleen, squinting her eyes as though to look back through all the pages of her life. "Maybe for following my heart instead of her rules."

"You mean the Church's rules."

"I guess so. It was always put to me that way, but I always felt that there was something behind the screen. Peter says that my mother will never be able to accept the fact that I am in love, because it liberates me from her and the Church and gives me the kind of joy that she never had. He says that women need love, and that without love they turn bitter and begin to rot inside."

"How poetic," said David. "But a bit of a romantic exaggeration, don't you think?"

"Not really," said Sissy. "Women *do* need love. They need it so much, in fact, that they often accept dangerous imitations. My feeling, as you know, Kick, is that you may have fallen in love with a dangerous man, a kind of Don Juan, who is more interested in his own conquests than in the women that he conquers. He's found you very exciting because you've been a great challenge. But once he's got you, perhaps he'll need a new challenge?"

"I'm willing to gamble," said Kathleen.

"The stakes are pretty high," said David. "There's your family to consider, and his, of course. His daughter is just coming of age and his wife is ill. It's pretty selfish of him to put his own pleasure before such responsibilities. It seems to me he's that way about everything. Since the end of the war he hasn't done anything for his country, nor has he shown any interest in politics, unless it's some local issue that will affect him personally and financially. You have to admit that he is rather self-centered and self-serving."

"I don't have to admit anything," she said. "Peter has had personal and family problems for a long time. I think he's made an honest effort to come to terms with them. Nothing has worked out. His decision to start a new life makes a lot of sense to me, and I am willing to take personal risks to share that life."

"Even if it means being a spiritual outcast?" said Sissy.

Kathleen took a deep breath and let it out in a sigh. "It's not what I want, but if that's the way it has to be --" Her lips trembled and she seemed on the verge of tears, but she smiled as if to fend them off.

"I hear the weather in America has been awful," said diplomatic David.

"It'll be fine in Palm Beach, but it was horrible this winter in Boston and New York. There have been twenty five snowstorms in Boston and that big one in New York that broke all records since the famous Blizzard of '88. Maybe Mother Nature knows I'm coming and is setting the stage for the big drama." She laughed and, for a moment, she seemed like her old self.

It was always a dramatic change to go from the chill and dampness of England to the bright sunshine and warmth of Florida. For Elizabeth Cavendish it was an absolute revelation. She lounged by the pool in a conservative one-piece bathing suit that revealed the whiteness of her soft skin and her uncertainty about the whole idea of sunbathing. "I can't believe it's February," she said, squinting towards the sea and then glancing back at the Spanish style villa with its arches and tiles. "I feel rather strange lying here in the sun. I should look like a boiled lobster in an hour or so."

"Good!" said Kathleen. "We'll have you for dinner. It's my birthday, you know."

"Oh, God, how could I have forgotten," said Elizabeth. "The twentieth of February. Of course!"

"It's being at sea. You lose your sense of time."

"Will there be some sort of party?"

"Not really, just the family. There are usually enough of us around to have a party. We've always been that way, sort of an exclusive club, family only. I don't know why. I don't think my father really approves of parties, and my mother would rather be a guest than a hostess. She likes to dress up and make public appearances. She used to take her mother's place on the platform when her father was active in politics"

"Is he still alive?"

"Yes. Old Grandpa Honey Fitz is still going, and still singing 'Sweet Adeline.' He really knew how to enjoy life."

"Sometimes I think the Irish have more fun than the English," said Elizabeth, "but I don't dare say things like that at home. You know how they feel about the Irish. Not your family, of course, Kick. They're quite removed. American really. In fact, when your mother visited us in September, everyone thought she was quite nice and incredibly attractive for her age. She looked more like your sister than your mother."

"Don't say that, Liz."

"Why?"

"Because everyone says it and I'm tired of hearing it. Of course, it's exactly what Mother wants to hear. I think she competes with her daughters to show the world how young and energetic she is. I think she's jealous in some funny way, and I get the brunt of it because I'm the oldest, now that Rosemary is out of it."

Elizabeth's eyes followed the progress of a motorboat that crossed their postcard view, leaving a trail of white that caught the sun. For a moment she seemed hypnotized, and then she said, "We were like your family in some ways. Clannish, I mean. Often alone. God, how I hated those luncheons and dinners at Chatsworth when Grandfather was still alive. Nobody seemed to have anything to say. We went on like that in silence for what seemed to a child like hours. As you know, my parents preferred to live at Churchdale Hall, and we all loved it because it felt like our home. We never liked Chatsworth. It seemed haunted by the sad old Duke and Grannie Duchess."

"Your mother and father have been very good to me," said Kathleen. "You all have. I don't think I could have stayed in England if it weren't for my wonderful in-laws. Your father is such a charming old eccentric, always fussing with the garden and talking politics."

"Did Billy ever tell you how he gardened by torchlight during the war? And how his sister Dorothy Macmillan did the same thing, using the lantern of a miner's helmet? You have to be really passionate about gardening to do that."

Kathleen laughed and then frowned. "I guess he never got over Billy's death," she said.

"No," said Elizabeth, "and I don't think he ever will. For both my parents a light went out when Billy died. The rest of us may recover in due time. We're young and life goes on, but it's different for them."

"Yes," said Kathleen. "My father is like that too, permanently hurt by the loss of Joe, though he puts up a good front now. For some reason my mother does not seem as deeply wounded. Perhaps it's her powerful faith in God." There was just a hint of sarcasm in her voice.

"I hear that women can deal with death more easily than men," said Elizabeth. "I think it's true, don't you?"

"Please don't ask me about the truth, Liz. I'm much too confused. The less I think about it the better. I've come here to tell my parents that I plan to marry Peter, which is going to upset them terribly. And then I'm going to ask them to forgive me. I must be insane. If they don't kill me I'll be way ahead of the game."

Kathleen's birthday came and went and was swallowed up in several weeks of recreation and social life that distracted her from her mission. There were dinner parties and dances, endless rounds of golf and harmless flirtations at the beach in sunshine so reliable that it was soon taken for granted. It didn't take Kathleen long to see that Jack was as good as his word. He had kept her secret. Her parents did not seem to suspect a thing. Her father was busy with all his ventures and with his role in the Marshall Plan. It was an election year and Harry Truman was going to have to make use of all his connections if he was going to beat Thomas Dewey, the likely Republican candidate.

Elizabeth was interested in the American way of pleasure, but suffered a bit from sunburn and homesickness. "It's great fun," she said, "but the days all seem to run together. When we first arrived I was afraid that it might rain; now I wish that it would. When are you going to talk to your parents?"

"I don't know. Every time I think there is an opportunity, something comes along to ruin it. Maybe I should just give up. Maybe I should run away with Peter and then send them a post card from Bermuda. *Just married. Having a wonderful time. Glad you're not here.*"

Elizabeth looked horrified. "You can't do that!" she said.

"Why not? I will if I have to."

"But there are too many people involved, including both our families. Can't you see the headlines? *Lady Hartington Elopes with Lord Fitzwilliam.* Mother would die of embarrassment. And then, of course, you and Peter would be exiled forever from civilized society."

"I was only joking, Liz. I'm not completely out of my mind. Not yet, anyhow."

The days passed. Kathleen took long walks alone and tried to rehearse her dramatic confrontation. She tried a hundred different ways of breaking the news to her parents, but nothing seemed quite right. She tried to imagine their arguments against the marriage so that she could prepare herself, but her rebuttals seemed feeble compared to her mother's righteous rage. She was confused and frightened and time was slipping away. "Why don't we take a trip to Washington and New York," she suggested one day to Elizabeth. "I'd like to talk to my brother and a few good friends like Charlotte and Patsy and maybe John White, who is back at the *Times-Herald.*" And then we'll do New York in style -- the Plaza, the shops, the theatres. Elizabeth loved the idea and agreed that a change of scene would do them good.

Before long they were part of a lively dinner party in the Georgetown house where Jack and Eunice lived in controlled confusion, the trademark of the young Kennedys. Among the guests that night were Senator Joseph McCarthy, who was interested in what Jack had to say about the Communist menace, and Robert Sargent Shriver, who was interested in Eunice. After listening to her talk about her job at the Justice Department and the wonderful work being done by the Christophers, Shriver said, "At the rate you're going you'll have the country fully reformed before your summer vacation."

In a private comment to Kathleen, Jack said, "Eunie doesn't know it yet, but Dad has decided that Shriver's the guy she's going to marry. And you get credit for spotting him years ago."

"He'll be perfect for her," said Kathleen, playing the role of an old match-making duchess."

Jack was amused. "You know, you're getting to look more and more English every time I see you. And more and more classy. Who does your diamonds, Lady Kickie Poo?"

"A few tokens of someone's appreciation," she said with a wink and a smile."

"I can't imagine who you're talking about, but when are you going to drop the bomb?"

"I don't know, Johnny. I'm scared."

"Well, if you chicken out, I bet Frank Waldrop would give you your old job back at the *Times-Herald.*"

"Don't think I'm not tempted. Those were some of the happiest days of my life."

"We'd all love having you back in town. You could even move in here with us, if you wanted to."

She kissed him on the cheek. "You're sweet, Johnny, and I'm crazy. I guess I'm going to go all the way this time."

When they reached New York, the first phone call that Kathleen made was to her friend Charlotte, who was more like a sister to her than Eunice. Even though Charlotte was Catholic, Kathleen felt she could tell her the whole story of her involvement with Peter. "Meeting him has changed my whole life," she said. "Now I know what love is really all about. I didn't know. I really didn't know. I remember how we talked about this one summer. God, it must have been the summer of your sister Anne's marriage to Henry Ford II. I was one of the bridesmaids. It must have been 1940."

"It was," said Charlotte, allowing Kathleen to go on.

"I remember saying to you that I thought love must be that thing that made you forget yourself completely, like a religious experience. And I remember saying that it had never happened to me. For years after that I lived in the secret fear that it never would, that I was cursed in some way and I would never be visited by love. My compensation would be a fine marriage, perhaps a title and all that goes with it. And now it's all come around together. There's Peter, who loves me and offers to change his life to have me. And there's wealth and position and the good life. Of course, people will talk, but once we're married they'll forget all the gossip and scandal. Very little of it is true anyway. Peter is not a reckless playboy and I am not ruining his marriage. It died during the war, I think, just as mine did."

Charlotte looked troubled. "I don't know what to say, Kick. I suppose I ought to just congratulate you and wish you well, but it all strikes me as rather

293

messy. I mean, he's still married. You only have his word that he will soon be divorced. There may be legal complications. Who knows, there may even be a reconciliation."

Kathleen shook her head. "Impossible. It's over. If you could spend five minutes with his wife you would agree with me."

"All right, then, even assuming that the divorce is possible, what sort of a marriage could you have? The Church won't accept him, a divorced protestant! I can't imagine what sort of compromise you can work out that will keep you in good standing as a Catholic."

"We'll think of something. Perhaps his church will marry us and I can live in sin until I'm old and need a way to find forgiveness. Anyhow, I sometimes have my doubts about the authority of the Church."

"There are other problems, too, Kick. Practical problems. Think of all the people who will be hurt by this. Your parents, Peter's wife and daughter, the Duke and Duchess of Devonshire, who have been so kind to you. And what about your social life? Where will you live? What if your friends turn against you? Will you become part of that migrating international set that goes from racetrack to casino to parties in Paris given by Aly Khan?"

"No, it won't be like that," said Kathleen. "We'll settle down on one of the estates, perhaps in Ireland, but we'll have the use of Milton at Peterborough, which is not all that far from Newmarket and Rockingham, his horse farm. His great passion is horseracing. And then there will be London. I may keep my little house in Smith Square. He's talking about buying another townhouse, something larger and more elegant. It will be a wonderful life. Really it will! I don't know why anyone should object." She stiffened suddenly and frowned. "Damn it, Charlotte, my husband is dead and Peter's marriage is dead. What are we supposed to do? We are in love. Can't we be allowed a second chance at life?"

Charlotte relented. "I'm sorry," she said. "As your good friend I had to say these things because you're so much in love that it may be difficult for you to think about them."

 "Oh, I've thought about them all right, especially about my family, and most especially about my mother. But I've also thought about myself as an old lady who once gave up the man she loved when she was just twenty-eight years old. Try that one on for size, Charlotte McDonnell Harris. You're already married and happy. You don't have to look forward to fifty years of regrets. I know now what I never knew before -- that love is more important than *anything* else in the whole world. And I mean *anything*."

"I'm not going to argue with you about that, Kick, and I have to admire you for fighting for what you want, but I just want to say one more thing before you run off into the world like a wild woman. When you were talking about how you and Peter were seeing each other secretly, I had the impression that the illicit nature of the affair actually excited you. Is that possible?"

"I haven't thought about it that way," said Kathleen, " but now that you mention it -- yes, it is exciting. It's very romantic. Maybe it's the suspense or the forbidden fruit or the sense of danger. It's fantastically arousing."

"Sexually?"

"Yes. It would embarrass me to tell you what we do in bed."

"I won't even try to imagine," said Charlotte, "but did it ever occur to you that you might have chosen this kind of affair in order to take revenge on your mother, perhaps for opposing your marriage to Billy?"

295

"I have thought of that, actually, but I don't think so. I met Peter quite by accident and it was love at first sight."

"But you must admit that it's a little like saying to her, 'If you objected to sweet Billy Cavendish, let's see how you like my rich, lusty, protestant, married lover.' What's more, it seems to me that there are some similarities between your womanizing father and your womanizing lover."

"All right, Carlotta, don't get Freudian on me. Let's just say that my mother has never really approved of me, going back at least to the time that she yanked me out of the public school in Bronxville and sent me away to a convent school. I'm sure it was because of the boys who started to come around to see me. I've tried to please her, but nothing seems to work."

"Marrying Peter is certainly not going to please her."

Kathleen looked confused for a moment. Then she said, "Well, I don't give a damn anymore what she thinks. And after I tell her about Peter it's probably all going to be over anyway. She'll never forgive me."

Charlotte tried to comfort her, and, with the help of some champagne, she actually succeeded.

One of the people Kathleen planned to see in New York was her childhood friend Jackie Pierrepont, who had become a Catholic convert during the war and ran a bookstore that featured Catholic authors. It was a place where some of their old Irish-Catholic friends were inclined to meet. Charlotte often stopped there when she went into the city. When she mentioned Jackie's name in passing, it occurred to Kathleen that he might be useful.

"Well, well," said Jackie, when Kathleen walked in. "What brings you to the Big Apple?"

"I flew in from London just to visit you, darling."

"Don't you look gorgeous," he said, leading her to the back of the shop where they could sit and talk.

"You Pierreponts say the nicest things. I hope you don't mind if I get right to the point. I'm meeting someone for lunch and I'm running late."

"Whatever you say, Kick."

"My parents are going to a big event this coming weekend. It's the reopening of the famous Greenbrier Hotel in White Sulphur Springs, West Virginia, where they honeymooned in 1914. About three hundred people have been invited by the owner Robert Young. The place will be loaded with celebrities, including the Duke and Duchess of Windsor. I want you to be my escort. And don't you dare say no!"

"I wouldn't dream of it, Miss Scarlet," he said in an amusing Southern drawl. "I mean Miss Kennedy. I've heard about the Greenbrier affair, of course. They say it's been done up as a Southern mansion, complete with Negro slaves. I'd love to go."

On Friday they boarded the special train for guests provided by Robert Young. It picked up passengers all along the route to White Sulpher Springs. There was a party atmosphere on board. Kathleen and Jackie had drinks and caught up on the news of all their old friends. He told her the story of how he shocked his prominent protestant family by converting to Catholicism while serving in the South Pacific during the war. And then she shocked him by blurting out her own story. "I'm in love with a married man, whose wife is an alcoholic."

She went on, and he listened open-mouthed. "Do your parents know all this?"

"No, but I'm planning to tell them."

"This weekend?"

"Yes. I may not get another chance. I'm leaving for England next week. They're going to be very upset."

"The understatement of the year, Kick! "

"You won't say anything, will you?"

"Of course not. Just be careful. Don't do anything that you might regret."

"The only thing I might regret would be allowing myself to be talked out of marrying Peter Fitzwilliam. I won't let it happen. They'll have to burn me at the stake to stop me."

"I don't think they do that sort of thing anymore," he said.

She laughed, her honey-red hair touched by the flickering light from the window, through which she could see the world flashing by.

The first night passed without an opportunity for Kathleen to talk with her parents, who seemed intoxicated by the nostalgia that the gathering evoked. There were old friends, old stories, memories of good times and bad. They waltzed in their formal clothes, a pre-war generation that was peaking out and starting to make room for younger people. The elegance of the Old South, though only a stagey renovation, seemed to lift their spirits and feed their aristocratic longings.

She watched her parents dance, their feet gliding, their smiles fixed. It looked like love, but wasn't it only a ritual dance in a glittering ballroom? And then she had the sinking feeling that they were strangers, people she never really knew, except as parents. They were born in the nineteenth century, and here they were halfway through the twentieth century in a world that had been changed irrevocably by two world wars. Everything was moving so fast. For a moment she felt dizzy. And then she saw a picture in her mind of Peter and Olive dancing in another ballroom in another country. Jackie broke into her reverie with a smile and two glasses of champagne.

That night also passed without a clear opportunity for her to explain herself to her parents. That left only one day and one night. She had climbed up on this high diving board and there she was, frozen in fear with time running out. She had to gather enough courage to jump or she had to admit defeat and climb down.

The next evening, she walked boldly into their suite as they were dressing for dinner. "What is it, dear?" said her mother, looking at her through the mirror in front of which she checked her appearance. Then she turned to confront her directly. "What's wrong, Kick? Are you ill?" Rose looked stunning in her emerald green dress and diamond adornments.

By comparison, Kathleen felt drab in a pale pink dress that did not go well with her Palm Beach sunburn. She tried to speak, but she felt her throat thickening with panic. She swallowed hard and said, almost inaudibly, "I have something to tell you." Her heart was pounding against her ribs and she could almost visualize every bone in her body.

She was interrupted by her father, who came in from the adjoining room, still adjusting his black bow tie. "Oh, it's you, Kick," he said. He glanced at Rose and caught a sense of alarm in her face. "What's going on?"

"Nothing," said Rose. "Kathleen has a bit of a headache, that's all."

"No, Dad, that's not it. I don't have a headache. I have a problem, and I have to tell you both what it is. Don't interrupt. Just listen to what I have to say. I've been putting this off for a long time because I know you won't like it, but here it is. I'm in love with a wonderful man in England. He is Lord Peter Fitzwilliam. Anglo-Irish, protestant, and married." She did not pause, though she saw the wide-eyed look of horror on her mother's face. "He

299

was a hero in the war, and his wife proved to be unfaithful to him and an alcoholic. They are negotiating a divorce, after which we plan to get married." She bowed her head, as if to wait for the first stone to be cast.

The first voice she heard was her mother's. She spoke with firm separations between her words: "Kathleen are you out of your mind? You almost ruined your life by marrying out of your faith the first time, and now you want to go a step further towards perdition by marrying a divorced man. It's out of the question. Your father and I will never give you our approval."

Kathleen looked up, her eyes blazing and tearless. "I'm asking for your love, not for your approval. I'm going to marry Peter whether you approve or not." She glanced at her silent father and she could see that he planned to let Rose do the talking.

"How dare you ask us for anything in this madness? How can we love a daughter who is hellbent on hurting us and destroying her own life? Do you have no sense of shame or responsibility? A woman who breaks up another woman's marriage is nothing more than a --"

"Don't say it, Rose!" warned her husband in a subdued voice.

"And what about us?" she said. "What about your brother's political career? The newspapers will have a field day with scandal like this."

"I'm sorry, Mother," said Kathleen, twisting a handkerchief in her hands as though she might tear it to pieces. "I don't mean to hurt anyone. I just have to lead my own life, that's all."

"Well you can't lead your own life. You're not living alone on an island. You *must* consider the feelings of your family. If you don't, then, by God, you will no longer be a member of this family as far as I am concerned. You will no longer be my daughter, and I will treat you as if you had died.

Furthermore, I will see to it that you are stripped of any income whatsoever from this family. And if your father will not cooperate in this then I will leave him. And he knows what else I can do. I would rather see the whole structure of this family come down than to let you get away with this outrage. Now go somewhere and think about it. Pray like you've never prayed before, and when you come to your senses we may have something to talk about."

Kathleen left without saying another word. Her mouth was as dry as dust and her head felt as though it might explode. She found herself outside on a lawn looking back at the Southern mansion that shimmered and glittered in the night like a dream. *White Sulphur Springs*, she thought, looking beyond the mansion to the stars.

Back in Washington, Kathleen rushed off to see Patsy Field, without even stopping at Jack's house in Georgetown to see if Elizabeth had arrived from New York. She had to think out loud by talking to someone who understood her. She told Patsy in detail what had happened at Greenbrier, practically acting out the scene, as if to rid herself of the whole event. "I've never seen my mother like that. I expected her to be angry, but she was in a blind rage, ready to consider me dead if she couldn't control me. I don't understand. She's my mother. How can she talk that way?"

"She must be a very unhappy woman, who never had the kind of love affair that you described to her," said Patsy. "She must have noticed your passion and the light in your eye."

"You mean it shows?"

"Of course it shows, you idiot. Anyone can see that you are a woman in love, and everyone knows that there is no one happier or crazier than a woman in the grip of that intense feeling."

"I used to think that she was just jealous," said Kathleen, "but now I can see how she has lived all these years, looking after her husband and children out of a sense of duty, but experiencing no deep personal sense of happiness. She looks so calm on the outside, but inside she is furious."

"You would be too if your religion forced you to stay with a man you didn't love and bear him nine children while he was constantly committing adultery practically before your very eyes."

"I couldn't have done it," said Kathleen. "And I'm not going to let my religion keep me from marrying the man I love. I'll be damned if I want to wind up like her."

The next day Kathleen also talked to her old friend John White, Patsy's brother. They were sitting in "the cave," John's old room in his sister's house, and they were reminded of the good old days when they worked for the *Times-Herald*. She spoke as freely to him as she had to Patsy. She could see that he was a little jealous, and she was glad. "I don't suppose you'd consider giving up this Prince Charming for a second rate journalist with an old car."

She shook her head but smiled affectionately.

"In that case, I suggest you give up your religion and marry the prince. Just keep one thing in mind. It's real life you're talking about, Kick, not a high-school crush. Make sure it's what you really want."

Kathleen and Elizabeth stayed in town for another few days and got caught up in the social activities of the Kennedys and the Whites. Eunice blamed Kathleen's deplorable behavior on John White, who, she insisted, destroyed her faith in Catholicism. Under pressure from her mother, Eunice insisted on making an appointment for Kathleen with Monsignor Fulton Sheen in New York. Elizabeth Cavendish found the whole young crowd in Washington interesting and exciting. And John White found Elizabeth pretty exciting, but there was no time to pursue the matter.

The night before Kathleen left for New York she and Patsy sat up late in the big bed, like a pair of school girls, and talked about the future. Kathleen was eager to get back to England and excited about a trip that she and Peter were planning to take to the Riviera in May. "Peter's been on safari in Africa," said Kathleen. "I can't wait until he's safely back in England. And I can't wait until this whole ordeal is over. My mother is not going to quit, believe me. I know how she does things. She got to Eunice, and Eunice made an appointment for me with Monsignor Fulton Sheen. I don't want to go, but I don't know how to get out of it. He's a very persuasive speaker and a good friend of my mother's. You may have heard him on the radio. I just can't stand the idea of another inquisition."

"Why don't you just call up and cancel the appointment?"

"At this hour? It must be past midnight."

"Honey, it's two o'clock in the morning, but what's the difference. Leave a message. There's bound to be a night operator at the diocese office."

She made the call and it was surprisingly simple. "I feel a lot better," she said. "Maybe I can get some sleep now."

Before she turned out the light, Patsy said, "Don't worry about your family. I'm sure that in due time they will come around. Perhaps even your mother, once the others do."

"Do you think so?" said Kathleen, her eyes half closed.

"I'm sure of it," said Patsy.

A few days later Kathleen and her sister-in-law were aboard the *Queen Elizabeth* for the five day journey to England. Kathleen stayed on deck to watch the great ship eased from its West-Side berth into the Hudson River, from which it made its way into New York Bay and then out to sea. The people on the shore who waved goodbye grew smaller and smaller, until they disappeared. And then, as the whole skyline of Manhattan faded into the haze that veiled the city, she had the feeling that she would never see it again.

CHAPTER TWENTY

A week later she was back in London. Peter too was back from a long journey. They met as though they were the only two people in the world and all the wells had run dry except their own. He arrived at Smith Square late at night after a long drive and swept her into his arms. "I missed you in my bones," he said. "I must be absolutely addicted to you." He kissed her lovingly, held her away to look at her, then hugged her again.

She was small in his arms, and she felt his strength. She inhaled the familiar fragrance of his clothes and skin. "Yorkshire!" she said. "You smell like Yorkshire. I love you."

She took him by the hand and led him to her bedroom. "Don't you ever go anywhere without me again." She pretended to scold him and then kissed him on the mouth suddenly, hungrily.

"It was you who had to visit your family," he said.

"Well, it may have been for the last time."

"What happened?"

She told him about her mother's reaction. "It was horrible. I was absolutely terrified. I thought she might actually kill me."

"What about your father?"

"He said nothing. He just sat there in silent agreement. And we haven't talked since. My mother said she would see to it that the entire family would have nothing to do with me, but I can't believe that my father would go along with that. Before the big scene, he told me that he would be in Paris on business in mid-May, and that he would give me a call. Things are different now, but if he calls it will be a good sign."

"Yes," said Peter. "It might lead to some kind of reconciliation."

They were in bed, propped against pillows and smoking cigarettes. The smoke was ghostly in the light of the lamp, and the whiskey glistened in the small crystal glasses. "It's my mother I'm really worried about now," said Kathleen. "I keep feeling that she might find a way to stop us, but there's nothing she can do, is there?"

"No, darling," he said, "there's nothing she can do, but I think we should announce our engagement as soon as possible, perhaps during or after our trip to France. It would be nice to be away so that the press can't find us, but it might be wise to appear as proper as possible. There's going to be an awful fuss about this."

"Maybe I can arrange something with Marie Bruce. She's incredibly good to me. Perhaps I can persuade her to take me in and be my chaperone, as if I need one with you. When we're together, you're the one who needs protection." She leaned against him and put her arm across his naked chest.

"We've only got two weeks before we fly to Cannes," he said. "I've charted a DeHavilland Dove for the trip, a two-engine eight-seater with pilot and co-pilot. Perfectly safe and very private. In Cannes, of course, we'll be staying with friends, so we won't have to worry about the press."

"It all sounds so wonderful. I'll have to shop and pack and have my hair done and catch up with two months of mail and house business and see old friends and, God, it's all too exciting. Are you planning to go to Newmarket next weekend for the season opener?"

"I have some business to settle and some good runners going. Why don't you come with me?"

"I'd love to, but do you think it will be all right?"

"At this point I don't think it will make much difference who sees us. Everybody goes to the races. It's a public event, and I don't think we'll be making love in the paddock."

"Don't be too sure, Mr. Commando. Horse-racing can get me pretty excited."

Kathleen had lunch with Marie Bruce, and they had a marvelous time working out the details of their conspiracy to avoid the press. "When do you think you'll be making your announcement?" said Marie.

"About a week after we get back from Cannes. We're leaving on the thirteenth, about ten days from now, and returning on the seventeenth. It may be a long engagement, but at least the rumor-mongers will know what our intentions are."

"Good. Very good. I'll take a small house abroad in my name. We'll not only hide you from the press, but give the world the impression that everything is being done in an orderly way. A reception would probably be unwise. Too much exposure. And there is the delicate question of the first Mrs. Fitzwilliam. Three months after the divorce is final might not be an inappropriate time for a gathering."

"I'm sorry that you and Mother are no longer friends," said Kathleen. " I feel responsible in a way."

"Nonsense, child," said Marie. "You're mother's a difficult woman. She never forgave anybody who had anything to do with your first marriage, but let's not worry about that now. We're on the brink of a romantic adventure, and I am almost as excited as you are, my dear."

"I would feel a whole lot better about all this if my father would call or wire to tell me he accepted my decision or wished me well."

"If he doesn't call," said Marie, "I suggest you try calling him when he's in Paris. He's not going to hang up on you. In fact, I bet he'd be delighted to hear from you."

"I 'll think about it," said Kathleen.

She went back to Smith Square by way of Westminister Abbey. She lingered in the church for a while, listening to the whispers of history. She was not especially interested in architecture, but she liked the "feeling" of the place. There was a time when she dreamed of being married there. It was not likely to happen this time either, she thought.

She walked home briskly in the early May mixture of sunshine and clouds, her mind focused on her trip to the Riviera with Peter. How wonderful it would be to get away from it all and to be together with a sense of freedom. In her mind she was packing for the trip. She considered several daring evening gowns and garments. She would include two exciting negligees, the pink peignoir and the black garter belt. Peter liked that sort of thing. She smiled, remembering her flannel nightgowns and bootees.

She removed her hat as soon as she entered her house. Ilona appeared with a nervous expression on her face. She was saying "There's someone here to see you," but Kathleen's eyes swept past her and saw a slim woman all in black who looked exactly like her mother. It was impossible, of course, since her mother was in Palm Beach. But then the woman spoke in her mother's voice and said, "Hello, Kathleen. Are you surprised to see me?"

It was like seeing a ghost. She could feel her heart beating in her ears and neck. Finally, she was able to say something. "How did you get here?"

"The same way you did, dear. I took a boat. I was so upset by our last encounter that I called the travel bureau the very next morning. Now that we've both had time to think, perhaps we can have a sensible conversation about this scheme of yours."

"Yes. Yes, of course, Mother," she said, stunned and frightened by her appearance.

"Shall we prepare dinner for eight o'clock, Lady Hartington?" said Ilona.

It was Rose who answered. "That would be fine!"

"Did you have a nice trip?" said Kathleen awkwardly.

"The weather was fine, if that's what you mean," said Rose, "but I've been worried sick from the moment you told us about your affair with Peter Fitzwilliam. I still can't believe that you plan to go ahead with this relationship."

"Would you like some tea?" she said in a pale, automatic way.

"Yes, let's have some tea," said Rose. "Tell Ilona to serve it in the sitting room upstairs, and tell her not to disturb us."

"Yes, Mother," said Kathleen, hating herself for sounding like a schoolgirl at Noroton addressing the mother superior.

She found Ilona. "We'll have tea in the sitting room," she said, "and keep out of sight. My mother is going to spank me."

"Will you be all right?"

"I guess so, but if we need anything outside, send your sister."

"I understand," said Ilona.

Rose took off her veiled hat and revealed her face. She looked totally composed, as though she were sitting for a portrait in her black dress and pearls.

"Will you be going to Paris on this trip?" said Kathleen.

"I'll think about that later," said Rose. "I came here with only one thing in mind. I must persuade you to give up this insane plan of yours. Give up this married man. He's not yours and never will be, in the eyes of God. What kind of a marriage can you ever expect to have? A marriage built on sin and deception and adultery? You'll never be happy. Never! Not in this world or the next. It is my duty as your mother to stop you before it's too late."

Kathleen folded her hands in her lap and bowed her head. Each sentence was a whiplash, and she took it as though she deserved the punishment, but was secretly determined to go on being defiant.

Rose paused to sip her tea and to study her daughter. Her posture was bird-like. She was perched there on the edge of the sofa, her back straight as a rod, her whole body disciplined, her eyes steady and cold. "Tell me, Kathleen," she said, "what do I have to do to convince you that I am dead serious? I do not intend to leave this house until you promise me that you will give up this man, or, at the very least, that you will wait a year before making any announcements or committments. Do you have any idea how embarrassing and damaging this idiotic affair can be for all of us? There are already rumors afloat. Did you know that?"

"Yes," she said, "in England."

"I mean in America, and close to home. Did you know that the girls at Manhattanville have been giggling over the rumor that Kathleen Kennedy has been having an illicit affair with a wealthy and titled Englishman? A married man. A gambler and womanizer. A man without principles of any kind. Ruthless. Dissipated. Perverted in his desires."

Kathleen looked up. That last stroke of the whip was too much. "Stop it, Mother," she cried, the tears flooding her eyes. "Stop it! Stop it! You don't even know him. How can you say these things?"

"Oh I know him all right. I know his kind. Men like him love power. Money and property and women. That's what drives them and excites them. And to them women are like money and property, all extensions of their inflated egos. God asks us to set aside our personal desires, to ignore the demands made by the *self*. But these men keep trying to conquer the world. Some women find that exciting. Perhaps *you* do."

She went on this way through tea and dinner until midnight. And then she stood up suddenly and said,"I'm going to bed. I'm exhausted, and I imagine you are too. Perhaps this ordeal will kill us both, and God will have found another solution for you."

During the night the weather turned bad. The windswept raindrops ticked against the window. She knew that the assault would begin again in the morning, and she decided that she would try passive resistance. She would let her mother talk until she was talked out. Her strategy made her mother angrier. "I know what you're up to," she said. "I'm no fool. I remember how stubborn you were when I punished you, how you submitted your body but not your heart. You have to realize, Kathleen, that I did not come here to punish you but to save you. I'm not your enemy. I'm your mother. So, don't play your little-girl games with me. Grow up and pay attention. You are about to ruin your life and damage the reputation of the whole family."

Kathleen was forced to reply. "I'm not being childish and I'm not being stubborn. I'm twenty-eight years old, Mother. Peter and I have decided to get married. It was *our* decision to make and it wasn't easy. But it was *ours* not yours. In a way this is all none of your business. You can't use threats to get your way. At Greenbrier you forced me to choose between Peter and my family, and I made the only choice I could possibly make, because I can't give in to force and because I know that what I am doing is the right thing."

Rose got up from the breakfast table and marched back and forth. "How in the world can you say that? How can you say that you are doing the right thing when you are committing adultery and breaking up a marriage? Do you have no sense of shame? Have you completely lost sight of your religion?"

311

The battering began again and Kathleen retreatd to the livingroom. She slumped into a chair and tried to escape from the sight and the sound of her mother. "Look at me, Kathleen," she kept shouting. "Look at me. Look me in the eye and tell me that you do not feel guilty about what you are doing. And now I suppose you're going to run away and do your dirty thing somewhere with that man. I suppose you have an arrangement to meet him and would love to get rid of me. Well, don't count on it, because I'm not finished with you yet. I have a lot more to say and you're going to listen."

She made her threat good. She seemed to have a list in her mind, something perhaps that she wrote down on the boat and committed to memory. She cited chapter and verse on religious issues. She reviewed again her threats of disinheritance and her description of her family united in their condemnation of her. "They all agree with me," she said. "Every single one of them."

Kathleen looked up, her face stained with tears that had dried. "Not Johnny," she said.

"Yes, even Johnny. I don't know what he told you, but he agrees that this marriage would be a disaster for all of us, including him. How would he explain you to his constituents? What will he say when they ask him about the nasty newspaper reports. And you know how nasty those people can be?"

Her gaze drifted aimlessly away to the rug, the furniture, the curtains, the dull light at the window. She had no idea what time it was. Hours passed, then days. Sometimes they ate in silence, sometimes she was allowed to sleep. Ilona whispered to her, "You mustn't let her do this to you."

"I'll be all right," said Kathleen. "She'll give up soon and go away. I've beaten her and she knows it, but I can't send her away. I can't reject my family. If they choose to reject me for doing what I think is right, then the choice is theirs."

"I understand," said Ilona. "And if there is anything I can do --"

"I'd like you to stay in the house somewhere, just in case."

In the middle of the night someone was pushing at her. When she opened her eyes she could see that it was her mother and that it was not the night but early morning. She tried to roll over and sink back into sleep, but her mother wouldn't let her. "Come on, get up, child," said Rose. "I'm going to give you one last chance and then I'm going to leave. And if I do it will be the last time that you will ever see me."

The last day of Rose's visit was the worst, but still it did no good, and finally they were both exhausted. The next morning Rose announced that she was leaving and asked Ilona to help her with her bags. "There's a car coming any minute," she said.

When it arrived, she looked at Kathleen and said,"God knows I tried my best. You think you have won, but you are a lost girl, and I will mourn for you." And then she was gone.

Inside the house Ilona comforted Kathleen, and then scolded her gently for having put up with "four days of that awful tyranny. You are twenty-eight years old and a British resident. I don't understand how she can talk to you that way, even if she *is* your mother. But come now and have some tea. You will be feeling better soon."

Kathleen sat there shaking her head in disbelief. "I have to call my father," she said. "Before I do anything else I want to talk to my father."

She went upstairs to her study and eventually got the call through. It was early in the morning in Palm Beach. She told him what happened. He said, "I'm sorry, Kick. I tried to stop her from making the trip. I told her it would do no good. I was going to call you when I got to Paris. You know you're still my favorite girl and I love you. I was hoping you would come to see me there, at least for a day or for lunch or something. I'll be pretty busy. Maybe we can work something out. What do you say?"

"Of course I'll come Daddy," she said. "Whenever you say."

"Call me at the George Cinq Hotel on Thursday the thirteenth or early Friday."

"We'll be in Cannes that weekend. We can fly to Paris. Do you mind if Peter comes along? He wants to meet you. Please don't say no. You'll like him, honest you will."

There was a pause in which air seemed to be rushing through the phone lines. Then she heard him say, "You know I can't turn you down when you ask me that way. Sure, Kick, bring him along. Let's make it lunch Friday about one at the Ritz."

She kissed him long distance, said goodbye and hung up. Then she ran downstairs full of excitement to tell Ilona. "Oh, I know he'll like him; I just know he will."

"Of course he will," said Ilona with her big Hungarian smile.

CHAPTER TWENTY-ONE

Peter was in Ireland most of that week, and did not call until Friday night. She told him about her mother's visit. "There was no point in trying to discuss things with her. She was going to have her way or she was going to punish me. I couldn't give in. It was awful."

"What an incredible woman," he said, "but good for you, darling, for standing your ground."

"I was so upset that I called my father," she said. "If he was as adamant as my mother, I think I would have shriveled up and died. It would have been very difficult to go through all this without a kind word from at least one of them, but he was very pleased that I called. He invited me to lunch on Friday in Paris. And, believe it or not, he invited you as well. He wants to talk things over and maybe find a practical solution."

"What a good piece of news, Kick. It's just *terrific*, if you don't mind my using your favorite word. I promise to be on my best behavior."

"Just don't drink too much, darling. He's a bit puritanical about such things."

"He doesn't sound very Irish."

"Well, nobody's perfect, darling, except you of course. What time are we leaving tomorrow for Newmarket?"

"Early."

"Not my favorite time, but I'll be ready."

He appeared in a dark green sports car with large wire wheels. "It goes like the wind," he said. And it did -- into the magic mist of the eighth of May. "Look at those hills. Mist rising through sunlight. J.M.W. Turner. Do you like his paintings? I'll buy you one as a wedding gift."

"If we live to have a wedding."

"Don't say that, darling. We're going to live forever."

Once again everything seemed to be happening at high speed -- the drive, the races, the trip to Cannes, the flight back to Paris to meet the ambassador, and the early announcement of their engagement.

The opening at Newmarket was a social event. Peter went off trom time to time to mingle with owners and trainers, while Kathleen sat in his box and chatted with friends. It was not a scene that could evoke much comment. Those who might have noticed any special intimacy between them already knew what was going on.

Afterwards they stopped off at Milton to visit Peter's cousin Tom, who lived in one of the wings of the large house. He was delighted. "We're flying to Cannes for the weekend," said Peter. "On Saturday we'll hop up to Paris to have lunch with Mr. Kennedy. I've got to persuade him that marrying his daughter is not the kiss of death."

"Well," said Tom, "you've had your way since you were a nasty little boy, so I guess there's no stopping you now. Your mother seems to think that this charming girl will be your salvation, and I'm inclined to agree. But how will you ever persuade Mr. Kennedy?"

"I don't know. I may have to offer to build him a church."

"He's too rich to be interested in bribes," said Kathleen.

"Sorry! I didn't mean to be offensive."

Tom intervened with a bottle. "One for the road?"

And then they were off again, into the dusk, the car's lights searching out the uncertainties of the road, the wind filling them with careless excitement.

Back at Smith Square they made love and slept and then made love again in the morning.

Ilona shook her head at the two large suitcases that Kathleen had filled for her weekend trip. "So much for so few days?" she said.

"I want everything to be perfect," said Kathleen. She looked neat and lovely in her navy-blue suit and pearls.

It was Thursday, the thirteenth of May, and they were waiting for Peter. Their plane would be leaving from Croyden, at the southern edge of London. When he arrived, it was as if he had run all the way. "We're a bit late," he said, "but I think we'll be all right." He glanced at her luggage. "Now I know why you imported that enormous American station wagon."

His driver carried out the bags and they were off, Ilona on the sidewalk waving furiously, Kathleen tossing her a kiss. "We were supposed to take off at ten thirty," he said. "We'll be lucky if we get off by eleven. Townshend will be annoyed. He's a very punctual man, RAF pilot and instructor in the war and all that. Goes a bit much by the book, but he's one of the best. He wanted to be in Paris by noon and out again by twelve thirty. Something about the weather."

At Croyden they were hustled out to the DeHavilland Dove. It was a compact two-engine plane with excellent radio and navigational equipment and a good record for short runs with as many as ten passengers. The propellers were already spinning as they approached, and they held their hats through the dust blown back at them. Inside, they were given separate seats just behind the cockpit for better weight balance, and were warned to keep their belts fastened when there was any sign of turbulence. There was a door between them and the cockpit, but it was left open, so that they could all talk to one another. Arthur Freeman, the radio man, occupied the seat next to Townshend.

317

"There's been a report of some serious weather activity in the Rhone Valley," said Townshend, talking to them over his shoulder. "That's why we're stopping in Paris. It's going to be a bit tricky, especially since we're behind schedule already."

They landed at Le Bourget at twelve forty-five. Peter glanced at the clear sky. "Looks fine to me."

"The problem is not here," said Townshend. "It's between here and Cannes. I'll get all the up-to-date reports and meet you back here in half and hour, forty minutes at the most."

When they were alone, Peter and Kathleen looked at each another and shrugged. "Do you suppose we can get something to eat around here?" she said. "I didn't have much for breakfast."

"Airport food is not worth eating, even if you can find it," he said. "Why don't we just get a taxi and have a quick lunch at the Cafe de Paris? I'll ring up some friends of mine and ask them to meet us there."

"I don't think we have time. Townshend's in a hurry for some reason."

"Townshend can damn well wait. His plane is just a taxi in the sky, as far as I'm concerned. Anyhow, an hour is all we need." He took her by the hand and there was nothing more she could say.

They found a taxi outside the terminal and drove away from the drab, treeless landscape of runways and storage tanks. It was a short ride into the center of the city. Intoxicated by the beauty of springtime in Paris, they embraced and laughed in the taxi.

There were two men and a woman waiting for them at the Cafe de Paris. The men were involved in horse racing, and they all spoke English well but with a French accent. "You are wonderfully unpredictable," said one of the men. "We never know when you are going to appear. And here you are. *Voila!* "He raised his glass.

To Kathleen they all seemed to be talking at once, including the waiter who took their orders. "And another bottle of the Bordeaux," said Peter.

Two hours later they were driven at high speed back to Le Bourget, with three people jammed hilariously into the back seat of the open car.

Peter and Kathleen found Townshend in the operations office. He was furious. "That wasn't a very wise thing to do," he said in a clipped military tone. "Forty minutes does not mean two hours. Why didn't you tell me what you were going to do?"

"Sorry, old boy," said Peter. "Got a little carried away. Didn't think it would make that much difference."

"The update of the forecast is very bad. The meteorologist here reports deteriorating conditions over the Rhone Valley, with a dangerous thunderstorm moving in about five o'clock. It's a three-hour flight to Cannes, and it's now about three o'clock. We can't possibly beat that weather system. All commercial flights passing through that area have been cancelled and private planes are strongly advised to do the same."

"It can't be all that bad," said Peter. "The weather's perfect right here. How much worse can it be a few hundred miles away?"

"It's a fast-moving storm with heavy rains and strong winds. That area is mountainous. It can be very treacherous in such weather."

"Look, Townshend," said Peter. "I'm terribly sorry about all this. I'm willing to take the full blame. But, really, it's only a prediction. It's liable to be nothing but a little rain and wind. The Dove's a very sturdy aircraft. I think it could take a bit of turbulence, especially since you're only carrying two passengers."

"It would be very risky."

"We're on the good side of the weather, and can always turn back if things look truly awful," said Peter. "If necessary, we could even make an emergency landing."

"I'd rather not have to do that," said Townshend. "And I'd rather not have to lay over in some strange town. I've got a schedule to keep and other bookings to consider."

"We're wasting time arguing. If we took off right now, we'd be in Cannes by six o'clock. Perhaps the forecast is a little off. Why don't we start out and check with Lyon by radio as we get closer to the storm. I'm willing to give it a try, and you can be sure that I'm not going to risk my life when I am about to marry the most wonderful girl in the world. What do you say? Once we leave the ground, I promise you that I will not utter another word. You'll be completely in charge."

Townshend hesitated and seemed to be consulting his flight plan. "It's damned foolish," he finally said, "but if we're going to give it a try, we'd better get moving."

They took off at three twenty. It was a normal take off, and by the time they were over Fontainbleau they were cruising at nine thousand five hundred feet. They all seemed to relax, and there were stretches of silence, except for the droning of the engines and the sound of the radio, which reminded Kathleen of a badly scratched phonograph record. She tried to doze, but it was not possible. Peter leaned forward to chat with Townshend and Freeman. Their voices were a comfort and a threat all at once. She liked the masculine sound, but she could not hear enough to understand what they were saying. Peter leaned back and gave her a reassuring smile.

By four fifty they were in thick clouds and could hear distant thunder. The lightning that they could not see was picked up by the radio. They were no more than an hour and a half from their destination, and Freeman was on the radio, trying to get a weather report from the Lyon station. "ETA 1830," he said several times, because of the bad reception."Come in Lyon. Conditions at Cannes ETA 1830." The voice on the scratchy record replied with a description that apparently Freeman understood.

"See what they say about the Ardeche Mountains," said Townshend.

Freeman tried, but his contact was gone. He kept trying, but he couldn't get through. "What's wrong?" said Peter.

"Atmospheric interference," said Freeman. "It should pass." He tried other frequencies, but was unable to get a response.

"A hell of a time to lose ground contact," said Peter.

"We could try going over or under the cloud bank," said Freeman.

"I don't dare get off this course," said Townshend. "We're flying blind. There might be a mountain top under us, and who knows how high we'd have to go to get over this storm. I'm keeping her at ten thousand feet. If we haven't drifted too far, we know we have no obstacles. Keep trying that damn radio."

"You may be going into the eye of the storm," said Peter, and Kathleen caught his sense of danger.

"That's a risk we'll have to take. Our instruments are not reliable in this atmosphere. We'll have to hold her steady until we know where the hell we are."

Freeman went back to his radio, chanting like a primitive priest, his voice becoming more urgent as the turbulence increased. Peter and Kathleen were buffeted about. He reached out to take her hand. The whole cabin of the plane shuddered. Kathleen went pale. She felt her lips forming a silent prayer. "Don't worry," said Peter. "They've got her in hand. It can't last much longer. We ought to be seeing daylight any minute now."

He was interrupted by Townshend, who suddenly shouted, "Oh, my God!" They followed his gaze and saw looming in front of them a swirling wall of black clouds. "We've got to go down," he said. "Wherever we are, we've got to go down."

The Dove plunged into the violent storm and began sliding and falling and rising hundreds, even thousands of feet, as though it were a tiny boat in an immense hurricane. Kathleen closed her eyes and pleaded with God."Don't let it happen. Don't let it happen. You've done enough. Don't let it happen again."

The plane seemed about to break up, but it didn't. It seemed to be able to survive whatever destructive force nature hurled at it. Twenty minutes into the storm they were still alive, though the rain beat down on them and the wind tossed them roughly through the sky. "We've got to bottom out. We've got to break clear," shouted Townshend, wrestling with the controls.

Suddenly, the plane fell through the bottom of the storm and the world became visible again. For a brief moment Kathleen felt the fluttering wings of hope in her breast. And then she could see that they were falling towards a mountain ridge. "Pull her up," roared Townshend, pulling back on the stick with every ounce of strength in his body. Beside him Freeman was pulling desperately at the elevator cable that had come loose from the foot pedal. He could feel the plane straining to come out of the dive. And then something gave way, and to their horror they saw the right wing rip off and disappear behind them. Then an engine tore loose, then the tail section. For a few seconds Peter and Kathleen were able to fix their eye on each other. Then the wounded Dove spun out of control and crashed into a mountain.

CHAPTER TWENTY-TWO

The Kennedys offered no arrangements, and Kathleen was buried in the Cavendish cemetery near Chatsworth. Two hundred of her friends rode the special train with her to Derbyshire after a high mass in London. The only member of her family who was there was her father, too devastated even to speak. It was the Duchess of Devonshire who provided her epitaph:

JOY SHE GAVE
JOY SHE HAS FOUND

Two months later, in the summer that Kathleen would never see, her brother Jack walked on the beach. It was a misty morning and the sea and sky were one. Not a single day had passed without his thoughts turning to his sister. He heard her voice across the wide expanse of water. He heard her laughter, saw her flashing eyes, her honey-colored hair tosssed in the wind as their boat leaned on the long tack for home. He felt bound to her by more than blood. They were spiritual twins. A part of himself had fallen from the sky when she fell, descending through lightning like a struck-down angel. Had he failed her in some way, he wondered. He had been called a hero, but it was she who had the real courage. She had followed her heart; he had abandoned his. He whispered a few words to the dawn and then walked back along the beach -- alone.